A FLY ON THE WALL

by Elizabeth Longrigg

CHAPTER ONE

If it is possible for a human being to be a fly on the wall anywhere, it is possible in the Senior Common Room of Emmaeus College, Camford. The windows are heavily shaded by the prolific growth of an ancient, climbing, twining fig tree, and the panelling of the room is darkened by the smoke of several centuries of fires and burning tobacco: pipe tobacco, after-dinner-cigar-tobacco, male tobacco; maleness and staleness; millions of minutes of low-key down-toned masculinity, which has left its dark patina on the dim panelling that seems to recede into ever dimmer corners of unfathomable shadow.

In one of these corners something white flickered and crackled occasionally to the accompaniment of a low mutter:

'Seventy point five. Just as I expected.'

It was Peregrine Forsyth and the University Gazette. He was engaged in his favourite study: the obituaries. Not that he was taking much account of the names of the famous or obscure individuals whose departure from the common rooms of this world were recorded there. It was their age on departure that interested him. He had an indelible conviction that the allotted lifespan of Man is now, always has been and moreover always will be, three score years and ten, whatever meddling medical men and statisticians might say. As The Gazette obligingly records the ages of departed Camfordians each week, Peregrine was able to add them up and average them out, and the blitheness or bitterness of his ensuing mood was a clear indication of the proximity of his average to the figure of seventy.

It happened not infrequently that a couple of longaevous clergymen - nearly always clergymen, Peregrine reflected sourly, showed what idle, protected lives the beggars led - would put out the average rather badly by surviving well into their nineties. Whenever this was the case Peregrine would begin eyeing his younger colleagues to see if they were showing any symptoms of redressing the balance in the near future.

Narrowly he eyed a pair of chess players sitting at a fine, round, eighteenth century table, beautifully be-drawered and inlaid, and generally unnoticed by the habitual occupants of the room. Unhealthy looking beggar, that young Otis; all that curly hair might make him look juvenile but he was too fat, much too fat. Looked like a cross between a classical Jove and a Rubenesque cupid. Never be able to stand up to any real exertion - all that surplus weight. Florid, too. Not a good colour.

'Check!' said Otis.

Peregrine emerged verbally from the enveloping shadows.

'Can't understand you, Otis.' Men of Peregrine's generation addressed each other with surnames only. 'Healthy young fellow like yourself sitting on your arse all afternoon playing chess. Bad for you. I'll give you a game of squash before dinner.'

Otis turned, rather startled, in Peregrine's dimly lit direction.

'Oh, Pewegrine! I didn't wealise you were there!' For all his bulk his voice was high and light, and his pronunciation of 'r' something between an impediment and an affectation. 'I weally don't think I can manage a game this evening. Shona's having a dinner party and I'll have to get the dwinks weady."

'Nonsense,' responded Peregrine, 'Shona likes you to play squash.

You told us she'd bought you the gear to encourage you to play more.' Hector Otis sighed heavily. 'I weally can't think why,' he muttered rather pettishly. 'It's a pwetty pointless occupation, weally, only fit for the dimmer undergwaduates. No, weally, Peregrine, not this evening.'

And he returned his attention to the game more suited to his tastes and temperament.

Hector's father had been a schoolmaster of the old-fashioned kind, with a fair knowledge of the warlike exploits of the Greeks and Romans and an indelible admiration for the manly virtues of muscular Christianity. His eldest son had, of course, been named after the Trojan hero who seemed to him to have been the embodiment of both. The fact that the fall of Troy antedated the birth of Christ by a few hundred years had never been regarded by him as a relevant factor. Hector Otis had, while a schoolboy, attempted to live down to his father's image of him, and had early succeeded, at least in the way of size, but had eventually shown himself to be far more academic and far less muscular than his father had bargained for, and the fact that he ever attempted to take any exercise at all was possibly due to residual feelings of guilt at his inability to shine on the field of sport as his namesake had shone on the field of battle. About his lack of Christianity he felt no guilt whatever, though he had often wished he'd been given a more genuinely Christian name; nobody would have noticed a failure to live up to that. He listened to his father's lamentations over the decline of classical studies with a half-consciously realised satisfaction that each successive generation of undergraduates was less likely to perceive the disparity between him and his Homeric namesake.

Peregrine turned his attention to the other chess player, an elegantly aging, finely-boned Doctor of Music. His eyes were deep-set and heavy-lidded. He had a habit of looking intently into the middle distance as if catching the echoes of ethereal harmonies, and was generally known as 'the archangel' by dons and undergraduates alike, partly because he could have sat for a Renaissance painting of the expulsion from the Garden of Eden, his expression of remoteness and faint distaste for everything around him giving him just the right air, but largely because his name was Gabriel. He had a strangely ugly wife and an only slightly less ugly mistress, who, as she was also a don, was frequently to be seen in his company at faculty parties. She was rather hearty and very forthright, and their relationship was a relatively well-kept secret because nobody could believe it. Peregrine was impatiently dismissive of him. He was almost at retiring age and hence would do nothing useful to diminish the average age of human demise even if he were to join the permanent members of the heavenly faculty of Musicology the next day. Besides, he was probably one of those delicate-looking blighters who creak on to make ninety- five. Peregrine sighed discontentedly. He really shouldn't complain. Today's average of 70.5 was most satisfactory; but on the other hand there had been a plethora of nonagenarian bishops in the previous couple of issues, and something lower than 70.5 was needed redress the overall balance. He moved to the bookshelf to extract the copies of the last two Gazettes, just in case he'd made a mistake. As he did so a lean, rangy figure with unkempt black hair hailed him from the corner of the window-seat.

'What's the matter Peregrine? Averages not too good? It might interest you to know that I've reached half my allotted span today. It's my birthday.'

Peregrine eyed him with more interest than he had hitherto felt in this untidy person with his shabby corduroys and baggy jackets and tieless shirts.

'Hmph,' said Peregrine. He did not wish his colleague a happy birthday. The Archangel looked up vaguely from his chess and said 'Dear me, is it really?' as if it was a matter for commiseration, and continued looking into the distance until Hector Otis said crossly 'It's your turn, Gabwiel!'

Peregrine returned to his corner with the two extra Gazettes and gazed thoughtfully at the thirty-five year old. Yes - that would bring the average down nicely. Never thought of him before, somehow. Not in the common room as much as some of the others. Supposed to be a bit of a womaniser. Must be why he's known as 'the Wolf'. Lone wolf, too, of course. Bad at attending meetings; very remiss.

Just then the Wolf, whose cognomen was due to his lupine appearance as much as to his sexual or social proclivities, left the room as abruptly as his rather loping gait made possible. The clock ticked, the smoke rose to the heights and recesses of the dark panelling and settled there. A few papers rustled. Chessmen moved silently.

Suddenly all heads turned to the window. A slim man who had been reclining on the window seat with his feet up on a not much smaller table, removed them with alacrity, stood on them and broke the silence with 'Do you see what I see?'

Heads already turned craned further; two more men rose to their feet to peer through the fig leaves at two figures who crossed the lawn and went through a small door in the high stone wall of the college garden.

'Hmmmmm!' said the slim man, as he reclined again and replaced his feet on the table. Peregrine had not needed to crane and rise. The view from his corner was in direct line with the door in the wall and he had no difficulty in ascertaining that the figures were those of the Wolf and a slim young blonde girl of undergraduate or early graduate age. Some sly smiles were exchanged.

Somebody said 'Well well!' And the archangelic doctor said 'Dear me!'

Peregrine said 'Hmm' too, though his thoughts were not on quite the same lines as the others'. Just the thing. Of course. Those loose-living fellers often went out rather suddenly. Heart strain, probably. Not really likely to be syphilis these days. Too many meddling doctors about dishing out drugs. Very rarely got to the tertiary stage. Still, he must look up the symptoms again. He felt strangely cheered.

'Funny the way these modern languages people behave,' remarked the slim man, who was a historian. 'Long hair, barely shaved half the time. No tie.'

'No ties, either,' interjected the Economics don, 'at least, none that seem to have any hold on them.'

Arthur Middleton was heavily bespectacled, short-back-and-sides, prematurely middle-aged and never deserted by an expression of owlish earnestness which had almost certainly been with him from early childhood. His remark was greeted with grunts and chortles of amusement and he went quite pink in response.

'I don't think it's funny! This sort of thing is one of the intolerable concomitants of the residual upper-class laxity that infects this university. It's all part and parcel with having college servants to serve our meals and wait on us and clean our rooms and it's thoroughly demoralising and corrosive to the whole social order!'

'Dear old Arthur,' said the slim man tolerantly, 'at least he doesn't laugh at his own jokes. He's usually the only one who doesn't see them.'

Peregrine had been too absorbed in his own musings to listen. Arthur Middleton was the kind of speaker who often drove his listeners deep into their own musings. There was a story going round the university that he was the only don in Camford to have actually gone to sleep in one of his own lectures, but nobody in Emmaeus believed it because they couldn't remember ever having seen Arthur go to sleep at all.

Suddenly a voice boomed from a portly man:

'Ties are very important. I wouldn't be seen without one myself and moreover, I will not teach undergraduates who come to my tutorials tieless.'

Apparently Arthur was not the only one who had failed to see the joke; Julian Holloway-Smythe hadn't even heard it.

'Weally, Julian! Whatever do you do about it then?' asked Hector.

'When?' said the English tutor, who had already opened his mouth to continue his discourse.

'When they come to tutorials without ties, of course.'

'Why I simply say: "My dear chap, you haven't got a tie! You must have forgotten it! How dreadful for you. Now go into my bedroom over there and inside the wardrobe door you'll find a vast selection of ties. Choose any one you like and put it on." And they do, you know. If they happen to choose one I'm not particularly attached to I make them a present of it. And they never come to my tutorials without a tie again; never again!'

And with this satisfactory exit line he left the room.

'Dear me,' sighed Gabriel Taylor, stroking his right ear with his fine-fingered hand, 'the emptiest vessels make the loudest sound.'

CHAPTER TWO

The Wolf, whose name was in fact Everard Lucas and who liked to be called Everard by everybody except the college servants, was telling his blonde companion that she obviously needed some help with her thesis and the only time he could spare was after dinner, so what about 8.30 - in his room? Everard was not in fact, despite his college reputation, getting on quite as well with this young graduate as his colleagues suspected; but he was by no means averse to fostering their suspicions. He was well aware of his nickname and lived up to it as obviously as possible. He was also of the opinion that his first name, subject of ribald jokes at school, was not unuseful in the pursuit of objects to foster his reputation. Certainly, women did seem to react to it. Subconscious probably; Freudian. Even quite young women had no innocence these days - well, not the attractive ones, anyway. He always got a perceptible reaction, if not invariably of the most flattering kind, when he responded to their calling him 'Mr Lucas' by looking into their eyes and saying 'Everaaard' with a drawl on the last syllable.

He stood now, in Camera Square, listening with rather less than one ear as Emily Matheson listed the difficulties of her work a little nervously. He was thinking what a prim old-fashioned sounding name she had for a girl who looked like a Nordic actress. For all her appearance of sophistication she was hesitant and unsure of herself. He decided on a tolerantly-amused smile combined with donnish superiority:

'That doesn't suit you? You don't like the idea?'

He lifted an eyebrow and the girl looked a little foolish and flushed as she searched for the appropriate reply.

'Oh - ah - no of course not, I mean yes it does. I don't like to take up your time - after dinner especially...'

'About 8.30, then.'

'Yes. Thank you so much, Mr Lucas.'

He couldn't resist it. He gave a slant look into her eyes and drawled

'Everaaard'.

The man on the window seat, who had first called attention to Everard and his companion, continued to recline with his feet elevated to table height and his hands behind his head. He wasn't greatly pleased, for all his show of interest. Well of course, yes, he was interested. Call it sour grapes, if you like. Or sour figs. He looked mistily at the leaves surrounding the window. Not that there ever were any figs on that thing, and if there were they'd be sour enough; but it was barren, a barren fig tree. He seemed to have heard that phrase before - couldn't quite place it - yes, barren, like him and Barbara: married twenty- three years and never any offspring. And there was that wulverine Everard with three dark shaggy-haired sons, as like him as possible, given the age difference, and he let his wife bring them up practically single-handed while he raced round pursuing other women.

'Woger!'

The sound of his name, however mispronounced by Hector, roused him from his bitter musings.

'No!' he answered.

Roger liked to be different. Hector, however, was accustomed to this response from him and took no notice.

'Gabwiel won't play with me any more because I keep winning. Will you have a game?'

'Certainly not. I'd beat you too easily. Aren't you going home to help with the dinner party? I seem to remember you saying Shona hadn't been well.'

'Oh, not weally,' replied Hector carelessly, 'she had a miscarriage a couple of weeks ago, but we didn't want to put off the dinner party. The pwofessor's coming and a chap fwom the university pwess.....'

'So you're going home early to help!'

Hector laughed.

'Not too early! I don't want to get there until everything's weady for me to put the dwinks out, and anyway...'

He'd been about to say that he'd used it as an excuse to get out of playing squash with that old fossil Peregrine, but he remembered that Peregrine was probably still lurking in his shadowy corner and changed it to 'anyway there's something I want to listen to on Radio 3; I genewally listen in the afternoons, I find it vewy welaxing'.

He rose, looked into the corner, saw that Peregrine was still there, and added: 'Pwaps I'll go home after that. I've put off my evening tutowial, of course; far too taxing when one's having a dinner party.'

He lumbered out and let the door close noisily behind him.

'Oh drop dead!' said Roger through his teeth.

Peregrine emerged from the shadows again:

'What was that, Roger?'

'Mind your own business' was Roger's - not unusual - response. 'What's the matter? Not feeling too great?' asked Peregrine, approaching him with some appearance of solicitude. He decided that Roger must be nearer fifty than forty, and the sort of chap who never has a day's illness. Still, you never knew. Perhaps that deliberately cultivated rudeness of his was the product of some undiscovered malady that would carry him off well before retiring age. 'Working too hard, are you? You're dealing with the new appointments, of course, now I think of it.'

'What? Oh yes, the Medical Research Fellowship and Everard's lecturer. Can't think what Everard needs a lecturer for; surely he can do the teaching himself or farm it out to graduate research people.'

'Oh I don't know,' said Peregrine thoughtfully, 'there's a lot of language teaching in his subject - you know, mere language, not literature, and he doesn't like teaching that; he's not keen on the medieval options, either. A young junior lecturer isn't a great expense to the college'.

'Actually the applications are still coming in. I've passed them all on to Everard and he hasn't even spoken to me about them yet.'

'Ah, but he has to me,' Arthur Middleton butted in importantly, 'he wants to appoint a woman.'

'A what?' Roger's feet made a lightning descent from the table and he leaned on the window seat at a dangerous angle. 'A WHAT did you say?'

Peregrine noted with satisfaction that his face had gone a peculiar colour.

'Yes, he told me,' continued Arthur, delighted at having secured the fascinated attention of his audience. 'He rang round to all the women's colleges telling them to send any suitable candidates along - well, at least, you know, to invite them to apply - as women would be considered for the job even though the Gazette advertisement only mentions men.'

Roger gazed at Arthur, incredulous.

Peregrine chuckled, 'Well, Roger, that's what you get for putting it all on to your junior colleague. But don't worry, all is not lost, you only have to consider a woman. Though mind you, there's nothing in the statutes to say a woman can't be appointed as a lecturer; it's only as undergraduates and fellows that women are barred.'

Roger said nothing at all. He left the room and went outside into the main quad and walked round it slowly several times in order to ask himself why he should be seething with anger. Much of it was due to Everard's going behind his back. Just what he would do of course. Typical Everard! Impulsive, opinionated, underhand. He'd always talked about wanting to have women in the college and voiced disapproval at the - as he termed it - antiquarian stance of the fellows who refused to contemplate the idea. Such discussions had usually degenerated into the bandying of ribald comments as to why Everard might be so keen to get women in and no serious attention had ever been given to the subject.

Objectively, Roger had to admit, the idea had its merits. He'd taught a number of women himself and had been impressed by their diligence and ability; though he'd always said - like most of his male colleagues - that it was ninety per cent diligence and ten per cent ability. Must allow for the notion that men could always do as well or better if only they'd work as hard. But what really stuck in the gullet was the thought of women invading the SCR, feminizing that men's club, that male inhabited and male dominated territory. How could you swear comfortably and be normally rude to your colleagues, be natural at all in fact, with a woman sitting there listening?

He despised his colleagues who treated their wives badly. He himself, like many childless men, was extremely protective of his own wife. But when it came to the daily presence of a woman in one's centre of communication and recreation! Rationalising his anger did little to diminish it. He was now angry with himself. He couldn't really approve of his reactions, but he couldn't alter them, either. He left the quad and the college, crossed the wide street and went into the University Bookshop to find some distraction in the new books section. On the table displaying recommended new writings the one that immediately caught his eye and refused to let it go was *The Descent of Woman*.

The same afternoon, Everard's wife Jean was sitting on a hard chair near a large table in a dark kitchen. The table was covered with the debris of more than one meal mingled with papers, books, envelopes with or without their original contents, all heaped in miscellaneous profusion. Along the window sill was a row of variously sized flower pots. Some of them contained strange growths, but in general they held a higher proportion of cigarette butts than of greenery. Jean was staring in the direction of the potted butts and rocking back and forth silently and rhythmically on the hard-bottomed chair.

The shouts and squabbles of small children were clearly audible from outside, but she was oblivious of them. She was working herself into a fine state of mental torment as she inwardly contemplated Everard's probable activities and her own situation. He had made no secret of his interest in the blonde graduate, or in anybody or everybody else. He'd always made it clear that she could do the same whenever she wanted to. Monogamy and jealousy were out of date and hopelessly bourgeois. She'd agreed. In some ways she still agreed - objectively. But she'd been pregnant three times in four years and one doesn't really feel like having affairs when pregnant; nor when nursing a child, nor when carting them about - nor indeed at any time when tied to a family of demanding male children, living in the depths of the country without being able to drive. Going anywhere meant hauling three children and a pushchair on and off infrequent buses. It was hopeless to do anything. But she must combat this misery with some exertion. She wasn't stupid. She had a good degree, as good as Everard's.

Intellectually they were very equal. She could...

But one of the children burst into the kitchen, howling dismally and holding up a bleeding hand. She could do nothing but bandage it up, comfort the sufferer, give them all something to eat, minister as always, however inefficiently, to their physical needs; perpetually compelled to do what she did badly to the exclusion of what she could have done well.

Shona Otis was preparing for the dinner party. Her house was modern and spotless. Her kitchen gleamed with stainless steel and shining utensils and the other effects of sound expenditure and diligent exertion. The dinner was well under way. The dining table was set with the best silver and the wedding present crystal glasses. Hector disapproved totally of the way some dons lived in filthy, evil-smelling houses and squalid chaos. Shona's housekeeping abilities, considered hopelessly boring and bourgeois by the Lucases, were a source of considerable satisfaction and self-congratulation to the Otises.

Shona, however, sighed with rather less satisfaction than usual. It had taken two days to get things to this stage because she wasn't feeling well. That miscarriage had been very upsetting. Not only was it a physical setback and a jar to her otherwise healthy constitution, but Hector -

well, she mustn't complain.

Of course he was disappointed. They only had a daughter so far and he was anxious to have a son. And of course he couldn't be expected to realise how she felt about it. Strangely enough they'd been having a dinner party when it happened. Just as well the eating part of it had been finished. She'd hoped to be able to go on until the guests left, but it had been impossible. She'd had to make an excuse to get Hector into the kitchen and whisper to him. He'd been very good about looking after the guests for the rest of the evening while she'd driven herself to the hospital. Still, it had made things awkward for him.

Well, at least nothing like that could happen tonight. If only she didn't feel so dull and tired. She'd have to pull herself together and be as interesting as possible to the professor and the publisher. That was the worst part. Capable in the kitchen, organised in domestic matters, Shona found conversation on such topics as the state of the economy or the problems of the third world tedious and demanding.

She switched on Radio 4 and spread out The Times on the kitchen table in the hope that either of them would provide inspiration for possible conversational gambits if Hector were not near enough to provide them. Radio 4 issued an unuseful rendering of Country Gardens and Shona tried to absorb the foreign news in The

Times, but before she realised it she found herself taking in every detail of a small column about a wife putting rat poison in her husband's food.

'How appalling!' she thought satisfactorily as she read to the end and wished they took a paper more devoted to the reporting of such matters than The Times.

She heard a car crunch on the gravel of the drive, whisked the paper off the table, swiftly folded it into a neat square and put it into the proper place for today's paper: on the shelf under the recipe books. It didn't occur to her to wonder why she felt guilty and surreptitious. Hector opened the kitchen door.

'I've come home early to do the dwinks,' he announced.

'Oh thank you, that is good of you. The ice is ready in the deep freeze and the lemon's in the fridge and I've got the glasses out and polished them.'

'I hope you remembered to get some more tonic water!'

'Oh no, I didn't. O, I'm so sorry, Hector. I'll go and get some immediately, even if I have to borrow it - but I need to keep an eye on the dinner - oh dear -'

'I'll get it,' said Hector nobly, and with a less than pleasant hint of condescension. 'I suppose you'll start saying you can't think of everything!'

'Oh Hector, I don't say that. It's just that I haven't been as well as usual ….'

'Now we don't want to go over that again,' responded Hector with a grimace of distaste, and he stumped back to his car with the air of a man who knows his duty.

CHAPTER THREE

The dons were having lunch in the long room adjacent to the SCR. It was hung with portraits of former occupants of the college who were not sufficiently important to have a place in hall, despite the fact that they were all men. The dons sat at the long table with their newspapers folded and placed or propped at angles, and as they consumed their jugged hare they read while chewing or swallowing and engaged in a little desultory conversation between mouthfuls.

There was every outward appearance of the normal, ordinary, lunchtime scene, but in fact there was a tension in the atmosphere. The shortlist for 'Everard's lecturer' had been made up to include a woman, and she had been interviewed that morning by Roger Tomlinson, Everard and the Rector. The Rector didn't count. He had little interest in the matter and almost equally little say. He rarely penetrated the senior common room or the dons' dining room, preferring to have lunch and usually dinner with his large, bossy, organising wife in their large and draughty lodgings. The other inmates of the college regarded this as totally inexplicable by ordinary criteria; but ordinary criteria are rarely applied in Camford, where there is probably less attempt made to account for foibles than anywhere else in the civilised world.

It was to Everard and Roger that the occasional speculative glance was directed. Neither of them had so far satisfied anybody's disguised curiosity. Everard because he was hugely enjoying the situation and was particularly fond of jugged hare; and Roger because he was at a loss to comprehend his own reactions and was in the process of considering them too deeply to wish to talk about them. He couldn't disguise from himself the fact that the woman they had interviewed had impressed him. More than that, astonished him. Of course, he told himself hastily, she was older than most of the men they'd seen, almost as old as Everard himself. Any man with comparable experience and qualifications would have been in a steady, secure job by that age and unlikely to apply for a mere Lectureship.

Peregrine, whose averages had been particularly pleasing that week - a couple of accidents had brought the figure right down to 55.6 - was sufficiently expansive to voice the question that had long been hanging inaudibly in the air:

'Well, Roger, and how was the ravishing redhead?'

'How do you know she's a redhead?'

'Oh, just happened to be in the lodge when she came in and asked the way to your room. Wasn't the only one hanging about there at the time, either, was I, Hector?'

Hector pinked perceptibly.

'Oh was that her?' he responded. 'Yes wather noticeable. Looks quite wipe, doesn't she?'

'I don't know what you mean by 'ripe' but she's certainly intelligent. Gave clear concise answers to all our questions, and obviously a very experienced teacher, too.'

'Yes, wipe. Vewy expewienced!'

'Dirty sod,' replied Roger matter of factly, and went on, 'you can pick a person who's used to teaching. Interesting, really. I asked her if she experienced any particular difficulties in teaching men and do you know what she said?'

'I can imagine.' Hector began a giggle, but seeing that the rest of the table were paying genuine, interested attention to Roger, he stifled it quickly and fell in with the prevailing attitude and allowed Roger to continue. 'She said "Well, you do have to be more polite to them." Amazing, really; it's just what we find when we're teaching women.'

It was, in fact, this statement above all others which stuck in Roger's mind. Impressed though he'd been, at first unwillingly, though with increasing interest and admiration as the interview progressed, he had somehow clung to the special-difficulties-when-teaching-men question as a final demolisher. Had the answer been 'None' it would have been a mark of inexperience, insensitivity or insincerity; had it been almost anything else it would have betrayed a lack of competence or confidence; but to have precisely the one factor he had always found a nuisance in dealing with women pupils given in answer to a query about a converse situation! He had been floored, stymied, almost as astonished to hear his own sentiments issuing from the mouth of delicate-featured young woman as if they had suddenly been given vocal expression by a creature of a different species. He'd suddenly found himself defending her against Everard's trick question: 'Could you teach the special papers?'

'That would depend on the options,' he'd heard himself interject before giving her time to say anything unfortunate.

'What about the early Philology?' Everard had continued in a honeyed voice. Roger knew what was happening. Everard had no interest in or regard for early philology; he always very actively discouraged any pupil of his from reading it. He certainly did not want any lecturer he appointed to teach it. But the girl had mentioned a dislike of philology in her application and he wanted to lure her into the trap of saying she'd be willing to teach it and then render her embarrassed and confused by cross-examining her about the discrepancy between her application and her answer. Roger had found himself surprisingly short of breath while she paused to consider her reply. Everard's smile had widened to a leer; he enjoyed making women feel confused and foolish. But when the answer came it was direct and unconfused:

'No. I couldn't possibly tackle that, I've no interest in it at all.'

Everard had at least had the grace to laugh at the demolition of his trap.

'Well, I'm delighted to hear that!' he'd said.

Roger had found himself not merely breathing freely again but even in a state of near exultation at this superiority to Everard's devious ploy. To his colleagues round the table he now spoke aloud:

'I think we'll have to give her the job.'

There was nothing so vulgar or so openly expressive of emotion as a gasp of disbelief, but some stares of almost amazement reached Roger from both sides of the table. Everard laughed at his colleagues' incredulity.

'You see!' he announced with the air of a showman, 'even old Roger! "Fondly overcome by female charm." Oh you'll all come round to it. Well,' looking at Julian Holloway-Smythe rather pointedly, 'with one or two exceptions, perhaps.'

'There's such a thing as human intelligence,' Roger remarked rather acidly, 'which can be recognised and appreciated in spite of the body it inhabits.'

'I don't know why you should say "in spite of" Roger, we're living in *nineteen* sixty-seven, not *eighteen* sixty-seven,' Arthur Middleton butted in. Arthur Middleton always had the air of butting in, however legitimate his right to speak. 'In Russia women are considered exactly equal to men and do precisely the same kind of jobs without ...'

'Yes Arthur, we know, we know,' Roger responded somewhat wearily, 'I didn't mean "in spite of" in that way exactly.'

'No, but it indicated that you were surprised at human intelligence in a woman, didn't it? Even so it's more liberal than I would have given you credit for a month ago.'

Arthur prided himself on the liberality of his own opinions. He felt a sense of social guilt because he led his life and drew his living in one of the oldest and in many ways most exclusive universities in Europe, and he endeavoured to compensate for this by enjoying it as little as possible. Every vacation he turned his back on the misty spires of Camford and journeyed resolutely to the less tourist-infested industrial cities where he took photographs of multi-storey carparks. He had a large collection of these, all postcard size, and each day for six days a week he showed a different one in a frame on his chimneypiece. On the seventh day the car parks gave place to an earnest looking young woman with severely centre-parted hair and a number of very noticeable teeth. She was Arthur's fiancée. Some of his colleagues had been rumoured to say that they avoided his room on a Saturday because the car parks were considerably less depressing, but most of them never noticed the difference. The story of the regularly alternating photographs was in fact most appreciated by the college servants who heard it from the elderly servitor who cleaned Arthur's room. A dim awareness of Arthur's fiancée passed through Roger's mind and he wondered if she had been chosen for her intelligence, as no other sort of attraction was very apparent. Perhaps that accounted for Arthur's present attitude.

'How's your fiancée these days, Arthur?' he asked.

'Oh, very busy as usual. She's had some very distressing cases lately.'

'Cases?' Roger couldn't remember what she did.

'Yes, cases. You do know she's a social worker, of course?'

'Of course.' Roger wondered how he could have forgotten anything so inevitably apt.

'Ah yes,' Peregrine chipped in with sudden interest, 'she works in one of those industrial areas where the infant mortality rate's a good deal higher than the national average, doesn't she?'

Arthur responded by launching into a generally condemnatory diatribe on the sufferings of the underprivileged, to which Peregrine ceased to listen once the early mortality rates gave way to the psychological effects of living in an urban environment.He went back to contented musings on the obituaries in the most recent Gazette. It had been a particularly satisfactory entry: no fewer than forty-nine deaths recorded and the average age 55.6! Really, the way things were going it would be difficult to get up to the three-score-years-and-ten average, rather than down to it.

'I suppose we'll have to dine the woman,' Julian Holloway-Smythe boomed into the silence that had ensued after the final paragraph of Arthur's peroration on the inner cities.

'Well of course,' grinned Everard over the bones of his hare.

His eyes narrowed with amusement as he gauged the reactions of his colleagues.

'That's a point, you know,' Julian continued. 'I don't mean the pre-appointment dinner; that's a once-only anyway. But what about dining nights in general? We can't have her coming in every night!'

'Surely there's plenty of time to discuss details like that!' Roger said testily.

Here the Bursar, who was relieved to find the matter at last entering his territory, made his definitive statement: 'No, we certainly can't have her coming in to dine in the normal course of things. Not at all. Definitely not! You can't have a dinner with one woman! Not a college dinner.'

The bursar was a gentleman of the old school. He dressed with impeccable anonymity. An Old Harrovian of more breeding than brain he had had a mediocre career in the navy and also maintained, from a gentlemanly distance, a large farm in the northern reaches of the country. From the navy he had somehow drifted back to his old college to become Bursar. He was rather good with money. He had quite a lot of it. He lived in a moderately sized manor house in a village near Camford with his impeccable, self-effacing wife and their two daughters. In the vacations they all retired to the farm in the northern reaches to walk the moors, inhale the healthy air and view the perpetual improvement of the pigs. One of his best pigs had won a number of important prizes and the Bursar had rewarded the animal by having a reasonably well-known artist paint its portrait. The portrait hung in his room in college, in pride of place above the chimneypiece, unchallenged by any competitors. There was not so much as a photograph of his wife or daughters to be seen. Even the actual presence of the Bursar himself provided little competition for he was the kind of man in whom no feature is memorable. Visitors to the college, guests of other dons, showed a remarkably consistent inability to remember his name, the colour of his hair, whether or not he wore spectacles, or in fact any other detail about him apart from his interest in pigs, which had, at least, the value of the unexpected.

'Ladies' guest nights!' he exclaimed suddenly.

'Ah yes, the women's nights,' echoed Julian Holloway-Smythe with only the lightest hint of correction in his voice. He was sure one never talked about 'ladies' except in their hearing; but he felt a mite less sure of himself than usual when correcting an Old Harrovian.

'Time we got round to having them regularly. Last college in Camford to have one, weren't we? It seemed to go pretty well. None of them passed the port the wrong way.'

'I thought we'd agreed to have two a term?' said Roger.

'Yes, and you were against even that, I gather!' Everard's laugh had a slight edge. The way Roger was behaving since they'd interviewed the woman anybody would have thought it was his idea.

'You wouldn't know,' Roger retorted, 'you never come to meetings. You've been fined for it, haven't you?'

'I said "I gather",' Everard was quite unchastened.

'So what about her coming to those and those only? Surely you can put up with her at two dinners a term when there are other women present anyway?'

And so it was resolved, mainly because the situation was too unfamiliar for any immediate objections to present themselves.

CHAPTER FOUR

Julia Leslie was nervous; no, apprehensive would be a better word. Tonight she was to dine in that all male preserve, Emmaeus College and be the only woman there, the only woman who'd dined at that high table, apart from some guests at their first ever Ladies Night only the previous term. She was not even sure whether this meant she'd been given the job. Was it a final test of her suitability? Her dress was probably all wrong. Not enough sleeve, but what else could she put on? With the children to feed and clothe and very little money coming in, she couldn't expect to have a vast supply of clothes. She looked at her watch. Hell! Getting nearer the time and her husband not back with the car yet. He must realise she'd be in a state. She ran down the steep narrow stairs, which ended only a leap from the open front door, went out and peered anxiously up and down the street, a narrow straight street rendered perpetually sunless by the disproportionate height of its terraced houses. There was no sign of Jeremy or the car and the babysitter had been there for ages already.

'Anything the matter?' The quiet, concerned voice of their lodger, Tim. He'd been polishing his dark blue Beetle a couple of doors away and Julia had been too preoccupied to notice him.

'Oh Tim! I've got this important dinner in Emmaeus tonight - you know - about the job and Jeremy said he'd be home to take me and there's no sign of him.'

'I'll take you. Don't worry. Of course you don't want to be late. Have you got everything? I hope you won't be too squashed in the Beetle.'

'Oh you are kind. How thoughtful to ask if I've got everything. Jeremy just keeps telling me to hurry and never mind anything else.'

'Yes,' said Tim. He was concerned about other people by nature. He was particularly concerned about Julia and what he deemed the selfish and inconsiderate treatment meted out to her by her husband. 'Of course you can't hang about getting steamed up before such an important thing. It won't do at all. But it's all right. You'll be in plenty of time if I take you now.'

Tim was a graduate nearing the end of his D.Phil thesis and he understood the complexity, scarcity and importance of university appointments. Jeremy, on the other hand, had been invited to apply for his Prep. School job by a friend of the family and had been appointed accordingly.

Julia was in good time. There was nobody to meet her and she stood outside the porter's lodge feeling conspicuous and irresolute. The porter eyed her with more distaste than curiosity. He opened the slide window in front of him and was about to issue a stern reprimand about the college being closed to visitors when she smiled at him. He was surprised into changing the 'c' of college into 'can I help you Miss ...er Madam?'

'Oh, I hope so. I'm to dine here this evening and I don't know where to go.'

'Oh there you are,' came a breathless voice from just inside the quad before the porter had time to answer. 'Hasn't Everard ...er anybody met you?'

It was Roger. 'I'm the Senior Tutor. Saw you at the interview, of course'

'Yes, indeed. Good evening. I hope I'm not late. Should I have been somewhere else? I'm sorry I didn't know ...'

'Not at all, not at all. Quite all right.'

Roger was cursing the necessity to be polite to a woman while angry at Everard's failure to do the proper thing. Everard should have been in the lodge waiting for her. But that was Everard all over: engineering a situation to make other people feel as awkward as possible, putting the unfortunate young woman he regarded as his future 'assistant' at a disadvantage right from the start. Everard himself loped into sight round the chapel corner of the quadrangle, accompanied by Emily Matheson. He left her standing there and, without quickening his pace, came towards

Roger and Julia. His eyes flickered over them both.

'Aha, Roger. Couldn't wait to do the honours, I see'

'Couldn't wait for you to do them!' retorted Roger, prevented by Julia's presence from saying something much more uncomplimentary. 'Well, let's go into the SCR for a glass of sherry.'

Emily Matheson, still standing under the apse of the chapel feeling excluded and inferior, watched them disappear through the small door in the opposite corner of the quadrangle.

Inside the dark panelled SCR stood a number of black-gowned figures. Julia suppressed a gasp of dismay. Of course she'd forgotten they wore gowns for dinner in men's colleges. She hadn't brought hers.

'Oh - you haven't got a gown,' said Everard. 'Never mind. Pity to cover you up, really.' His eyes flickered over her again.

Julia responded with a calm, steady gaze. She was beginning to get Everard's measure and had no intention of being embarrassed or intimidated by him - gown or no gown. Roger, unaware of this, hastened to her aid by offering one of the several 'extra' gowns that hung just outside the Common Room for the benefit of dons and guests who might have forgotten theirs. Julia hoped he wasn't thinking, "how like a woman!" and put it on gratefully. She needn't have worried about the almost sleeveless dress: the sleeves of the gown were large and long.

Introductions and sherry over, the butler came in, stood at the foot of a small wide staircase with shallow, polished, wooden steps and announced 'Dinner is served.'

'Now, my dear,' Julian Holloway-Smythe detached himself from the gowned group and endeavoured to locate Julia's elbow through the long black sleeve, 'do be careful on these stairs: frightfully slippery. When we had a Women's Night last term the Rector's wife came down a regular arser. Didn't hurt her, of course, far too tough!'

Some of the older dons cast Julian a look that was intended to indicate their opinion of his using unsuitable language in front of a woman: at the same time feeling annoyed that her presence rendered the cautionary glances necessary. She was certainly going to be a nuisance. They sighed.

Seated at high table, Julia felt more comfortable. She'd been to college dinners before, in her own and some of the more forward-looking men's colleges which had been holding Ladies Nights for some years. She was not unaccustomed to formal dining either; partly from having a mother who set great store on formal dinner parties and partly from working as a waitress during university holidays when she was a student. There was no point in worrying about being the only woman: one would normally have a man on either side anyway. Everard, on her right, was actually making an effort at polite small talk. This was unusual for him, though he knew how to do it when necessary. He had been just a little disconcerted by Julia's response to his up-and-down eye flickering. Her steady eyes had given a clear message: 'I know your sort and the kind of game you're up to and you're wasting your time.' Well, time was something he had plenty of. She was being appointed for three years. He must remember that she was nearly as old as he was, married, and not to be treated like a pupil.

Peregrine watched her from a distance and decided that she wasn't very likely to help his averages by dying before she reached three score years and ten. She was pale, of course, the more so in contrast with the black gown, but it was the kind of pallor that went naturally with that dark red hair, not the sickly kind. Women lived too long these days, anyway, now that they didn't die in childbirth. They were the ones responsible for pushing up the averages. It hadn't occurred to him before that the obituaries in the Gazette dealt with a far higher proportion of men than of women - at least seven times higher. His jaw dropped so far that he stopped chewing his baked venison. He had to admit it made a difference. Human lifespan had to include both sexes. Funny how, when one thought of people one didn't normally think of any but male people. His jaw tightened on the venison again, but somehow it seemed to have lost its savour.

Julian Holloway-Smythe eyed Julia Leslie with overt appreciation, a fact not lost on his colleagues. He was amused. They're all thinking: 'What's that old queen doing? He's never liked women.' Can't one appreciate a pretty face in either sex, especially at my age. Not that pretty's the right word. There's a depth in that face, intelligence, repose. "That repose which stamps the caste of Vere de Vere." Poor old Tennyson. Wrote a poem about a perfectly foul Lady Clara Vere de Vere who induced - or seduced - the local lads to fall in love with her and then left them in scorn to die of broken hearts. Sort of Victorian "Belle Dame sans Merci". And almost the only line of it anyone remembered was that one about class! Still, class is what this girl's got - though one doesn't dare mention it these days with the Common Room and hall half full of oiks holding their knives like pencils.

He looked at certain of his colleagues with distaste. Himself originally a scholarship boy from a grammar school, he had come up to an Camford full of elegant, nonchalant, public school men, whose manners, attitudes and accents it had been essential to imitate if one were to be accepted anywhere. He'd been imitating them for so long that he regarded them as first rather than second nature to him: after all, he'd been using them more than twice as long as the alien manners of his origins.

The Old Harrovian Bursar, who was considerably less class conscious than Julian, merely gathered without thinking about it that Julia was the sort of young woman who might have been at school with his daughters; and took no further interest in her. Clearly she would present few problems at Women's Guest Nights and could probably be easily overlooked at other times.

Hector Otis decided that she was beginning to look vaguely familiar, though less obviously "wipe" than a woman of 33 might be expected to look. He knew he didn't appeal to that type of woman; he'd been spurned by a number of them before - and since - he'd married Shona. He really preferred plain, figureless, slightly academic women; they were so much more grateful for his attentions. Of course there was the buxom barmaid type too - but that was something else, more separate from home and college life. Hector smiled reminiscently.

After dinner Everard took Julia to his room for a chat. 'Well,' he remarked as an opening gambit, 'I've had some difficulty reconciling what people from your college have told me about you and what I've heard from our mutual friend Alison Greer.'

The name shed a sudden ray of clarification in

Julia's mind. Of course! Alison Greer was hardly a friend, more an acquaintance and erstwhile neighbour who always knew a lot of nasty things about a lot of people. Of course! This was the Everard Alison had talked about at length. Julia hadn't known his name apart from 'Mr Lucas' until tonight. The story flashed through her mind. His way of 'confessing' to his wife that he'd had a woman to stay with him while she was away was to leave his diary, with fairly full details, in a prominent place! Ingenious really, because Jean had suffered the added indignity of doing something underhand, not quite the thing, when she read the diary and found out about it.

Everard looked at Julia with the air of one interviewing a candidate for Camford Entrance.

'What do you think about it? Do you think you'd agree with Alison's assessment of you?'

Julia did not imagine Alison's remarks about her were likely to be any more charitable than about anybody else.

'I should think it extremely unlikely,' she said.

Everard laughed just as he had in the interview after her lucid answer to his trick question. 'Oh! You didn't fall for that one! Yes, I like Alison, but she has got a rather malicious sense of humour.'

Yes indeed, thought Julia; and greatly wanted to say she hoped the things Alison had said about him were as untrue as the things she'd said about her; but then she hadn't got the job offer on paper yet and she needed it so badly. How silly he is, she thought. Even if I didn't know Alison all too well, he's told me my college's opinion was the opposite of hers - and I'd never have got this far without good backing from college.

Everard was staring at her trying both to discomfort her and read her thoughts - without any success in either endeavour - when the telephone rang.

'No,' he said into the receiver, 'not necessary at all. I'll take her home.' He turned to her again.

'Roger seems to be very protective about you: wonders if you need him to take you home. Doesn't seem to trust me. You haven't got a car, have you?'

'No, not here. Our lodger dropped me in his.'

'Ah!' said Everard, baring his teeth in a grin. 'Your lodger!'

Julia cast her eyes mentally if not physically to heaven. Oh God! she thought. Don't tell me we are going to have jokes about 'Roger the lodger the sod' in the inner reaches of academia. I can't bear it.

Aloud she said, 'Yes. It's always embarrassing to admit it, but we need one to help pay the bills.'

'Why is it embarrassing?' enquired Everard.

Julia felt she'd been polite for long enough. 'Because silly people make such boringly inevitable remarks about it,' she replied.

On the way home Julia summoned enough courtesy to enquire about Everard's family. He said he was going home early because his wife wasn't very well. Julia hoped it was true and that she might eventually manage to think better of him than she did so far.

CHAPTER FIVE

A couple of days later Julia received a formal letter from Emmaeus College offering her the lectureship. That was the gist of the first paragraph. The second paragraph Julia had to read twice before she could believe it. It said succinctly: 'As this lectureship was advertised in The Gazette with a man in mind, we trust you will take it without the living out allowance.'

When Julia received that letter "Women's Liberation" was barely in the process of invention. The days of the Suffragettes were long past. She felt alone in her anger, felt personally downgraded and belittled. She seized paper and a pen. As she did so a flash of lightning glared momentarily into the room and a roll of thunder hurtled across the sky.

'Good,' she thought grimly. She always found storms exciting. 'That's just how I feel!'

Furiously she wrote a letter to the college demanding to know whether her sex rendered it unnecessary for her to have food and shelter and enough money to provide them.

'I've never thought much about women's rights

before,' she continued, 'but the insensitive audacity of such an offer as your letter contains is enough to make me chain myself to the college railings and demand equal treatment with men of my age and education.'

I'll have to tone that down a bit, she thought, but I'll write it all as it comes and get it out of my system.

The storm abated sooner than her wrath; but she managed a letter of less virulent tone with a relatively courteous beginning and end and went straight out to post it before she was tempted to think better of it.

Roger received the letter the following day and the news of its contents soon went the rounds of the Senior Common Room. Reactions were varied. The old guard were astonished and affronted that any woman should have the temerity to suggest rejecting their exemplary offer on any terms.

Hector Otis said, 'Well weally!'

The Archangel said 'Dear me' and decided not to ask his mistress what she thought of it. He had an uncomfortable suspicion that she might be more disapproving of the college than of the young woman's reaction. And that might lead to unpleasantness. Unpleasantness was something Gabriel avoided whenever possible. The Bursar was particularly piqued. It had been his suggestion. A young Australian lecturer had the temerity to say 'Good on her!' just loudly enough for half of the lunch table to hear. Some none-of-your-business glances were thrown in his direction, but Everard said, 'I agree, Bruce. Shows guts. Why should she take less than we'd offer a man?'

'Absolutely.' Julian Holloway-Smythe realised that his championing of this young woman was causing surprise, and he enjoyed surprising his colleagues. They all thought him a reactionary, dyed-in-the-wool traditionalist, he knew. Serve them right if they had to change their little minds. Far too complacent, most of them; set in their judgements of other people.

Roger said nothing. He was the one who'd have to deal with the matter and he was genuinely puzzled. It had never occurred to him that the girl, or anybody else, would think the offer strange or controversial. Still, he did have to admit she showed spirit.

After lunch he telephoned Julia to arrange a meeting about it, giving a time. She was sorely tempted to respond that she "had no superfluous leisure; her stay must be stolen from other affairs."

She managed to keep it back and simply said she was teaching at that time; was there any other possibility? Again Roger was surprised. Of course, term was still going on; it was obvious she had a lot of teaching for her own and some other colleges: he'd read it all in her dossier. Still this was obviously so much more important. She was showing herself to be a bit more high-handed than they'd bargained for. Eventually a mutually suitable time was arranged.

But Roger was disturbed, disappointed. She'd seemed so vulnerable at the dinner. Of course women could be a nuisance with their vulnerability, like his wife, sometimes. But it did make one feel, well, large and strong and necessary. And here she was standing up to them all and even asking for a time that suited her. Well, she'd have to take the job without the allowance and come down off her high horse. Anyway, it was the wish of the Bursar and the older and more prominent Fellows of the college.

Julia appeared promptly. She was still too angry to be nervous. Moreover she had a Cause.

Roger began calmly by saying: 'Aside from the question of the living out allowance, do you want the job?' '

'Yes, I do. I want it and I need it'

'Would you take it without the allowance?'

There was a pause. Julia thought it was unfair that she should be asked this question prior to any discussion.

'I can't,' she said. 'It would be letting the side down.'

'The side?' Roger was genuinely thrown.

'Women,' said Julia briefly. 'It's the principle of the thing.'

'But you're married,' said Roger.

'So are you, I gather, and most of your colleagues'.

'My wife doesn't work'

'Surely some of the other wives do.'

'Well - they still don't earn a lot,' said Roger deprecatingly, and then rather guiltily remembered that one or two were women dons who earned, in their women's colleges and with their university lecturerships, as much as their husbands.

'My husband's a prep. school master,' said Julia. 'Do you know how much they earn? Well, it's a pittance.'

She didn't add that a good percentage of the pittance disappeared in the school bar, though this was a strong contributory factor to her need for the job.

'Moreover,' she added, 'I've got three children and have to pay somebody to look after them while I work.'

Roger hadn't considered that and he suffered a brief pang at the realisation of the limitations in outlook his own childlessness imposed. Nevertheless he brought out his main card.

'After all you can't possibly live in.'

'Surely,' replied Julia with calm equanimity, 'that is a very fundamental reason for giving me an allowance on which to live out.'

She tempered this with a smile and a glance of amusement rather than triumph. Her face was lit up with liveliness. She was enjoying this volley of words so much she had become almost forgetful of its purpose and importance, almost heedless as to its outcome. She knew she had trumped an ace and was exhilarated. She rose to leave, feeling that the final word had been said and there was no point in saying any more. Roger opened the door for her with polite murmurs about 'seeing what we can do.'

Then he returned to his patched leather armchair feeling a little shaken. He felt he had been playing a game against himself: a game he had wanted his opponent to win.

Julia got her living out allowance and the job.
'Poor old Roger,' said Julian Holloway-Smythe. 'Fondly overcome by female charm!'
'Don't be ridiculous,' said Roger stiffly. 'It's the principle of the thing.'

CHAPTER SIX

The heavy grey concrete buildings of the women's college where Julia had been an undergraduate loomed large over the summer garden party on the college lawn. It was a fairly new, relatively benign, forward-looking college that prided itself on receiving the sort of women other colleges rejected, like nuns and married women. The garden party invitations even included the husbands and small children of its alumnae, and catered for the latter by providing ice-creams and donkey-rides and balloons and tubes of bubble mixture. Husbands, however, were not catered for in any way appreciated by Julia's. The only drink on offer, apart from the children's orange cordial, was tea. He considered it unmanly to go to any party where alcohol was not provided. So Julia alone had dressed their three children in their cleanest and best and wheeled them all, in a pushchair meant for two, the mile and a half from the tall terraced house in the narrow street. She generally enjoyed the annual garden party. Jeremy was not the only absentee husband and there were often surprise meetings with contemporaries and, more recently, former pupils, most of whom seemed to have grown shockingly old-looking in a remarkably short space of time. A few were accompanied by friends or boy-friends, often much more amiable than husbands, thought Julia. This time there was the addition of kind and interested greetings from the dons of the college, even the Principal.

'We're very proud of you, my dear. Such a wide field. And a men's college. Of course I think they wanted a married woman. More suitable. But you are to be congratulated!'

How odd, Julia thought. I'm the same person as I've ever been, but they're treating me quite differently. I've been teaching for this college for half a dozen years and they've never taken any notice of me before. Of course it might have been different if I'd been married to a don.

A contemporary of Julia's hailed her.

'Hello Julia! How nice the children look. What was the Principal talking to you about? She was looking particularly gracious. Have you published a book or something?'

'Not much chance of that with these three and having to teach whenever they're being looked after. No, it's just that I've got a lectureship at Emmaeus.'

'Oh! Just that! You must be the first woman to get beyond the lodge of that college and you say that it's just that you've got a lectureship there. You'll be working with that exciting Everard Lucas, won't you? Lucky you! I know a lot of people who find him very attractive.'

'Heavens! Do they really?' Julia was a little shocked to realise that her own feeling for Everard was the kind of antipathy that borders on revulsion. 'Oh dear!' she murmured, too involved with this encounter to avoid being accosted by Alison Greer.

'So!' said Alison, almost accusingly. 'You're to be Everard's new lecturer, I hear. How on earth are you going to manage with all those children?'

'Much the same as before, I imagine, except that I'll have help full time as I won't be teaching at home.'

'Oh, you can't afford that! It's far too expensive. You'll be spending your whole salary.'

'Possibly, but it's better than having no job and being condemned to an existence of unrelieved household drudgery. Anyway, I'll be earning more than I do now.'

'Well, yes, and much more than Jeremy earns, no doubt. Of course it's a much more prestigious job, too. How does he feel about that?' Alison's eyes lit up with a malicious interest that was not dispelled by Julia's not very truthful reply that Jeremy was delighted.

'I can ask him myself.' Alison's tone implied that that might be more to the point. 'We often see him in the pub, usually complaining that you "won't come out". Surely you could leave the children on their own for an hour or two once they're asleep?'

Alison's husband was a don some twenty years older than herself and they had no children.

'No,' said Julia plainly. 'I couldn't. Besides, that's when I do my reading and marking and so on; between getting them to bed and going to bed myself.'

Pushing home the heavy pushchair, laden with three tired children, Julia tried to dispel her disquietude. Alison certainly had the knack of hitting on the sorest points: Jeremy's lack of money, ambiguous attitude to Julia's appointment, and increasingly frequent absences from the house. "Mothers look after children when they're little and fathers when they're older" was his regular response to any complaint. I don't suppose he'll be there when I get back, she thought. He wasn't. Tim, however, was in the kitchen washing up the few dishes from his bed-sitting room lunch.

'Julia! You look worn out. Sit down and I'll make you a cup of tea. Wasn't the garden party a success? I'd have thought they would all have been congratulating you!'

'Well, yes, they were. It's odd how they suddenly find me so much more interesting just because I've got a job in a men's college. Some of the comments were a bit snide, though.'

Tim undid the children from the pushchair and

sent them into the garden to play.

'There's one good thing about a terraced house,' Julia commented, 'lock the back door and the children can't get out into the street. You know they're safe in the garden.'

'Nothing wrong with living in a terraced house anyway.'

Tim had himself been brought up in one by his intellectual, proud, poor, state school teaching parents.

'Jeremy thinks there is. When he was a little boy, he says, he wouldn't have been allowed to speak to children who lived in a house like this.'

'Why are you living in it then?'

'His father bought it for us. Outright. No mortgage. I think he thought it was quite good enough'

'So it would be with a bit of decorating and the garden not so overgrown. Oh – I know you can't do it.'

Tim was anxious not to impute any fault to Julia.

'You do too much anyway. And of course the children have a lot of fun in all that tall grass.'

'I know. It's awful. The neighbours don't like it. The seeds from the weeds blow into their gardens. But the day we moved in we were out in the garden and people from about five houses down called out to us and waved. Jeremy just walked inside and slammed the door and I had to wave and shout back with desperate heartiness to compensate.'

Julia laughed a little at the recollection, but Tim found it less than amusing. He changed the subject.

'I've got a new record. Britten's Sacrifice of Isaac. Come and listen to it when the children are in bed. You know you really should have a record-player when you're so keen on music. I know you've got a lot of records.'

'Oh yes. I had most of them before I was married. I thought Jeremy liked music. He had a record of Mozart's Horn Concerto which he played the first time I had tea with him. I didn't know until much later that it was the only classical record he had and his family had been very snooty about his "going intellectual."'

'But what happened to the record-player?'

'Jeremy's was borrowed – and didn't I tell you the story of what happened to mine?'

'No. What?'

'Oh, it wasn't so long ago. I heard the boys talking and Richard saying, "It's your turn now, Jamie; you stand on it and I'll turn it round". And that was the end of it really'

Tim thought disgustedly that the amount Jeremy spent on drink and dining out in a month could well pay for a new one; but if Julia could consider it light-heartedly, so much the better.

The summer vacation had progressed into autumn and Julia had heard nothing from Emmaeus College or Everard Lucas. She decided to drop in, casually as it were, get the feel of the place and visit the library; find Everard if possible and ask when she might be expected to turn up for lunch.

She stepped through the wicket in the main gate and into the gloom of the lodge. The porter was not one she'd seen before; a man of red-faced ferocity, he barked

'College is closed to visitors!'

Julia felt less within her rights than when she'd been invited to dinner.

'Well, actually, I'm looking for Mr Lucas.'

The porter's generalised ferocity took on a more ominous tone of extreme, personal disfavour.

'Mr Lucas,' he announced, looking down on her with contempt from the superior height of the porter's window, 'is in the buttery – having tea with his WIFE and CHILDREN.'

Julia coloured at the realisation of the guilt imputed to her. How embarrassing! He thinks I'm one of Everard's spare women! They must keep turning up here asking for him. But I can't explain who I am without appearing to answer a direct accusation, and that was only an implied one. So she merely said 'thank you' as coolly, she hoped, and politely as if he had given her precisely the information she had asked for, and left the gloomy lodge for the sunlight of the front quad, with its bright flowers and perfect lawn, its glowing, honey-gold stonework. She could see the entrance to the buttery, but she had no intention of interrupting the family party. The library might be a better bet – if it was open. It was. The heavy nail-studded door creaked into a two-tiered building with an iron-railed gallery giving access to shelves of darkly bound volumes. There was an air of musty tranquility. Julia took a book from a lower shelf and turned to sit at the long table going down the centre of the room. She was startled to hear a cultured feminine voice:

'You can't come in here, I'm afraid,' it said. 'The library's open to members of the college only.'

'Oh! I do beg your pardon. I didn't see you. I should introduce myself. I'm the new modern languages tutor – well, that is – I think my appointment dates from the beginning of September, but nobody seems to be expecting me.'

'Well, certainly nobody's told me anything about it. But why be surprised? They never do.'

'I'm so glad you're the librarian,' Julia responded, sensing an ally. 'I didn't think there'd be any other women – except some of the college servants, of course. Or are they all men too?'

'Oh, the scouts!' The lady of the library used the

proper Camford word for college servants. 'No. Most of them are women. So much cheaper, you see! And I'm not the librarian, I'm afraid. The librarian's a Fellow of the college and he's also the chaplain as it happens. I'm just the dogsbody who guards the place and gets the books in and out. Pauline Dickenson, at your service!'

'Julia Leslie. How do you do! I expect we'll see each other a good deal – though I'm not completely sure when I ought to start coming in. I only "did some teaching" for my own college and never ventured into the place until I was summoned to the meeting in the week before term began; but I felt I should come in earlier here.'

'Well, don't worry about anybody expecting you. Just come in and make your presence felt. It'll do them good.'

Pauline made the tone of the last three words sound very much as if she'd said "It'll serve them right".

Heartened by the encounter with Pauline Dickenson, Julia emerged into the sunlit quad just in time to see Everard Lucas, a small woman in torn jeans and three dirty, shaggy-headed boys of organ-pipe similarity, disappear round the chapel corner. So there are the wife and children, she pondered. Good heavens. They look as if they'd have lice. She gave a slight shudder of revulsion. Not the sort of children she'd want near hers.

'Hello! What on .... what .... have you been doing with yourself?' It was Roger's voice at her left elbow. He'd clearly been about to ask what on earth she was doing there and then thought better of it.

Julia was not unamused.

'I was passing. I thought I'd try and find out when I should come in.'

'Oh. Have you seen Everard?'

'Well yes. But only in the distance. It seemed to be a family party.' Roger made a mental note to attack Everard for his remissness in failing to contact his new lecturer.

'Come in on Monday,' he said. 'That's when term begins, not full term, of course, that's more than a fortnight away, thank heaven. But we should have your room fixed up by Monday. Ask the porter to put a call through to me and I'll come and meet you at the lodge.'

'Oh thank you. You're so kind. You always seem to appear just when I am at a loss what to do next.'

Rather embarrassed, Roger muttered a gruff disclaimer and left the quad with unnecessary haste. Julia made him feel uncomfortable. Well, of course she would. Bloody nuisance, women. College should be a men's club where we can get away from them. He went into the library and greeted Miss Dickenson absent-mindedly.

'I've just met the new woman lecturer.' Miss Dickenson's cultured voice had a slight edge to it. 'Nobody told me about her. I all but turned her out of the library.'

Roger stared at her without replying. Odd, he'd never thought of her as being a bloody nuisance in a men's club. Well, of course she had her place. She belonged in the library. As far as he'd ever been concerned, she didn't have any existence out of it. He shrugged, both in answer and to free himself from an uncomfortable sensation.

Everard drove his aged Range Rover into the village and down the drive to the ramshackle house he and his family inhabited. He noticed neither the weeds in the gravel of the drive nor the peeling paint on the front door. Jean noticed them but felt inadequate to do or say anything about them. She'd enjoyed the tea in the college buttery with the boys and had no wish to dispel the harmony of the moment. Everard could be fun when he chose to extend his charm to his family. It tended to happen when there was somebody else in the background to put him into a good humour; when he was either anticipating or relishing some new conquest; but ten years of marriage to him had reduced Jean to a philosophy of thankfulness for small mercies. Theirs was an "open marriage"; they had an agreement that they were both free to go to bed with other people, provided they didn't get emotionally involved. The worst sin was jealousy. Jean gave a sigh and reached for her cigarettes. She watched Everard playing with the boys and braced herself to react suitably to his casual mention that he "had to go back to college" that evening.

Emily Matheson had spent most of the summer vacation at home in the United States and Everard had largely forgotten about her until he had received a letter in college indicating her return to Camford and her need for his advice. Their encounters so far had been limited to a lunch and two after-dinner sessions in his room. Everard's behaviour had been, he hoped, at once enticing and disarming. He was adept at what he called "verbal flirtation". This was particularly useful for lunches and tutorials. The next stage was the "nearly but not quite" approach. This had worked well with Emily. In showing her a passage in a book or discussing a particular paragraph of her own work he had stood over her or sat beside her, enjoying her quickening of breath and uncertainty as to his next move, and just when she was expecting an arm round her shoulder or a hand on her thigh, would nonchalantly resume a lolling position in his own chair, from where he would look at her quizzically and smile as if with inner amusement. Emily had not been quite able to hide her disappointment.

Emily knocked at the door promptly at 7:45. Everard stood up as she came in. He was not in the habit of standing up for women; certainly not for women he was supervising or teaching, but Emily's appearance took him unawares. Her blond hair, perfect from an expensive cut, was brighter and her Californian tan deeper than after an unbroken year in damp and cloudy Camford. She was wearing a plain dress, fitted to the hips and revealing her delicate symmetry, then flaring to a modest length just below her knees. Everard gave her an involuntary blink of undisguised appreciation and had to force himself to remember that he ought to look sardonic and superior. Authoritatively he took charge of the situation.

'I'm going to take you out to dinner. It's too beautiful an evening for work now. We'll see about that later.'

His sudden, acute desire for her was almost matched by his desire to show her off; he wanted to be seen in charge of this perfect creature. Pity he didn't have a sleek sports car with an open top. That was the right setting for a gem like Emily. Like many Camford dons he was not materialistic. Cars in themselves interested him very little, but now he decided that his battered family car, unshining and littered with the debris of sweet papers and crisp packets, normally unnoticed by the parents of small children, would not do for the drive to a country restaurant that he was intending. A surge of excitement overwhelmed him. Would that old fool Julian Holloway-Smythe have left the keys in his Triumph as he usually did, thinking it safely enough stowed away inside the walls and locked gates of the college? He guided Emily down the clattering wooden stairs and into the lodge.

'Wait here for a moment while I decide where we are going.' He sped into the back quad, saw Julian's Triumph standing, as usual, with its nose towards the giant doors of the north gate. It was open, of course; not much point in locking it with the hood down. Old Julian pretended he lived in a stately home and was invulnerable. Well, of course, a college was rather like that, come to think of it. Now – keys? Yes, in the glove box. Everard loped back to the lodge and Emily.

'Yes, it's OK,' he said as nonchalantly as he could with his heart pounding, both from unwontedly swift movement and exhilaration at his own daring. Of course he was only borrowing the thing. If he were to ask Julian, he'd probably lend it to him.

'Come and sit in the car while I get the gate open.' Like all college Fellows he had keys to the massive medieval doors which folded back to the stone walls with surprising ease and silence. He drove the car out on to the pavement of the wide street, closed the door again and got into the car beside Emily.

'This is almost like a North American car,' Emily purred approvingly, 'except of course that I feel a little disorientated sitting on this side and not driving.' Everard noted the clichéd observation but was swiftly deciding that Emily's company and appearance rendered it tolerable when she continued: 'I've been driving an open-top automobile all summer.'

'Your own?' hazarded Everard.

'Well no. No, it belongs to a friend.'

'A boy-friend?'

'Uh… well, more an older man friend. He's over thirty. I used to go out with college boys before but now I've been here in Camford I find older men so much more… interesting.'

So that's it, thought Everard. She's got a lot more poise and polish than she had last year; she's lost that gawkiness tall girls often have before they've grown into themselves and she doesn't seem to be scared of me any more. He turned as if to look sharply to the left and caught Emily's knowing reminiscent half-smile. A flash of envy, even jealousy, of the 'older man friend' increased his desire for the girl and his awareness of it. They were on the edge of the town, leaving the lights behind them.

CHAPTER SEVEN

Jean Lucas was trying to put the boys to bed. They didn't want to go and were being as difficult, balky and demanding as possible. Three against one she thought is simply not fair. If only Everard could be here sometimes to exert some authority and provide physical help. She continued mechanically with the business of running a bath and trying to retrieve last night's pyjamas from a muddle of sheets and blankets on unmade beds. The 'if only' had started her on a reverie of wishful thinking. If only I could find somebody who'd love me and help me and cope with the children for my sake and carry home some of the shopping and make the boys behave better… The mythical perfect husband took a vague shape in her mind: not too young or old; not so clever as to put her down all the time, but clever enough to appreciate her own intellect; patient, good tempered, devoted… appearance not important. I sound like something out of a lonely hearts column, she laughed to herself. Anyway, such men don't exist.

In the tall house on the north side of the narrow street Julia was also putting children into bath and bed. Her husband was also absent but she was being helped by Tim. The children were cavorting about naked, laughing and squealing with delight as Tim swished water into the bath and made steamboat noises and shouted instructions to the 'crews'. Julia merely provided towels and sleep-suits and left them to it while she prepared dinner for herself and Tim. Dinners didn't come into Tim's rights as a lodger but were a tacit reward for his help. Besides he was company and, as often as not, did half the cooking himself and most of the clearing up. 'Which is a lot more than Jeremy ever does' Julia thought rather grimly. If Jeremy weren't so attractive to look at and so good in bed there'd be little point in having him as a husband.

Everard and Emily, in the illicitly borrowed sports car, sped into the country. Everard was in a state of high excitement such as he had never experienced since his earliest days as an undergraduate. The combination of his own daring, the power and prestige of the sleek fast car and the erotic signals he was receiving from the apparently emancipated Emily, produced an electrical atmosphere charged at the same time with heightened perception and a sense of escapist unreality. Having dinner was going to be a tantalising delay when all he wanted to do was stop the car on the side of the road and leap on the girl. He sighed in frustration and drove into the courtyard of a small stone building, half concealed by picturesque vegetation, which housed an exclusive - and very expensive - restaurant. The car glided into a dark space between a Bentley and a yew hedge and Everard had hardly brought it to a halt before he put an arm round Emily, touched her left breast lightly with his right hand caressing the nipple delicately as he kissed her, tantalisingly gently, once, then with a small protrusion of his tongue, twice, then as she was responding with a gasp of pleasure said quietly 'Dinner first!'

The first course was king prawns served in their shells, in a garlic and lemon sauce. Emily picked them apart delicately, leaving a not inconsiderable amount of the flesh in the tails. Everard picked one from her plate, held it to her mouth and said 'Suck it!'. Emily lowered her eyes, took the prawn tail in her own hand, and as Everard held his own hand over hers did as she was told.

'Delicious, isn't it?' murmured Everard.

'Delicious,' Emily sighed with an almost imperceptible shiver of anticipation.

A main course and a bottle of wine later, Everard and Emily returned to the car hand in hand. After a swiftly light caress, Everard drove out of the courtyard and sped back to Camford, increasingly anxious over the undetected return of the car to its rightful place and increasingly aware of his aching desire for Emily, whose right hand was stroking the back of his neck with delicate fingertips. At last the great college gate had been opened and closed again; the car had come to rest in its place on the cobbles and Everard and Emily hurried with a wholly indecent haste to Everard's room at the top of the clattering wooden staircase, the room where the leather sofa was large and long. Everard pulled Emily close to him, swiftly undid the long zip at the back of her dress, eased it over her shoulders and let it slide to the floor. He held her at arms length for a moment, relishing the sight of her in a barely necessary bra and - to his mind - wholly unnecessary knickers, then removed the top garment before laying her on the sofa and removing the bottom one, and Emily accommodatingly bent her knees and raised her legs to aid this manœuvre.

Jean Lucas, exhausted by her efforts with the children, having at last got them all into their respective beds, sank gratefully into her own, the king-sized one she shared with Everard; she briefly wondered where Everard might be, set the alarm clock, put her pillow into a comfortable position and fell asleep almost immediately.

Julia and Jeremy lay in their large double bed in the room above the kitchen which Tim had cleared and tidied after the dinner he and Julia had shared. They lay well apart and spoke with quiet voices and veiled animosity, Jeremy unsuccessfully attempting to hide the slurring of his words.

'So you enjoyed the dinner?' said Julia - more as a statement than a question.

'Yes, it was very pleashant.'

'Tim helped me with the children and cleared up after dinner.'

'I wish you wouldn't let him have so much to do with the children!'

'Why?'

'Well, for one thing, he's teaching them all to say "pardon".'

'If you were here more often, I wouldn't need him to have so much to do with the children. I appreciate his help too significantly to worry about a few "pardons".'

'When I went to my first prep school, the headmaster slapped me across the face for saying "pardon".'

'I know. You've told me that story before. It's very distressing but only shows how horribly wrong the headmaster's priorities were.'

'All the same - it won't do, you know. They'll be talking about the "toilet" next. Obvious that that chap's never been to a boarding school.'

'And it's equally obvious that you were at a boarding school far too long.' Julia turned away from her husband leaving a cold gap in the bed between them and trying to close her ears to his almost immediate inebriated snoring.

CHAPTER EIGHT

Julian Holloway-Smythe looked up from what he called the luncheon table as Everard Lucas entered the dons' dining room.

'Hah! Lucas!' he hailed him. 'Coming to the Women's night?'

Everard, his mind on Emily whom he had already invited, smiled what he imagined to be a sardonic smile of reminiscence and anticipation.

'Of course,' he answered. Julian was officially in charge of the Women's nights which everybody else called Ladies' nights, and always tried to make sure that they would be well attended.

'Come and have sherry with me beforehand; I'm inviting our own woman, Julia, and her guest, which is really what you should be doing, but I don't imagine you've had the nous to think of it.'

Certainly, Everard hadn't. He was far too involved in his affair with Emily to give any thought to his junior colleague outside the necessities of their working relationship.

'You bringing a woman yourself, Julian?'

'Aha! wait and see!' was Julian's reply.

Everard had been a little wary of Julian since the

car episode, and had shown this, unconsciously, by an increase of hauteur and coolness towards him. For all that he'd returned the vehicle to the place safely and without incident or detection, the cold light of dawn and reason had found him far more disquieted at the enormity of his offence in taking a colleague's car without consent, than at his seduction of Emily. In fact the latter was a source of pride rather than compunction of any kind. Julian had absolutely no suspicion that his car had been driven by anybody other than himself, but there was that in Everard Lucas's attitude to him which annoyed him: arrogant, unkempt, fellow; too utterly heterosexual; too casual in all his attitudes. He badly wanted to do something snide to get under that apparently rhinocerine skin. And he'd hit on a very good idea. Just the thing.

'Oh frabjous day!' he said to himself. 'Calloo, callay' he continued to quote, and suiting action to remembered words; he chortled in his joy.

Julia's husband was not at all pleased that she was going to the College guest night with Tim.

'What do you mean, you can't ask me?'

'I told you it's simply not done for men to take their wives to guest nights or vice versa. It's practically forbidden, in fact. Surely you don't mind me going with Tim. It's not like taking some stray man you don't know. Besides, look how often you go out to dinner without me.'

Jeremy's immediate impulse to say 'That's different' was stifled in time for him to change it into 'That's di-decided, then. But why don't you take another woman next time? Some of your friends must be dying to go.'

'I'll see what this is like and then think about it,' said Julia coolly. Having a job with male colleagues was making her look at Jeremy more objectively. Jeremy felt this and became increasingly defensive.

'I expect he'll say "pardon" all the time and ask for the "toilet",' he sniffed.

'A good half of my colleagues do that anyway,' retorted Julia. 'Well, say "pardon". They don't need to ask me or anybody else where the lavatories are. Though the Bursar was quite embarrassed about telling me which one I could use, especially as it's miles away from anywhere I'm likely to be for any other purpose!'

'Does the Bursar talk about "toilets"?'

'Oh no, he's an Old Harrovian'.

Everard was favouring his wife and family with his presence at supper. His affair with Emily was having such a mellowing effect that some of his good humour was even overflowing in Jean's direction.

'By the way,' she ventured, deeming the time and Everard's mood ripe for revelation and request, 'I've been invited to your ladies' guest night next Wednesday, so I hope you'll be coming home that afternoon and be able to take me to College with you.'

Everard was aghast. He saw his plans for himself and Emily blighted into extinction. He had only just sufficient presence of mind to render his expression blank and his voice casual.

'Really?' he said. 'Who's invited you?'

'Julian Holloway-Smythe.'

The cunning devil, Everard thought; he'd looked as if he had some malicious trick up his sleeve. 'Oh, yes, of course. Didn't I tell you I was taking one of my graduates? Girl I'm supervising. Usual thing to do, you know.'

'Oh yes,' said Jean, trying to sound equally casual and as if she didn't know all too well, 'I knew you'd be going too so I arranged a babysitter.'

The supper continued with the clamourous squabbling of the children taking a large enough share of their parents' attention to hide the fact that the atmosphere had altered and the tension between them aggravated.

Tim drove Julia to the dinner in his small aged car.

'I've arranged with the porter to let us park in the back quad,' Julia told him.

'You must have got on the right side of him then.'

'Well, yes, I hope so. Though he still tends to address me as "Sir - er Madam". But we swap stories about my children and his grandchildren, so he regards me as a human being. I daren't mention children to any of my colleagues. If I ever do, a sort of glazed look comes into their eyes and the subject's changed immediately.'

Tim was busy negotiating a squeeze between a bus and another car and wasn't listening.

'Pardon?' he said.

'What!' said Julia, acidly, more influenced by Jeremy's strictures than she would have been willing to admit.

'I was always taught it was rude to say "what",' said Tim.

'Yes, I've no doubt you were!' Julia was on edge. These social occasions were far more difficult and fraught with pitfalls than any day to day encounters, and teaching, where she felt completely in control, was a delight in comparison. 'I'm sorry, Tim. I'm not looking forward to this dinner. It's quite nerve racking, being the first one.'

Tim made allowances and soothing noises; but he felt a little put down all the same.

Julian Holloway-Smythe welcomed them into his rooms with elaborate courtesy. He cast a practised eye over Tim and decided immediately that he was 'not public school' and must be condescended to, and another eye over Julia, wondering what she was doing with 'a chap like that'. Jean arrived next, alone. Everard was waiting in his rooms for Emily. He'd timed her arrival exactly so that he could have a few minutes alone with her after sending Jean over to join Julian.

Jean was quite as much on edge as was Julia. She mistrusted her husband's motives in appointing a woman lecturer and had no idea how to approach another woman in a guise so unfamiliar. She was even more distrustful of his relationship with women graduate students, but at least on more familiar ground, especially as their thesis subjects were likely to be akin to her own and she could show a knowledgeable interest in them. Socially she was her husband's inferior, not being 'public school' stock, but in Camford's Academia this was rarely a problem: so many high-up academics were American or Colonial (so-called) or advanced from humble British origins via Grammar Schools and scholarships. She occasionally had some feeling that Everard had married her to spite his family and to show off his relatively newly acquired Socialist principles, but it was hardly a major issue. There were more important things at odds in their relationship.

Nevertheless, in the presence of Julian Hollow-Smythe's affectedly Old School jargon and formality, Jean found Julia's totally unaffected "how do you do" a little off-putting, and Tim's equally unaffected and clearly sincere "pleased to meet you" both genuine and reassuring. She gave him a rare smile of fellow-feeling, and they were already engaged in conversation when Everard and Emily came into the room. Conversation ceased. There was nothing so obvious as a gasp from anybody, but the impact of Emily's beauty was apparent. Flattered by what she saw as her entrée to Senior Common Room society, and elated by her relationship with Everard, she had excelled herself in the understated perfection of her makeup and the expensive, but revealing, simplicity of her dress. Julian Holloway-Smythe kissed her hand with ostentatious Olde Worlde chivalry; Tim was considerably awed and said "pleased to meet you" in a dazed voice, several seconds after being introduced, and Jean, having a sense of empathy with Tim, immediately echoed his words, thus eliciting a very black look from her husband, who was conscious of Julia's critical eye sweeping him and his wife and his guest in one comprehensive glance. "Married-beneath-him-and-making-up-for-it" that glance conveyed and its purport was not lost on Everard. He was angry with his wife, proud of his guest and discomfited by his colleague, all at once. Tim, however, turned a grateful countenance on Jean which confirmed their fellow-feeling as the most 'normal' people in the gathering, and they resumed their conversation happily.

CHAPTER NINE

Julian Holloway-Smythe shepherded his group of guests over to the SCR; not, of course, that either Everard or Julia, or indeed anybody but Tim, needed shepherding, but once in the role of host, Julian played it to the full. They entered the dark panelled room where an unnecessary but attractive fire was shining in the stone fireplace; they were introduced, as appropriate, to the other dons and their guests, and stood about in an awkward series of silences interspersed with general pleasantries expressed in cleverly adapted clichés. Dons are not, on the whole, skilled in social chit-chat, and the ladies' guest nights were still a new enough phenomenon to generate an atmosphere of unease, at least until the alcohol levels had been topped up by more than a couple of glasses of sherry. Hector Otis had brought an old flame of his called Charlotte. He had some hopes of rekindling this flame, and indeed only that morning he had awakened to announce to his wife, somewhat petulantly: 'Oh dear! I was dreaming I was in bed with Charlotte!'

Shona had felt a sharp pang of unhappiness before being reminded of a song one of her brothers used to sing as a naughty schoolboy.

Charlotte, the harlot, the cow-punchers' whore,

You could have her for thruppence or sixpence or more...

Shona couldn't remember any more of the words, if indeed she'd ever known them, as her brother had usually been stopped and slapped or otherwise punished before getting any further. To Hector's surprise she'd burst into a nervous giggle; it was not the reaction he would have expected. This early morning scene played itself over in his mind as he stood next to Charlotte in the SCR trying to think of something witty and amusing to say. The entrance of Everard and Emily had not helped. Emily's Nordic beauty and Everard's proprietary attitude to her drew envious looks from all the males. None of the other women present could compete, with the possible exception of Julia, whom they were all used to seeing, and her beauty was of a more delicate, less obtrusive kind. 'More intellectual really,' thought Roger as he viewed the scene from a little way off. 'More of an acquired taste' he added to himself, 'but once acquired ...' He stopped himself in mid-thought and turning abruptly to the duties in hand went among the guests. Julian was warning Jean of the slipperiness of the wooden staircase and repeating his story about the Principal of a women's college falling a regular - he was about to say "arser", thought it was not quite suitable to the company and was struggling for a more suitable word when the butler appeared and announced: 'Dinner is served.' Without mishap, everybody filed up the stairs, two-by-two. Hector was telling Charlotte how somebody had once had the temerity to liken this procession to the animals going into the ark. 'Too banal a cliché, don't you think,' he concluded.

'Well,' Charlotte mused as they stood in their places and she was able to view the dons and their guests, 'they don't exactly look like pairs, do they?' Her eyes flickered from the ethereal-looking Gabriel beside his loud, fat mistress, to swarthy, slightly stooping Everard and blond, upright Emily.

'Oh, I don't know' lisped Hector with a smile approaching a simper, 'I think some of us could pair off very happily!'

Charlotte glanced at his smug pink face and hoped he wasn't thinking of her and himself. Roger, acting for the absent Principal of the college, picked up a small wooden hammer, struck a small wooden dish with it, and as the sound reverberated round the ancient hall said distinctly: 'Benedictus benedicat', using the old, anglicized pronunciation of the Latin words so that the last two syllables sounded like "Die, cat!" - a source of mirth to generations of new undergraduates.

There was a sudden din of scraping chairs and everybody sat down. Charlotte was on Roger's right and Jean on his left. Opposite him, Everard was torn between wanting to concentrate on Emily alone and being forced to pay attention to the chaplain's guest, a voluble woman research fellow who was convinced that she had discovered the identity of the Dark Lady of Shakespeare's Sonnets and was pouring a resumé of her irrefutable proofs into the unwilling ear of her table neighbour. On the other side of the chaplain a heavy-looking woman with an equally heavy Teutonic accent was asking him in puzzlement:

'Zis Dark Lady, vot iss it? Iss it a ghost?'

The chaplain explained that it was generally supposed to have been Shakespeare's mistress.

'His mistress?' The speaker glared at the chaplain in disgust. 'Vot? You pry into ze private life of zis man?'

The chaplain murmured that "This man" had been dead rather a long time and didn't seem to have made any bones about his feelings for the Dark Lady even in his lifetime. The Teutonic lady, however, continued to express strongly her disappointment and disapproval of the Camford academics whose studies took such a form.

The entrée consumed, the fish course was

brought on. There was a whole fish on each plate, a dark-skinned, shining fish complete with tail and head and an eye gazing accusingly at each diner. Emily looked at hers with a shiver of revulsion.

'What's the matter?' Everard saw her reaction and felt a little sadistic, rather than protective. 'I know how well you cope with prawns - even king-sized prawns! Surely you can manage a little fish!'

'It's the eyes' Emily replied faintly. 'That eye staring up at me makes me feel awful!'

On her right the elderly don who'd been making a show of fatherly interest in her all through the first course, caught the word "offal", as Emily had pronounced it, and hastened to assure her that there was 'nothing wrong with offal! Nothing at all. Food fit for kings. But this is not offal, my dear, not in England anyway. Great delicacy, especially the eyes. Now when you take the eye out, be sure to eat the bit just behind it - see!' He demonstrated by prizing the eye out of his own fish and pointing with his fork.

Everard noted Emily's discomfiture and enjoyed the superior feeling it gave him. He liked to patronize his women. He looked over to where Julia was sitting and saw that she was handling her fish expertly. 'She would!' he thought, annoyed. So far he was finding it difficult to feel superior to Julia, despite the seniority of his position in the college. He decided not to see how his wife was coping and turned back to Emily, whose wine glass had been refilled by a college servant. She was downing the wine with gratitude and rapidity. "Good" thought Everard - and then remembered his wife's presence - and said "Fuck!" very gently under his breath.

Emily cut the head off her fish, hid as much of it as possible under the garnish and struggled to eat a few mouthfuls of the body.

Course after course appeared, expertly served from the left of each guest by suitably vested college servants. At last the signal was given to rise. Roger struck the gavel against the wood again and said 'Benedicat Benedicato' which sounded like "Benny die cat Benedick Cato". A former head of the college had once had two cats called Benedick and Cato, but only the more serious-minded undergraduates had found that amusing.

'Now, you must keep hold of your napkin,' Everard explained to Emily, 'because you'll need it for dessert'

'Dessert?' she queried, 'but we already ate dessert.'

Everard always enjoyed this part of dinner with a guest unfamiliar with the ways of college high tables. 'What we had before the savoury was pudding. Dessert is fruit and so on, but mainly fruit. People who have two or three more courses after the main meat course distinguish them by name, but most people only have one, so they call it anything. But now we take off our gowns and we all go into the dessert room and sit beside somebody different, somebody we didn't sit beside at dinner.'

Everard was pleased and not surprised to note that there was already some subtle but appreciative hovering round Emily. With the exception of Roger, who had already appropriated Julia, and Tim, who had thankfully rejoined Jean, all the men seemed to be jockeying for a position near the Nordic blonde. The Teutonic lady had noticed this and was regarding Emily with obvious dislike, while the literary female specialist on the Sonnets of Shakespeare pondered, not for the first time, on the unusual sensitivity and discrimination shown in his choice of a dark-haired woman as his mistress.

Hector had made considerably less headway than he had hoped with Charlotte; he felt aggrieved. Dammit, she was still single, wasn't she?. He'd expected her to be pleased and flattered by his gallant attentions, and instead of that she'd turned them off neatly, asked a lot of rather searching questions about Shona, and implied quite overtly that she was very glad not to be in Shona's shoes. He decided to show her that he greatly preferred Emily, anyway.

'Here's matter more attractive,' he murmured. Economist though he might be, Hector prided himself on keeping up with the arts, regularly went to the theatre in London and Stratford, and had, he considered, little need to brush up his Shakespeare. Roger fortuitously placed him next to Emily at dessert. Emily, having swallowed as much white wine as the servitor could pour in order to wash down the fish, had become thirsty enough to take an equal amount of red wine with the venison, and was beginning to feel a floating sense of unreality as she contemplated yet another table loaded with lighted candles, beautiful old silver and, this time, artistically piled heaps of fruit. She tried to focus, both visually and aurally, on Hector who was explaining how the port must always be passed to the left and that she should pour herself a glass and then pass it on immediately - though, of course, she could have Madeira if she preferred. 'Oh, port. Thank you.' Emily did as she was told and was vaguely aware of placing some grapes and a slice of pineapple on her plate. Everything seemed to be at an unusual sort of distance away. She took a sip of port. She'd never had it before. It tasted delicious; sweeter than the red wine at dinner and somehow very soothing. She ate a little fruit and had another glass of port as soon as it came round. Hector was talking volubly and rejoicing in what he took to be her wide-eyed gaze of rapt attention. Actually her smile was due to the euphoric effect of the port and her attentive appearance to her efforts to keep Hector's features in focus. The port came round for a third time and with it a small casket of fine old silver.

'Wass this?' asked Emily with a careful attempt at clarity. Hector was delighted to explain the use of the fine, brown, odorous powder.

'It's snuff' he told Emily. 'A way of getting the effect of tobacco without smoking it.'

'I don't believe it,' Emily gasped. 'You guys - people - still use snuff here? I thought that was finished in the eighteenth century! Oh no, I couldn't, no thank you.' Emily passed on the nauseating substance and did her best to suppress the realisation that she was feeling rather nauseated anyway.

Everard had watched this little scene with a smile of amusement, partly Emily's reaction, and partly at her thwarting of Hector's obviously intended explanation. It was funny, he reflected, how much men enjoyed explaining things to attractive young women and yet got so impatient when explaining anything to their wives. When the snuff came to Julia, Everard's smile broadened.

'This'll put her in her place,' he thought. Julia, however took a small pinch of the powder between her right thumb and forefinger, deposited it on the back of her left hand and from there sniffed it delicately and successfully into each nostril. Everard's smile faded. Roger, taking the snuff-box from Julia's left hand, said 'I see you're no stranger to snuff.'

'No,' Julia replied 'though it's a while since I've taken it. When I was an undergraduate I used to have my own mixture made up for me at Fribourg and Treyer's. I rather liked "Prince's Special", too. Is this one a college special?'

Roger, who had never really thought about it before, murmured an affirmative and pondered on the many facets of Julia's personality.

They rose from the table. Hector solicitously put a hand under Emily's elbow to steady her. Everard saw this and glowered. Tim and Jean were still too eagerly engaged in conversation to notice anything else and Roger drew his attention away from Julia only in order to initiate the withdrawal to the next stage of the festivities: coffee and brandy or whisky in the SCR. The fire was still burning brightly and the atmosphere was in every way warmer and more relaxed than it had been over sherry.

'It seems hours since we were here before,' said Julia to Roger, 'and yet, in other ways it's passed amazingly quickly - especially the dessert.' Julia turned her rare smile on Roger. He heard himself say, 'Coffee? Brandy?' abruptly, and without waiting for an answer he turned away.

Hector Otis brought a large brandy to Emily only to find that Everard had already put one into her hand.

'Never mind,' he said benignly. 'Have both.'

A misty thought suggested to Emily that he meant both himself and Everard, as well as both glasses of brandy and she gave a little giggle. Hector was delighted and only with difficulty did he remember his own guest. He introduced her to Julia and watched with relief as they appeared to get on well together. Sometimes, he reflected, it was quite useful to have a woman member of Common Room.

The coffee drunk and the conversation dwindling, at least in some parts of the room, moves were made to go. Jean reminded Everard that it might be a good idea to go and relieve the babysitter.

'Shall we drop Emily off on the way?' she asked.

'Yes, of course. But she's left some books and things in my room,' said Everard. 'You wait here while I take her over to get them.'

Jean watched him go over to where Emily was sitting and prize her away from Hector Otis and a couple of other men, to whose conversation she was apparently listening with interest.

Tim was watching Jean and he saw her mouth compress into a sad smile. He went up to her, touched her arm and said 'I'd like to come and see you and meet the boys.'

Everard guided Emily across the quad, up the stairs and into his room. She needed guiding. Once in his room he took her in his arms and gave her a long expressive kiss. Emily pulled away from him. She looked horrified.

'I'm going to vomit!' she said.

With all speed and none of the nonchalance of his usual loping gait, Everard opened two doors and pushed her into a little room, next to his, which contained a lavatory and a sink with taps.

'In here!' he said. 'Quick!'

For several minutes Emily was very sick. Eventually she emerged. 'Ugh!' she said.

'All right now?' Everard was a little anxious. He put his hands under her elbows to hold her up, but she sank quite gracefully to the floor.

'Ugh,' she said again - and passed out completely.

For the second time that evening Everard said "Fuck!" And then reflected bitterly that it was an expletive particularly inappropriate in the circumstances.

CHAPTER TEN

The only people left in the SCR were Roger, whose duty it was to stay until everybody else had departed; Julian, who couldn't leave until his guest did; Jean, who was waiting for Everard with increasing unease and irritation; Tim, who had no intention of leaving while Jean was still there, and Julia, who was waiting for Tim. Finally Everard appeared. He managed to muster up a semblance of insouciance as he spoke.

'I don't really know what to do. Emily seems to have lost consciousness.'

Tim laughed and Roger couldn't contain something of a guffaw. 'Passed out, you mean! Well, I can't say I'm surprised the way you kept plying the girl with drink. Serves you right.'

'I can't just leave her there,' said Everard crossly, annoyed at his colleague's attitude. 'You take the car back, Jean, and relieve the baby-sitter, and I'll stay in college - well - at least until I can get the girl home.'

'Oh, I can't take the car Everard. I've had too much to drink. And anyway, you'll need it to take her home in - and ...' Jean would have liked to say it was most unsuitable for Everard to spend the night with Emily in his room, however drunk she might be, but faltered into silence.

'I'll take you home, Jean.' said Tim. 'I'll drop Julia off first and then take you.'

'Oh, that's so kind - but it's in the opposite direction and a long way and ...'

'Nonsense,' said Julia quickly. 'Of course Tim can take you home, and don't worry about dropping me off ...'

'I can take you,' said Roger. 'It's on my way anyhow; then Jean can get back to her baby-sitter all the sooner.'

Julian Holloway-Smythe, aware that his plan to queer Everard's pitch by inviting his wife to the dinner was not entirely successful, had by now had enough of the "women's night", enough of his guest and more than enough to drink, said his effusive goodnights and went thankfully to bed.

Everard went slowly across the quad again and wearily ascended the seemingly innumerable stairs to his room. Emily was snoring very slightly. He threw his black university gown over her unconscious curves, registered a faint hope that she might recover sufficiently to be of some use before dawn, slumped on to the sofa and went to sleep himself.

Roger drove slowly the longest possible way to

Julia's house. He was excited by her nearness and happy in her company; feelings he had not experienced for many years, had in fact almost totally rejected or forgotten.

'Did you enjoy the guest night?' he asked her.

'Some of it. There were some rather tense moments, I thought, in spite of the vast amounts of alcohol consumed. Everard's guest made quite a stir, didn't she?'

'Hmph! Archetypal dumb blond in spite of her academic pretensions. But trust Everard!'

'I'd rather not, I think.' Julia laughed lightly, then added more seriously, 'I'm sure his wife doesn't.'

'Can't think how he gets away with it – the way be behaves to girls – other women – in front of his wife. Must be deeply hurtful and embarrassing for her.'

'I don't think people do get away with these things, not for ever, anyway. Disappointment and distress, anger and resentment build up and up until eventually the volcano blows its top and out comes the lava and kills off everything in its path.'

'A very graphic image! You're a wise woman for your years.'

'I've been married for quite a few of them.'

Roger glanced at he quickly. 'Happily?' he enquired.

'In the main – like most people, I suppose. We've

got less in common than we thought we had when we got married – but men like Everard make me realise how lucky I am really. Besides, I believe "once married, always married" so one just gets on and makes the most of it.'

'Is this belief on religious grounds?'

'Not really.'

'You're not a religious person then.' Roger had long since given up any practice of the religion he'd been brought up in, apart from obligatory appearances in the college chapel, and found himself hoping that Julia was similarly emancipated.

'I'm a Catholic atheist.'

Again, Roger glanced sharply at Julia. Could she be serious?

'I'm quite serious.' Julia answered his glance. 'I believe as much as I believe anything that Catholicism has the answer – all the answers. I believe in its rightness. But I believe it intellectually. I haven't any faith. "Haven't got the faith" as Catholics say. Faith's a gift and I haven't been given it. Not yet, anyway.'

'So you believe that marriage is forever indissoluble?'

'Well, not a civil marriage, necessarily, but a religious one, a sacramental one, as the Catholic church teaches.'

Roger was far more interested in the state of Julia's own marriage than in the Roman Catholic

Church's views on the subject of matrimony. 'So where does that put you? Presumably you were not married in a Catholic church – or before a Catholic priest?'

'Oh no. In an Anglican one with all the trimmings; both our families insisted on it. I think I do regard it as sacramental and binding, though Anglican ideas are rather mixed about it.'

'You and your husband come from much the same kind of background then?'

'Yes – and I think that's important. Marriage is a very social thing, isn't it? It's so important to agree on how one brings up and educates one's children. Though my husband's much more fussy about details than I am; but that's because all his experience is based on schools rather than a university. Of course he's got a Camford degree – but I don't think he mixed much, in all his three years, with any men who hadn't been to his school or a similar one. Of course it's not fashionable to say such things these days – but one must be realistic.'

The conversation had taken altogether too serious and philosophical a turn for Roger's liking. Julia tried to lighten it a little .

'I don't suppose I'd be talking like this if I hadn't had too much to drink at that dinner! How you men can cope with two guest nights a week is more than I can fathom. I think one a term will be enough for me!'

Roger surprised himself by saying: 'Oh no. You must come to both.'

'Here's my house,' said Julia with some relief. She was beginning to find Roger not unattractive and that, she thought, was not a good idea. 'Thank you for being so kind to me – not only this evening but all the time. People told me you delighted in being rude and abrupt, and I thought it was true at first – but you're much nicer than that, like Mr Darcy!'

'Mr Darcy?'

'You know – in *Pride and Prejudice*. Thank you again. Good night.'

Roger's wife was not asleep when he gently opened the door of the bedroom.

'You're later than usual, aren't you?' she asked

'Yes. That bloody sod Everard brought in some young woman graduate and gave her far too much to drink, and then there was a problem about getting some of the women home. Blasted nuisance. I always said the whole thing was a sodding ridiculous idea.'

He undressed swiftly, got into bed and turned out his bedside light with what sounded like an angry snap; but he was aware that his anger was only a pretence and that he felt some unidentifiable emotion of elation, almost excitement. He preferred it to sleep; wanted to enjoy it while it lasted. More than an hour later Roger's wife was awakened by the sound of the bedroom door opening and closing.

'Oh, that stupid man,' she said aloud. 'He must have had too much to drink. If I don't go down and get him some bicarbonate of soda there'll be hell to pay tomorrow.' For a few minutes she fought the desire to go back to sleep and leave Roger to his own devices, then she put on a dressing gown and slippers and shuffled downstairs.

Roger was in the easy chair in his study, reading. 'I couldn't sleep' he said, rather defensively. 'I need to read something soothing.'

'What is it?'

Roger's answer sounded faintly ashamed. '*Pride and Prejudice*' he said.

Tim's car chugged gently along the country road. "Sputter, sputter little car" he sang. "How I wonder what you are." He and Jean had reached the stage of companionship when continual conversation is no longer necessary.

'Funny we should come from the same part of the world,' Tim mused aloud.

'Oh, it's so nice to know somebody who's lived in Penrith,' said Jean. 'People down here have never heard of it.'

'People down here think Carlisle's a historian with the wrong spelling' Tim laughed. 'There's always been this thing about North and South!'

'Oh yes. Even Chaucer gives northern students funny accents and puts them into rather gross comic situations. So it goes back at least as far as that!'

'I feel very happy with you, Jean.'

'I do with you, too. Very – well I was going to say comfortable, but that sounds much too middle aged...'

'I know what you mean. I'm glad.'

'I don't even feel upset about Everard now. In fact, I've only just remembered to think about him.'

'Will he come home tonight?'

'I don't know. Probably not. He often sleeps in college when he's been to a guest night – or working late – well, that's what he says.'

'I wish we knew for certain he wouldn't be home.'

'Why?'

'Don't you know?'

'What?' Jean did know, but preferred to hear it from Tim.

'I want to stay with you.'

'Oh, Tim – you can't!'

'No?'

'We've only just met.'

'I feel as if we have known each other for a long time.'

'Oh, I know. I do too – but it's too soon. We might regret it.'

'Are you worried about Everard? You've told me you've got an "open marriage".'

'Yes, that's true… but I've never…, well, I've never really wanted to before.'

'But you do now?'

'Yes; but I'm afraid of spoiling it all.'

The little car humped into the Lucases' untidy back yard. Tim stopped the car and put a hand gently on Jean's arm. 'You're right,' he acknowledged quietly. 'I'm being too precipitate. I don't want to do anything that makes you feel unhappy. I don't want to risk spoiling it either. Can I see you tomorrow?'

'I've got to pick up the boys from school in the afternoon.'

'How will you get there?'

'Well, if Everard doesn't come home I'll have to go by bus.'

'That must be very exhausting.'

'I'm fairly used to it.'

'I'll come in the early afternoon and take you in the car.'

'Come to lunch, then?'

'Lunch seems a long time away – but all right.'

'I must go in now.'

'Kiss me first.' Tim kissed her mouth, lovingly, protectively, then her eyelids, then her mouth again. She was not unresponsive. He managed not to say 'let me stay' and murmured only 'Till tomorrow, then,' and watched Jean let herself safely into the house before he drove out of the bumpy yard and back on to the winding lane.

Julia pottered about in her kitchen before going upstairs. She felt she'd behaved rather badly with Roger, been rather pert, in fact, talking about his expected rudeness and surprising lack of it. She'd be embarrassed to see him again now. That's what came of drinking too freely at the dinner – even if she had only drunk about two thirds of the amount most of the men had put away. And some of the women, she reflected with amusement, thinking of Emily. She undressed in the bathroom to avoid waking Jeremy and then quietly opened the door of the nursery to see that the children were safely and soundly asleep.

'Mummy!' said a little voice, plaintively.

'Yes, darling. It's all right. Go to sleep.'

'I can't go to sleep. I haven't seen you all day and all night.'

'Oh, precious one, Mummy's tired and has to go to bed.'

'I want a cuddle.'

Julia felt a pang of guilt. Having a man's job and going to guest nights was all very well – but of course it was less than ideal for the children. She got into the child's bed and folded him in her arms.

'It's all right, darling. Mummy's here.' Richard put his thumb in his mouth and sucked it contentedly. Julia kissed the top of his head, rested her own head on his pillow and immediately fell asleep.

CHAPTER ELEVEN

Everard awoke, with a crick in his neck and a pain in his back, to the realisation that something was moving on the floor of his room.

'Ooooh,' it wailed. He sat up suddenly, remembering what it was.

'Emily!' he said. The desk lamp was still on and he watched Emily fumblingly disengage herself from the folds of his gown. She wailed again.

'How are you feeling?'

'Offal,' said Emily. 'Just offal.'

'One does feel awful with a hangover. But I expect you've had one before and recognise the symptoms. Do you remember anything about last night?'

Emily burst into tears. Everard felt impatient. Tears were all very well in a woman in the right setting and the right circumstances, but – he looked at his watch – at twenty past six in the morning when one was aching with weariness and discomfort and had a mouth like the bottom of a birdcage and expected silent sympathy rather than noise and responsibility, tears became very unattractive. Everard winced as Emily wailed again. Her voice seemed to have acquired a nasal quality, he considered.

'Oh, I feel absoloodly mordified,' sobbed Emily.

'Mortification of the flesh is supposed to be salutary in some quarters,' Everard responded, 'or did you in fact say "modified"?'

Emily stared at him, aware only that his tone was that of a tutor rather than a lover, and a somewhat sarcastic and intolerant tutor at that. Everard decided it was time to force himself into a better humour.

'I'll make us both a cup of coffee and then take you home before it gets any lighter.'

'Oh, I need to go to the bathroom.' Emily got to her feet unsteadily.

'Whatever for?' asked Everard, genuinely surprised. Emily looked puzzled and a little embarrassed. 'Oh!' exclaimed Everard. 'You mean the lavatory! Do you remember where it is?'

Emily did, all too well.

'Of course I do. And I want to wash up, anyway.'

'Wash up? There's nothing to wash up. We haven't used the cups yet and my scout always washes them up.'

'I mean,' Emily spoke slowly and distinctly, 'I

wanna wash my face and hayands.'

Even at 6:30 a.m. Everard was struck by the linguistic interest of the situation.

'I see! Wash up means wash the dishes in England, but in America ...'

'Yes,' interrupted Emily 'In the States it means get yourself washed.'

Everard decided not to keep Emily away from the lavatory any longer by observing aloud that in England "get yourself washed" meant to employ someone else to do it, but he mused on it silently, considering how right Oscar Wilde was about the English and Americans having everything in common except language. He seemed not to have noticed it before, but in fact, at this time in the morning, he was wondering what he did have in common with Emily apart from sex, and neither of them was in the mood for that.

They drank their coffee in a dispirited silence. Then Everard wrapped Emily in his gown again and took her across the main quad and into the back quad to his battered, sweet-paper and crisp littered vehicle. No chance of Julian's sports car this time.

'I've got the old fetch-the-children bus tonight,' he apologised in a hoarse whisper which sounded slightly aggressive.

Emily prised Jean's spine-protruding umbrella from the front passenger seat, sat down and with some difficulty found enough space for her feet among the litter of fruit-drink packets, crisps, sweet papers and the odd apple-core. She looked sideways at Everard's gaunt and beard-shadowed features and wondered how she could ever have considered him romantic or attractive.

Emily's digs were no distance away and Everard hardly had time to consider the best way to say goodnight to her, especially as the lightness of the sky and the growth of his beard would have made "good morning" more appropriate. He passed his left hand over his stubble and decided not to kiss her. It would leave her guessing anyway. He firmly refused to entertain the thought that she might turn her face away. It was odd how her voice had jarred on him this morning; he'd only found it attractive before.

'Stop! It's here!'

Emily interrupted his thoughts, sounding alarmed and anxious not to be driven any further than necessary. Everard stopped. Emily immediately turned away from him and fumbled fruitlessly with the wrong handle on the door.

'Oh, how do you open this thing?' Her voice sounded panicky.

Everard had to stretch his left arm over her to open the door for her. She shrank back into the seat and gave a small grimace which Everard was at a loss to interpret.

'There you are. Panic over,' he said in tones intended to be kind. 'Out you get.'

Emily remembered her manners sufficiently to feel she ought to say "thank you", but it stuck in her throat.

'Oh, I don't know what to say!' It came out as half whisper, half wail. 'No need to say anything. Go and get some proper sleep.'

Emily unwrapped herself from Everard's gown, threw it into the car, banged the door and ran stumbling up the path to the house. Everard watched her with no emotion but a slight sense of relief. He sat without moving and pondered the pros and cons of going home or back to College. He had tutorials at ten and eleven o'clock and none in the afternoon. Better go back to College, doze a little more, shave with the emergency razor he kept there. He could have breakfast in College, do his teaching and then go home. Just as well ordinary suits were worn at weekday guest nights and not black tie. He might have to brave a certain amount of banter at breakfast, but that he did not mind. He was all for letting his colleagues believe that his night had been much more exciting than had, in fact, been the case – especially that bugger Julian. Everard felt a qualm of guilt at the thought of Julian and gave a slight shiver as he wondered whether his inviting Jean to the "women's night" had been revenge for the "borrowing" of his car. He still felt it was too heinous a deed to get away with and was convinced that retribution must be waiting, however patiently, in the wings.

Shona Otis watched Hector drop his pyjamas on the floor and put on a clean pair of underpants. He really was getting much too fat. She was not sure whether to be worried because of the strain on his heart or pleased because it would render him less attractive to other women.

'How was Charlotte?' she asked aloud, adding 'the harlot' under her breath.

'Oh,' Hector pulled on a string vest and his fat pink face emerged out of it, 'she was fwightfully gwateful to be asked to dinner. I think she still wather likes me, you know. Poor old thing.'

Jeremy Leslie woke up drowsily at five to seven, put out an arm to touch Julia and found space. Not only space, but cold space. He sat up suddenly and switched on the light. A horrible thought struck him. Of course! She'd gone to that blasted college dinner with Tim! Where the bloody hell was she? In Tim's bed? Far too friendly, that chap. Far too familiar. He'd thought so before. He went hot and then cold. He wanted to rush up to Tim's room and fling the door open. Then he decided he really didn't want to. His heart pounding, he pulled on his paisley dressing-gown over what Tim had once referred to as his "public-school pyjamas" and realised that he had to have a pee before he did anything else. He went into the bathroom. Julia's dressing-gown was normally hanging on the back of the bathroom door when it was not in their bedroom. No sign of it. He went into the bedroom; it was not there either. Back in the bathroom he saw that Julia's clothes were hung over the towel rail and the side of the bath. Oh God! She must have undressed before going up to Tim's room. His heart pounded more furiously. Outside the bathroom door he stood on the landing rendered immobile by the conflict between his desire to race up the stairs and "confront them" as he put it and an equally powerful desire to escape the situation and go in the opposite direction. He felt numb and leaden. Then he heard music from the kitchen. Radio 3. Julia always listened to Radio 3. Well, at least he could investigate that first. He went downstairs very quietly, keeping to the wall side to minimise the creaking. The kitchen door was ajar and he could see Julia in her dressing-gown pouring a cup of tea as she hummed to the music on the radio. She looked up and gave a start as she saw him.

'What's the matter?' they both said, simultaneously.

'Why did you start like that?' demanded Jeremy.

'"And then it started like a guilty thing Upon a fearful summons"' Julia quoted. 'You look as if you'd seen the ghost of Hamlet's father yourself – or some other ghost. You're as white as a sheet.'

'What guilty thing?' said Jeremy grimly. Schoolmaster he might be, but his knowledge of Shakespeare was limited. 'Where've you been? Where's Tim?'

Suddenly Julia realised the reason for Jeremy's angst. She burst out laughing and flopped into the nearest chair.

'Oh really!' she exclaimed wiping tears of laughter from her eyes and laughing again. 'You didn't think ....! Oh, you are the absolute limit!'

'I don't see what's so funny. You didn't come to bed all night!'

'Oh Jeremy, don't be so ridiculous. Oh of course ... I never thought ...' Julia burst into more gales of laughter. 'Richard was awake when I went into the nursery and I was so tired I went to sleep while I was giving him a cuddle. I only woke up about twenty minutes ago. Well, I must say I'm flattered that you're so concerned – but really – I mean Tim!! Actually, he didn't even come home with me. He took Everard's wife home. I think he's taken quite a shine to her.'

'So how did you get home?'

'Oh, the Senior Tutor – that chap Roger I've told you about – gave me a lift. He's actually very nice when you get to know him.'

'Hmph. Bloody dons. Think they own the world. None of them knows what it is to do a proper day's work, either. If they had to work half as hard as we do ...'

'Oh please, Jeremy. Not at this hour of the morning. And try not to be so snarky about dons. It sounds like sour grapes. Have a cup of tea!'

'No thanks.'

Jeremy knew he ought to feel relieved and able to laugh at his unfounded fears, but instead he felt angry and aggrieved. He was proud of Julia's academic job – indeed bored everybody at school by dragging it into too many conversations, but somehow he felt much less sure of her than he had before; she was different, too independent, had too much of a life of her own outside his orbit. He stumped upstairs to dress while Julia got the breakfast and dressed the children.

At half past eight Everard, feeling a good deal more comfortable after some more sleep and a shave and a wash, strolled over to have breakfast in the dining room where dessert had been eaten the evening before. He was assured by the servant on duty that there was plenty of food and there was certainly plenty of space as only the unmarried dons lived in college. Julian Holloway-Smythe looked up from his newspaper.

'Well, well, well, Lucas! And how's the blonde bombshell?'

Everard smiled the particular smile which he considered his most inscrutable, especially when accompanied by a slight droop of the eyelids.

'She seemed fine when I took her back to her digs.'

'And what time would that have been?'

Everard increased the smile and the eyelid droop and said nothing.

Peregrine Forsyth eyed him silently for a few seconds and then said, 'Not looking too fine yourself, if I may say so.'

'How satisfactory for you, Peregrine. Here I am, only lived half my allotted span, and giving you every expectation that my excesses will carry me off at any moment. That would bring down your averages nicely, wouldn't it? I hope you regard me with proper gratitude!'

'Quite right, Forsyth,' Julian addressed Peregrine heartily. 'Need fast-living young-dying chaps like Lucas here to counteract the women.'

'What women?' Everard asked, puzzled. Neither Peregrine Forsyth nor Julian Holloway-Smythe had ever showed what he considered a normal interest in women.

'Oh, didn't you know?' Julian answered. 'Forsyth's only just realised there are more than twenty times as many men mentioned in the Gazette obituaries as there are women. And since he has a scholarly regard for accuracy he feels he ought to include them as part of the human race – and that's upset his averages. Blue-stocking women are as bad as clergymen; they all seem to go on into their nineties.'

'Oh, cheer up, Peregrine,' said Everard. 'There's a generation of women coming up who are as fast-living as the men; though I dare say you'll feature in the obituaries yourself before many of them oblige you by dropping off early.'

Everard's second tutorial finished just after twelve; it was not a stimulating tutorial and Everard decided that he was too tired and not hungry enough to wait for lunch in college and that he'd go straight home and rest. He yawned his way over the ten miles that separated his village from Camford and thankfully turned into the bumpy yard of his home. To his surprise it was already occupied by another car, a small beetle-like car. Oh, fuck! he thought, Jean must have somebody to lunch. He went into the kitchen. Something about it looked different but he couldn't think what. Then he heard voices from the sitting room: Jean's and a man's. His intention to creep upstairs unperceived and go and lie in or on his bed gave way to his curiosity. The man's voice sounded familiar but he couldn't quite place it. It was an educated voice with a northern accent – if such a combination's possible, he thought sourly. He went into the room. Tim and Jean were sitting on the sofa side by side. There was nothing directly compromising in their position, but they both looked immensely happy and were so taken up with each other that neither of them noticed Everard immediately. When they did realise his presence in the doorway, their reaction was as if to a stranger who had interrupted the normal course of life. Tim felt inclined to say "Can I help you?" while Jean addressed her husband.

'Why have you come home?'

Everard was completely nonplussed and realised that he had no idea how to express his reaction either to the question or to the whole situation. He had been too preoccupied with his own life and work even to remember that Jean had gone home with Tim the previous evening but now, seeing him as another man in his house, talking cosily with his wife, he felt a sudden twinge of anger and jealousy. So far all the exercising of "open marriage" rights had been on his side. In principle he had always decried the "double standard" and would have maintained hotly in any debate that women should have the same rights, be judged by the same standards, as men ... but when he saw it happening in his own house, he was astonished by the strength of his reaction, the power of his anger. He had immediately jumped to the conclusion that Tim had spent the whole night in the house; it would not have occurred to him to think otherwise. He stood in the doorway unable to speak, feeling himself alternately hot and cold.

'Tim's come to lunch,' Jean said casually. 'He's going to help me collect the boys this afternoon. I didn't think you'd be back.'

'Really?' Everard's voice rose to a sneer. 'So I've come back to bring you the car and missed my lunch in college to no purpose!'

In fact it had never occurred to him that Jean might need the car and he had given the matter no thought whatever until she spoke of it, but it gave him an excuse for his displeasure and a means of rendering Tim redundant at the same time.

'Well, we're just going to have lunch. If you want some it's ready.' Jean felt unwontedly secure and unabashed by Everard's manner.

'No, thank you,' Everard was surprised to hear himself saying. He was tempted to say "I know when I'm not wanted" but that was too childish, too petty. Instead he said, 'I'm rather tired after last night – I'm going to have a rest.'

He'd found this line to have good effect on previous occasions: the half-admission of extra-marital adventures disarmed criticism and made

Jean's suffering in silence both pleasing to his ego and soothing to his conscience. This time he felt it also added a touch of "two can play at that game". He went upstairs leaving Tim and Jean to lunch together.

CHAPTER TWELVE

Julia had completed a full day's teaching, collected the children, given them tea, bathed them and put them to bed. She was now cooking supper for herself and Jeremy, who was not yet home. He often stayed late at school, a lateness he usually ascribed to reports or marking or meetings. The fact that the school had a bar, which was certainly open every noon and night if not actually in the mornings, was probably, Julia considered, more accountable. She'd often welcomed Tim's company and help in these tiring evening hours, but since the dinner in college she'd seen a good deal less of him. Consciously, emotionally, she was not aware of missing his presence or his company but she was aware of a greater tiredness than usual, of the children being more difficult, of the time between her arrival home and Jeremy's seeming longer. She put it down to the demands of working in college and the strain of being the only woman there and feeling perpetually self-conscious, gauging the effect or possible effect of everything she said and did in the company of her colleagues to an extent that was not necessary or natural in ordinary life.

Jeremy arrived home, cheerful and expansive, shortly after half past eight.

'What's for dinner?' was his greeting. 'How's your day been?' he continued, and then, without waiting for any answer, 'Sorry I'm a bit late – had to go over a few things – never get any time during the day: teaching, marking, something every minute. Not like you dons with the odd tutorial here and there and loads of free time. Yes, I know it's different for you because you've got to see to the children, and speaking of that I've got a surprise for you!'

'What kind of surprise?' Julia hoped a faint hope that he might be going to offer to see to the children himself one evening.

'Well,' said Jeremy, dwelling on the word to heighten the suspense, 'you know Ma Barnes, who teaches German?'

'Yes, I think so; that rather strident woman with the sudden rush of teeth to the mouth.'

'Yes, you could describe her like that.' Jeremy found he resented the criticism of his colleague. Julia was altogether too haughty about his colleagues, he considered. 'Well, some German friends of hers have have got a twenty-year-old daughter who wants to learn English in Camford and I said she could come to us as an au pair girl.'

'What? Here? Living in? Well, I really think you might have asked me first. I'm not sure that I want an au pair and anyway, where on earth could we put her?'

'She'll have to have Tim's room, of course. Tim will have to go.'

'Oh indeed? Well I must say that's most unfair on Tim; and how, moreover, are we going to manage without his money?'

'We surely don't need it so much now you've got a proper job.'

'But we'll have to pay an au pair.'

'Oh, not very much,' Jeremy replied airily. 'You could give her some English lessons to make it worth her while.'

'Thank you. It's hardly my subject and I know very little German.'

'But if you can teach French, surely you can teach English!'

'I don't exactly "teach French" as you put it; my pupils already know quite a lot of it when they come up.'

'Oh, you're just being difficult. I thought you'd be really pleased. Here I am finding somebody to help you. You're always saying you need more help.'

'I'm always saying I need more help from you. Tim does a lot more to help me than you do.'

'Does he indeed!' Tim's helpfulness and prowess in matters domestic had often irritated Jeremy and fuelled his suspicions that Tim might be too interested in Julia. He was sure that no man could willingly do such chores unless he had an ulterior motive.

'Is he in, by the way?'

'I don't think so. Why?'

'Well, we'll have to tell him to find somewhere else to live.'

'Oh, really, Jeremy. I don't like the idea of that at all.'

'Don't you? I wonder why not!'

'Because he's always been such a nice person to have in the house.'

'Nicer than me I suppose you mean.'

'Oh Jeremy. Don't be silly. You know very well what I mean. We've been very lucky to have such an ideal lodger and here you are wanting him to go.'

'Well we can't have him and an au pair and the au pair's a must. Ma Barnes is going to ring you to go over the details.'

Feeling too tired and dispirited to argue any further, Julia dished up the supper. A step was audible on the linoleum of the front passage-way and a cheerful whistle of "A north-country maid". Jeremy leapt from the table and into the passage-way.

'Ah! Tim old thing! Just in time to have a bite of supper with us.'

It was generally Julia who invited Tim to meals, so he was a little surprised at the invitation, if not the greeting from Jeremy. He murmured his thanks and said he'd already had some supper.

'Well, a glass of wine, then.'

Tim smiled. This was more normal. Jeremy almost invariably offered wine to any and every visitor to the house. It provided an excellent excuse for him to open a bottle, most of which, with any luck, he'd be able to drink himself. Jeremy's taste in wines was not towards the cheaper end of the market, and Tim knew that Julia worried about what she saw as an unnecessary extravagance. He wanted to refuse the wine, too, but Jeremy was already halfway down the stairs to the cellar, not having waited for an answer at all. Julia met Tim's eye and gave a shrug and a sigh.

'Oh, do have a little bite to eat, Tim. There's loads. And besides, it's really nice to see you.'

Tim sat down at the table, made sure there really was plenty of food and immediately got up again to get himself a plate, knife and fork and save Julia the effort of providing these for him. Jeremy emerged from the cellar with a bottle of wine and proceeded to enlighten Tim with details of its origin, vintage and so on. Tim, who preferred beer, remained relatively unenlightened. He was thinking that it must be quite a few days since he'd really spoken to Jeremy and Julia, though he hadn't realised it before. He'd been taken up with seeing as much as possible of Jean. He'd had another lunch with her; met her boys; taken them home from school; helped Jean bath them one evening when Everard was not there – though Everard had in fact been there rather more than he might have expected.

'Tim, old chap!?' Tim realised that Jeremy was speaking to him. 'The fact is, you see, Tim,' Jeremy continued, 'we think Julia needs more help now she's got this job ...'

'You think,' Julia murmured.

'I mean, Mrs Davies only comes during the day when Julia's not here, and it would be better to have somebody living in all the time, you know, to help in the evenings and babysit and so on.' Jeremy's ideas as to the kind of help needed were rather limited, 'and we've decided to have an au pair girl.'

'You've decided,' said Julia more distinctly than before. 'It's merely an idea, Tim. Jeremy's only just mentioned it this evening. The woman who teaches German at his school wants to place some German girl with an English family here and thought it might suit us to have her. But I'm not at all sure I want such a person ...'

'I've told Ma Barnes!' Jeremy interrupted with some force. 'I've told Ma Barnes we'll have the girl.'

'Oh, I see!' Tim was suddenly aware of the reason for Jeremy's hearty greeting. 'So you'll need my room, won't you?'

Jeremy was relieved at Tim's swift perception of the situation. Few of his colleagues would have been so quick on the uptake.

'No, really Tim,' Julia said anxiously, 'nothing's finalised; nothing's decided at all, in fact.'

'Please don't worry, Julia, I do understand and you do need somebody to help more. I'll start looking around and we'll see how it goes. There's no need to do anything in a great hurry, is there?'

'Well,' said Jeremy 'This German girl –'

'No,' said Julia 'Of course there isn't. Even if this girl of Jeremy's does come ...'

'She's definitely coming, all right,' said Jeremy. He and Julia were both speaking at once.

'It doesn't matter.' Tim spoke over them both. 'It really doesn't matter. You're not to get upset because of me. I've been very happy here but it was always on the cards that you might need the room. Please!'

Jeremy and Julia stopped. It was clear that Tim was not upset. He looked perfectly happy and serene. He was, in fact, pleasantly envisaging the possibility of getting a room in or near Jean's village.

Emily was in her college lodge among a group of students. She became aware of an Australian voice addressing the porter.

'Excuse me,' it said politely, 'have you got any Durex?' Conversation among the students ceased abruptly. The porter glowered angrily. The Australian girl was aware that she had caused an adverse reaction, but clearly had no idea why.

'This envelope won't seal,' she said by way of explanation.

'She means sellotape' said Emily hastily. Emily had had similar, if less embarrassing, experiences with the names of recently invented products. 'I've got some in my place,' she said kindly. 'Come over with me and you can use it.'

'Oh thanks. You're American aren't you? It's nice to meet some- body who isn't English; the way they act sometimes you'd think I'd said something terrible. What did you say they call durex here?'

'Sellotape.'

'Oh, yeah. Like they call a lux a hoover – and Lux is a washing powder.'

'Why sure,' Emily answered, 'only the problem is this time that over here Durex means condoms – what we call rubbers.'

'Oh no! I can't stand it! Do you mean I went up

to the porter and asked him for a condom?! How embarrassing! I'll never dare speak to him again!'

'You weren't to know. Don't let it bother you. It'd be the same for one of them asking for a rubber in the States when they mean an eraser, that is. I'm Emily, by the way, Emily Matheson.'

'What a nice name. Mine's Nerelle. Say "what?" They all do, over here.'

'Is it a very usual name in Australia?'

'Well, at least everybody's heard of it.'

'Here we are. Would you like a cup of coffee?'

'Yeah, thanks. I've got to get over that big blue.'

'Big blue?'

'Yeah. It means a blunder, like the one I just made about the sellotape.'

Emily laughed. 'Well, I have some here, anyway. And at least you'll know what to ask for in a shop.'

'Thanks. You're lucky being an American. Nobody expects you to change your accent. We just sound like we're speaking bad English.'

'They can be the same to us, believe me. My supervisor now.' Emily thought rather grimly about Everard. 'I said I was "mordified" and he thought I said "modified".'

'Why were you mortified? Are they that bad when you take your work to them?'

'Well ...' Emily found herself more able to confide in this stranger than in her English acquaint-

ances. 'It was when I was out with him, frankly,'
'You went out with your supervisor?!'
'Yes – well – a few times. I don't think it was a big success. I thought he was really something at first, but – have you noticed, some English men don't seem to be too careful about personal freshness?'
'Yeah, that's right. They don't seem to know about deodorants.'
'Well, there was one time he reached across me to open the car door and the odour was really terrible. It put me right off him. Well, that and other things.'
'Is he still your supervisor? I mean, isn't it embarrassing after you've been out with him?'
'I'm going to try and change to another one.'

The dons of Emmaeus were at lunch. Most of them had newspapers folded and propped to readable angles. Everard put out an impatient hand to reduce a bump in his Guardian and knocked over a salt cellar.

'Sod it,' he said. Julian Holloway-Smythe regarded him with the superiority of an equable man in the presence of another's ill-temper. 'One of your happier days, I see Lucas,' he said.

Roger looked up from his Times.

'Oh, he's always like that, aren't you Everard. What's the matter? Got out of the wrong side of somebody's bed?'

'Do I detect a note of envy?' Everard was rarely at a loss for a suitable response. 'As a matter of fact I am about to teach my least favourite pupil. Organ scholar. The college habitually takes on these dimwits simply because it's deemed necessary to have somebody to play the organ in the chapel. The whole system should be abolished in my opinion.'

'And the chapel demolished, no doubt.' Julian Holloway-Smythe was a High Churchman and a regular attender at chapel services.

'Certainly,' responded Everard 'It's ridiculous to keep up that outmoded charade when we need the space for more useful activities – such as teaching.'

'You teach in your room, surely.'

'Tutorials, yes. But there's almost nowhere to teach classes, except for that dismal dungeon in the back quad basement.'

Roger was inclined to agree in principle; but as a rule he preferred not to agree with Everard, so he said only 'Demolition might be considered a rather drastic measure.'

Everard finished his lunch and loped across the quad to the lodge. He was conscious of a pervading sense of irritation bordering on anger. It was days since he'd seen Emily or had any contact with her at all. There had been no note or sign from her to thank him for the college dinner and all the trouble he'd taken over her. He was not really sure whether he wanted to see her again, but felt she ought to want to see him. He had hoped she would last at least until the end of term; he hadn't anybody else on the horizon. Perhaps there'd be a letter in his pigeon-hole, delivered by late morning messenger. He went to check with the porter. There were some faculty envelopes, but nothing of any interest. As he left the lodge he saw Roger going into the chapel.

'That's odd,' he thought 'I don't remember seeing Roger going into the chapel on any but obligatory occasions.'

He climbed the stairs to the tower room and, once there, looked thoughtfully out of the window that commanded a view of the main quad. He saw Roger emerge from the chapel, in company and apparently absorbed in conversation with Julia. They stopped just outside the chapel door and continued to talk. Everard watched them with interest. Julia was a very good-looking girl, especially when her face was animated, as it was now. The sun glinting on her dark red hair didn't do any harm to her appearance, either.

'Old Roger seems to fancy her,' Everard thought to himself. 'Fat chance he's got.'

Roger had gone into the chapel purely on an impulse, provoked no doubt by Everard's talk of demolition.

'Iconoclastic bugger that Everard,' he thought. 'The chapel may not be one of the most notable in Camford, but it's fifteenth century and beautiful in its own way. The stained glass makes it a little dark, certainly, but on a sunny day like today, the windows are very striking ...'

'Oh!' he said aloud 'I'm sorry. I didn't see you.'

He had vaguely noticed that there was somebody emerging from the choir stalls, but spoke only when he realised that it was Julia. 'Well,' he continued, 'and what's a Catholic atheist doing in here?'

'I often come in here. I like it. Besides, it was built by Catholics for Catholics and I admire their conviction – and their architecture. There are not many places where it's so quiet, either.'

'I'm sorry to disturb you.'

'I was on my way out. But I'm glad to see you. I haven't had a chance to thank you for taking me home from that dinner.'

'As a matter of fact,' Roger said rather quietly, 'I'm going to a mixed guest night in another college where I have dining-rights. Would you like to come?' He could hardly believe he'd said it. Until then he had had no intention of going. They emerged into the sunlight.

'I'd love to, if I possibly can,' Julia replied. 'When is it?'

They were discussing the suitability of the date and agreeing on a meeting time as Everard looked sourly at them from his tower. He heard a knock on his door and his pupil came in. He was not the most attractive of young men and he had the self-satisfied air of one too stupid to have any notion of his own limitations. Everard picked up the essay he had previously received from him and held its few pages at arm's length.

'Now what,' he began slowly in tones of over-solicitous interest, 'is your own opinion of this essay?'

'Well – I think I've covered all the main points and dealt with everything necessary.'

'Indeed?' Everard's tone gave nothing away. He continued. 'Well, this is what I think of it!' and he tore the essay across and across again and handed it to the bewildered young man. 'Go away and write something a little more worthy of a place in this university.'

When the pupil had departed, wordless but enraged, to recover his voice in the JCR bar and spread the story through the college, Everard went to the window again and looked gloomily on to the glowing stone of the quadrangle and decided he might as well go home.

CHAPTER THIRTEEN

Everard was hovering in the quadrangle when Julia went over to lunch. She noticed him standing in the corner by the entrance to the lunch room, as she could hardly fail to do since he stared at her from the moment she was within eyeshot. This was obviously intended to be intimidating and though it made Julia feel self-conscious it also gave her time to summon up the resolution not to be intimidated. Everard greeted her with a supercilious smile and the delivery of an obviously prepared sentence: 'The men are absolutely vituperative about that language test you set them!'

'They needed it,' Julia replied briefly.

'Really!' Everard's downward intonation was dismissive. He followed Julia into the lunch room. 'They say it's just the sort of thing you'd expect in a women's college.'

Roger, on the way to the table with his first course, caught the last words and deduced from Everard's tone that he was bent on being unpleasant. 'What's the sort of thing you'd expect in a women's college, Everard?'

'Oh—you know—madly over-teaching: girls' grammar school type learning tasks and tests of all things!'

'Well you must admit the women's colleges get results,' Roger countered.

Hector Otis looked up from his soup, 'No doubt about that,' he chimed in, 'I can't imagine Shona could ever have got her degwee if she hadn't been fwightfully well taught. She's never done anything with it since. But weally, Julia, you shouldn't give yourself so much extwa work, and so dweadfully borwing, setting and marking tests.'

'Medieval texts are a great deal easier to master if one has a proper understanding of the basics of the language,' Julia answered.

'Anybody who's going to get a First will learn for himself,' Everard asserted. 'You'd do better just not to get in their way.'

'That may be true,' said Julia, 'but what about the ones hovering between a Second and a Third? Proper teaching, showing them how and what to learn, is going to make an enormous difference to them.'

Everard stared at her in genuine surprise. 'Oh! Those people!' he gave the suggestion of a shrug indicating that such pupils mattered not at all and were merely to be tolerated rather than taught.

Julian Holloway-Smythe joined in the discussion. 'You certainly shouldn't overtax yourself, my dear,' he said kindly if condescendingly to Julia, 'the glory of the tutorial system is that they can teach each other. 'Put a dim chap in with a bright one and he'll learn a lot.'

'I haven't found that to work very well,' Julia responded with some temerity. Julian Holloway-Smythe was a very senior Fellow and she but a very junior lecturer. 'It tends to make the dim one feel inferior and does little for his confidence or improvement.' Julia was surprised at her own daring in arguing the point, but she cared passionately about teaching and regarded it as part of her vocation to enable her pupils to achieve the very best of which they were capable and to do so with a sense of pleasure and fulfilment. She was dismayed that none of her male colleagues seemed to share her attitude.

'Oh weally, Julia,' Hector Otis spoke somewhat impatiently, 'you can't put two dim men together in a tutowial; that would make it so dweadfully borwing for the tutor.'

'Oh, I don't know,' one of the older Fellows, a teacher of the most modern aspects of English literature, broke in jovially, 'what you should do is have the brightest and best in the first tutorial of the week – they'll be the only ones who've done the work by then anyway – and for the rest of the week you can use all the stuff they've come up with on all the others. It saves you an awful lot of work.'

'I've no doubt it does,' Quentin Crawford spoke from the heights of Classical Philosophy, 'yours being such a taxing and impenetrable subject! So much so that some colleges don't teach it at all.'

A few insufficiently suppressed chortles were the main response to this statement. There was still a large following for the old Camford view that it was no province of a university to teach people their own language and what was written in it, and that anybody who could not come to know by the light of nature all that was necessary and valuable in English had no right to be at a university at all..

'But that reminds me,' Quentin Crawford continued, still speaking to the English don, 'what's become of that exhibitioner we handed over to you to do a pass degree? How's he getting on?'

'What's that?' Julian Holloway-Smythe voiced the astonishment of many, 'an exhibitioner in Classics doing a pass degree? How on earth did that happen?'

'I have to admit he was our mistake. He got good marks in Entrance, his Greek and Latin looked decidedly better than average, but set him an essay topic and he simply can't write a word.'

'He still can't,' said the English don gloomily. 'I set him a simple essay on King Lear and he wrote exactly four lines.'

'Perhaps you should send him to Julia,' Everard spoke with sarcastic smoothness, 'she's so devoted to bringing out the best in deplorable people.'

Roger gave Everard an angry look and Hector Otis and some of the others smirked. Julia felt her own anger rising at their attitude, both to herself and to the unfortunate exhibitioner, so sadly and apparently inexplicably lapsed from his earlier academic potential. She let her glance sweep over Everard and the smirkers, rested it on the English don and said seriously 'Yes, do. I'll see what I can make of him. I'd be interested. He must have something in him to have got so far.'

Hector Otis sniffed, 'You must be a workaholic!'

Roger looked anxious. 'You've already got a heavy teaching load.'

'I can manage one more hour a week,' Julia smiled in reply. 'I don't play chess or squash!' Still smiling she looked at Hector Otis, who sniffed again.

Having found that the pass degree exhibitioner was called Daniel Watkins, Julia left a note in his pigeonhole telling him to come and see her with any work he'd done recently. He duly appeared at 12 o'clock the following day. Julia gave him a glass of sherry, glanced at his four lines on King Lear, and asked him why he didn't want to go on with Classics. She used "didn't want to" designedly, to imply lack of volition rather than inability and resulting pressure from on high. It worked.

'I never did want to do it,' he replied, 'but I got good marks and they made me.'

'Who made you?'

'Oh, at school. And my parents, because of what they said at school.'

'You mean they made you take A levels and Camford Entrance?'

'Yes. I never wanted to. I wanted to leave school at sixteen and work in a nice little office somewhere. But they made me stay.'

'Well, you can surely go and work in an office after you leave here; and you'll have more choice if you've got a degree.'

'I suppose so; but it seems a waste of time.'

'I don't believe you'll always think so; and now you are here you might as well enjoy it. What sort of books do you enjoy reading?'

'I don't know. I've only read the things they made me read.'

'You've never actually read a book for pleasure?'

'No, I don't think so. There wasn't time with all the other things.'

'Well, you have got time now. Let's see if we can find something you'll enjoy. How about the Pooh Bear stories?'

Daniel Watkins stared uncomprehendingly.

'You've heard of them?'

'No.'

'Well, as Blackwells' is just round the corner I think we can go and get a copy now. Then we'll come back and talk about it a little and you can read some stories for your next tutorial.'

Daniel Watkins did read the stories. He read all of Winnie-the-Pooh in the first week and all of The House at Pooh Corner in the second. He enjoyed them. He began to be able to say why they were funny and what was interesting about the characters and construction and storytelling technique. He even managed to write about them. From then on the progress was rapid. By the end of the term he had progressed to the William books and by the end of the year he was genuinely taking real pleasure and interest in Jane Austen and the less depressing novels of Hardy. He had in fact learnt to read!

Julia always regarded him as her greatest triumph. Whatever work he ended up doing as a living he would be able to enjoy his leisure and enlarge his horizons by means of books.

CHAPTER FOURTEEN

Tim and Jean had had a very good lunch, cooked by Tim. Moreover, all the dishes had already been washed and put away. In a very few days Jean's kitchen had become a different place. The plants no longer drooped over cigarette ends and their dead leaves had been removed. The sink was clean and the taps shining. Jean bore steaming cups of real coffee to the table.

'You are a wonder,' she said 'when you've cooked a meal the place is tidier than when you started'

'I just wash up as I go. Anyway you've done a lot yourself.'

'I seem to have got more interested all of a sudden. Thanks to you.' Tim laughed happily.

'You make me feel very appreciated,' he said.

'You are very appreciated!'

'Good. Now let's go and look at that granny-flat they've got on offer at the farmhouse. It sounds excellent. Self-contained, quiet, all mod. cons and no more than I've been paying for one room in Camford.'

So they finished their coffee and set off for the farmhouse in Tim's car.

Everard arrived home with a bag full of books and the beginnings of an article he was working on. He rarely worked at home and was not very willing to ponder on his reasons for doing so that afternoon. He was surprised not to find Jean there but decided she must have gone early to fetch the boys. He sat at his desk, cleared enough space on it to put down his notes and a couple of relevant books, and felt totally disinclined to do any more. He wandered into the kitchen to make some coffee. Blast! Where was that jar of instant? He could usually see it among the numerous other objects littering the surfaces. He looked round, puzzled, and decided to get a new jar out of the cupboard. To his surprise the half-empty one was there too. 'Bloody silly place to put it' he muttered. He made his coffee, stirring it violently with a large spoon which he then left on the work surface to join the swill of brown liquid spilt from his cup. He went and sat at his desk again and realised he should have told Jean he was coming home so that she wouldn't have needed to take the bus to fetch the boys. Too late now. Anyway, she shouldn't have left so early. He gave a sigh, put his coffee on a pile of papers and forced himself to look at his article again. He was still at his desk more than two hours later when he heard the slam of car doors and the treble voices of his children who barged through the back door, talking excitedly. Jean followed and then Tim. Everard went towards the back door to meet them.

'Hullo!' said Everard, rather too heartily, looking at Jean. There was a brightness in her expression, in her whole demeanour, that almost startled him. But when she looked at Everard her face went blank. 'Well,' he said, as if joking, 'you needn't look so shocked to see me!'

'Shocked?'

'Yes. For want of a better word.'

'Oh! You're not normally home at this time.'

'I came home early to let you have the car to fetch the boys; but of course you weren't here. Hullo Tim.'

'No. Tim took me to fetch them, as you see.'

'How very kind. You must have been very early if you went to get them by car.'

Neither Jean nor Tim replied to this indirect question. They both found they felt reluctant to say anything about the granny-flat at the farmhouse just out of the village, though it had exceeded expectation as to its suitability and Tim had arranged to move in as soon as possible.

'I'll get the boys' tea' said Jean. 'You will have some tea, won't you Tim?'

'Well, if that's all right, love.'

'Oh!' said Everard 'It's "love" is it?' He tried to sound as if he were showing a detached interest.

'Everybody calls everybody "love" where Tim and I come from,' said Jean. 'It's considered normal to be friendly.' She went to put the kettle on. 'Oh, for heaven's sake, Everard,' her raised voice was impatient, 'why can't you make a cup of coffee without spilling it all over the kitchen?'

Everard stared, opened his mouth, closed it again and finally said 'I thought you'd got over worrying about things like that long ago.' He'd wanted to say 'You sound like your horribly houseproud, lower-middle-class mother,' but Tim's presence inhibited him. The implication was, however, clear from his tone. Tim was already laying the table. Everard retreated as far as the kitchen door and watched for a minute or two. 'How does that bugger know where everything is?' he wondered. Aloud he said 'I've got to get on with my article. You can call me when it's ready.' Jean gave him a look of contempt.

'Thank you!' she said.

Jean and Everard sat eating their dinner in silence. They always had dinner quite late when Everard was at home; he considered it vulgar to eat before 7:30 at the very earliest, and it was usually nearer 9:00 than 8:00 when Jean, after putting the boys to bed, had the food ready for the table. Sometimes she complained of being too tired to enjoy eating anything by then, but Everard's response was always 'Why don't you do more of the preparation part earlier? After all, you've got all day!' But now their silence was not of the tense variety; it was due on Jean's part to her preoccupation with Tim's flat, her mental picture of him, living there, her own feeling of – what was it? security?- in having him so near at hand. Everard could sense her preoccupation with something from which he was excluded, and he was also aware that she looked more like the woman he had fallen in love with and married than the harassed mother of three demanding children, as she normally did. She was really, he decided, a very attractive, very desirable woman.

He got up from the table, put his plate into the sink, went behind Jean's chair and putting his hands on her upper arms, kissed her lightly on the cheek. Jean started as if awakened from a happy dream. Everard took her head in both hands and kissed her mouth firmly, then more firmly. Jean responded only by holding his wrists and trying to force his hands away, leaning away from him as far as she could. He removed his mouth a fraction but, as she began to speak, put his thumbs into the corners of her lips and kissed her again, intruding his tongue. Jean gave a sound between a choke and a groan and began to struggle. Everard let her go, suddenly and impatiently.

'What's the matter with you?' he asked. 'You used to like that!'

Jean sat silent. She was astonished at her own reaction. 'I don't know,' she said finally. 'Perhaps it needs more working up to ... I ... I was surprised.'

Everard took her by the shoulders and hauled her into a standing position. He shook her, none too gently and said 'Let me surprise you further!' in a voice whose cultured tones were at odds with his feelings. He knew he wanted to shake the daylights out of her, throw her on the floor and force himself on her. He bent, hoisted her on to his shoulder in a fireman's lift, carried her into the sitting room and threw her down on to the sofa. She had stopped struggling and was staring at him, frightened.

'Don't ...' she said.

'Don't what?' Everard grinned broadly, put his hands on her breasts and pushed her further into the depths of the decrepit sofa.

'Don't wake the boys!' Jean heard herself saying. Momentarily she wondered why she should have said such a thing, unaware that her basic instinct to protect her children was governing her reaction to Everard's violent behaviour and making her willing, against the grain, to absorb it herself.

Everard pulled off her shoes and flung them down with a thud and another thud. He peeled off her trousers, tore at her knickers which, being in bad repair, came away at the seam, pushed her legs painfully wide apart and held them there as she gave a sob, then inserted himself in a series of strong angry thrusts.

When Tim got back to the tall house in the narrow street after a long evening's academic work, Julia was doing some washing in the kitchen.

'Hullo Julia. Jeremy not here?'

'Oh, he's gone to bed. He said he'd had a tiring day at school.'

Or a tiring evening in the bar, thought Tim. 'Well, you certainly do need some more help,' he said. Here you are still working when you must have had a long day yourself.'

'Oh well,' Julia replied philosophically, 'at least it's a change. I don't think I'd trust anybody else to do the washing properly anyway.'

'You're too much of a perfectionist,' said Tim, not without admiration. 'But I hope you will let an au pair help you; and speaking of that I've got news. I've found an ideal place, a self-contained flat in the country.'

'Oh Tim!' Julia felt a pang of regret. She had

hoped it would take some time for Tim to find anywhere suitable. 'However did you manage to find something so quickly?'

'Jean told me about it; you know, Jean Lucas. It's a granny-flat in a farmhouse near her village. Well, it was, but the granny's just died, apparently and they want to let it out. Of course it's some way out of Camford but it's quiet and reasonably priced and I've got the car.'

'Well, I won't say I'm delighted because I'm not. I'm really sorry you're going; though I am glad you've found such a good place – and I don't suppose you'll find Jean's proximity a drawback!'

Julia gave Tim a sideways look and a smile. 'Why Tim! I believe you're blushing! Now that's an unusually attractive sign in a young man these days.'

'I'm not all that young,' said Tim. 'Anyway, I can move this weekend, if that's all right with you.'

'Of course it is. But we'll miss you, you know.'

'Oh I'll keep in touch, of course. And there's a particularly good pub in the village, right on the green and with a big garden as well. You and Jeremy must come out and bring the children.'

'Now that is a good idea – and guaranteed to appeal to Jeremy!'

Everard's anger evaporated with his lust. He

rolled off the sofa and on to the floor, then sat up to look at Jean and began to stroke her hair.

'Now wasn't that fun?' he said. Jean gave him no answer but turned her head away. He kissed her hair and her ear and then stood up, did up his clothes and went to the kitchen. Jean heard him doing the washing-up. She felt mentally numb and emotionless, and physically cold. Beginning to shiver, she picked up her scattered clothes and shoes, took them up to the bedroom and went straight to bed. When Everard came up some half hour later she pretended to be asleep. He got into his side of the bed with unusual care and quietness, lay on his back and put his hands behind his head. He decided that he didn't like himself very much. He'd tried to persuade himself that his behaviour was a caveman act, a simulated rape to give spice and variety to the otherwise over-familiar patterns of marital intercourse; but he knew it was not true. It left him with a great sense of guilt; far more guilt than he had ever felt when betraying his wife with another woman, though the present memory of some of those occasions was an added burden. He rolled his head against his hands to shake the memories away. 'Post coitum omnia tristia' he mouthed, whispering to himself. Post-coital depression. Not something one hears a lot about these days, though apparently some men always suffered from it. Glad to find a merely physical cause for his state of mind he gave a sigh and slid his head onto his pillow and tried to sleep.

Jean woke to see Everard looming over her. She stared at him as if wondering who he was.

'I've brought you a cup of tea,' he said, 'You stay in bed. I'll see to the boys this morning.'

Astonished, Jean sat up. Everard had barely been so considerate when she'd just had a baby, not so willingly considerate, anyway. She took the tea silently and Everard went downstairs again. He seemed not to have expected her to say anything. She was glad of the tea. Getting up was always a struggle for her. Moreover, she wanted to think – an activity almost impossible while preparing children for school. Slightly to her surprise she found she was not thinking about Everard but about Tim; Tim moving into his flat in the farmhouse; Tim very near at hand; Tim, kind, sensitive and understanding, helpful and undemanding… She tried to think how she felt about Everard. She ought to feel strongly about him, one way or the other. She put down her empty teacup, looked at Everard's side of the bed and picked up his pillow. It was none too clean. She smelt it, made a wry face and threw it away from the bed. She thought of Everard sleeping in that bed with other women – a thought she had rarely let herself entertain because of the anguish it brought with it. But today she felt nothing; no anger, no anguish. Only a kind of freedom, an increasingly happy freedom. Everard couldn't hurt her any more. She merely disliked him.

CHAPTER FIFTEEN

Julia was preparing for the dinner with Roger. She'd already fed the children and bathed them and Jeremy was telling them a story. He was good at telling children's stories and the appreciation he received went some way towards placating him for having to come home early and babysit. Nevertheless, he was not at all sure that he approved of these college dinners including women: lone women with no husbands present to look after them. Julia addressed him from the door of the nursery.

'Do I look all right?'

'You always look all right, you know that.'

'You look lovely, mummy,' said Richard.

'Who's all this dressing-up for?' Jeremy asked.

'What, not who. I told you it's a college dinner, at Roger's "other" college – where he's got dining rights.'

'Oh yes – very grand. I expect you'll have marvellous wine – not that women know how to appreciate it. Now, I'd really enjoy it.'

'I'm sure you would. But you don't exactly go without, do you!'

Jeremy had already decided to go down to the cellar immediately Julia had left the house but preferred not to mention it.

'Anyway, you really do look nice. That black and white shows up the colour of your hair, somehow.' He looked at her appreciatively and congratulated himself on having carried off against some odds, a woman of her distinction. The doorbell rang and Julia ran down to answer it. Jeremy watched from the top of the stairs, curious to see what Roger Tomlinson looked like. Julia opened the door.

'Oh, Roger, do come in for a second. I'll just put my coat on. Jeremy, darling, come down and meet Roger.'

Roger watched Jeremy run lightly down the stairs. 'Nimble and neat,' he thought, 'clearly an athlete, and very good-looking with all that bright blond hair and perfectly placed blue eyes.'

'How do you do,' said Jeremy, and the men shook hands while Roger murmured the appropriate response and wondered whether he ought to say something about how much they appreciated Julia.

Jeremy's qualms about Julia accompanying Roger to the dinner subsided. He was reassured to see that Roger was quite ugly and decidedly undersized – only about as tall as Julia. He smiled charmingly and wished them an extremely pleasant evening in his best public school manner.

As Roger's car threaded its way cautiously along the narrow street he said 'Good-looking chap, your husband.'

'Well, I think so, of course; but nanny would have said "handsome is as handsome does". In fact I say it to him myself quite often!'

'Oh, you had a nanny? Was your mother working?'

Julia laughed. 'No, I'm afraid not. She could have been a musician but never wanted to be more than an amateur. She had a very active social life, played a lot of bridge and so on. Still does, in fact.'

'You don't come from an academic family, then?'

'No. They think I'm an absolute freak. My father talks about "you intelleckshels" and my mother says despairingly "darling – you're such a bluestocking". She used to tell me it was a terrible disadvantage being so intelligent and she only hoped I could be intelligent enough to hide it.'

'How do they feel about this job?'

'Well, oddly enough, quite pleased. A proper job makes them feel there might be some point in women going to university after all. And they're surprised but gratified that their friends seem impressed.'

They drove into the car park of St Mary's.

'This college is frightfully grand, isn't it?' asked Julia. 'I never thought a lot about such things as an undergraduate, but one's more aware of them now.'

'Don't worry. A guest night at one college is much the same as at any other. There is a difference at dessert here, however, but I'll tell you about it when we come to it.'

The usual preliminaries over, Julia found herself seated at high table between Roger and a man not much older than herself who was introduced to her as "Dr Merton – Psychology". He was a plump young man with a serious air of self-importance.

His opening gambit had clearly been mentally rehearsed. 'So you're one of the first of the few!'

'I'm sorry?' Julia queried.

'A woman don in a men's college.'

'Oh, I see. But I hope I'm the first of the many.'

The psychologist gave a dismissive shrug.

'Well, of course, there are few universities outside Camford that are not completely mixed. But then Camford is very special. How do you feel about being a lone woman among men?'

'Well, all the men are different, of course, but there is a certain demarcation. I divide them into "pre-war men" and "post-war men". The pre-war men, who are all public school or indistinguishable from public school men, treat me in a rather courtly fashion and always make me feel very conscious that I'm something set apart, as it were; but usually the post-war men treat me like a human being.'

'I suppose by that,' the psychologist responded gravely, 'you mean that they treat you like a man.'

Julie felt a spurt of anger.

'No,' she replied. 'I do not mean that. A human being is not necessarily an adult male one.'

The psychologist regarded her with a mixture of surprise and pity, and she regarded him with a mixture of contempt and rage, decided that it was not worth the effort of any attempt to explain what she meant, and turned to Roger, who began to explain that at this college, instead of a college servant hovering around the table to refill the wine glasses, each diner had a carafe of white wine and another of red wine at his place.

'So you must be sure and not hold back,' he continued, 'because otherwise the white will be whisked away at the end of the fish course and the red at the end of the meat course.'

Julia was feeling quite shaken, not so much by the attitude of "Dr Merton – Psychology", as by her own reaction. She felt the same onset of fruitless, uncontrollable anger as she had when initially offered her job "without", as she was not a man, "the living-out allowance". She reached for her carafe, poured a large glass of white wine and swallowed it with impressive rapidity. She poured another.

Roger recognised something aggressive in the action. 'Of course you don't have to drink it all if you don't want to.'

'Thank you,' said Julia, with an edge to her voice. She wanted to add that she was perfectly aware of the fact and did not appreciate being treated like a child at a special treat party. 'I can't imagine you'd say that to a man,' she said. Roger tried to envisage a situation in which he might, but was quite unable to.

'No, I believe you're right; though I'd never thought about it before. I suppose we're not used to seeing women pour their own wine. There's this idea that they have to be strenuously urged to have more than the most minute amount.'

'Oh, it's all part of the charade: men being strong and masterful and daring and women drawing back from temptation with a kind of modest coyness. Yugh!'

'I didn't realise you were such a feminist – though I suppose I should have.'

'I didn't realise it either. It's come as quite a shock, actually. I would have thought it to be the result of a rational, deliberate mental process, whereas it's much more a matter of immediate emotional reaction.'

The psychologist, who had been listening to this conversation from Julia's left, opened his mouth to join in, but Julia turned such a withering glance on him that he thought better of it. She turned back to Roger.

'Well, at least I can talk to you about it more or less calmly: you've always listened and tried to see one's point of view and acknowledged that there are simply things you hadn't thought about before, and that you're willing to think about now.'

'That's true. I'm not merely willing, I'm interested. I feel I'm coming to understand and embrace – figuratively, you understand – another half of the human race which, perhaps reprehensively, I've come into remarkably little contact with up to now. I'm married, of course, but I went to single sex schools, a single sex college; I haven't a sister or any daughters. Yes. I've been very limited. Of course there are college secretaries and female scouts; but somehow one thinks of them largely in their context. One can't feel quite like that about a colleague. Interesting.'

Julia poured the last glass of red wine from her second carafe. She was feeling a good deal more mellow. Dr Merton – Psychology – whose left hand conversation had long since languished decided to tackle her again. Although she was, he considered, one of those annoyingly intellectual women, she was also undeniably attractive – and besides, she'd had the last word so far.

'Is your husband an Oxford man?'

'Yes, this college, actually.'

'What subject?'

'Geography.' Julia watched his face for the expected reaction.

Members of the Arts faculties regarded Geography as a barely respectable subject but then psychologists might be different. They were not highly regarded by readers of the humanities either.

None the less, when he responded his expression registered a flicker of superiority. 'Is there a big Geography school in this college?'

'Oh! He doesn't teach in this college. He was an undergraduate here. He's a schoolmaster.'

'Really? Public school?'

'No, prep. school.'

'Dear me. That can't be very intellectually stimulating.'

'Possibly not. But then my husband isn't very intellectual.'

'How very surprising!'

'Why?'

'Because you very obviously are.'

'Oh, well, you see, I married a dumb blond.' Dr Merton stared at her, open mouthed, with a mixture of horror and astonishment.

'You can't really mean that seriously?'

'Why not? Plenty of intelligent men marry dumb blondes, don't they?'

The gavel was struck, the diners rose, the chairs

resounded on the wooden floor and the psychologist was spared the embarrassment of his failure to find a suitable reply.

Napkins in hand, the dons and guests walked along a narrow passage that seemed like a parapet on the edge of a roof in order to arrive at the room where they were to enjoy the display of more college servants, more college silver and dessert. Instead of a large table, however, a number of small tables were set out round the vast room. Between the tables on either side of the wide stone fireplace was a triangular structure resembling a bi-sectioned hill, its sloping side bearing steel tracks and weights and chains as if in readiness for a small cable car. Julia, pleased to have escaped from Dr Merton – Psychologist – stood next to Roger as they waited to be assigned to tables and table partners. To Roger's satisfaction several of the dons edged towards them with an eye to being well in the vicinity of Julia. They melted into the background, however, discomfited, when the head of the college invited her to share his table on the right hand side of the fireplace, within reach of the long wooden triangle.

'Now what do you suppose that is?' he asked Julia as they arranged their napkins over their laps.

'Well, it rather reminds me of a cable-car, but I don't quite know why.'

'Ah! Very astute! It does indeed work on exactly

the same principle: as the left side goes down, the right side goes up, and vice versa.'

'Oh! Of course!' exclaimed Julia, full of the delight of discovery. 'It's the famous port trolley, isn't it? I've heard of it, but I had no idea what it really meant. It's because you pass the port from table to table here, isn't it?'

'Exactly. And the distance across the fireplace is such as to necessitate another means of locomotion – and there it is! The bottle is placed in that metal cradle and slides down to the lower end where we can reach it, while the other metal cradle goes up to receive the bottle on its next round!'

'How very ingenious! Not, of course, that from one side of the fireplace to the other is a very long way to walk with a bottle. But this is much more fun.'

When the port bottle reached the bottom of the hill for the second time it contained only just enough port for Julia's glass.

'Ah, now!' the head of College explained happily, 'you're very lucky, my dear. You've achieved what's called a "buzz". It means you get an extra glass of port!'

'Oh dear! I'm not sure that that's a very good thing. I seem to have drunk an awful lot already.'

'Oh, but you must have your buzz!' Julia felt as if all the eyes in the room were turned to her; clearly this was something regarded as meritorious and worthy of respect.

'That's right. Drink it down,' she was told. She did so and another bottle of port appeared and another glass was poured. Despite considerable practice acquired by way of drinking, on occasion, about half as much as Jeremy did, Julia began to feel decidedly unsteady and found herself wishing for the evening to be over. It was not quite true that this guest night was the same as any other – but enough was enough. She maintained a chatter of small talk, however, until the signal was again given to rise, napkins were left behind, and everybody filed into an immensely spacious room where they were served coffee and brandy or whisky. Julia declined the spirits but thankfully drank a cup of black coffee; drank it so rapidly in fact that she had finished it before most of the men had started theirs. This gave rise to the familiar comment that women could drink hot things men couldn't touch. The psychologist murmured that women had a higher threshold of pain than men and a discussion arose as to the truth and reasonableness of this assumption while Julia drank another cup of coffee and sank into a leather sofa beside Roger.

'Would you like brandy or whisky?' he asked her.

'Oh, neither thank you. I've had too much to drink already. It's only the coffee that's keeping me from collapsing.'

'You don't look as if you're in danger of collapsing. You look wonderfully lively and collected. You must know that you've been greatly admired this evening. My colleagues are looking on me with envy and respect.'

'How flattering. But then it's easy to be lively in intelligent, appreciative company.'

'Did you enjoy talking to that psychologist on your left?'

'No, I didn't. He merely inspired the liveliness of considerable annoyance. I mean your company, of course.'

Julia gave Roger a sideways smile and then happily finished her coffee. She was aware that she had definitely had too much to drink and was letting herself go in a way she would never do normally. Roger was proving to be so much more likeable, more attractive than she'd ever considered him to be previously. She had the sensation that they were isolated in that spacious room, miles apart from the other human beings islanded in their vast armchairs.

'Do you still think I'm like Mr Darcy?' Roger ventured.

'Mr Da ... Oh! of course, in *Pride ad Prejudice*. That was terribly rude of me. I'm really sorry.'

'I'm not. I think you were quite right. As long as you realise that you're Elizabeth Bennet.'

'Oh, very well. You mean when Mr Darcy describes her as "tolerable" but "not handsome enough to tempt him". Yes, I can probably manage that.'

'You know very well that's not what I mean. I'm talking about the development of the relationship, not the first impressions.'

Julia's coffee cup rattled on its saucer. 'Oh dear,' she murmured. 'I think I'm losing my grip – on my coffee cup and on reality. I really have had far too much to drink.'

'You probably think I have too.'

'One wouldn't dare suggest such a thing; but perhaps it would be a good idea for me to go home.'

'All right. I'll take you home if you really want to go so early.'

'Please.'

As they walked through a piercingly cold wind the few hundred yards to the college car park Roger held Julia's arm. She felt she ought to resist, but decided it was more dignified not to. She sank into the passenger seat immediately Roger opened the door of the car. In the driver's seat Roger looked at Julia, leaned towards her and then decided that if he were to try to kiss her it might shatter the delicate atmosphere. Sighing, he started the car as quietly as possible.

CHAPTER SIXTEEN

Hector and Shona Otis were preparing for bed. Hector went straight upstairs with his pint of kitchen water. He never drank water from a bathroom tap. Shona folded the newspapers and put them away; turned off the lamps and the television and made sure all the plugs were disconnected from the wall sockets. She took Hector's cup and saucer and wineglass into the kitchen, washed them and put them away and began laying the table for breakfast. Hector called impatiently from the top of the stairs

'Shona! Huwwy up! You always take so long to come upstairs! I don't want to be asleep and have you coming up late and disturbing me!'

Shona hesitated. If she left the tablesetting now she'd have to get up ten minutes earlier in the morning and she hadn't been feeling very well in the mornings recently. Reluctantly she decided to leave the table setting. Quickly she made sure that all the electrical appliances were switched off at the wall, turned off the kitchen light and made her way upstairs.

Roger and Julia, still in Roger's big car, were driving in silence. Julia felt she had said enough to show Roger that her assumption of the role of Elizabeth Bennet could be taken no further than her rejection by Mr Darcy. Roger felt that his acting the part of Mr Darcy, while it shielded him from outright rejection in his own person, gave a lightness and humour to the situation, a sense of mutual and exclusive understanding between him and Julia and at least an even chance of furthering the relationship. He stopped the car outside Julia's house on the north side of the straight, narrow street. Julia leaned forward a little to open the car door and Roger slid his left arm round her shoulders. Julia put up her left hand to detach his arm, only to feel the tight grasp of his fingers.

'Mr Darcy would never have done this,' she said, though she found the grasp exciting.

'Mr Darcy may have had ten thousand pounds a year and a park more than ten miles round, but he didn't have a car!'

Julia turned to Roger with a smile and he kissed her a little tentatively, then more confidently, then with something of the emotion he was feeling.

Julia drew back, stared at him in dismay. 'Oh heavens. You're attractive. You're amazingly attractive!' And she opened the car door and almost fell out of the car in her haste to get into the house and out of danger with all possible speed.

Roger drove home slowly. He could feel his heart racing and his face smiling and he had neither the wish nor the ability to control these involuntary but immensely pleasurable reactions.

Shona Otis woke unwillingly to the sound of her alarm clock, ten minutes early. She stared at it, puzzled for a few seconds, and then remembered the breakfast table. She sat up quickly and was aware of a wave of giddiness and nausea. She sank back on to her pillows with a slight moan. Hector had barely stirred at the sound of the clock. He was sufficiently used to that to block it out of his consciousness; but the extra movement and the moan were enough to rouse him.

'Whatever's the matter, Shona?' he asked crossly.

'Oh, Hector – I don't feel very well. Awfully sick.'

'Well for goodness' sake go to the bathroom and be sick in there.'

'It must be – I think I'm probably pregnant again.'

'Oh dear!' Hector was torn between his impatience of any sort of illness, especially in his wife, and his hope for a son to carry on his not very common name. Another miscarriage would be unfortunate. Shona's doctor had told her last time that she'd feel better if she got up slowly and had a cup of tea and a biscuit before rushing about making a cooked breakfast. Hector had pooh-poohed the idea and said the doctor was a nitwit out to make other men's lives as uncomfortable as his own. But then Shona had lost the baby.

'Oh dear!' Hector repeated. 'I suppose I'd better get you a cup of tea and a biscuit.'

'Oh, but I haven't finished setting the table ...'

'Never mind the table. You must be careful. You know what happened last time when you would keep dashing about!'

Having shifted his twinge of guilt on to his wife Hector felt almost magnanimous and went downstairs to make tea and look for biscuits with quite a good grace.

Lunch was in progress. Julia came in a little late and took a seat at the bottom end of the table. She was glad to see that Roger was near the top; she didn't want to sit too near him. Everard Lucas, sitting opposite Roger, noticed how his eyes followed Julia's every movement while his face was carefully expressionless. He also saw Julia's eyes flicker towards Roger and quickly drop their glance as she bent towards her plate, hiding a half smile. Roger, with the intention of acting very normally, addressed Everard.

'Are you dining in on Sunday?'

Everard would have been surprised at Roger's query had he not had a shrewd suspicion of his motive.

'No,' he answered. 'Jean's going out to dinner with some women friends of hers so I said I'd see to the boys. It's often difficult to get a babysitter on a Sunday.'

Hector, who was sitting next to Julia, was struck by this unusual sign of paternal responsibility in Everard and proud of his own exertions in that field.

'I took my wife a cup of tea in bed this morning' he confided. Julia gathered from his tone that this must be a matter of special significance and not a normal occurrence.

'It she not well?'

'Actually,' Hector was glad of a feminine ear, 'we think she's pwobably pwegnant. You know, things that should have happened haven't happened and this morning she felt weally sick.'

'She must have been awfully grateful for the tea.'

'She wanted to get up but I wouldn't let her. She had a miscawwiage last time and I do want a son to cawwy on my unusual name.'

'Yes, I'm sure you do. Congratulations – if and when appropriate. But won't your wife object to having it known quite so early?'

'Why should she?'

'I think most of us prefer to keep quiet about a pregnancy until it's getting obvious. Perhaps we don't want to tempt fate – or we just feel rather conspicuous.'

'Oh, well, I wouldn't know about that.'

Hector looked a little piqued. Julia thought that there might be a good many of his wife's feelings that he wouldn't know about, but merely expressed the hope that all would be well this time and the conviction that tea and biscuits in bed every morning would help considerably, at which Hector regained his complacency. Julia was glad to discontinue the conversation and think her own thoughts under cover of concentration on The Times crossword which was uppermost on the neatly folded newspaper by her plate. She had received a letter from Roger in her pigeonhole just before lunch and had only had time to read it hurriedly before ramming it into her handbag. She was both intrigued and disturbed. In addition, Tim was moving out at the weekend and the German au pair moving in. Term was well under way and the momentum of teaching and marking increasing. She could do without additional complications. Stifling a sigh she made an effort to finish her lunch. She had little appetite but was too well trained to leave anything edible on her plate. Julian Holloway-

Smythe was observing her.

'Ah!' he boomed 'Un soupir étouffé. Did you know – now this will interest you, Mrs Leslie – that there was a colour fashionable in the late eighteenth century called soupir étouffe?'

Julia hastened to make a show of interest.

'Really? Whatever colour was a "stifled sigh"?'

Julian replied, gesturing with a fine-boned hand, the little finger raised delicately. 'The palest, palest possible shade of mauve.'

'I'm afraid it wouldn't suit me very well.'

'Oh yes, I think it would my dear.'

Julia rose, took her copy of The Times and escaped to the SCR.

She was surprised when first Peregrine Forsyth and then Everard came and sat beside her. Peregrine was looking at her with some interest.

'You're very pale today,' he said. 'I hope you're not finding us all too much of a strain.'

'Take no notice of Peregrine,' said Everard. 'He's the one who can't stand the strain of extending his averages to the female of the species. We must have a chat sometime about the translation classes and how the men are getting on in your side of things. What time do you finish teaching? I'll come over to your room, with some papers I want to go through with you.'

Julia was murmuring suitable acquiescence and gratitude when the butler came into the room with a large handbag which he carried almost at arm's length as if to dissociate himself from the alien object. He handed it to Julia. 'I believe you left this in the luncheon room, Madam.'

Julia thanked him and marvelled how on earth she could have forgotten anything containing such important material as Roger's letter.

'Now I wonder how he knew whose it was?' Everard said acidly.

In her own room Julia read Roger's letter again:

Dear Julia,

Or should I write "Dear Miss Bennet" as we both feel safer hiding behind our adopted personae as if we were acting in roles which can be shaken off whenever we leave the stage. Be that as it may, we must somehow meet and talk. Can I take you out to dinner? Dinner in a restaurant this time, not in a college. Please don't say no. Unresolved as things are now, we shall be embarrassed meeting in college. Tell me a day and time suitable for you. Let me hear from you soon – please.

Sincerely, Roger

Julia read the letter again – and again. Her immediate reaction was to write back and say "no, certainly not". But the sentence about the embarrassment of meeting in college was sufficient to make her pause. She had already experienced it at lunch; and meet in college they must, unavoidably. She decided on an equivocal answer which could still lead to a final refusal. After tearing up several attempts she wrote

Dear Roger,

Thank you for your letter. I should have written to you anyway to thank you for taking me to dinner in St Mary's. It was an interesting experience in every way. I hope you'll forgive me for saying I particularly appreciated the port trolley!

As to your most recent invitation I can as yet say nothing because an evening out always necessitates so much organisation at home. Perhaps I could let you know next week.

'So far so good – but how shall I finish it?' Julia asked herself. It seemed very feeble merely to echo Roger's "Sincerely". But after rejecting "Yours" and certainly "Yours ever" as in danger of being misinterpreted she wrote "Sincerely, Julia" after all and put the letter into a suitable envelope which she decided to take to the porter's lodge on her way home. She still had two hours of teaching to do. Unlike almost all her colleagues Julia taught in the afternoons whenever possible. This was regarded as very strange; afternoons should be a time for relaxation – recharging the batteries as it was often said; for writing letters or going to meetings at most. Besides, the undergraduates wanted to play games, didn't they? Most of Julia's pupils in fact didn't and a few of them even wanted to go to lectures which always took place in the mornings, though they were discouraged from this by Everard. 'I can teach them anything they'll ever hear in a lecture' was one of his favourite statements. He and some dons did often teach for an hour before dinner, however, an hour when a good deal of alcohol was consumed by dons and pupils alike, mainly in the form of sherry, though some tutors preferred gin. Julia's own tutor in her college had been so generous with the gin that her pupils never forgot the twelve o'clock or six o'clock tutorials from which they reeled euphorically regardless of the actual merits of their work.

Everard knocked on Julia's door as her pupils left at ten past five. She was unsure whether to offer him anything. It was too late for tea and too early for drinks. Besides she wanted to be home in good time to relieve Mrs Davies, so she merely started talking about work; teaching and pupils. Everard cast a glance round the room, looked at Julia's desk, let his eye rest rather obviously on the letter addressed to Roger and then nonchalantly sat himself on the bed which did duty as a sofa. As a very junior don, Julia had a room which was exactly like any undergraduate's and could indeed revert to being an undergraduate's room whenever she might be moved to another.

'I want to show you these papers' said Everard. He held them where she could see them only if she sat on the bed beside him. His ploy was so obvious that she decided to show him that physical proximity to him was a matter of total indifference to her and would not arouse the faintest frisson of interest. She felt she was achieving this very successfully as they were discussing the papers in totally neutral tones when suddenly the door opened without any preceding knock and in the doorway stood Jeremy, glowering like thunder. Julia was so bent on showing no reaction of any sort to Everard that she showed none to Jeremy either, but remaining exactly where she was.

'Oh Everard, you know my husband Jeremy, don't you?'

Everard, for all his usual panache, was caught unawares and looked decidedly sheepish. He wondered whether Julia had expected her husband, or even deliberately asked him to come at that time in order to protect herself and trap Everard into a compromising situation. Julia was, in fact, as surprised as Everard by Jeremy's sudden appearance, but a good deal less put out. She wanted to burst into fits of laughter as she had when Jeremy suspected her of spending a night in Tim's room. It was so ridiculous. Everard awkwardly raised himself from the low, somewhat sagging bed; stood up; tried to think of something suitable to say; fell back on 'I think we've dealt with everything necessary', smiled into Jeremy's angry face and made his exit.

'So that's how you deal with your colleagues!' Jeremy snarled as soon as the door was closed. 'Sitting on the bed together!'

'Honestly, Jeremy, this is the first time Everard – or any other colleague, for that matter – has ever been in my room. Everard is an utter pain and I despise him. He engineered the sitting-on-the-bed business and I was successfully showing him that the nearer he is to me the less he does for me. He leaves me cold to the point of revulsion. But I presume you've come to take me home. Right?'

'Yes, and you'd better hurry because the car's illegally parked. I came in to pick up a lamp for the au pair's room.'

'How unusual of you. You never took any interest in it in Tim's time.'

'Tim mentioned that he'll be taking his lamp when he moves.'

'Well, as this girl's entirely your idea, I'm glad to see you're taking some responsibility for her comfort. But I've got to drop a letter in at the lodge on the way out.'

'Oh? Who to?'

'To the Senior Tutor. NOT Everard. Nothing interesting.'

CHAPTER SEVENTEEN

'Jean!' From halfway up the stairs Everard called up to their bedroom where Jean was preparing to go out for dinner.

'Where did you put those sausages for the boys' supper?'

'In the fridge, of course. And the baked beans are in the larder.'

'I'm not used to finding things in the right places.'

'You're not used to finding things at all. I'll be down in a minute.'

Everard banged about in the kitchen as he searched for food, utensils and related paraphernalia. Jean came and stood in the kitchen doorway.

'Why is it you always leave all the cupboard doors and drawers open?' she said dispassionately.

Everard had never thought about the matter before and wondered at Jean's thinking about it now.

'That's how I know which ones I've looked in, of course. Nobody knows where they'll find anything in this kitchen. You look different. That's not what you wore to the college dinner, is it?'

'No.' Jean decided not to mention that it was new.

'You don't usually dress up much to go out.'

'I don't go out much.'

'No, I suppose not.'

'If I did, you might be more used to finding things and getting meals.'

'I'm perfectly able to do both, thank you. Just leave me to get on with it. Go and enjoy yourself with your friends. I expect you'll have a happy evening capping complaints about your husbands and children.'

'Only about our husbands. I don't know when I'll be back.'

'It doesn't matter. 'Bye.'

Jean drove the car out of the bumpy yard and smiled more widely and happily with every turn of the wheel. She was reflecting on how funny it was that Everard should have simply assumed that she was going out with a woman or women friends. She'd never actually said so. Once she would have been needled at his lack of interest in her activities, but now, as she turned a sharp bend and off into a narrow lane she broke into a little laugh. The lane led to the farmhouse where

Tim had just moved into his new flat.

Tim opened the door as soon as he heard Jean's car. Jean saw him framed in the doorway as she drove up the last stretch of the lane and thought how very unlike Everard he was. Everard would never have done anything so obvious, so openly indicative of eagerness and affection. He would have been more likely to let her ring the doorbell twice before answering and enjoyed her expression of relief as he finally appeared. She'd long learned to repress any demonstration of fondness to Everard; but now she found herself almost running from the car to greet Tim, who stretched out his arms as he came to meet her.

'Oh Tim, Tim, TIM!' she said, and flung her own arms round him.

They went through the door together, almost sideways so that they lost as little contact as possible.

'Where are all the other people?' Jean asked – knowing full well.

'Other people?'

'Isn't this a house-warming?'

'I hope so.'

'Don't lots of people usually come to house warmings?'

'Not this one. This one's special. And besides, I've only cooked enough for two. Gin or straight on to wine?'

'Gin! How extravagant.'

'Not nearly as extravagant as a "lots of people" party.'

'But I will have to drive home – sometime.'

'There'll be plenty of time. Won't there?'

'I told Everard I didn't know when I'd be back and he said it didn't matter.'

'Well in that case you can certainly have some gin.'

Tim had the dinner so well organised that getting it from the kitchen to the table was no impediment to the happiness of the atmosphere. The blend of beautiful food, candlelight, firelight and companionship was so harmonious that there was no obtrusive element, only an undercurrent of excitement in the awareness of how special this occasion was and how significant its climax. They didn't quite finish the wine at the end of the meal; almost suddenly they both rose from the table, clasped each other and kissed a long, loving kiss and went into the bedroom hand in hand.

Julia had bathed the children and put them to bed and was telling them a story as best she could with constant admonitions to Jamie to stop standing on his head before he fell off the bed, and an ear open for the arrival of Jeremy and the German au pair whom he'd gone to fetch from the airport. For once the timing was right. Julia's account of Jack the Giant Killer had just hurled the giant to the bottom of the beanstalk and Jamie had at last restored his head to a normal position well above his feet and said 'Poor old giant', as he always did, when Jeremy's measured tones and others of a higher but more staccato voice sounded in the hall. Julia hastened to the top of the stairs and viewed the newly-arrived with some misgivings. The girl looked older than she had expected, was well-built and shapely, with hair a brighter shade of Julia's own colour and an expression which said boldly and plainly: "I'm very attractive and I know it". Julia had almost to force herself to continue down the stairs and go through the ritual of greeting and hand-shaking.

'This is Astrid,' said Jeremy proudly, as if he had single-handedly produced a marvel.

'How do you do, Astrid, I'll ...'

'I'm fine,' Astrid cut in to Julia's attempted sentence with an in- tonation that implied she would soon sort out anybody who said she wasn't fine.

'I'll show Astrid up to her room,' said Jeremy quickly, having mentally registered what Julia hadn't managed to say. 'I'll have to take her bags up anyway.'

'Oh. Thank you, Jeremy. Astrid, would you like to meet the children before they go to sleep? They're going to be interested to see you.'

Astrid gave a shrug. 'If you want' she said.

So the introductions were made on the way to the top of the house where Astrid's – formerly Tim's – room was situated. The children stared at Astrid and Astrid stared at the children who refused to say 'Hullo' as directed by their parents.

'Astrid's come all the way from Germany to help look after you,' said Jeremy. Jamie pushed himself up, leaned on one hand, looked Astrid up and down dispassionately.

'We don't like Germans,' he said.

'Jamie, how can you be so naughty!' Julia and Jeremy exclaimed. 'You've never known any Germans!'

'Well I don't like Germans now.'

Jamie delivered his last word and lay down again. Leaving Jeremy to redeem this inauspicious beginning as best he could, Julia gladly fled downstairs to put the light supper on the table and try to suppress her misgivings about the whole situation. When joined by Jeremy and Astrid some ten or fifteen minutes later Julia made a consciously strong effort to oil the wheels.

'Have you been to England before, Astrid?'

'Yes.'

'Oh? When was that?'

'Two years.'

'You were here for two years?'

'No.'

'Astrid was here two years ago,' explained Jeremy. 'She came to a language school in London for a couple of weeks. She's been telling me all about it.'

Jeremy was not displeased that Astrid seemed to communicate much better with him than with Julia.

'You must be older than twenty, aren't you?' Julia had decided that polite social exchanges were not the flavour of the day and she might as well find out what she wanted to know.

'I am tventy-fife.'

Julia turned to Jeremy. 'I thought Ma Barnes said she was twenty?'

'Yes, something like that. Early twenties.' Jeremy couldn't see that it mattered very much, but Julia, while hoping that maturity might be a good thing for somebody looking after children, also feared that a smaller age-gap between herself and the au pair might make the latter more difficult to handle.

'I'm sorry Astrid,' Julia turned to the German girl who was helping herself to some more salad, 'you must think we're very rude, discussing your age. It's just that I'd thought you were younger'.

Astrid smiled a smug little smile which conveyed clearly: "I'm younger than you are, anyway!"

'Can I haf some more flesh?' she demanded.

Jeremy looked startled and Julia, even though she knew Astrid meant "meat", felt slightly revolted and had fleeting thoughts of turning vegetarian.

In bed at last, just after midnight, as Jeremy had told Astrid she mustn't do anything to help that night and Julia had had to do all the clearing away and the dishes before settling to some preparation for the next day's teaching, Julia hoped Jeremy was already asleep; but of course he wanted to know what she thought of Astrid.

'I don't know yet. It's too soon to tell,' she prevaricated.

'Well I think she's a jolly nice girl.'

'So I gather.'

'I suppose you're determined not to like her because she's my idea.'

'It's not that at all, but having a complete stranger come into one's house to stay for an indefinite period creates a situation that needs careful handling.'

'My family always had people in the house working and there weren't any problems.'

'Your family had servants who came from generations of local people – and they didn't have to be conversed with at meals.'

'You've been bloody dffiicult since you've had this grand job of yours.'

'Oh please, Jeremy! Not now! I won't be able to do any job if I don't get some sleep. Let's just make the best of things and say goodnight.'

Jeremy turned on his side, away from Julia, and didn't say goodnight.

Through the open door of the bedroom Tim and Jean could see the last flickerings of the fire reflected on the wall of the sitting room.

'I'll have to go home, Tim.'

'Do you really have to?'

'You know I must.'

'Will you stay all night some time? Or don't you want to?'

'Of course I want to. I want to stay now.' Jean stopped herself from saying she wanted to stay forever: Everard and her higher education had given her a distaste for "sweeping statements".

'I was quite frightened about tonight,' Tim confided. 'Until you arrived. After that I was too taken up with you – with my feelings for you – to worry.'

'Why ever should you worry?'

'I was afraid I might not please you; that you might be disappointed.'

'Disappointed! Tim you are the most amazing, most marvellous lover. I couldn't have believed it was possible to come so often. And you never hurt me.'

'I should hope not.'

Speaking of hurt Jean remembered Everard. 'I've got to go back,' she said.

Tim noted that she said "go back" and not "go home" and he put the words carefully in a safe place in his mind so that they could be brought out and worked over at leisure.

'I'll make you a cup of tea before you go.'

'Oh Tim! You make me feel so at home. Up north we're always having cups of tea at any time of the day or night.'

'I know,' said Tim and he put the kettle on and began to sing:

>"A north-country maid
>Down to London had strayed
>Although with her nature
>It could not agree:"

And Jean, unwillingly putting on her clothes, joined in:

>"Oh she sobbed and she sighed
>And she bitterly cried:
>Oh I wish once again
>In the north I could be
>Oh the oak and the ash
>And the bonny ivy tree,

> They flourish at home
> In my own coun-tree."

Jean came into the kitchen and Tim stroked her hair, kissed her gently. 'Don't worry. We're hardy enough to flourish even in the south – if we stick together.'

'Yes. We're very good at doing that.'

They laughed childishly, embraced again, then sat on the sofa to drink their tea.

Everard found an evening spent feeding and tending the boys and putting them to bed more tiring than he would have wanted to admit. He decided that clearing up the debris of their meal was more than could reasonably be expected of him, left it and went to bed early. He woke in the morning to find that Jean was already downstairs making light work of the mess and humming cheerfully.

'You must have had a nice evening,' he greeted her.

'Yes, I did.'

'I couldn't do all this.' He indicated the kitchen with a sweep of his hand. 'Had to go over somebody's work I'm supervising.'

Jean smiled and went back to the tune she'd been humming. Everard looked at her closely. It wasn't the reaction he expected when he mentioned supervising: generally her eyes registered a little stab of anxiety.

'Can you stop humming that sodding tune!' he growled.

'What? Oh! didn't realise I was doing it.' And she finished the tune from the point of interruption, lingering on the words "In my own countree."

Lights were on in the lunch room at Emmaeus. The sky was dark outside and the rain falling heavily. Roger came in, shaking his wet hair and wiping his face with the back of his hand.

'Foul!' he said. Julia looked up from her end of the table and smiled at him. She felt more able to do so without self-consciousness when he appeared in a condition unusual enough to be noticed. Roger caught her eye and gave a slight look of query. He'd left a letter in her pigeon-hole asking whether she could arrange to have dinner with him on Tuesday or Thursday or Friday. He didn't expect her to have had time to answer it, and hoped her smile was not merely directed at his wild and wet state. Julia dropped her eyes and was on the point of sighing when she remembered how a previous sigh had been remarked upon by Julian Holloway-Smythe and reflected that it was not pleasant to be conspicuous in any way. No wonder the royal family developed poker faces.

Everard came in looking as glowering as the weather. He had received a note from Emily Matheson informing him that she was applying for a change of supervisor. It had contained no apology and no mention of their relationship. He glanced across the table at Julia and considered that she was looking totally serene. "Self-satisfied bitch!" he thought. "Nothing disturbs her". He went on to fantasize about making her fall in love with him and seeing what it would do to her peace of mind and her attitude of impervious control. Julia became aware of his concentration on her in time to catch something of it before he looked away. She had always found him unattractive, but there was now a malevolence in him that was disquieting. Unconsciously seeking an ally she looked towards Roger. It had not occurred to her before that a friend at court might be necessary for survival in a college. Roger's letter, rammed into her handbag after a hasty scan, began to seem more comforting than disturbing.

Roger decided not to have any coffee after lunch. He could never drink it as fast as Julia could and he wanted to be able to leave the common room immediately after her in order to extract an answer to his letter without waiting for her to write. Julia did, in fact, down her black coffee in record time and was outside in the quad when

Roger caught up with her. His rapid exit was not unnoticed by the other occupants of the common room.

'Woger's in a huwwy,' said Hector Otis.

'Nobody can think why, of course,' said Everard sourly.

'Dear me. Poor fellow!' said the archangel.

Peregrine reflected that Roger was looking distinctly harassed and that it couldn't be doing his heart any good.

Roger, now crossing the quad with Julia, felt a shortness of breath and an increased pulse rate which might have made him agree with Peregrine's reflections, had he known them. Julia decided not to beat about the bush.

'Thank you so much for your invitation. I ...'

'Yes?'

'I'll try and arrange for Thursday. But I'll have to see how willing or able the new au pair is to cope in my absence. Can I let you know on Monday?'

CHAPTER EIGHTEEN

Julia spent most of Saturday catching up on the week's washing and housework, trying to initiate Astrid into the mysteries of the washing machine and vacuum cleaner, keeping the children happy and occupied and worrying about how to answer Roger's dinner invitation. Jeremy's prep school demanded his presence on Saturdays for lessons in the morning and games in the afternoon and Julia found Astrid less taciturn and more amenable in his absence. She wondered briefly whether Jeremy would again come home earlier than usual now that the au pair was installed and reflected wryly that at any rate he'd spend less in the bar if that were the case. Her preoccupation with Roger was taking the edge off her anxieties about Jeremy. Her immediate instinctive reaction was to say no; no dinner; no anything. No. But the recollection of Everard's antipathy, her apprehension of loneness and insecurity in an alien environment if she were to jeopardise Roger's undoubted protection of her, combined with an increasing and undeniable sense of his attractiveness, tempered the negative reaction into one of doubt and indecision.

Jeremy did come home earlier than usual, but Astrid announced that she was going out, so he and Julia put the children to bed together for once and had a late supper à deux. It was pleasant. They drank a bottle of wine between them, left the dishes, went to bed and made excellent love. Julia lay awake for a little while afterwards thinking how beautiful Jeremy was and what an excellent lover and that marrying him hadn't been such a mistake after all. She decided not to go out to dinner with Roger.

On Sunday morning, however, after getting the children's breakfast, potting them, washing them, dressing them single-handed while Jeremy stayed in bed and Astrid, clearly determined that Sunday was a non-working day, showed no sign of emerging from her attic room, Julia's resolution was wavering.

'I can't cope with this,' she thought. 'I don't even know how I feel from one minute to the next. There's nobody I can talk to about it, but I can't cope with it on my own.'

When Jeremy yawned his way into the kitchen at ten o'clock she said 'I'm going to take the children to mass.'

Jeremy stared. 'What on earth for?'

'I think they ought to go. And you never take them to church.'

'They're too young.'

'I don't think so. The earlier the better. And they're not stupid.'

'Isn't it enough that they're at a Catholic nursery school – well, Jamie and Richard are.'

'It's only a lay-Catholic nursery school; most of the other children who go are taken to mass every Sunday by their parents. Anyway, I want to go myself.'

'Oh, so that's it. All this high-minded talk about bringing the children up with religion and definite principles is just an excuse for you to go.'

'If that were the case I'd go on my own, wouldn't I? And leave you looking after the children.'

'Well, you can't have the car.'

'All right then, I'll push them all in the pram. I'm used to that.'

So Julia packed the three children into the pram and pushed them all the two miles to St Francis Xavier's in good time for the eleven o'clock mass. She lifted them in turn to the holy water font and guided their hands into the sign of the cross; told Jamie that no, the candles were not for blowing out, they were signs that people were asking for the prayers of a saint.

'Don't they tell you about it at school?' she asked him.

Jamie's response was to pick up a new candle from the box. 'Can I light one?'

'All right. What do you want to ask for?'

'A kitten."

'Wouldn't you rather ask to be helped to be a very good boy?'

'No. You can ask that. I want a kitten.'

Julia took two candles, helped Jamie to light one and Richard to light the other from it. Then they went and sat in a pew not too far from the altar.

'Mummy!' said Jamie.

'Yes, darling?'

'Did you ask for me to be good?'

'Not exactly. More for us all to be good.'

Jamie looked shocked. 'But you're always good,' he said.

Julia pushed the the loaded pram into the narrow street at the end of the trek back from the church. Emma had been asleep since halfway through the mass and Richard and Jamie had been sufficiently awed by the ceremony, lulled by the music or amused by the books they'd borrowed from the large basket at the back of the church to be surprisingly quiet. Julia had more opportunity to observe and reflect than might have been expected. As she approached the house she saw that the car was in its place, taking up almost the whole of what should have been the front garden.

'Oh well,' she thought. 'It's really more trouble getting them in and out of the car than it is pushing them.'

'Well,' said Jeremy, emerging from the sitting room as they went in, 'did you enjoy it?'

'Yes, thank you. We all did, didn't we?'

'I lit a candle, daddy. I'm going to get a kitten,' said Jamie.

'So did I. I want a kitten too.' Richard often let his younger brother take the initiative.

'Don't tell me you've promised them kittens to get them to mass!'

'Of course not. It's what they prayed for.'

'So what if they don't get them?'

'One has to learn to face up to life's disappointments.'

'Mummy said prayers to be good,' said Jamie.

'For us all to be good, Jamie,' Julia corrected.

'Well' Jeremy sniffed 'At least that sounds a little less like Father Christmas's Grotto.'

'Has Astrid shown any signs of surfacing?'

'Not that I know of. I've been out to get a Sunday paper,' Jeremy added inconsequentially. 'Where did she go last night anyway?'

'I've no idea. Why?'

'Oh perhaps Ma Barnes asked her round or something. Anyway, what's for lunch?'

'I'll do some sausages; something quick. Going to a high mass doesn't leave much time for lunches.'

'I really can't imagine why you went. You can hardly feel you belong there. They're nearly all foreigners or Irish – and mainly working class.'

'Our society is mainly working class. That's one of the things I like about Catholicism: it reflects society as it is and doesn't just cream off a group of conformist, like-minded, middle class people.'

'You don't even believe in it.'

'I wish I did. I feel the need of it. This life's often too difficult to cope with alone.'

'Alone? How can you say you're alone? You've got a husband and three children!'

'Yes,' said Julia, and set about cooking the sausages.

Shona Otis lay in bed where her husband had uncharacteristically ordered her to stay while he "saw to things". As well as the now customary tea and biscuits, he had also brought her some breakfast: cereal and toast. It had of course taken longer than he'd reckoned on and he was only now out to buy the Sunday paper. Shona was aching to get up and organise the kitchen for lunch; she was agonising over the possibility that he'd left something on that should have been turned off. Then her mind wandered into an anxiety that his unwontedly solicitous behaviour was the result of guilt. Had he been seeing Charlotte? Or somebody else? Then she heard him pound his way up the stairs and he came in looking disgruntled and clutching the Sunday Telegraph.

'They've run out of The Times,' he complained, 'so I had to buy this rag.'

Shona glanced at the headlines and picture on the front page and decided it was an improvement. By the time Hector reached the kitchen again she was immersed in the hitherto secret love-lives of once famous personages and almost content to leave Hector in charge of the lunch.

Jean spent Sunday mentally reliving the evening of the Sunday before. There was no immediate hope of repeating it as Everard was not willing to miss another Sunday guest night and was dining in college. Contact with Tim had been limited to telephone calls and one brief afternoon meeting. Nevertheless her increasing detachment from Everard and imperviousness to his moods and his remarks about attractive secretaries and research students made her happier than she could remember being in all her married life and rendered Everard baffled and wary. He had not tried to make love to her again, and was aware that some effort to win her back to any desire for him might be needed; but the situation was unfamiliar and he felt at a loss. He began preparing for the college guest night earlier than usual and made less than his accustomed fuss about finding cufflinks, black tie and relatively clean white shirt in the chaos of their bedroom. Jean saw him leave the house with only a vague "goodbye" and no query as to when he'd be back. Half an hour later the telephone rang. It was Tim.

'Has Everard gone out?'

'Yes. About half an hour ago.'

'Good. Shall I come and help you put the boys to bed?'

'Yes please.'

'Then I'll cook you something nice.'

He arrived fifteen minutes later, bearing bags of things to cook and a bottle of wine. The boys were delighted to see him; bedtime for them was more fun than fuss and by nine o'clock Tim and Jean were having their companionable supper.

'When are you going to come and stay with me?'

'For a night you mean?'

'Preferably longer.'

'Oh Tim – I don't know.'

'Well, I can wait.'

'How long can you wait?'

'As long as it takes. I don't want anybody else so I'm content to wait for you.'

'It's difficult enough to get an evening away, let alone a night.'

'Couldn't you say you were going to your mother's?'

'I usually take the boys.'

'Even an evening would be nice.'

'I'll try Wednesday. If Everard insists on going to the Wednesday guest night I'll get a babysitter.'

Hector and Shona were in their tidy sitting room, Hector glowing with achievement and righteousness after his memorably successful day of household tasks and Shona unable to shake off her suspicions as to his motivation.

'You've really done wonders today, Hector,' she said.

'Oh – just a matter of applying intelligence in a practical direction,' responded Hector smugly.

'Well, nobody can doubt your intelligence.'

'I hope not.'

'There are some Camford dons who don't seem very intelligent when you meet them.'

'That's true enough. Geographers, for example, and some of the scientists – well – I suppose they must be all right in their own field but some of them can hardly speak or write English!'

'Isn't that new woman lecturer's husband a geographer?'

'Oh, him. He's a schoolmaster. Can't think why she married him.'

'He's very good looking, isn't he?'

'How do you know what he looks like?'

'I've only had him pointed out to me. When I was in college for a wives' lunch somebody saw him going across the quad and we all went and had a look at him.'

Hector sniffed. 'Men never think about whether other men are good looking or not. We wouldn't know. Anyway, it's not relevant.'

'It's the first thing men notice about women, though!'

'Well, of course. That's quite different.'

'Why should it be?'

'Because it's important how women look.'

Shona had never been a beauty and was almost inclined to be flattered that Hector might ever have thought her one when he elaborated.

'Not as important as money and good family, of course – for a wife, that is. And safer for a wife not to be beautiful, really.'

Hector took another long swallow of the good wine he felt he richly deserved after his day's labours.

'Is she thought to be beautiful?' Shona asked tentatively.

'Who?'

'The woman lecturer. Julia Leslie.'

'Oh I don't know. Depends if you like red hair and a pale face. Some people certainly seem to, though.'

'Who does – do?'

Hector gave one of his tenor giggles. 'Old Woger for one. Follows her like a spaniel. Thinks nobody notices – poor old chap.'

'Not Roger Tomlinson?! I can't believe it.'

Hector's giggle rose to counter-tenor. 'Yes, we all think it's fwightfully funny. Except Everard. He's wather sour about it. Of course he expected her to fall for him – out of gratitude for giving her the job I suppose!'

'So has she fallen for Roger, then?'

'Not noticeably. Nothing obvious about her, weally. Except that she doesn't like Everard. Moves inches away when he goes anywhere near her. Poor old Everard. Not used to that!'

'No.' Shona had always felt, along with some of the other Emmaeus wives that Everard was rather attractive and exciting. 'Ooooh.'

'What do you mean "ooooh"?' demanded Hector.

Had Shona been talking to another woman she would have said that she found Roger's interest in Julia, and Julia's lack of interest in Everard, very intriguing and that she was dying to hear more; but she was not accustomed to a conversation of this kind with Hector – or with any other man. She was, in fact, surprised at Hector's showing any interest in the subject or admitting that it was discussed among his colleagues.

'It's really interesting.'

Hector began to feel that he'd revealed too much about the inner workings of the Senior Common Room and decided it was time to go to bed.

Once the children were in bed and quiet, Julia settled to marking and preparing work for Monday's classes and tutorials. She and Jeremy generally had a late tea with the children on Sundays and only a light snack for supper. Jeremy had, however, murmured something about work almost immediately after tea and disappeared. It was now nearer nine o'clock than eight and there was no sign of him. Julia sighed and reflected that at least she could get on with her work unhindered for the moment and had better make the most of the opportunity; but she was tired and found herself reading the same paragraph of a pupil's essay over and again because her thoughts kept wandering away before she could reach the end of it. Increasingly they were wandering to the subject of what she was to say to Roger. "Well," she thought sadly "at least I'm not so taken up with wondering what Jeremy's doing."

At last in desperation she went into the kitchen,

took the timer from its place and set it down immediately in front of her work. With a fierce twist she set it for seven minutes. 'By the time this rings,' she told herself, 'this essay must be completely marked!' It was. She then applied herself to the rest of the work with increasing energy and satisfaction. When at last she had finished and was putting her books and papers away – and there was still no sign of Jeremy – she told herself that she'd been ridiculous to worry about going to dinner with Roger; that there was nothing in it at all and only the opportunity to make that clear was needed. Perpetual stalling would mean perpetual anxiety and indecision. She finally climbed the stairs to bed hoping that in the morning she would feel as calm and confident about it as she did now.

CHAPTER NINETEEN

Jean and Tim stood in Jean's kitchen enveloped in each other's arms and swaying companionably and rhythmically from one foot to the other as if pretending to dance. Neither wanted the evening to end.

'I wish we could go to bed,' said Tim.

Jean tightened her arms' clasp and tucked her head between his shoulder and chin.

'We can't, though, can we; not now. Anyway, with the boys here, I couldn't .... I wouldn't like to ....'

'I know,' Tim stroked her hair. 'Don't worry; I do know. We can wait till Wednesday. Somehow! It's better if I go now before Everard gets back. Things might be difficult for you if any suspicions are aroused.'

Jean sighed. 'You know I don't want you to go.'

'I don't want to go either.'

They resumed their former encircled swaying, neither wishing to break away. Perhaps fortunately a howl from upstairs parted them. They kissed swiftly before Jean went to deal with the problem and Tim went to his car.

At lunch in Emmaeus the following day Julian Holloway-Smythe was conducting his usual post mortem on the formal Sunday guest-night. 'You seemed to be enjoying yourself, Lucas,' he boomed at Everard.

'Good choice of wines don't you think? I thought the red particularly pleasant. Not surprised you did such justice to it – AND your guest. Brave of you to bring in a Tory M.P.'

'Very brave.' Arthur Middleton, a staunch member of the Labour Party broke in with an audible sniff. 'Flaunting the old boy network isn't as popular as it used to be.'

'Thank you, Arthur,' responded Everard in deceptively silky tones. 'Surprised to see you at a guest night at all, actually. Thought you disapproved of such things!'

'They wouldn't exist in an ideal state. They stink of privilege.'

'They employ a lot of people.'

'Most of whom could be better employed.'

'Doing what, for example? Building multi-storey car-parks, I suppose.'

There was a ripple of laughter from those in earshot. Arthur Middleton's devotion to multi-storey car-parks was a college joke. Arthur flushed outwardly and fumed inwardly, thought some high-minded thoughts about his incurably bourgeois and materialistic colleagues and said no more.

Peregrine Forsyth, arriving late, flustered into his usual seat.

'The butler's not quite his usual self today,' he murmured. 'Looks decidedly dyspeptic.'

'Too many heeltaps, probably – plus the odd bottle we didn't drink at all,' somebody else commented.

'Actually, he's not very pleased with me, I'm afraid' said Everard.

'Really? Why?' Peregrine was disappointed that the butler's indisposition might not be entirely due to illness.

'Well, I came in early last night and had a look at the dessert table. It was really very inadequate; it didn't have that cornucopia effect that a properly stocked dessert table should have. So I asked him to put a bit more fruit on. After all, the visual impression is as important as the gastronomic,'

'You had a nerve,' said Roger drily. 'No wonder he's looking dyspeptic.'

Arthur Middleton saw an opportunity. 'There was far more on that table than we could possibly eat; I suppose it didn't occur to you to think about the amount of waste?'

'Talk about waste!' retorted Everard. 'That's one of the problems. The college servants eat half of it before it can get on to the table!'

Julia who had been following this conversation was aghast at Everard's attitude. 'So you consider it waste if the servants eat it?!' she exclaimed.

Realising the implications of his remark and unable to retract it, Everard – unusually – showed his chagrin by turning a dull shade of chestnut red and failing to make a reply.

Arthur Middleton was delighted and beamed approval on Julia as he spoke. 'Some of us here have more liberal views!'

Julia was angry with herself for making her hostility to Everard so apparent. She glanced at Roger who seemed to be making a very small effort to hide a smile. Hastily she turned to Hector Otis and asked if he'd been at the guest night. Hector, delighted at the opportunity to vaunt his virtuous day's housekeeping, which he would not have been so happy to admit to his male colleagues, replied in as conspiratorially *sotto a voce* as his reedy voice would permit.

'I spent the whole day doing the house and cooking for Shona! She needed a west. I didn't let her do anything. It's surpwisingly easy weally, but women make such a fuss about these things. I suppose you're too much occupied domestically to come to many guest nights.'

'I'm only allowed to come to two a term: only the ladies' guest nights.'

'Oh, of course, I'd forgotten.'

'Thank you.' Julia was genuinely gratified, but Hector mistook her response for sarcasm or a coquettish show of feminine pique and replied crossly

'One can't remember everything!'

'Oh. Oh dear, I didn't mean it like that. I was pleased that you'd forgotten that I was ....' Julia hesitated to say 'a woman' and ended feebly 'that I was .... different.'

Hector slipped very perceptibly into his chatting-up-the-little- women mode and simpered '*viva la difference!*'

Julia sighed. She fiercely wanted to thump the table and shout out that she was a rational human being and capable of rational, intelligent conversation without being simpered at. Hearing the sigh and totally unaware of its cause Hector gave Julia a sideways glance.

'Woger's to be seen at most of the guest nights' he said, with a hint of significance. To his surprise – and her own – Julia laughed. Hector stared at her, as did several others, who looked up from their newspapers or aside from their conversations in surprise. Well, so much for poor old Woger thought Hector. But Julia was laughing at herself, at the fact that the mention of Roger immediately dissipated her angry claim to rationality.

'Pride goeth before a fall,' she found herself thinking.

Surely nothing could have been more irrational than her whole weekend's absorption in the problem of Roger's dinner invitation and her inability to find a consistent answer to it.

Roger himself, engaged in conversation with Everard, heard Julia's laugh but was more affected by its attractive quality than curious as to its cause. Everard was making a show of asking for advice about small second-hand cars, which meant he wanted it known that he was considering buying one for Jean.

'Not too small,' Roger was saying. 'Tend to be tinny; not safe enough.' His mind wandered into a fantasy of buying a car for Julia. Everard perceived that Roger had no particular interest in his choice of car and addressed Arthur Middleton.

'Know anything about cars, Arthur?' he queried.

'Only that people who dine with Tory M.P.s have at least two,' Arthur sniffed.

'You and your fiancée have got one each, haven't you?'

'Well, she needs one, of course. Social workers can't go visiting clients in distant housing estates and such places without a car.'

'And what do you need one for?' said Everard. 'But of course privileged car owners are necessary to justify the existence of multistorey carparks, aren't they?'

Julia left the lunch table as soon as she could and decided to go straight back to her room, foregoing the usual cup of coffee in the Senior Common Room and thus avoiding Roger. She hurried across the quad telling herself all the way that she was being cowardly, and she was breathless with anxiety and relief by the time she closed her own door on herself. She switched on the kettle to make some instant coffee and before it had come to the boil there was a knock on the door. Julia felt her heart thudding and was inclined to give no answer and pretend she was not there. A louder knock followed. The kettle began to hiss with steam, a sound probably inaudible through the door but a deterrent to Julia's pretence of absence.

'Come in,' she said.

She was unsurprised to see Roger in the doorway. He hesitated, unaware of her reaction.

'Come in,' she repeated. 'Have a cup of coffee. The kettle's boiling.'

Relieved, Roger entered the room and sat down.

'Only instant, I'm afraid. Milk? Sugar?'

'Milk to cool it, please. I know you don't take either; not after lunch or dinner, anyway.'

'After dinner?' Julia, her mind on the Emmaeus common room momentarily wondered when he'd seen her drinking coffee after dinner but was immediately reminded of the sofa in the Senior Common Room at St Mary's when she'd been struggling to hold on to her coffee cup and her balance.

'Oh – of course.'

'You haven't forgotten that you have been to dinner with me?!'

'Of course not.' Julia felt unwontedly inarticulate and to compensate continued. 'I know I had rather a lot to drink, but I do remember it, all of it. Total recall, in fact.'

'Will you have dinner with me again? Or were you trying to avoid giving me an answer by fleeing across the quad instead of having coffee in the common room?'

'I think perhaps I was. I hadn't decided on my answer.'

'And now?'

'I would like to have dinner with you again; but I want to meet your wife first.'

'What?' Roger, whose wife had not been taking a large part in the upper reaches of his consciousness, was completely thrown. 'Why?'

'Well you've met my husband.'

'But – haven't you met her?' Roger was vaguely aware that somehow all the college wives knew each other. But then of course Julia was not a college wife. 'No. I'd forgotten. I hadn't thought. It hadn't really occurred to me. Surely it's got nothing to do with ....'

'Our going out to dinner together? Perhaps not; but surely it's a fair condition. I'd like to meet some college wives; my position's rather isolating. Only two ladies' guest nights a term – and a rule that nobody brings his own wife.'

'You're a clever woman.'

Julia had completely regained her composure; more than that she was positively elated at having suddenly and inexplicably found so immediate, if temporary, a solution to her "Roger problem". Roger regarded her with wry admiration.

'A very clever woman. Thank you for the coffee. I'll be in touch.'

He left the room swiftly. Hearing his footsteps clattering down the uncarpeted stairs, Julia sat back in her chair with a happy sigh of self-congratulation.

Everard sat brooding in his room. He had been aware for some time that Julia did not find him attractive, but her attitude at lunch had revealed a degree of real dislike for which he had been unprepared. He told himself it might have been different if he'd been less taken up with Emily Matheson at the beginning of term. That was a washout, he thought sourly. Moreover, he hadn't found a replacement for her. Don't tell me I'm losing interest, he thought, not yet. Almost in spite of himself his mind wandered to Jean. The idea of buying her a car of her own had occurred to him only as he was seeking a means to recover from his discomfiture over the dessert. He was at a loss to know why he had thought of it. He hadn't felt very comfortable with Jean lately.

'Can't seem to get through to her,' he murmured aloud. He felt overcome by a kind of numbness, an inability to think or act. He put his head back, closed his eyes and went to sleep. He dreamt that he was driving a fast, low-slung car and beside him was a young woman with blond hair flying in the wind. Then he was being overtaken by their old car, high and square, and Jean was sitting in the passenger seat, not driving. He couldn't see who was driving, but Jean looked down on him as they passed, saw him, but without registering emotion of any kind, looked away as the car sped into the distance while he had great difficulty in making his sleek new car put on any speed at all, however hard he stepped on the accelerator. He woke up suddenly, shivering.

CHAPTER TWENTY

Jean had decided not to mention to Everard that she was going out on Wednesday evening and getting a babysitter. The Wednesday guest nights were not as formal as the Sunday ones and he would not be coming home to change into a dinner-jacket. Tim was coming to fetch her, as Everard had taken the car to college. Jean gave the boys their supper early, got them ready for bed and let them sit watching television until the babysitter arrived. She was a girl of sixteen whose parents kept the village pub, just across the green. She was used to noise and late nights and not too bothered about when she got home.

'I'll pay you now so that you can go home if my husband gets back before me,' Jean said to her. 'I'll give you enough for four hours and if it's any more than that I'll drop it in to you tomorrow. Is that all right?'

'Fine. No problem.'

Jean gathered her scattered belongings from

various parts of the house and was ready to leave immediately when Tim's Beetle car puttered into the yard before seven o'clock. He had no need to move from the driver's seat. Jean was ready to open the passenger door even before the Beetle stopped. Almost in one movement she sank into the seat and put her arms round Tim. They kissed happily. Tim then turned the car and they bumped out of the yard, negotiated the road and the lane and speedily arrived at Tim's farmhouse flat.

'It's too early for dinner,' said Tim.

'Yes,' said Jean, 'much too early.'

Hand in hand they almost ran into the bedroom, shed their outer clothes and collapsed on to the bed, laughing and panting. Tim undid Jean's blouse.

'Oh, I've been wanting you so much, so much.'

Gently but swiftly they helped each other remove their remaining garments until they lay together enjoying the uttermost contact of their naked bodies.

More than an hour later Tim brought two glasses of wine into the bedroom and he and Jean sat up side by side to drink them.

'I've just turned the oven up. We can have dinner in a few minutes.'

Jean laughed. 'How can you be so amazingly organised?'

'Well, I have an incentive. Shall we dress for dinner?'

'We'd better. It's a bit cold to eat unclad.'

'Maybe in the summer sometime. It could be fun.'

Everard returned from his dinner earlier than usual. His guest had seemed rather hard work and the food less good than usual, though the bowls of fruit at dessert had been full to overflowing. This made them difficult to manage. Everard's own guest had suffered the embarrassment of dislodging a precarious apple which had rolled on to the table and upset somebody's glass of port. Peregrine Forsyth had given Everard a meaningful stare and the butler, dealing with the spillage as discreetly as possible, had fixed an accusing eye on him. After coffee in the Senior Common Room Everard had declined both brandy and whisky in order to make it awkward for his guest to accept any and that got rid of him with little delay. Home quite shortly after ten o'clock, Everard was more than surprised to find a babysitter in occupation instead of Jean.

'Has something happened?' he asked her. 'Where's my wife?'

'She's still out,' was the reply. 'She said I could go if you got back before she did.'

'What time did she leave?'

'About seven. She's paid me for four hours.'

'Did she say ...' Everard wanted to ask 'where she was going' but suddenly decided he was unwilling to reveal his ignorance of Jean's whereabouts, so instead he struck his head with his fist somewhat over heartily and continued 'of course! I'd forgotten all about it. She wouldn't have expected me back before eleven. I mean she didn't expect ... Yes – there's no need for you to stay now. No, don't worry about the money – it must be over three hours, anyway.'

So the babysitter got back to her parents' pub before closing time.

'You're early,' said her father.

'Yes. Mr Lucas is home.'

'That's unusual!'

'Yes. He seemed a bit drunk.'

'I'm not surprised. They drink more in those colleges than people do in pubs – more's the pity.'

Everard felt unable to go to bed – he prowled round the house purposelessly until he asked himself what he was doing and was unable to come up with an answer. He was not willing to admit that he was looking for clues as to Jean's activities. He wished he had asked the babysitter how long ago Jean had booked her for the evening. He felt particularly aggrieved that he'd come home early and Jean was not there to appreciate the fact. It didn't often happen; he was usually late and Jean had always been there when he got back. In bed asleep as often as not. He decided to wait up for her.

Tim and Jean ate their dinner and drank their wine by the light of the fire and four candles. Lingering over the last glass Jean ran the tips of her fingers lightly over the back of Tim's hand.

'I love your hands,' she said. 'So strong and deft and sensitive.'

'Like yours,' said Tim.

'I can't bear to say I must go. But ...'

'Not yet.' Tim took Jean's hand, stood up, pulled her gently to her feet and towards him and said 'After!'

Quite unable to summon the will to resist Jean allowed herself to be led back into the bedroom. There they stayed, making love, talking, dozing, utterly happy in each other's company and aware of little else until finally they agreed reluctantly that it was impossible for Jean to stay all night, and Tim helped her to dress, dressed himself and drove her home.

Jean unlocked and opened the back door as quietly as possible, given the age and state of the lock. She could see that there was a light on in the sitting room. Surely, she thought, Everard must have got home and relieved the babysitter. She looked at the clock in the kitchen: two forty-five. Jean took off her shoes and advanced cautiously to the door of the sitting room. A long low masculine snore revealed Everard's presence. Jean's immediate reaction of fear at the possibility of his waking suddenly to find her in her outdoor clothes was tempered with a desire to shake him roughly awake and tell him how she hated him with his drunken snoring and how happy she'd been with someone else and how she couldn't bear to live with him any longer. But she only gasped at her own temerity and went noiselessly up the stairs to their bedroom where, without turning on the light, she undressed with haste and lay in bed trembling, more frightened at the strength of her own emotions than of Everard.

Everard himself woke slowly to a realisation that he was cold, uncovered and uncomfortable. It took some minutes for him to remember where he was and why he was there. Waiting up for Jean to come home was so new an experience that he could hardly believe it. He looked at the time. Almost three o'clock! He felt angry, suspicious, shocked, apprehensive and helpless. He had no idea where she'd gone or how she'd gone. He'd had no inkling that she was intending to go out at all. He sat up suddenly. Would she come back? He loped across the room and up the stairs to their bedroom where he flung open the door and switched on the light almost simultaneously. He'd intended to look and see what Jean had taken with her, but instead saw her in bed with her arm over her eyes against the sudden light. Irrationally, he felt more angry than relieved.

'Where have you been?' he demanded.

'Where have you been, more like it,' Jean responded. 'And keep your voice down, you'll wake the boys.'

'I've been home for hours. I was waiting up for you.'

'I didn't see you.' (True she thought to herself. I only heard him).

'I was in the sitting room.'

'Hmmm!' said Jean in a tone implying "that's-a-new-one-and-I-don't-believe-it".

'You must have seen me.'

'I didn't go into the sitting room.'

'I left the light on.'

'I'm so used to you leaving lights on I don't notice them.'

Everard began to feel that he was the one on the defensive. It was, of course, the more normal situation. Jean turned away from him and the light and made a pretence to settling back to sleep. Everard undressed slowly, wondering why he felt unwilling to probe any further into the mystery of Jean's activities. He must have slept more heavily than ... Jean could have come back quite early ... He began very dimly to realise that if anybody were to be guilty of staying out very late for very questionable reasons he'd much rather it was himself.

CHAPTER TWENTY-ONE

Jean slept deeply for about three hours and then woke with surprising suddenness. Her heart was pounding and she felt a sense of panic. This was not an unaccustomed feeling. She knew she had to run over the possible causes in her mind until an extra twinge of distress told her that she'd hit on the right one. Most often it had been suspicion or evidence of one of Everard's affairs. But this time she believed he'd been at a guest night and come home relatively early, and anyway she no longer cared. She now found – had found for some weeks – that she could contemplate Everard's activities in that field with no other emotion than faint disgust. Still, she might just check with the babysitter and find out what time he had come home. The babysitter! Jean's heart gave the expressive lurch that told her she'd hit on the cause of her sense of panic. How was she to explain her supposed belief in Everard's absence at the time she came home if the babysitter had not obviously been there? Why on earth has she not told him she'd known he was already home, snoring on the sofa? Her resort to attack as the best means of defence had been instinctive and no doubt combined with the bitterness accumulated in many a lonely evening, tied to the house and the children, when Everard had in fact come home very late. Phrases like "the biter bit" and "what's sauce for the goose is sauce for the gander" from the folk wisdom of her childhood came into her mind and she found herself smiling broadly. If Everard starts asking questions about it I'll laugh in his face, she thought. Even if he kills me for it I'd rather it was this way round.

Roger was having breakfast with his wife. His newspaper was propped in front of him. Barbara was used to this and occasionally wondered why she kept to the routine of getting up to have breakfast with him. She was immensely surprised when he suddenly said 'Isn't it about time we had a dinner party?'

'Whatever makes you say that? You're generally very resistant to our having parties.'

'Don't we owe rather a lot of invitations?'

'No more than usual. But do you really want a party now, with Entrance Exams practically upon you?' Roger remembered using Entrance Exams as an excuse not to have parties in previous years.

'Yes, you're right. I'd forgotten. Perhaps a drinks party. Less time-consuming.'

'It's not like you to forget Entrance.' Barbara looked at him speculatively, decided not to ask him how he felt and went on. 'Wouldn't it be better to wait and have one at or after Christmas – even New Year? After all, everybody else must be very busy now.' Roger gave no answer. 'Surely you agree,' Barbara continued, increasingly surprised. 'It's quite obvious from previous years ....'

'All right!' Roger interrupted with unnecessary vehemence. 'I'm sorry I mentioned it at all.'

'But Christmas or New Year would be ....'

'Subject closed!' said Roger. Then to compensate and appear less irritable he added, 'Remind me about it in a week or two.'

Roger drove to college angry with himself for so uncharacteristically forgetting about the nearness of the Entrance Exams, angry at his own irritability and even more angry that the cause of it was the unlikelihood of his meeting Julia anywhere but in College in the immediately foreseeable future.

Roger had barely reached his room when the college secretary rang him with information, questions and requests about the Entrance Examinations. She hinted that she had rather expected him to be in touch with her about them.

'They've been in a separate compartment in my

mind,' Roger answered a little testily, 'a special compartment.'

He was soon inundated with details and paperwork. When he looked up from his desk he was surprised to find that it was one o'clock and he was hungry. Lunch was a less leisurely affair than usual and over coffee the conversation, when not too specific, ranged round the merits of examinations and interviews as part of the selection process, the point and purpose of scholarships, closed and open and the fairness or otherwise of the whole system. Arthur Middleton was vociferous on these topics, especially when baited by Everard who expressed opposing views with an air of calm certainty. 'I don't know why you're so opposed to scholarships, Arthur,' he purred, 'they were designed to give clever boys from poor families the kind of education other people had to pay for.'

'We're talking about now,' responded Arthur, 'not the middle ages. What happens now is that rich boys, whose parents can afford to send them to public schools, where they stay for years and years, are specially coached to shine in entrance scholarship exams. Boys from state schools that have almost never sent candidates to Camford simply can't compete; can't be expected to.'

'Well, what about the closed scholarships? They are strictly limited to certain areas of the country for each college, so there must be more opportunities for local state school boys.'

'There's at least one public school in most areas,' Arthur retorted 'and public school boys are so much more sure of themselves in interviews – oily tongued lot,' Arthur added 'like you' under his breath and regarded Everard with aversion.

'Surely,' Everard continued, 'the best candidates are, simply, the best candidates, regardless of what makes them so. And you know it isn't exactly a boy's fault if his parents are so misguided as to give him a public school education; how many of us choose for ourselves where we are to be educated?'

'Besides, you know, Arthur,' Julian Holloway-Smythe entered the conversation, partly in order to avert one of Arthur's diatribes on privilege which he'd just opened his mouth to deliver, irrelevant as an answer though it might be. 'Besides, you know ...' Julian Holloway- Smythe repeated '... when we have a toss up between choosing a public school chap and a state school one, all else being equal, we always choose the state school one on the grounds that he must have better potential to get so far with fewer advantages. Fundamentally it's potential that matters.'

There was a silence. Julian Holloway-Smythe was generally regarded as a snob of the deepest dye who supported "the Establishment" in all its manifestations, though it was an open and never referred to secret that he himself, state school educated and with a resounding Devonshire accent, had come up to Camford on a closed scholarship. He had, however, shed this persona so completely that some of the younger dons didn't believe the story anyway.

Roger, who had been immersed in the contents of a very large buff envelope, gave a deep chuckle as he handed these over to Arthur. 'Take a look at this if you want to contemplate the ultimate in closed scholarships.'

Puzzled, Arthur looked in turn at a birth certificate, a marriage certificate and a detailed and official looking drawing of a shield, coloured a pale blue and sporting a cockle shell.

'What's all this got to do with scholarships?' he inquired, somewhat defensively, in case any or everybody else knew.

'This scholarship is open to "The lawful son of armigerous parents".'

'Of what parents?'

'Armigerous.'

'What does "armidgerous" mean?'

'I suppose,' Julian Holloway-Smythe said smoothly, 'one could say "armiggerous", depending when and where one learned one's Latin.'

'Hence the coloured shield,' said Everard, as if he'd known all along. 'It's a coat of arms. "Armigerous" means a person, or rather family, with their own coat of arms. Hence also the birth and marriage certificates: to show he's a lawful son, not illegitimate.'

Arthur wrinkled his nose perceptibly and handed the papers back to Roger as if they were something out of a refuse bin. 'You mean to tell me somebody's actually applied for this scholarship?'

'Yes. For the first time that I ever remember.'

'Some Etonian, I suppose!'

'Well yes, as a matter of fact.'

'But you must remember,' said Everard with pretended sententiousness, 'that he can't help it!'

Julia, where she sat shrouded in a darkly panelled corner, stored all this as conversation fodder for entertaining her father-in law when he came to stay over Christmas, not that she was uninterested in the entrance procedures for their own sake. She and Everard had to work together to choose the men who would be reading modern languages at Emmaeus for the next three or four years. They were to have a meeting at the end of the week when the scripts would have been received and, in the main, read. The prospect was in many ways intriguing: meeting and assessing the candidates whose work one had read was much more stimulating than the pure paperwork of examining A-levels, for example. Working with Everard might also be interesting, if not entirely pleasurable; combining these activities with preparations for a family Christmas was a task demanding organisation, concentration and considerable stamina. Julia sighed inaudibly, decided to finish as much of her normal work as she could and left the room as inconspicuously as possible. Even Roger did not notice her departure and was surprised and a little disturbed to realise she was not there when he himself left a few minutes later.

Everard was home early that evening and appeared to be in a particularly good temper. He always enjoyed the prospect of Entrance. He loved the sense of power it gave him, the feeling that he was controlling the futures of other men. His assumption of the influence he would have on the minds of the young men he chose to teach was greatly exaggerated, but his assessment of the effect on their lives that acceptance or rejection from Camford University would produce, was less so. Not that the truth or accuracy of his opinions had any bearing on those opinions themselves; but accurate or not they were the cause of his euphoria. He treated Jean to an account of the "the lawful son of armigerous parents" who would, if accepted, be one of his pupils. Jean, relieved that his mind seemed to be entirely on college affairs, promoted that topic of conversation with a more lively interest than usual. She reflected that Everard could, after all, be very entertaining when he chose to be, and told herself that he was unlikely to maintain any interest in her comings and goings, or the presence or absence of baby-sitters, or any other such domestic affairs.

They finished dinner amicably and when Jean got up to clear the table and do the dishes he said, 'Leave all that. Let's go to bed.'

Jean gave a gasp and willed herself not to stiffen perceptibly. She was shocked. She had been talking to Everard as if she were one of his colleagues. She had simply not been thinking of him as a husband. She realised clearly that she had lost all or any desire to consider him as such. Through her mind, however, flashed the consequences of resisting him: the likelihood of his violence; his suspicions of her late night activities. She was not ready for any revelations about her relationship with Tim. She stalled.

'I've still got a lot to do.'

'You used not to bother about such things.'

'That was because you didn't – and didn't want me to. I wasn't happy living like that. It went against the grain.'

'No need to go to extremes.'

'Washing half a dozen plates can hardly be called extreme. They'd all be done done now if you'd help instead of standing there arguing.'

'Please,' said Everard.

'What?' Jean turned round and stared at him in astonishment; he'd said something so totally uncharacteristic.

'Please,' Everard repeated.

Still staring, Jean put down the dishes and allowed herself to be led from the kitchen up to the bedroom.

'I don't know what to do,' she kept thinking, 'I don't know what to do.'

As Everard began to undress her she shuddered involuntarily. He was about to ask what was the matter: cold? apprehension? pleasure? revulsion? He was too afraid that it might be due to the memory of their last sexual encounter to voice any question and decided to make it so much a matter of pleasure that the other possibilities would disappear. He'd always been able to give her pleasure. Well – nearly always. Jean moaned, momentarily giving credence to Everard's confidence in his ability to make her happy. But then she turned her head away from him sharply. He found the unwillingness exciting – increasingly exciting – and he grasped both her arms just above the elbows and pinned her down forcibly, then as she struggled, forced his knee between her knees, then the other knee until he was actually kneeling on her outspread legs. She cried out in pain as he swiftly thrust into her. His own orgasm seemed longer and more intense than anything he had ever experienced, and he neither knew nor cared what she experienced of pleasure or pain.

CHAPTER TWENTY-TWO

Entrance was under way. Julia and Everard were in Everard's room at the top of the gatehouse tower discussing the candidates prior to interviewing them. So far everything was proceeding more amicably than Julia could have hoped.

'It's so different from a women's college,' she was saying, 'so different from my college anyway. Only seventeen people applying. We used to have about two hundred applicants to reduce to a short list of twenty-five or more. But then ours is supposed to be rather a "women's subject" isn't it? And, of course, with so few women's colleges in relation to men's the numbers are bound to be very different. Here's a chap with a gamma on his general paper – and we're going to interview him! We used to use gamma as a general signal to mean "hopeless, don't think of interviewing".'

'Oh, we'll interview all of them.'

'Did you read that strange essay on Heredity by the boy who seemed to think it meant being born male or female and ended his work with a diatribe on the awfulness of being a woman and his gratitude for having escaped such a fate?'

'I certainly did. I wondered what you'd make of it'

'I'll be interested to see how he reacts when he realises one of his interviewers is a woman. I'll have to be particularly pleasant to him so that he doesn't think it's the reason for turning him down – if we do turn him down.'

'I fear we may. He can't be very bright if he thinks heredity means gender. His other papers don't show a very intelligent regard for relevance either.'

'The Rector sits in on our interviews, doesn't he?'

'Oh yes. There's always somebody, as it were, neutral. The Rector often reads some of the answers to the general paper questions and asks the candidates the odd thing about them.'

'What's his own subject?'

'History. Not that I've ever heard him talk about it!'

'I don't think I've ever heard him talk at all.'

'Well he only appears at meetings and guest nights, and you can't come to many of those.'

The Rector, Everard and Julia were sitting in strategic places in Everard's room. They had been interviewing candidates since early – for Camford – that morning. Everard had apparently acquired a large clock to grace the occasion; at least Julia had never noticed it before. It had a sonorous and intrusive tick which became oppressively apparent during the silent pauses while nervous candidates were trying to think how to answer questions. Julia was rather nervous herself, initially. She had marked Entrance papers for her own college but never taken part in the ensuing interviews. The presence of the Rector was a little daunting and the tick of the persistent clock seemed not to synchronise with natural speech rhythms. The "lawful son of armigerous parents", whose application for this archaic closed scholarship had so amused or incensed members of the SCR, was early on the list. He announced, with little invitation, that he was 'not just a dilettante Etonian', that he 'really wanted to work and get a good degree …', only to be halted in mid-flow by Everard asking him to define 'dilettante'. He was only briefly discountenanced and made a good recovery. 'Oh, you know, partying and clubbing all the time and never doing anything useful.' Everard asked whether he knew any Italian. 'Well, not really. Always try to get by on French – and English, of course!' Julia's opinion that he sounded decidedly 'dilettante' – even if he didn't quite know what it meant – was not greatly altered by the rest of the interview, though the young man was undoubtedly charming and articulate and probably not likely to be troublesome.

'May as well take him,' said Everard after the door had closed behind the Etonian. 'He'll be lively in tutorials. We'll see him again this evening.'

Next came the candidate who had confused heredity with gender in his long and heartfelt essay on the frightfulness of being female. Julia was interested to see him. She had visualised a hefty rugger thug and was surprised to find that he was of relatively slight build with a pale complexion and a fine head of curly blond hair. His eyes opened in wide amazement at the sight of Julia and his mouth opened even wider when the Rector invited her to begin the questions. Julia wondered whether his attitude to the female might have been engendered by a reaction to accusations of 'girlishness' or doubts about his own masculinity. She decided to put him as much at ease as possible.

'You wrote a very interesting essay on heredity, Mr O'Donnell.'

The pale complexion was immediately suffused with crimson down to, and no doubt beneath, his collar line.

'I never thought it would be read by a female,' he managed to say, between a stammer and a gulp.

'Well, please don't worry. I thought it showed some quite sensitive understanding of the difficulties faced by women. I see you've done an A' level in English as well as French. Have you ever read any of Byron's *Don Juan*?

'I can't say I have.'

'Well Byron has some rather similar thoughts about women: "the real hardship of their she-condition" he calls it. I'm sure you'd find it interesting.'

Mr O'Donnell's crimson began to subside and he coped with the rest of the interview as well as anybody with his limitations might be expected to do.

The afternoon's work over and all the candidates interviewed, there was to be a short break before dinner, then dinner and the second interviews from eight o'clock onwards, of the seven or eight men most likely to be selected. A long day. Julia picked up her coat rather awkwardly and as she did so a shower of clothes pegs fell out of the pockets. She then remembered shoving them in there the previous afternoon when grabbing in some of the children's washing as the rain started to fall.

'Oh dear!' she said, thinking it slightly funny. The Rector and Everard, however, looked pained, almost embarrassed, as if she had committed some decidedly grave social faux pas. 'Oh dear!' she repeated and put on her coat and thrust the pegs back and escaped from the room feeling guilty and diminished.

Entrance finally over and eight candidates out of

the seventeen applicants informed that they had been accepted to read Modern Languages at Emmaeus College, Julia turned her whole attention to preparations for a family Christmas. As both her parents and Jeremy's were divorced and not on speaking terms with their former spouses, Julia's mother and Jeremy's father were to join in the festivities. There were presents to be bought, cake and mince pies to make, larger supplies of food to be got in and somehow stored in a house with a too-small refrigerator and no larder. In the low, dark cupboard beside the boiler, the salt went wet and the flour mouldered. Julia remembered with a slight shudder the second Christmas of her married life when Richard was a baby, how her father-in-law had sent in advance a vast, uncooked ham. No doubt he was trying to recapture the great country house Christmases of his youth, hoping to reenact something of them now that his son was married. She had stared at the ham in dismay. It was twice the size of any cooking vessel she possessed. In desperation she had decided to boil it in the twin-tub washing machine. It had been a matter of turning it on and off judiciously to prevent it from boiling over, while keeping it hot enough to cook. The steam produced had infested the house with moisture and even the stair rails had dripped dampness for days. Then there had been the turkey, ordered from a former servant of Jeremy's grandmother's, and clearly the biggest and best of the birds she had reared with loving care through the year. It had arrived on Christmas Eve and Julia, undoing the parcel, had let out a scream of horror just as Jeremy was going out "to meet somebody".

'What on earth's the matter?' he'd demanded, displeased at the impediment to his exit from the domestic scene.

'I can't bear to look at it,' Julia had gasped as the creature flopped over and off the kitchen table complete with feet, neck, head, eyes and beak and every other appurtenance of liveness except its feathers. Fortunately Jeremy, accustomed from his early youth to gutting rabbits and pigeons that he'd shot on the family estate under the tutelage of the gamekeeper and his son, found a dead turkey relatively easy to deal with and made fairly short work of ridding it of its inedible elements. Even so, it was still so enormous that nothing else could be put in the oven with it, not even a tray of potatoes, and it had cooked very unevenly. It had to feed only three adults and a child still at the mushed-up food stage. Julia gave a reminiscent sigh and reflected that since the death of the turkey-rearing family retainer, she had at least been able to choose her own turkeys, tiring though it was to cart them home. She also thought a little sourly of her mother-in-law's boast that she had 'never in all her life, cooked a Christmas dinner.'

Astrid, being German, had a proper sense of the importance of Christmas preparations and she had of necessity become more used to the house and the children during Julia's involvement with the Entrance examinations and interviews. She had even had the children help her make delicious little biscuits in interesting shapes. Julia decided that she was improving on acquaintance and, remembering the awfulness of coping unaided with shopping, cooking and very small children, was not sorry to have another woman in the house to help her.

She had become so embroiled in family life and so distanced from college and her colleagues with all their vagaries that when a card arrived conveying not Christmas greetings but an indication that Mr and Mrs Roger Tomlinson would be 'At Home' from 6 – 8 p.m. on Boxing Day for drinks, she reacted with a sense of something like shock that that situation was still to be dealt with and had not gone, would not go, away. Clearly Roger had engineered a suitable means for Julia to meet his wife well before the next term began. She could not quite remember whether she had agreed to go out to dinner with him on that condition, or merely to thinking about it, though she had a suspicion that it had sounded more like a conditional acceptance and that Roger would consider himself rightfully piqued if she did not abide by it.

Jeremy was delighted when she showed him the Tomlinsons' invitation, though Julia tried to play it down and even murmured that she didn't particularly want to go.

'It should really read only Mrs Roger Tomlinson At Home – not Mr and Mrs,' she remarked, rather hoping to provoke Jeremy into one of his descents into snobbery. But he was ignorant or heedless of the niceties of invitation wording, which he regarded as the prerogative of the women of the family, and both flattered and interested at the idea of meeting numbers of dons on a relatively equal footing. He and Julia had not infrequently been invited to parties given by the parents of his prep. school pupils, many of whom were dons, but the purpose of such invitations had been to reinforce the importance and specialness of the party-giver's offspring rather than for any pleasure to be gained from meeting the Leslies for their own sake. The discrepancy between the relative importance of dons and schoolmasters had been borne in on Julia when a hostess inquired whether she had a great deal to do with the school in any capacity.

'Not really,' Julia had replied. 'I teach in Emmaeus College.'

The hostess had appeared utterly aghast.

'Oh heavens!' she exclaimed. 'I had no idea! And I've asked you here with all these undergraduates! I do apologise. I hope you don't mind.'

Julia murmured the appropriate disclaimers and managed not to say that the company of undergraduates was much more tolerable than the implication that a schoolmaster and his wife were so far inferior to a don.

Julia propped the invitation card against the spice jars on the kitchen chimney-piece and decided to think nothing further about it than the writing of a proper reply – in the affirmative.

CHAPTER TWENTY-THREE

Jean had prevailed on Everard to look after the boys while she went to the hairdresser's. He had, in fact, been so totally astonished that she wanted to go to such a place that he had been unable to come up with a ready excuse.

'But you never go to the hairdresser's!'

'I have been before. I can't cut my hair myself.'

'Why does it need cutting? It looks normal to me.'

'It's getting thin and straggly on the ends. Alison Greer has hers done frequently.'

'When do you ever see her?'

'Well, they have got a weekend cottage in this village!'

Everard was well aware of the fact and had, from time to time, felt some interest in Alison Greer, but her husband was never far from her side and her interest in men was so general that he was doubtful of any success in that quarter. None the less, he felt he knew Alison better than Jean did.

Unbeknown to Everard, Alison had 'befriended' Jean when they first came to live in the village. That is to say, she had taken to dropping in on Jean at coffee time when she was in the vicinity and had nothing better to do. She had expressed disapproval of neighbours "going round to each other's houses all the time" and made it very clear that the dropping in was not to be reciprocal. Jean had at first welcomed her, glad of a woman companion of roughly her own age and education. Alison had been easy to talk to, good at asking pertinent (though Jean sometimes felt impertinent) questions, sympathetic over the sufferings of women and the tiresome ways of men. So when she had 'dropped in' one morning to find Jean in tears it had not been difficult for her to wheedle out the cause, and Jean had confided the finding of Everard's diary revealing the stay of another woman in the house during her absence. Alison had expressed kindness and consolation, but also stressed that that could never happen with Henry (her not-so-young husband) and Jean had felt increasingly, after Alison's departure, that there had been more than a glimmer of malicious triumph thinly veiled in her attitude, and from that time had become increasingly embarrassed and ill at ease in her presence and taken to going out with the youngest child, not then at school, before the approach of coffee time, until Alison had taken to dropping-in on different friends and acquaintances, most of whom had been regaled with the details of Jean's confidences, under the guise of Alison's anxiety about her.

Jean, indeed, wondered why she had even mentioned Alison to Everard, apart from the fact that she knew Everard found her not unattractive and that she had occasionally gone to the same local hairdresser. The truth of the matter was that Jean and Tim had arranged one last tryst before he went away to spend Christmas with his family in the north of England. He would be away for two whole weeks and Jean felt completely desolate at the prospect of so long a separation from him; a separation, moreover, during which telephone calls would be difficult and letters all but impossible. She was really at a loss to know why the situation should have inspired her to do something so uncharacteristic as going to the hairdresser, but perhaps it was a measure of the different persona she was taking on in the warmth and reassurance provided by Tim's love for her, emerging from the repression she had been suffering in her relationship with Everard. Be that as it may, the visit to the salon, local and unpretentious though it was, had been a great success. Jean felt cosseted and rested as she relaxed under the drier with a cup of coffee and a pile of magazines to look at. An article in one of them particularly caught her eye. O Come All Ye Faithless it was entitled, and it took a slightly cynical, slightly comical, view of the miseries of unfaithful wives, bound to their families and separated from their lovers over the Christmas period. There was a description of such a woman sobbing into the grubby muddle of the family washing. Jean read with absorbed interest. Never in the habit of buying or reading magazines of this kind, she was amazed to find that feelings like her own were experienced by other women; that she was by no means unique, either in her situation or in her reaction to it. She felt cheered and encouraged by this revelation: one of a significant group, not somebody alone on the outer edges. She subsequently returned home feeling confident – even triumphant.

She was greeted by the boys with remarks that she looked different. They were a little disapproving. Mothers should not look different. Mothers should always look stably and unalterably the same. Differences were disturbing. Not that they were able to consider these ideas consciously or voice them in any way other than by saying "Mummy you look different". Everard saw that she looked different too but he realised that she had been looking different for some time even though he had done his best to ignore the fact. He decided not to give her the satisfaction of having him remark on it. Instead he indicated an open envelope with a card half out of it.

'This was dropped through the door while you were out,' he said. 'It's an invitation to a drinks party at the Greers.'

'Here or in Camford?' Jean looked at the card to see for herself. 'Oh, here in their cottage. I thought so. We probably wouldn't have been asked to one in Camford.'

'Now why do you say that?'

'Well, Henry's rather senior and I get the impression that we're regarded as young and rather inferior in the hierarchy of Camford dons. It's not as if you and he were in the same College. Alison certainly treats me as an inferior anyway.'

'Oh, nonsense. You're always imagining things like that!' Everard had never previously considered that Alison might regard him as inferior to her husband – that effeminate old stick, as he privately regarded him. He felt rather put out. Aloud he said: 'He's a scientist.' Unsurprisingly, Jean had not been following his chain of thought. She'd been more engrossed in one of her own.

'Pardon?' she murmured absently. Everard took her roughly by the shoulder and shook her.

'What's the matter with you?' he shouted. 'I thought I'd got you out of saying that years ago. I wouldn't have bloody married you if you hadn't got out of it. I thought you'd never say it again.'

'You sodding snob!' Jean looked him up and down coldly and disdainfully. 'Don't take it out on me because the Greers think you're inferior. You are inferior – to practically everybody.' She shook herself free of him, picked up her coat, slammed the back door behind her and drove the car out of the bumpy yard.

She reached Tim's farmyard flat much earlier than they'd arranged. He came out to meet her, looking anxious.

'Is anything the matter?'

'Why? Because it's so early? No. Not really. I hadn't even thought about the time. It was just that I couldn't stay in the house with Everard a minute longer. Oh dear! That was very irresponsible of me. The children haven't even had their tea.'

'Surely Everard can see to that.'

'Well ... I suppose ...'

'They'll soon let him know if they're hungry.'

'That's true enough.'

'He wouldn't go out and leave them on their own would he?'

'No. I don't think he'd do that. Besides, he hasn't got the car.'

'Well then. Don't worry. Come in and we'll make the most of the extra time.'

Everard paced up and down the kitchen, found it too small to be paced satisfactorily, opened the back door and tried pacing the yard instead. This he soon found much too cold and windy so he retreated inside and flung himself moodily on to the sitting room sofa, hitting the wooden rail of the sagging understructure uncomfortably as he did so. Noise was emanating from the boys' rooms at the top of the house and he realised that something ought to be done about them. What, he was not sure. He had no idea when, or even whether, Jean would come back. He could, he told himself, have forcibly prevented her from going, and he congratulated himself on his moderation rather than admit that he'd been too taken aback to do anything fast enough. Increased volume from above reminded him of present necessities and he was suddenly cheered – slightly – by the thought of a clever way of dealing with them: he'd take the boys out for a fish-and-chip supper! He bounded up the stairs to impart the good news and deal with the problems of raucous noise, potential damage and supper at one go. He even remembered to bundle the boys into duffel coats and scarves,for which they were thankful as they encountered the bitter wind in the yard. But then the youngest piped piteously. 'Where's the car Daddy?'

So accustomed was Everard to having the car 90 percent at his disposal that he hadn't even thought about it.

'Mummy's got it, hasn't she?' said the eldest. The others, realising that fish-and-chips were now out of the question, began to howl. Everard took them all back inside, feeling hopelessly trapped in an inescapable situation. A glimmer of paternal instinct and parental responsibility kept him from howling with rage himself. He began searching inadequately through the kitchen to find his wailing offspring something to eat.

They were finishing a strange medley of toast, Marmite and baked beans when there was a knock on the back door. Knowing it couldn't be Jean, but inexplicably anxious, Everard went and opened the door to see the babysitter from the pub. Everard stared at her uncomprehendingly and she stared back at him.

'Mrs Lucas told me to come at this time,' she said.

'Oh. Ah. Yes,' Everard was rather at a loss. He was tempted to let her come in and take over but felt too defeated by the events, or non-events, of the evening and the lack of any vehicle in which to escape and he found himself apologising. 'I'm afraid there's been a mistake. Mrs Lucas didn't realise I was going to be here. I'm really sorry. Er ... I'm sure she'll pay you something anyway. I expect she'll see you tomorrow. Goodnight.'

He closed the door wondering at his feeling of reluctance to let anybody into the house, and went back to the kitchen to try and find some more food to complete the boys' – and his – inadequate supper. It took some time, seemingly even longer, to get them to bed. They were grumpy and uncooperative and asked frequently, he felt accusingly, when Mummy was coming back.

Everard evaded the questions as long as possible, and finally snapped: 'Not until you're asleep.'

It was after nine o'clock before anything like peace and quiet was achieved and Everard went downstairs feeling drained and exhausted but still restless and at a loss what to do with himself. It didn't occur to him to do anything about the debris in the kitchen. He tried sitting down with a book but soon threw it aside. It landed on a pile of papers which then slid off the table. Among them was the invitation to the Greers' party. Everard studied it speculatively and decided it made a good excuse – reason – to telephone Alison Greer.

CHAPTER TWENTY-FOUR

Julia's Christmas, while free from the encumbrances of an over-large turkey or a vast ham to cook – she'd bought one ready to eat – was not easy. Astrid departed for Germany on the 23rd of December to be in time for the Christmas Eve celebrations at home, and Julia's mother arrived to stay on the 24th. She complained that travelling made her very tired but insisted on washing up after lunch while Julia stuffed the turkey, a moderately sized one from the covered market.

'Oh!' she exclaimed, 'You're putting rice in the stuffing!'

'Yes, with apricots and some prunes. It's only part of the stuffing.'

'How unusual! The rice looks very good. It's not sticky at all.'

'Oh, well, I learnt to cook rice from my flatmate Phyllis. She's a marvellous cook.'

'Oh, that Catholic flatmate you're always talking about. Did you? Well, I cook rice Mrs Beeton's way. I've never had any trouble cooking rice; I've always been able to cook rice.'

Julia realised too late that her mother had taken umbrage. Always jealous of Julia's friends, particularly those Julia admired for qualities her mother did not possess, the implication that Phyllis cooked rice better than she did was enough to initiate a long-lasting defensive reaction. Julia remembered her mother's glutinous rice concoctions and sighed. She would have to make amends by complimenting her extravagantly on something, anything, but she was then too tired and too busy to make the effort.

Instead she said, 'Would you mind having a look at the children? They're rather quiet and that's probably ominous.'

Her mother went into the sitting room and returned to report that they were doing nothing worse than sitting in front of the television.

'I thought you didn't approve of television,' she added. 'You used to say you wouldn't have one!'

'I'm afraid we got it partly to keep the au pair happy and help her improve her English. It was Jeremy's idea; he's the one who went and got it. Though I think he likes watching the sport himself. I must admit it takes a lot of the strain out of keeping the children entertained and occupied. It's much easier to get their meals when they're watching programmes than it used to be when they were coming into the kitchen all the time.'

'Well, of course,' her mother moved on to another topic. 'I can't think why you don't have a proper nanny – especially now you've got a real job at last. You have far too much to do with the children. These au pairs are all very well, but they lack experience; they can't really take over. And the one you've got isn't even here for Christmas!'

'If she were you wouldn't be able to stay in her room.'

'It's hardly my fault that you've got such a small house.'

'We're quite fortunate to have a house at all at our age, and it was Jeremy's father who bought it for us – as Jeremy doesn't let me forget.'

'Is he coming tomorrow?'

'Yes, in time for lunch. Then he's staying a couple of nights in the little hotel round the corner.'

'He seems to come fairly often. Doesn't he ever stay with Jeremy's sister?'

'Well, you know, she can't cook to save her life, and he doesn't like her husband at all. I don't blame him. Paul's rude and demanding and arrogant and overbearing and makes no secret of the fact that he hates having guests in the house. He won't even have his own mother staying there if he can help it.'

'I'm not sure that many young people know how to make their mothers feel really welcome these days! I'm going to have a rest. You know how travelling always makes me exhausted'

Julia made suitably soothing murmurs and was glad, despite the help with the dishes, to have the kitchen to herself again. She had only the basics of a light supper to prepare and everything would be as ready as possible. She hoped Jeremy might come home in time to see to the children for a little while so that she could have a rest herself. She very much wanted to go to midnight mass, especially as there would be little chance for her to go on Christmas morning, with lunch to cook.

Jeremy did come home, at about 3 o'clock. He had clearly had a lunch comprising a large proportion of liquid.

'Godda have a rest,' he said as he stumbled in. 'Ver' ver' tired.' And he bumped his way up the stairs colliding with the bannisters at irregular intervals. Very soon the reverberations from his snoring filled the house. Julia hoped her mother was already asleep and couldn't hear it, and herself went into the sitting room to sit down at least and get what rest she could while looking after the children.

At 10:30 in the evening Julia and Jeremy crept into the children's room and replaced the empty pillow-slips hanging up by their beds with full ones. Everything else was ready. Back in the sitting room, Jeremy announced his intention of going to bed. He was still, he said 'ver' tired.'

Julia's mother said she wouldn't stay up long either, and Julia said she was going to mass, and would they please give an ear to the children.

'You can't go to mass, Julia,' her mother stated firmly. 'You'll be exhausted.'

'Well, I can't easily go tomorrow.'

'I don't see why you need go at all.' Jeremy was, he considered, being sensible.

'It's not as if you were a Catholic, like that old-maidish, marvellous cook, flatmate of yours.' Julia's mother had never liked Phyllis. 'I suppose that's where you got all this nonsense from. It's not as if it's in the family!'

'More's the pity!' said Julia, finally exasperated. She was on the point of adding that some Catholicism in the family might have reduced the number of divorces but thought better of it and merely spoke firmly. 'It's the one thing that I, myself, particularly want to do this Christmas, and I think it's little enough to ask, seeing that the children are asleep and there's nothing more to be done.'

She left the house and drove into the town, now relatively empty and beginning to sparkle with frost. She felt a sense of exhilaration and escape. She was early, but it was necessary to be early if one didn't want to stand, squashed in a side aisle without a seat. She sat down and found herself smiling as she basked in a sense of calm and well-being such as she had not felt for – she tried to think how long, but decided it was better to appreciate the happiness of the present rather than contrast it with any other time. She loved the mass, not only for the beauty of the church, the flowers, the candles, the vestments, the music, but for the tradition and timelessness of it. She watched the stream of hundreds of communicants going up to the altar rails to receive the sacrament and longed intensely to be one of them. 'But I can't,' she murmured. 'Not yet.' She was sorry when the priest sang 'Ite Missa est' – 'Go you are sent forth' – the last hymn was sung and the mass was over. Coming to the back of the church in the slow shuffle necessitated by the crowd of worshippers and the bottle-neck of the exit doors, she dipped her fingers in the holy-water font and made the sign of the cross. As she did so the woman immediately behind her said 'Hello!' in a voice of surprise. She turned to see Pauline Dickenson, the Emmaeus librarian. Simultaneously they said 'I didn't know you were a Catholic!' At which they both laughed and said 'I'm not'.

'Well,' Pauline continued, 'not quite. I'm taking instruction but I haven't been received yet. I've "come over" as they say from Mary Mag's down the road. You know – Anglo-Catholic. My father was an Anglican clergyman.'

'Oh, that's interesting.' Julia felt unaccountably delighted. 'I'd really like to talk to you about it some time. I'm – well, I don't quite know what I am. I was brought up an Anglican, but I don't think I'm a believer. Certainly I haven't been but I wish I was.'

'It'll come,' said Pauline cheerfully. 'It's a gift, faith. But you can pray for it, you know – even if you're not a believer.'

'Can I?'

'Undoubtedly. Try it. I'll look forward to seeing you next term. Meantime, have a very happy Christmas and a good holiday.'

'You too.'

Feeling that she had found an ally in an unexpected quarter, Julia returned home too elated to be weary and fortified against the rigours of a domestic Christmas Day.

CHAPTER TWENTY-FIVE

The Leslie children, like most others, woke very early on Christmas morning to open the presents bulging enticingly in their pillowcases. It was not long before they burst into their parents' room. 'Mummy! Mummy! Daddy! Look what I've got!' 'I've got slippers' this from Jamie,'and they're mouses with faces – and they fit!' He was immensely impressed that Father Christmas knew his shoe size. Julia, immediately awake, put on a dressing-gown and went into the children's room with them. Jeremy followed more slowly and Julia's mother appeared at the same time. "Granny Egerton" was very good at presents and enjoyed seeing them appreciated. Jeremy, who'd had little if anything to do with the providing of presents, was less able to sustain interest, even though the emerging toys, books, sweets and articles of clothing were as much of a surprise to him as to the children. His main task was to bring up a large pot of tea for the grown-ups.

'I don't know how you can be so bright so early in the morning, Julia' her mother remarked in one of the lulls when the children were so interested in their gifts as to be demanding no immediate attention. 'Whatever time did you get to bed?'

'It must have been a bit before two.'

'Well, of course, if you would go to that R.C. service.'

'Actually I found it both restful and stimulating. I think that's what's keeping me going.'

Jeremy came up with the tea, Julia went down to put the turkey into the oven, her mother began to find the decibel level of the children's delight, though gratifying, more tolerable at a distance, and went to her room to dress.

Breakfast time seemed to flow into coffee-time and then, with the arrival of Jeremy's father, into drinks time and then to the carving of the turkey and the serving of lunch, with all the accompaniments of crackers and paper hats and children's chatter, stilled only momentarily at the arrival of the brandy-flaming Christmas pudding. The grown-ups, at least the grandparental ones, enjoyed this with something approaching stoicism and looked forward to the late supper after the children had gone to bed. This they eventually did and almost im- mediately went to sleep, despite the discomfort of beds full of favourite objects from which they couldn't bear to be separated. Emma's most prized new possession was a black velvet coat, an extravagance of Granny Egerton's, which she insisted on having laid over the top of the bed-cover so that she could reach out and stroke it. 'My fur coat!' she murmured dreamily.

Julia's mother sat down to the nine o'clock supper determined to enjoy herself. The presence of a man to whom she was not related always acted as a stimulant to her, but she felt inhibited when surrounded by grandchildren and aged when addressed as "Granny". She had endeavoured to restore a more appealing image by changing into a chic, expensive and rather short-skirted dress and putting on some Chanel No 5. The truth was, however, that everybody felt a little jaded by the combination of incomplete recovery from the effects of the lunch time drinks and weariness, especially in Julia's case, after the labours of the day and the lack of sleep the previous night. Besides, when her mother was in scintillating form she was more than a little inclined to scintillate at the expense of any other woman who happened to be in the vicinity.

'Well, Julia,' she began, 'I must say that for an intellectual you're not a bad cook.'

'Thank you, Mater,' said Julia resignedly. She recognised her mother's ploy of praising her and putting her down at the same time.

'Absolutely. Hear, hear! Amazing ... especially

considering ...' Jeremy's father genuinely appreciated his daughter-in-law's cooking, though what he was considering was less clear.

Julia knew she should say something gracious about learning it all from her mother, but in fact she had learned more from a necessity to improve on her mother's cooking than otherwise.

'Not many Camford women like you,' Jeremy's father continued. 'Not in my time, anyway. Didn't really notice university women. Imported gels we knew from home or London. Never thought of taking women undergraduates anywhere. Not worth looking at. All mousy hair and spectacles.'

'There you are, Julia,' her mother pounced predictably. 'I told you you shouldn't wear spectacles. Nobody in our family ever did until you decided you wanted some.'

'Needed some, Mater.'

'Nonsense. You wanted to look like those tiresome friends you had at school. Though why any girl should want to look like a blue stocking is more than I can comprehend.'

'I couldn't see the blackboard and I had to read with one eye covered.'

'Well, I've always been perfectly all right without them. Anyway, it doesn't do to see too much, does it Pa-in-law?' She always called him Pa-in-law (pronounced 'Pahnlaw') since he'd told Julia to do so. Jeremy's father was dimly aware of having stirred something up and felt he ought to make amends. As he rarely finished a sentence even when he did know what he wanted to say, all he managed was 'Well, but, however ....'

'No doubt,' said Julia, hoping to bring the topic to a conclusion, 'your generation all agree with Dorothy Parker's maxim that "Men don't make passes at girls who wear glasses", and of course the whole purpose of a girl's existence is to have men make passes at her!'

The irony was lost on Julia's mother. 'Well, at least you don't wear them all the time,' she conceded.

'They're increasingly necessary now that I need to see from a distance what the children are doing.'

'Now really, Julia. It's time you had a rest from the children. You've had quite enough to do with them all day. And there are three of them. Of course they're frightfully sweet but one can't deny they're deeply exhausting! I really do think ... a proper nanny ... You always had nannies, didn't you, Pa-in-law?'

'What? Oh! Of course, yes, but Cynthia couldn't ...' There was an awkward silence. Jeremy's mother Cynthia had abandoned the family home to live with probably not the first in a long series of lovers when Jeremy was four and his sister six. She had not spent a great deal of time with her children even before leaving and had seen them only on rare occasions between long intervals thereafter.

'Have another glass of wine er ...' Jeremy had long since been asked to call his mother-in-law "Marcia" but could rarely bring himself to say it.

'Yes, indeed.' Jeremy's father looked relieved and revived at the same time. 'Come along now. No heel-taps.'

'I've never really understood that expression,' Julia mused, 'though I'm sure I've come across it in a book. One of Peacock's, wasn't it Jeremy?'

'Yes. Probably. They're all full of dinner-table conversations.' Julia turned to her father-in-law, hoping to engage his interest and promote a new topic of conversation. 'What does it mean, Pa-in-law?'

'Well really, Julia ... I would have thought ... I couldn't have imagined ... I mean honestly,' he blustered. Julia had often wondered how her father-in-law could possibly function as a schoolmaster as she knew that explaining things was not his forte, but had mistakenly imagined that heel-taps would not be beyond his scope.

Jeremy glowered at his father and more than adequately fuelled by the wine burst out: 'That's exactly the kind of answer you always give. You always did. Whenever I asked you something when I was a child you scolded me for not knowing the answer already and never told me it.'

His father glowered back at him from under his

eyebrows, opened his mouth as if to reply, but instead closed it on the rim of his wineglass and drained the contents.

'I'm sure,' Julia spoke evenly, 'I'm sure everybody considers that their parents made hideous mistakes in bringing them up; but the best way to get over it is to avoid making the same mistakes with one's own children.'

Jeremy's father bestowed an almost appreciative side-glance on Julia while continuing to glower at his son. 'Quite right,' he said. 'Never made the same mistakes with you my father did with me. Never sent you to the school I was teaching in. I was at my father's prep. school for years. No escape. Couldn't even think about home. We lived there. It was home – supposed to be. Any trouble and I always got the blame. "Send for Leslie," my father'd say. Then swish bang, swish bang. I never beat you either.'

'You sent me to a school where they did. That pervert of a headmaster had a whole drawer full of canes. And I was only six.'

'Well, at least I wasn't the headmaster.'

'We'll be sending our boys – all the children – to the school I teach in.'

'Won't matter so much – very big school – and you won't be the headmaster. Hope you haven't drunk all the wine I brought. Time for the next bottle, isn't it? Notice you've helped yourself to the last of that one.' Thoroughly in sympathy with his father on this issue at least, Jeremy hastened to fetch not one bottle but two. He handed the second to his father, along with an extra corkscrew, and some semblance of jollification was restored when the corks popped. The wine was poured – with a moderate amount proffered to "the ladies" – and the men addressed themselves to their main pleasure and solace in life.

In bed that night Julia woke gradually and unwillingly from a deep slumber, increasingly aware that Jeremy was moaning in his sleep, gnashing his teeth, then calling out 'No, no – please, no!' and giving out great gulping sobs. She shook him gently and spoke to him soothingly. 'Jeremy, Jeremy darling, it's all right, wake up, you're dreaming.' She almost said 'Mummy's here' as if talking to one of the children. Jeremy gave another sob and woke up trembling. She put her arms round him and repeated, 'You've been dreaming. It's all right now. I'm here, I'm here.'

'That terrible school,' Jeremy gasped. 'I was there. That headmaster, he was beating me because my mother had been to see me and left lipstick marks all over my face.'

'It's not happening,' said Julia. 'It's not real.'

'It was,' said Jeremy. 'She only came to see me once. I didn't know who she was. She looked so common. All make-up and huge tits. She kissed me and left the marks of her mouth on my face.

Everybody laughed. I was so ashamed. And it was so cold and I had earache and my hands hurt.'

'It's not like that now. You're not cold any more. You're here with me and I love you. Don't worry any more.'

Jeremy's trembling gradually subsided and he held Julia close to him and allowed himself to be soothed and comforted. Julia felt herself almost overwhelmed by her love for him and sighed deeply. She knew this was the basis of their relationship: he needed her and to be needed was the operative facet of her personality. It had worked very well until they had children. But Julia reflected that the children would grow up and gradually need her less, whereas Jeremy probably never would.

CHAPTER TWENTY-SIX

Jean and Everard had weathered Christmas better than might have been expected. Jean had come back from her extended evening with Tim feeling so secure in his affection, so glowing with pleasure and happiness, that she had felt not only armoured against Everard, but able to cope almost philosophically with the ensuing Timless fortnight.

Everard himself had had, he considered, a very satisfactory telephone conversation with Alison Greer, full of pleasantries overlaid with the kind of *doubles entendres* that seemed not unfavourable to a mutual understanding developing into something more interesting. He had been asleep when Jean returned, and in the morning had said nothing about her absence, apart from mentioning that the babysitter had come round and that he'd sent her away. Jean had said she'd deal with that, and they had subsequently even managed to arrange mutually agreed times to have the car and buy Christmas food and the final presents. Each of them concentrated on the mechanics of family life, on the physical and practical necessities of keeping their children occupied. Everard was, in fact, Jean reflected, less distant and dismissive than usual at such times and at least kept the boys entertained while she did the cooking and the background work. Now that she cared so little about him she was unhurt by his deficiencies and regarded any good thing he did as an unexpected bonus. She was not, however, looking forward greatly to the Greers' party. She generally found such occasions a trial. She had not grown up, as Everard had, in an atmosphere of partying and small talk and very soon after their marriage Everard had shown more interest in any and every other woman in the room than in her. Moreover, she was still embarrassed over her revelation to Alison of Everard's infidelity and felt or imagined a kind of contemptuous pity in Alison's attitude to her.

'I don't think I'll go to the Greers' party,' she told Everard.

'Why not? I said we'd go.' Everard looked surprised. Not that Jean's unwillingness to go to a party was anything new, but she generally said "Do I have to go?" and then succumbed to his demand that she should and would.

'I thought you liked Alison.'

'Oh – but we'll have to have a babysitter and it's easier not to.' Everard thought briefly of his intention to make Alison as interested in himself as the confines of a drinks party rendered possible; not that Jean's presence had ever hindered him in that kind of pursuit. Still, there was something in Jean's attitude these days that made her more of a force to be reckoned with. It might be preferable if she were not there.

'Suit yourself,' he said.

Strangely and unexpectedly, Alison herself 'dropped in' the following morning. 'We're having a few days break here after the hectic round of Christmas parties in Camford, and getting ready for our own, of course. The cottage one, I mean. We've already had one in Camford. We owe so many invitations. It gets too much, doesn't it?' Alison was aware that Jean's social life was nothing like her own and was not averse to pointing out the contrast. She looked at Jean narrowly. There was a kind of imperturbability about her that Alison found unusual.

'Have you been out?' she asked, almost accusingly.

'How do you mean? Why?'

'Well, you have the remains of a proper hair-do and you're wearing nail polish, or what's left of it!'

Everard having heard Alison's voice from the sitting room where he had been reading, came into the kitchen at that juncture. Jean was suddenly aware that they were all three staring at her nails. The nail polish had been a concomitant to the visit to the hairdresser, and she was aghast to see how she'd let it chip off unregarded since Tim's departure. Everard had not noticed it at all previously and wondered when and why she'd started using it, while Alison, missing nothing, was rapidly calculating combinations of two and two with a range of possible answers.

Jean began to laugh. 'How unlike me to have nails that arouse any interest,' she said, without satisfying Alison's curiosity. But Alison had turned her attention to Everard.

'I'm glad you're coming to our party. Most of the people round here are so boring. Thank goodness there'll be you to liven things up.'

Everard let his eyes flicker over Alison. 'Yes, let's hope we can do something about that!'

'I'm sure we can manage something between us,' Alison replied, laughing and letting her tongue protrude a little as she did so.

Jean suddenly saw why Alison had decided to 'drop round' after a long absence. She laughed again. Both Everard and Alison turned to look at her, startled out of their rapport with each other. Alison looked almost uncomfortable and rose to go. Everard saw her to the door and tried to put some feeling into "See you tomorrow", but the spell was broken and the moment gone.

He went back into the kitchen to see Jean, still sitting at the table, smiling into the distance. She had passed in a matter of moments from deep satisfaction at her freedom from any emotional attachment to Everard to a blissful recollection of her happiness with Tim.

'What are you smiling at?' Everard felt needled. Jean seemed to be developing an ability to diminish him.

'Oh!' Jean looked at him as if she'd been brought down to his level from another plane of existence.

'Oh!' she repeated. 'I must go and arrange for a babysitter for tomorrow.'

'I thought you weren't coming!'

'Oh no. I wasn't, was I? I've changed my mind. Why shouldn't I go out? I enjoy a drink, and there'll be plenty of that, if nothing else. Besides, it might be quite funny.' She laughed again and went to see about the babysitter, leaving Everard feeling oddly discomfited.

Jean took the trouble to renew her nail polish before the party and reflected as she did so that she was not dreading it as she used to dread such functions. She went over the plus factors she had acquired "since Tim". She had some clothes she felt happy in. She had got used to drinking and enjoyed it. She had become so detached from Everard that she would scarcely feel a qualm at his overtly lecherous behaviour with other women. Of course, if she were to be standing alone with nobody to talk to it might be slightly embarrassing, especially if the other women were to show an obvious lack of appreciation of his advances, as sometimes happened. If there was one thing worse than seeing women responding to him it was seeing that they considered him a clown who was making a fool of himself. Never mind. She'd have another drink and light another cigarette and think about Tim. She hadn't been back to the hairdresser, but she had washed her hair, and it shone and hung youthfully almost to her shoulders. She'd never really prepared for a party before, mainly because she'd resisted the idea of going until it was too late to do anything about it.

She was ready to go even before Everard was and therefore could not be subjected to any of his usual bullying to hurry her up, and arrived feeling confident rather than coerced. Henry Greer greeted her appreciatively.

'You look a new woman, Jean. The chores of Christmas clearly agree with you.'

The majority of the guests already assembled were nearer Henry's age than Alison's, so Jean had the advantage of being one of the youngest women present. The male halves of the several older couples took an immediate interest in her, and she was never without at least one of them to talk to. The drinks were strong. Henry Greer was well versed in college drinking habits and Alison had long been reacting against a teetotal nonconformist upbringing by consuming at least as much alcohol as her husband did. Everard considered most of the women disappointingly elderly and concentrated on Alison as much as her duties as hostess allowed. She considered it her right to command all the attention of the elderly husbands and was not pleased to find herself upstaged by Jean, so she responded to Everard's ploys and witticisms and double-edged remarks with more interest than might otherwise have been the case. By the time the Lucases left the party both Alison and Everard knew that they would be seeing more of each other in the near future. Jean had seen, from occasional glances through her group of older admirers, that Alison and Everard were talking to each other with little cessation and considerable animation, and she was wonderfully elated by the knowledge that she cared not at all.

CHAPTER TWENTY-SEVEN

Julia was glad she'd had little time to think about the Tomlinsons' party, though she was aware of contemplating it with more curiosity than trepidation. Jean Lucas was the only one of her colleagues' wives whom she'd met, and she'd been quite a surprise. Shona Otis she'd heard more about than any of the others, and was hoping to meet her and find out whether the reality matched her mental picture in any way. About seeing Roger in his home surroundings and meeting his wife she thought as little as possible. Jeremy's nightmare and memories of his appalling childhood had aroused all her affection for him and during the vacation, when she had no men to compare him with apart from his father, his deficiencies were less apparent. Besides, in the well-tailored suit he'd had made at the time of their wedding, and with his fine golden hair newly washed, he looked particularly attractive.

They arrived when the party was at the stage of

several small groups chatting quietly together. The room was large and high-ceilinged and there was a sense of space and comfort. They were ushered in by Barbara Tomlinson whom Julia liked immediately. She summed her up as slim, elegant, assured, intelligent and, on the evidence of her house and what she'd seen of its furnishings, practical and aesthetically sensitive. Julia was flattered that a man with a wife like Barbara could find her attractive, and hoped it was because of their similarities rather than their differences, apart from that of age. Barbara skilfully introduced Jeremy to one group of people and Julia to another. 'Of course you know Quentin Crawford, as he's a colleague, but you won't know our neighbours …' she continued with the introduction but Julia barely took it in, so aware was she that here was a colleague she seemed only to have seen at a distance. The neighbours murmured a few pleasantries to which she responded automatically, then turned to Quentin Crawford. 'It's very strange, but I don't think we've ever spoken to each other before'.'

'Oh?' he replied, looking down at her from somewhere above his Roman nose. 'Is that strange?' The neighbours, who'd already found him hard work, escaped thankfully, leaving Julia to pursue the conversation on her own.

'You're a classicist, aren't you?'

'Philosopher. But of course I teach the classics

people.' With an effort Julia put him into context. He always sat at the top end, as she thought of it, of the lunch table, whereas she herself sat very much at the bottom end. She had considered him very aloof and cold-looking and thought very little else about him.

'Is your husband here?' he asked.

'Yes, just over there – talking to Hector, and I presume, Shona, Otis.' Julia was tempted to take Quentin over and introduce him, but she could hear Jeremy animatedly perorating about the lazy ways of dons and how much less hard they worked than schoolmasters, and deemed it an inappropriate moment. She didn't mind subjecting Hector to Jeremy's hobby-horse; she had little respect for Hector and his father had been a schoolmaster anyway, so he knew there was some truth in it, however unpalatable it might be. She could not, however, face having this haughty man looking down his Roman nose at her husband, and instead asked him whether his wife was with him.

'No,' he replied coldly. 'She's at home looking after the children.'

'How many?'

'Three.'

'Oh. So have we. We met as undergraduates and married just after taking Schools.'

'We too.'

'Oh, is your wife an academic?'

'Well, she has a degree from Somerton.'

'Is she still in academic life? Teaching or anything?'

'No. She's well adapted to her sexual function.' Julia felt herself bristling with anger; was there no end to this appalling sexism, which she seemed to encounter at every turn? But aloud she said 'How very fortunate for her.'

'How so?' He sounded genuinely surprised.

'She presumably suffers none of the inner conflict and stress which inevitably assail women who try to combine the role of being a wife and mother – which I suppose is what you mean by "sexual function" – with a career.'

Looking even more surprised, but a shade or two less haughty, he regarded Julia with something more like respect than he had shown hitherto. 'You may well be right,' he said.

'Anyway, come and meet my husband.' Julia decided she no longer cared what Jeremy was talking about or what this obnoxious man thought of him, and made her way to where he was standing with the Otises. Quentin Crawford followed her but spent more minutes being enthusiastically greeted by Hector Otis, who had been rather nonplussed by Jeremy's peroration and was very relieved to be speaking to one of his own kind again.

Jeremy eyed Quentin with interest and whispered to Julia. 'Is that man a Wykehamist?'

'I don't know. Why?'

'Looks it. Couldn't be anything else.'

Quentin Crawford, who didn't regard Hector Otis as one of his favourite colleagues, turned to Julia. 'Let me introduce my husband, Jeremy,' she said. 'He seems to think you must be a Wykehamist.'

'How very perceptive! On what characteristics, might I ask, do you base this assumption?'

'Oh,' Jeremy replied cheerfully 'intellectual arrogance. It's written all over Wykehamists, especially the scholars. We can even see it in some of our boys before they go there; we can pick the ones who're going to get scholarships to Winchester.'

'And who are we?'

'Jeremy teaches at St George's,' Julia imposed.

'Indeed! Our eldest son's going there in September.'

'Weally, Julia,' Hector Otis sounded faintly aggrieved. 'You've never said your husband taught at St George's. Our children will be going there, of course!'

Julia perceived, with some amusement, that both Quentin and Hector, while somewhat aghast at her husband's lowly occupation, were nevertheless unwilling to alienate a possible, indeed probable, future teacher of their children. She turned to Hector's wife.

'You must be Shona; I've heard a great deal about

you from Hector and was hoping I'd meet you.'

'Does Hector talk about me?' Shona was surprised and not a little gratified.

'Oh yes, all the time. Well, to me he does, anyway. It's very refreshing. Most of them don't talk to me at all.'

'Don't they? I thought it must be really exciting, being the only woman among all those men.'

'Hardly. Everybody sits at lunch reading newspapers most of the time. I count it quite a red-letter day when somebody speaks to me. I often feel as if I'm invisible, no more noticeable than a fly on the wall. But that's preferable to being conspicuous.'

Roger appeared at Julia's elbow. 'You know very well you can't help being noticeable,' he said. 'Have another drink, Julia. Practically everybody's arrived now so I've at last got time to circulate. Come and meet some other people – and talk to me for two minutes on the way. How are you? I don't suppose you've had a chance to talk to Barbara.'

'Not yet, but I'd like to. Is Quentin Crawford a Wykehamist?'

'Yes, why?'

'Oh – my husband took one look at him and said he must be. This is the first time I've ever spoken to him!'

'Do you like him? Are you interested in him?'

'Hardly. He seems very arrogant and to have a low opinion of women.'

'Oh, I don't know!' Roger automatically rose to the defence of his colleague. While having no wish for Julia to admire Quentin, he felt she had no right to disapprove of him, either. Like most men he disliked hearing other men criticised by women – any women.

'What's his wife like?' Julia was intrigued to find out more about the woman so well adapted to her "sexual function".

'I don't really know. Not very noticeable, not very ... well not very anything as far as I remember. You'd better ask Barbara. The wives all know each other better than we know them.'

Julia reflected that the schoolmasters' wives she'd met at St George's were all far more loquacious, more vociferous, more powerful and dominant in every way than any of the dons' wives she'd met. They were, of course, much more integrated in the school community, much more a part of their husband's job, especially those who ran the boys' boarding houses. She herself felt an outsider among them because her husband was not a housemaster as most of the married masters were, and she was too much occupied with her children and her own work to attend all the numerous social functions, in which wives were almost invariably included. In a Camford College, however, wives were not to be asked to guest nights by their husbands, never to be seen at lunch or any other meal and had absolutely nothing to do with the workings of the college, though some might occasionally help entertain their husbands' pupils to lunch or dinner at home. Certainly Jean Lucas and Shona Otis seemed very muted, very much overshadowed in their husbands' presence – and Quentin Crawford's wife was relegated to total non-appearance. No wonder nobody in college had ever asked Julia about her husband. This she mused as Roger was diverted by somebody having to 'slip away early' and somebody else clearly wanting another drink. Barbara had just finished taking round a tray of the food and handed it to a helper, the daughter of the neighbours Julia had met at the beginning, to be replenished.

'At last!' she said, as Roger brought Julia to talk to her. 'One never has time to talk to people at one's own parties and I've been wanting to meet you properly.'

'And I you,' Julia replied. 'I'm very grateful to your husband. He's always been very kind to me.'

'Well, I wish he was to me!' said Barbara with a matter-of-fact, no-nonsense briskness. 'Not that I see a lot of him. He spends most of his life in college with his male counterparts. I'm left to run the wives' lunches and that sort of chore.'

Julia laughed. Barbara's manner clearly indicated that this was not to be taken too seriously and that she was, moreover, very much in control.

'You're Everard's lecturer, of course, aren't you?' Barbara continued.

'Yes, I suppose I must go under that title,' Julia responded and a little wryly. 'He's not here, is he?' She looked round the now crowded room.

'Certainly not,' Barbara responded, even more briskly, 'I wouldn't let Roger ask him. He behaved so badly last time he came I swore I wouldn't have him here again. That poor little wife of his; so embarrassing for her. I'm sorry if he's a friend of yours, but quite honestly I can't stand the man.'

Julia had drunk enough to speak boldly. 'I can see you have excellent taste.' It was a remark that could include the room, the food, the party in general, and while perhaps not entirely appropriate coming from a very junior lecturer to the wife of a very senior fellow, Barbara recognised a kindred spirit and was not displeased.

She laughed. 'You're a very good girl,' she said. 'I'm not surprised Roger approves of you.

By this time Jeremy had drunk enough, or rather more than enough, wine and was longing for some beer to wash it down. He approached Julia, holding up his left hand and tapping his watch and after the usual polite exchanges with their host and hostess they left the party.

Hector and Shona Otis stayed longer at the Tomlinsons' than almost anybody else. Hector had told almost all the other guests that Shona was 'only drinking very little' because she was in what he called 'an interesting condition', as perhaps they'd noticed. While not entirely unembarrassed by these revelations, Shona enjoyed being made much of by the women at the party, apart from Barbara, who remarked matter-of-factly 'I'm sure Shona has other qualities which are equally interesting. Never mind, my dear, you look very well and it doesn't really show. What else have you been doing?' Shona was spared the necessity of thinking up a reply as her hostess's attention was drawn to some departing guests. Nevertheless she continued to ponder on the question and turned to Hector a few minutes later saying

'What else have I been doing?'

'What else what?' he countered impatiently.

'I can't think of anything.'

'Well, don't then. It's time we were going, anyway. Nearly everybody's gone.'

'Julia seems very nice,' Shona said as they drove home. 'Do you like her?'

'Oh, yes, well I knew her before, of course. I used to go out with one of her flatmates.'

'Did you? I didn't know.'

'Yes. A Canadian girl. Vewy wich but wather inhibited. I didn't weally find her vewy interwesting. Julia's husband seems vewy borwing. I wonder how she came to mawwy somebody like that.'

'Well, he's very good-looking, isn't he?'

'Weally? I didn't notice. Of course men don't appweciate things like that in other men.'

'No. I suppose not. Everard Lucas wasn't there, was he?'

'Well, he and Woger don't always see eye to eye – and I don't think they do about Julia! I told you Woger's always following her about. I'm not surpwised she was invited!'

'Oooh, yes, I remember.' Shona decided to have a coffee morning and invite the college wives she knew best, steer the conversation in the Roger/Julia direction and find out as much more as she possibly could.

CHAPTER TWENTY-EIGHT.

Julia went into college a week before the official beginning of the Spring Term. There was a sizeable pile of envelopes in her pigeonhole, one of them – she was hardly surprised to see – addressed in Roger's writing. She decided to leave it until last, but once in her room, with the kettle on to make coffee, she found herself opening it immediately after dealing cursorily with a note about a faculty meeting. It was brief and to the point.

Dear Julia
My part of the bargain fulfilled; what about yours? Thursday of the week before term would be a good time. Come and have a drink in my room in College at about 6:45 and we'll go on from there. Pre-term "meetings" are in order, surely!

Julia sighed deeply, opened the rest of her post rather inattentively, drank a cup of coffee and pondered over a reply. 'It's got to be done before lunch,' she thought. 'I can't face meeting Roger until I know what to say. I wish I still had female flat- mates to talk to about things like this. Oh,' she suddenly wailed aloud. 'Fuck a bleeding duck!'

This exclamation unfortunately coincided with a knock on the door. It was Everard. He looked round the room as if expecting to see somebody else.

'Oh!' he said, 'You're on your own'

'Yes,' Julia wondered whether he'd heard her words or merely her voice. 'Why?'

'I thought I heard somebody else talking.'

'Only me. Talking to myself.'

'It didn't sound like you!'

'I was thinking myself back to my flatsharing days. I've changed since then.'

'For the better?' Everard regarded her quizzically; he'd almost slipped unawares into chatting-up mode.

'I don't know. That was probably the time when I was most myself.'

'Really? I don't quite follow you.'

'Before I left home I was a daughter. After I got married I was a wife and then a mother. The only time of real freedom in a woman's life is the period in between. I don't suppose men feel anything like that.'

'Well, I'm not conscious of having changed at

all.' Everard seemed to find the idea something of an affront. Julia stifled the desire to remark 'unfortunately not' and changed the subject, saying she supposed he'd come to discuss the term's tutorial arrangements. Everard had wanted to embarrass her about what he'd heard her say before the door was opened, but thought better of it. He found that she parried any attempt of his to talk on a more personal level by turning to objective generalisations. 'She sounds more like a bloody literary critic than a woman,' he thought. 'Can't get near her. Arrogant bitch.' But he continued to talk suavely and with some witty asides about their pupils and showed nothing of his annoyance.

When Everard had left there were still some three quarters of an hour to go before lunch. Julia felt too restless to settle to anything and acutely aware of the need to talk to another woman. She left her room and walked across the quad to the library. Pauline Dickenson was dusting books and bookshelves.

'Hello,' said Julia. 'Don't the scouts do that?'

'Rarely. And I can't trust them to do it properly. If they take the books out of the shelves they're quite likely to put them back in the wrong order.'

'I know what you mean. My mother had a help once who put all the books back in the shelf with the pages facing outwards and the spines inwards – so nobody could read the titles of course. I suppose she thought they looked tidier like that! More uniform, anyway. But college scouts must know better.'

'College scouts are not what they used to be. They spend their time flirting with the undergraduates – and some of the dons!'

'The bigger, richer colleges must still have some male scouts, haven't they? They did when I was an undergraduate. There were all those stories about them bringing the young men tea in their rooms in the mornings and if there happened to be a young woman in the bed as well they'd merely ask "And would madam require tea too?". One of my flatmates was keen to verify the story, but she was disappointed.'

'Oh dear. No tea?'

'No scout. She must have chosen the wrong college. Did you share a flat or a house with other girls when you were a student? I sometimes think it was the best time of my life.'

'You're fortunate. If I'd been a student I wouldn't be working as an assistant librarian in a small library in a small college. I was still at school when my father died and I've always lived with my mother.'

'How awful – er - awfully worthy of you.'

Pauline shrugged. 'Her health's never been good – and I haven't ever found the right reason or the right moment to leave her on her own. But there are compensations. It can't be as bad as an unhappy marriage.'

Julia was somewhat aghast to realise that in her view the awfulness of living continuously with one's mother up to the age of – how old was Pauline? forty? – made the unhappiness of a marriage pale into insignificance. She hoped she had not made too much of this visible to Pauline, and hastened to make amends in case she had.

'I'm sure you're right,' she said, as smoothly as possible. 'My mother's generation seemed to think marriage the be-all and end-all of a woman's existence, even though many of them had dreadful marriages themselves. My parents are divorced and so are my husband's. You know there's a medieval text – its title translates as Holy Maidenhood – written to encourage young women to a religious vocation. It says the gaining of any pleasure from marriage is like licking honey off thorns.'

'Licking honey off thorns,' Pauline repeated, with obvious satisfaction. 'What a striking image. Yes, that's very good. I shall remember that.'

'What does your mother think of your becoming a Catholic?' Julia asked, feeling that this topic might now be safely dealt with.

'Grieved, I'm afraid. Says my father must be turning in his grave and that she can't imagine where I got it from.'

'That's exactly what my mother said to me!' Julia

exclaimed. 'As if it's some hereditary ailment. But I don't suppose you're deterred by it.'

'Certainly not. I tell her she's lucky if that's the only thing she has to complain about; and it does distract her attention from some of my lesser foibles. Come what may, I'm to be received at Easter, and I hope you'll be there, and at the celebrations afterwards. You might have started taking instruction yourself by then.'

'Oh – I tend to feel like the seed that was sown among thistles: choked by the cares of the world.'

Pauline smiled. 'Ah well, we old maids have many disadvantages but I suppose, in general, that's not one of them. Our time is, relatively speaking, our own, and few people if any are dependent on us, unless our parents are very aged and very demanding – and that can happen to anybody.'

'That's true. And it's not as if you have to be perpetually trying to set them a good example!'

Julia could see that Pauline was not somebody she could discuss the Roger problem with. Nevertheless, their conversation was heartening and made her see her own life more objectively. 'I'm a free agent,' she thought. 'I'm not merely a wife and mother. I'm still me.' She thanked Pauline for her company and they agreed that it would be a good idea to meet for lunch away from college one day.

Julia left the library, emerged into the quad and decided not to write an answer to Roger's letter but to wait until he spoke to her in person.

CHAPTER TWENTY-NINE

Julia went in to lunch early and was sitting with the Times crossword propped up behind her soup plate when an intruding finger pointed to 1 across, then 1 down, then 2 across and announced the answers to each of them. Julia turned round to see Quentin Crawford taking the seat beside her.

'Oh! Hello!' she said in surprise. He answered by giving the solution to 3 across. 'Have you already done this?' she asked.

'No. I never look at a newspaper before lunch.'

'How annoying of you to do it so quickly! Don't you usually sit at the other end of the table?'

'I haven't a usual place.'

'I only saw you at the other end last term.'

'I was actually on leave last term, though I came in occasionally.'

Julia wondered why he hadn't mentioned that at Roger's party and decided it had been a ploy to make her feel beneath his notice; but then her attention was, in spite of herself, taken up by Roger coming into the room. She was always aware of his presence however much she tried to ignore it. He looked at her with questioningly raised eyebrows and she responded with a smile. He then noticed Quentin Crawford beside her and his eyebrows went down into lines of displeasure. He was followed by the Archangel who engaged him in conversation, and then by Hector Otis who was busy making some complaint to Everard who was close behind. Julia turned her Times to the front page to preclude any more crossword cleverness from Quentin. The butler appeared with a tall, bronzed, very good-looking young man who was clearly new to the college. 'Sit anywhere you like, Sir' the butler was saying, though at the same time ushering him fairly firmly to the lower end of the table. 'Er - perhaps here, by Mrs Leslie.'

The young man took the napkin the butler handed him and sat down gratefully by Julia. 'Hi! I'm Stuart, Stuart Gregson.'

'Julia Leslie. How do you do! Dare I ask if you're an Australian?'

'Right first time. I won't ask how you know!'

'It must be the tan that makes the rest of us look whitewashed.'

'Yeah, well it is mid-summer where I've come from.'

'Are you here on a Research Fellowship?'

'Yeah. Our academic year finishes in December, so I couldn't take it up till now. I'm here till this time next year.'

'I hope you'll enjoy it. People don't talk as much over lunch as over dinner; too busy reading newspapers. Not that I know a lot about dinners. I'm only allowed in on Ladies' Guest Nights.'

'Why is that?'

'I suppose it's because I'm the first ever woman don here. They need to get used to it by degrees.'

'What degrees?'

'Oh – no – I mean gradually. Our academic standing is not what matters, apparently.'

'I think that's terrible!'

'How kind of you. But don't stick your neck out. It wouldn't do any good. I'm sufficiently brainwashed to feel I'm lucky to be here at all.'

Sipping black coffee in the SCR, Julia sat in her usual dark corner feeling mercifully inconspicuous, knowing that Roger would follow her into the quad, and wondering what she was going to say to him. What would I have done as a flat-sharing single girl? she mused. Said no, of course, her mind answered; he's married. A man who was married, or even engaged, had always been an automatic cut-off. One of Mamma's maxims, learnt early, had had its effect. "There's only one word for a girl who goes out with a married man, and that's MUCK!" Not very happy muck, either, with blank weekends for the girl while the lover spent them with his family. But now, Julia went on pondering, she was married herself, and that was a very different matter. She was too engrossed in her musing to notice Everard until he was looming over her.

'Penny!' he said. Julia started and then realised who he was and what he meant.

'Oh? What? For my thoughts, you mean? I'm afraid they're worth a great deal more than that!' And she pushed back her chair and escaped from Everard's looming before he could answer. None of this went unnoticed by Roger, however, and he was at her heels almost before she'd emerged into the quad.

'Well?' he asked.

'Well indeed,' said Julia, 'I only got your letter this morning, so it's rather short notice. I'll have to see what's happening at home and tell you tomorrow.'

'You're stalling.'

'No, really. A woman with three children can't go out unless she's already arranged for them to be looked after. We're not really free agents, you see, in any way.'

'Can't you telephone home and say you've got a meeting in college and need to arrange things?'

'I haven't got a telephone in my room.'

'Why not? Everybody else has.'

'I suppose nobody's thought about it. It's only an

undergraduate's room, really, nothing special.'

'I'll have one put in for you immediately.'

'That would be kind. I can have messages sent from the lodge, of course, but I often feel the need to ring home just to make sure everything's all right. I suppose notes and messages have been the mainstay of Camford communications for so long that the telephone's hardly begun to take over. My father-in-law still sends postcards all the time instead of telephoning. He gets awfully cross if they're not delivered the same day.'

'Very unrealistic of him. But we're actually talking about dinner on Thursday aren't we?'

'I can only make arrangements tonight and tell you tomorrow.'

'I must make the best of that I suppose. You'll be able to ring me tomorrow, if I have anything to do with it.'

'Don't we have to ring through the porter's lodge?'

'Yes, I'm afraid so.'

'Aren't you worried that they listen to telephone calls?'

'I daresay they do. But on the whole they only gossip among themselves.'

'I wonder! Perhaps I'd better leave a note in your pigeonhole.'

Julia was home by 5:30 to take over the children

from Astrid, who was going out. At 7:30 she was reading them a bedtime story when Jeremy came into the nursery, red-faced, glassy-eyed and heavily redolent of alcohol. The children wrinkled their noses, stared at him with steady hostility and drew closer to their mother.

'How are you all getting on?' Jeremy managed to say, with an obvious effort to speak distinctly. Nobody answered. 'I said,' he raised his voice, '"how are you getting on?"'

'As you see us,' replied Julia, using a phrase she'd read in a Scottish novel and considered rather useful. Jeremy weaved into the room and patted Emma on the shoulder.

'Pretty thing!' he murmured. The child drew back, clutched her mother and began to cry.

'What on earth's the matter with you?' Jeremy shouted. He put out a forefinger and poked Julia fiercely in the chest. 'You're putting the children off me, aren't you? You and your precious job. The great Mrs Leslie who teaches in a men's college!'

'Jeremy, please! You're upsetting the children.'

'You've upset them, more like it. Don't take any notice of your mother, kids – she's pissed.'

Emma's cries became louder, Jamie covered his face with his arm, Richard continued his steady, hostile stare.

'It's all right children.' Julia tried to sound calm and reassuring. 'Go to sleep now. We'll finish the story tomorrow. Jeremy, will you go downstairs please. The children are going to sleep now.'

'Don't you tell me what to do! Who do you bloody think you are?'

'Please Jeremy! I'll talk to you downstairs. Why don't you go and have a glass of wine?' Julia could think of no other ploy to get him away from the children. Besides, she considered, he could hardly be worse and it would in fact be preferable if he drank himself unconscious. To her relief he left the room. The children emerged from their huddle and submitted quickly to being tucked into their respective beds.

Downstairs in the kitchen/breakfast-room Jeremy was drinking a glass of red wine, some of which had spilled on to the table. Automatically Julia took a cloth to wipe it up.

'What do you think you are doing?' shouted Jeremy.

'Wiping up this wine. It stains if you leave it.'

'It stains if you leave it! It stains if you leave it!' Jeremy mimicked in a high falsetto. 'Stop criticising me – nag, nag, nag –' he thumped the glass on the table, spilling more wine as he did so. 'Clever Mrs Leslie! She's the clever one! She knows everything!'

He picked up a saucepan and hurled it across the room, smashing a milk bottle which seemed to explode on the tiled floor into a shower of glass particles. Julia thought with dismay of the extra care that would have to be taken to ensure that no hidden pieces were a danger to the children. The floor would have to be swept, washed and washed again. Jeremy drained the rest of his wine.

'I'm going to bed,' he announced thickly. Julia followed him at a distance to make sure he went nowhere near the children. Within two minutes she heard him snoring. Clearly he'd gone to bed with all his clothes on. She returned to the kitchen and put her hands and head on the kitchen table, unable to face the task of glass clearing immediately. 'My God, my God,' she whispered, 'what have I done to deserve this? Those moronic schoolmasters must have been taunting him about his intellectual wife and probably casting some aspersions on his own intellect at the same time. How different my life here is from my life in college – and how Jeremy resents it! Oh God, what shall I do?'

Rather than answer the wider significance of the question she set about the immediate necessity of clearing the floor. She swept the myriad glass splinters into the dustpan.

'That's odd!' she thought. 'I'm calling on God as if I were a believer. Pauline must be right. I hope she is. There needs to be something beyond this.'

CHAPTER THIRTY

Julia spent the night precariously on the edge of her side of the bed, kept awake by her own thoughts and Jeremy's snoring. Eventually the thoughts confused themselves into a dream and she awoke at 7:00 hardly able to believe she'd slept at all. She got the children up and gave them breakfast. Astrid and Jeremy came down almost simultaneously, for which Julia was thankful. She felt she ought to speak to Jeremy but had no desire to do so.

Instead she addressed Astrid. 'Did you have a pleasant evening out?'

Astrid shrugged, pouted and said 'Oh yes' non-committally.

'Oh did you?' said Jeremy. Astrid merely shrugged again.

'Now, Astrid, on Thursday I've got a working dinner and a meeting in college. Can you cope? I can be home for a couple of hours in the afternoon.'

'Oh, yes,' said Astrid again.

'What about you, Jeremy?'

'What about me?!' said Jeremy.

'Will you be home to supper on Thursday?'

'I don't know yet. Probably not if you won't be here to get it.'

Julia was relieved. It would be preferable if he didn't come home until the evening was advanced and the children fast asleep. She was surprised at herself; surprised that her resolution had hardened; she had seemed to hear herself speaking to Astrid about the 'meeting' as if listening to somebody else. The words had apparently formed themselves without any deliberate intention on her part.

She went into college as soon as she possibly could, only to find a couple of workmen busy installing a telephone in her room. Oh! Roger is kind, she thought. He doesn't say he'll do things and then forget about them.

'It's all right, Miss,' one of the men assured her as she went into the room. 'Almost finished. Then you'll be able to phone up your boyfriend!' He gave a large wink with this information and Julia laughed, partly because it was already a little flattering to be taken for an unmarried undergraduate and partly because there was some truth in the statement. She had every intention of ringing Roger to thank him and to accept his invitation.

Everard's telephone jangled in his room as he was immersed in going over his first lecture for the term. He was not in the mood for telephone calls.

'Hello!' he said brusquely.

'Hello–oo,' replied a huskily seductive female voice which he didn't immediately recognise.

'Hello?' he queried with a who-is-it-or-is-it-a-wrong-number intonation.

'It's me, Alison.'

'Oh! Alison! Of course –. Somehow I don't quite associate you with this hour of the morning.'

'It's eleven o'clock!'

'Exactly.'

'Well how about associating me with tea this afternoon?'

'Tea? Where?'

'In your room of course. Surely people still have tea in Camford Colleges? And it's not only an undergraduate institution. Surely you like crumpets!' They both laughed.

'Yes indeed!' Everard found his mood had changed suddenly 'I'll have some sent over from the buttery. Will you be able to come at 4:00?'

'I certainly hope so!' was Alison's husky reply, and she put the receiver down leaving Everard to muse on something he'd thought little about for years – the notoriety of Camford college teas. Clever of Alison, he pondered, to evoke such associations in such a brief conversation at so unpromising an hour in the morning. Accustomed to managing such manoeuvres himself rather than to being on the receiving end of them, he was slightly aggrieved – almost, if he would have admitted it, shocked – by what he regarded as role-reversal, but also a little flattered and not without admiration for a kindred spirit, albeit of the opposite sex.

At lunch Everard found himself sitting next to Hector Otis.

'Did you have women to your room for tea when you were an undergraduate, Hector?'

Hector smiled a large smile of lustful recollection that was intended to convey to all his prowess in the field. 'Frequently!' he smiled.

Julia, overhearing from the other side of the table smiled at the recollection of her flatmate's account of avoiding Hector's advances at tea.

'Odd really,' Everard continued. 'Teatime hasn't a promising sound for seduction.'

'Well, considewing that everybody of the opposite sex had to be out of all colleges by 7:30 – 7:00 in some – and that even for people in digs there were fierce landladies, not to mention that dinner's much more expensive than tea ... and in the winter term it's dark by 4 o'clock. What's more comforting than a bit of cwumpet in front of one's gas fire?'

Roger looked across at Hector's complacent face.

'Filthy sod,' he said, affably.

Hector looked suitably flattered and Julia, watching him, had difficulty in preventing herself from laughing, knowing as she did of the disparity between Hector's projected image of himself as a Don Juan and the reality of the matter. She marvelled that any of his colleagues could consider him a man attractive to women, but reflected that one tended not to know these things about people of one's own sex. Hector was not, she thought, like Everard, whom though he might be repulsive to her, she could understand that some women would find attractive.

Everard returned to his room after lunch unwilling to apply himself to his lecture, important though this was so near to the beginning of term. His mind was more inclined to dwell on hearthrugs in front of gas fires in dimly-lit college rooms, and by the time Alison knocked, somewhat prematurely, on his door just before 4 o'clock he was quite in the mood to receive her.

'I suppose we have to have tea first.' he said.

Alison's response was a long, tongue-searching kiss.

'No!' she said, 'Afterwards.'

She undid Everard's belt and the top button of his trousers, deftly inserted her hand, palm side outward, and caressed his belly and then broke away from him swiftly, sat on the sofa and peeled off her stockings and knickers, undid her blouse, crossed to the hearthrug and lay down with one knee raised and the other bent a little outwards. Everard pushed down his trousers with frantic haste and thrust himself into her.

CHAPTER THIRTY-ONE

On Thursday Julia set off for home immediately after her 2 to 3 o'clock tutorial, having ended it exactly on the hour rather than ten or fifteen minutes later as she usually did. She was conscious of a mounting excitement at the prospect of dinner with Roger. It was a problem to find something to wear: interesting enough to look well in a restaurant yet sober enough to give credence to the idea of a working dinner. Not that she supposed Jeremy would be home to see her before she left, but Astrid might take stock of what she was wearing and in fact she herself almost believed in the "working" aspect of the occasion. She decided on a simple navy blue with touches of white. Astrid did notice.

'That looks nice,' she remarked, uncharacteristically, with an approving nod. 'Even ven you are so pale.'

Julia knocked on Roger's door exactly six

minutes after the expected time.

'You're late' said Roger, with a smile of welcome.

'Only a very civilised late' said Julia.

'You did it on purpose.'

'Indeed.'

'I'm not sure what that means, but would you like sherry or gin and tonic? I don't run to ice and lemon, I'm afraid.'

'Not very necessary in this climate and I'd love a gin and tonic. Thank you.'

Roger poured a generous one. 'Heavens!' said Julia, tasting it. 'There's more gin than tonic in this.'

'Well, take a few sips to make room for some more tonic if you like. But I think you need a good drink to help you relax. Did you have a difficult time getting away from home?'

'Not really. The au pair's looking after the children and Jeremy's sure to eat out as I'm not there to cook for him. Not that he needs an excuse to eat out.'

'He doesn't like your teaching here, does he?'

'He can be quite nasty about it to me, though I think he boasts about it to his colleagues – which isn't a very good idea either.'

'How do his colleagues react to you?'

'Some of them are quite pleasant, though they do rather go out of their way to show how knowledgeable and intellectual they are, which can be a bit of a bore. It's their wives who tend to be hostile.'

'They don't take kindly to a woman with a higher grade job than their husbands'?'

'Perhaps not. As they hardly talk to me I don't really know. They talk to each other as if I were not there. But of course most of them have houses full of boarders and matrons and cooks to run and take it in turns to ask each other to dinner-parties, so they've many things in common to talk about.'

'And how do you find *your* colleagues' wives? Are they hostile?'

'Well, yours certainly isn't, she was extremely pleasant to me. And Everard's wife's much nicer than ...'

'Than Everard?'

Julia smiled a little wryly at the implication that that would not be difficult and went on 'than I would have expected.'

Roger laughed and took Julia's now empty glass. 'Dinner!' he said, and held out a hand to help her up from the sofa.

'Thank you' said Julia. 'That gin was strong, but I'm not quite legless yet. Where are we going or is it a surprise?'

'A surprise' Roger replied. 'But I suppose you've been there before.'

'Before I was married and had children, perhaps.

I don't seem to have seen the inside of many restaurants since.'

Looking out of the restaurant's first floor window in one of the oldest stone houses in Camford, across to the floodlit tower of the largest and grandest of its colleges, Julia sighed happily.

'This is very nice' she murmured.

'And you have been here before?' Roger guessed.

'Yes. Quite often in fact, in my undergraduate days.'

'You must have gone out with rich young men.'

'I don't suppose I thought about it at the time. I certainly didn't appreciate it properly. It used to be very stuffy and old-fashioned-English. I remember eating very dry pheasant served by waiters who looked rather like bulldogs and were every bit as fierce. The lighting was very dim with one candle on each table – in a silver candlestick, of course. I once put the candle right next to my plate so that I could see to separate the bones from the flesh of my pheasant: there wasn't much difference in texture! A waiter immediately came over and put the candle on the far corner of the table again. It didn't enhance the relationship with the young man who'd brought me there. It all seems a great deal pleasanter now.'

'That's possibly because it's under new management, continental. So I hope it now has the opposite effect. Especially as you're here with a ... a _'

'A less young man' Julia finished for him.

'How very tactfully put!' They both laughed.

'Let's have the fondu as a main course' Roger suggested. 'It's fun as well as being delicious.'

'A fondu?'

'Yes. Not at all English or stuffy – and you cook it at the table the way you want it. But I'm going to have prawns with rice and aioli to begin with – that's if you don't mind the smell of garlic. It's not too strong; They don't chop it, they squeeze it though little holes in something called a garlic press ...'

'Oh Roger! A garlic press is one of the first things I bought when I got married.'

'Really?'

'Yes. My American flatmates taught me how to make garlic bread. I use it all the time – I love the smell of garlic. But I'm going to have the avocado. Quite the new 'in' thing aren't they?' Julia remembered hearing Alison Greer boasting about serving avocados at a dinner-party. She was enjoying herself a great deal more than she had expected to.

'I'm sure you're too sensible to worry about what is or isn't 'in"

'Oh, certainly. I eat the things I like, regardless of fashion. I can't stand food snobs – and you must remember that I 'prefer a plain dish to a ragout,' Mr Darcy!'

'As you told that appalling, gluttonous sloth of a brother-in-law of Bingley's!'

'Oh! How clever of you to pick that up! It's marvellous to talk to somebody who can understand one's literary allusions.'

'Thank you, Miss Bennet! I read P and P again quite recently' (And re-read it, thought Roger, more than once, with the pleasure of identifying Julia with Elizabeth Bennet.)

'But Mr Darcy could never have taken Elizabeth Bennet to a restaurant.'

'Did they have such things?'

'Not as such, I'm sure. The nearest thing was the Bennet sisters having the equivalent of a pub lunch together.'

'Restaurants must have been much less necessary when meals were cooked by servants.'

'True. And young, unmarried women can have had little choice in who was invited. Hence the incentive to get married and have one's own home to invite one's own guests to.'

'Surely you can do that now?'

'Yes. But the work entailed in giving a dinner party when you've got no cook and several small children to feed first … Oh! Here's the fondu. This is fun.'

The waiter set up the burner and the pot of hot

oil and Roger explained the technique of holding the raw pieces of fillet steak in it until cooked to taste.

(Oh dear – Julia thought. I'd better not say anything about having one of these at home. I've already admitted to being here before and possessing a garlic press. He must have taken my expression of surprise at having such a dish here for ignorance that it existed). So she listened carefully to his instructions and cooked the steak companionably, piece by piece, and thought at the same time that Jeremy must have bought the fondu set because he'd been introduced to it in this restaurant on one of his many sorties for a solitary, expensive meal. The thought by no means diminished her pleasure in Roger's company, though she was momentarily disturbed by the reflection that for a man to leave his wife at home and dine in a restaurant alone was not as bad as to dine with another woman. But Roger can afford it, she told herself, and Jeremy can't.

CHAPTER THIRTY-TWO

The coffee drunk, the bill (discreetly) paid, the luxurious and slightly exotic atmosphere of the restaurant absorbed, Roger and Julia walked back to college arm in arm. It was true that Roger had drunk more than half of the two bottles of wine they had consumed between them, but Julia had certainly had enough to render her considerably less inhibited than at the beginning of the evening and just a trifle unsteady without an arm to lean on. While they continued their game of Elizabeth Bennet and Mr Darcy, verbally and externally, Roger was pondering whether he dare ask Julia to come back to his room, and Julia was wondering whether she wanted him to ask her or not. Her body was urging Yes! Yes. Yes. But her mind gave her pause – what then? No. Aloud she said 'As my father hasn't sent the carriage for me I think I ought to take a taxi home.'

'Certainly not,' said Roger. 'You can't go home from a working dinner in a taxi. I'll drive you home.'

'Do you think you should ... I mean ...' Julia was actually thinking of the law's new stance on drinking and driving. People could even have their licences taken away, she'd heard; but she felt it was hardly suitable to point this out to Roger. He, however, took her hesitation as a sign that she was drawing away from him and unwillingly decided that to ask her to his room might spoil everything. It was too soon, greatly though so tame an ending to the evening went against his inclinations. Julia allowed herself to be propelled into the 'parking quad' of the college. They went straight to the car. She felt relieved that no decision was demanded of her, but at the same time sobered by disappointment.

Roger stopped the car a little way from Julia's house. They thanked each other for the happiness of the evening, kissed briefly and said goodnight. Julia walked slowly to her own front door, unwilling to open it. She had no sense of guilt or anything to hide apart from a sharp realisation of the contrast between Roger and Jeremy. Jeremy might be better looking, but with him there was a significant lack of "the meeting of true minds".

She stood outside the door for more than a minute, making a conscious effort to adjust her mental state, then finally entered the house to hear Jeremy's voice from the kitchen, correcting

Astrid's English, both of them laughing. They were sitting over a very nearly empty bottle of whisky, Jeremy looking rather flushed and Astrid a good deal more cheerful and responsive than Julia had ever seen her. They hardly noticed Julia, who murmured to them, filled a glass with water and took it upstairs to bed. She lay pondering on Roger's circumspection and her surprise at her own disappointment. 'Oh dear,' she finally moaned to herself, 'I'm afraid I like him all the better for it.'

Julia woke up suddenly for no apparent reason to see the luminous hands on her clock at 4:30. 'Oh dear!' she thought. 'This always happens when I've had too much to drink. I hope I can go to sleep again'. But instead she gradually realised that the other side of the bed was empty. And cold. She sat up and turned on the light. There was no sign of Jeremy at all. Her heart pounding wildly she lay down again to take stock of the situation. It had happened before that he'd come home very late. She remembered the last time she'd been pregnant, in winter, with snow lying thick on the ground. Jeremy had been out to dinner and she had agonised over the thought that he might have collapsed on the way home and be lying in a drunken stupor, dying of exposure. She'd been about to get up with the intention of going out to look for him when he'd come in, so drunk that he'd taken only half of his clothes off and then, because he could see two beds, tried to get in the wrong one and fallen on to the floor. But this time she'd seen him at home. In the kitchen. Drinking whisky with Astrid. That was odd because he always boasted that he never drank spirits – as if that meant that he never drank too much.

Julia's heart pounded more violently, throbbing in her head and her ears. She got up gasping for breath and padded downstairs to the kitchen. On the table were two glasses and the empty whisky bottle and a large hair-grip that she recognised as Astrid's. 'Oh God!' she muttered. She went into the dining room, then in to the drawing room. There on the sofa were Jeremy's jacket, shirt and trousers and sticking out of the trouser pocket a packet of durex, roughly torn open. 'Oh God, Oh God!' she breathed aloud. 'Help me to bear it patiently.'

She went upstairs again and lay on her bed, pondering the best course of action. By six o'clock she could bear it no longer and she went slowly up to the top floor where Astrid's bedroom was. She could hear Jeremy's voice – he was still, apparently, correcting Astrid's English. Without pausing, Julia opened the door. The light was on. Jeremy was in Astrid's bed. At the sight of her he stopped talking, but without closing his mouth. Astrid looked defiant and sulky.

Ignoring Jeremy Julia spoke to her in a voice of deadly quiet.

'Astrid, you will leave this house by 12 noon today and you will never come into it again. Do you understand me?'

Astrid turned down her mouth. 'Yes,' she said. 'I will go. I do not want to stay here."

Jeremy was staring at the floor. 'Jeremy,' said Julia, marvelling at the levelness of her own voice, 'take your things out of the drawing room before the children get up.'

Leaving the door open, Julia went down to her own bedroom and lay on the bed, shaking all over. Her instinct was to leave the house herself, walk away from the whole situation. She felt that her home had been polluted, rendered sordid and repellent. She heard Jeremy's footsteps. He paused outside the bedroom and then went downstairs.

Practical reality overtook her. She had to get the children up and dress them; give them breakfast, get the boys to school; find somebody to look after Emma. Mrs Davies. Thank heaven for Mrs Davies. It was one of her days. That would see them through the morning. She could cancel her afternoon tutorials. She contemplated the necessities of the day, mentally, but stayed on her bed, feeling too drained of energy to make any physical effort. 'I can't, I can't,' she said aloud, 'but I have to' and finally she dressed herself and went into the drawing room to make sure that Jeremy had taken his things away. He was there, lying on the sofa, crying. She closed the door quietly and left him there, deciding to tell the children that he wasn't well, if the necessity arose, and went up to the nursery to see to them.

In college in time for a cup of coffee before her first tutorial, Julia thanked God for a job to escape to. Then, while teaching, she became so engrossed in the subject and the stimulation of imparting her enthusiasm for it to her pupils that she forgot her troubles. At the end of the morning she left a note on her door cancelling the afternoon tutorials, and then went to the lodge to leave notes with the same information to the pupils involved. She was just going out of the wicket when Roger appeared and called to her.

'Julia! Aren't you going in to lunch?' She turned and he saw her face. 'What's the matter? Are you all right? Has something happened? Was it ...' he was going to say "to do with last night" but stopped, aware of the interested eye of the porter.

'Oh no – I – not really,' Julia stammered, uncharacteristically. 'Our au pair's gone – er, unexpectedly – so I have to go home and relieve the cleaning woman who's standing in – and then see to a replacement. But thank you for your concern. I'll get things back to normal as soon as possible. I must go now.' And she stepped through the wicket and into the street and away.

Roger looked after her for several seconds. He couldn't believe her explanation; she looked so ... he tried to think what she looked, but could only think of 'different'. He feared she must have had a terrible scene with her husband after going home the previous night. He went to lunch feeling slightly guilty and a little anxious and wondered how he could possibly contact Julia over the weekend and find out more about it.

Julia arrived home to find Mrs Davies jubilantly in charge.

'So that German's gone then!' she remarked, with something between a sniff and a smirk. 'Good riddance, I'd say. Huns! Never did like them, even before the war. Glad to see the back of her.'

'Do you know what time she left?' Julia asked.

'Just before twelve, it was. Just over an hour ago, I s'pose. Bet you're glad she's gone.'

Julia looked sharply at Mrs Davies, wondering how much she knew or suspected about the situation. 'Well, in some ways, certainly. But I had rather come to rely on living-in help since I've had a proper job. It's going to be difficult ...'

'Well now,' Mrs Davies interrupted. 'There's this lady that's been putting up at my place with 'er boy, Derek. Well she's a relation really – 'er mother was my auntie, like – and they was living in a tied cottage. Well, when 'er 'usband died they thought they'd of been able to go on living there, but now the landlord's gone and kicked them out and they got nowhere to live. If you was to 'ave them 'ere, like, she could do everyfink any pair girl can do and more.'

'But I've only got one room, Mrs Davies.'

'Oh, they'd manage. Better than with us where they're sleeping on the floor. I could tell 'er to come round and see you this afternoon if you like. She wouldn't need much pay because she's got 'er widder's pension.'

Julia sat down, heavy with relief and amazement. 'It sounds too good to be true. Please do tell her to come round.'

'Right then. 'Er name's Mrs Thomas.'

CHAPTER THIRTY-THREE

Everard went home on the evening of his "tea" with Alison feeling triumphant and benign. He even toyed with the idea of taking Jean out to dinner to celebrate. There would be a delicious irony in that. He would be celebrating and Jean would have no idea what; or, in fact, that he was celebrating at all. He chuckled at the thought. But when he entered the house calling out 'I'm home!' with unwonted joviality, he encountered only the babysitter. 'Where's my wife?' he asked her, annoyed with this setback.

'Oh, she left about half an hour ago. She said she didn't know when she'd be back. She said I could go if you got home before she did. But I haven't put the boys to bed yet. They're watching television.'

Everard was not pleased. An evening at home on his own was not what he'd had in mind. He would have dined in college if he'd realised sooner – but now it was too late. He knew it was no use trying to contact Alison: she was at what she'd described as 'a deeply boring dinner party' in Camford with her husband.

'Well, hang on here for a bit longer, will you?' he told the babysitter. 'I'm going out again.' He'd decided to do something he rarely did – go to the local pub for a meal.

It was a good pub, well placed on the edge of the large village green, very old and picturesque with its thatched roof and black beams, but with a comfortable no-nonsense interior, large wood fires and good plain food. It attracted both locals and the more discerning car-owning pub goers from Camford and the surrounding area and remained mercifully free of tourists. Everard took a pint of the – very good – local bitter to a small table and sat down to drink, study the menu and give a wandering eye to any unattached local talent.

A sudden burst of laughter drew his attention to a group of four young people some distance away in a diagonally opposite corner: two young men and two young women. As he looked at them the two nearest heads, men's, swivelled sharply away from his direction. Realising that he must somehow be the subject of their mirth he felt a little cold and conspicuous. He applied himself to the menu, but peering over it a moment later to see the four heads now fairly closely together he began to realise that two of them looked familiar. One belonged to Stuart – what was his name

– Gregson, the new Australian at Emmaeus, and another to Emily Matheson. The second girl raised her head suddenly, gave a stare in his direction and jerked her head down again. It took little imagination for Everard to suppose that Emily had been regaling her friends with some details of an encounter with himself.

He felt vulnerable and outnumbered and unwilling to remain where he was. Should he simply leave the pub or should he go over and speak to them with a good display of charm and superiority? Either way, any appetite he'd had for a solitary pub supper had diminished to zero so there was little to lose. He sipped his beer slowly. When three-quarters of it had gone he made his way to the group with an attitude of nonchalance and no haste and stood looking down on them until they stopped talking. Stuart Gregson regarded him with slightly puzzled half-recognition.

'Ah! our new Antipodean! ' Everard drawled. 'What brings you to this neck of the woods?'

'Oh, hi! I didn't realise you knew me – I mean I hardly feel acquainted with Emmaeus dons yet ...' Stuart had, of course, been enlightened as to Everard's identity by Emily, but had reckoned on himself being anonymous to Everard. He wondered whether he should merely answer on his own account or be matey and Australian and introduce the others. Either way he felt embarrassed, but decided on the latter course.

'Er – this is Nerelle, also from Australia, and Antony and Emily – from America ...'

'Ah yes, Emily!' Everard made his voice imply that he had only just remembered who she was. 'Drinking beer, I see. I do hope it doesn't make you sick!' Emily flushed very red.

There was an embarrassed silence. Everard drained the rest of his beer, put the glass on the counter, said a general 'goodnight' and left the pub. He felt he had triumphed sufficiently, leaving a decidedly deflated group behind him.

'What was all that about? asked Stuart.

'You didn't tell him did you' said Nerelle, 'you didn't tell him about his stinking armpits making you feel sick?'

Emily had, of course, been regaling her friends with a heavily edited account of an outing with Everard, implying that he had made passes which she had strenuously rejected; but now, Everard's attitude and Emily's reaction to him suggested other implications.

'I never expected he'd come and speak to us,' was all she said. 'He must have somehow known we were laughing about him; isn't that offal?'

'He's never spoken to me in college,' said Stuart. 'I thought he was much too grand to notice me. He always talks like someone very superior.'

'Yeah,' said Antony. 'These English guys are very good at that. But it doesn't do to take too much notice – and anyway, they do it worse to each other. The ones who've been at public schools really despise the ones who haven't.'

'Why?' asked Nerelle. 'What sort of schools did the others go to?'

'Grammar schools, mainly.'

'Aren't grammar schools public schools?'

'No. They're called state schools here. Public schools are the ones people pay for privately.'

'I'll never get the hang of this place. Nothing seems to make any sense. How can you tell the difference anyway? They all seem the same to me.'

'A lot of it's the way they talk. That guy Lucas is obviously a public school man. He's got that drawly talking-down-to-the-servants sort of voice. Hasn't he Emily?'

But Emily was anxious to put Everard out of her own mind and preferably everybody else's; and while some of the ebullience had gone out of her evening, she was finding a personable Australian of her own age group a great deal more interesting than a snooty old Englishman. She was listening to Stuart.

Everard wandered home slowly, enjoying his discomfiture of Emily and the feeling that he had employed exactly the right tactics. His sense of satisfaction almost compensated for the absence of supper – and the absence of Jean. He decided to make a virtue of it, let the babysitter go and put the boys to bed himself. He'd tell them a story and make them appreciate him. He suppressed a latent feeling that it might not be a bad idea to get them on his side.

Jean and Tim spent an evening of unalloyed mutual happiness. The time of their Christmas separation seemed to melt away to nothing. They spent a rapturous time in bed and the only bar to perfection was the knowledge that Jean must somehow tear herself away and go home.

'Stay all night,' Tim urged her. 'Why should you get back before breakfast time? You know you don't care what Everard thinks or says about it. You've got to think about leaving him – or getting rid of him.'

'Strangely enough I find it much easier to live with him now that I no longer care about him. I feel as if I've been set free, he can't hurt me any more. It's almost as if I've recovered from some long-term illness. And what if I did get rid of him altogether? How would we manage about the boys?'

'I'd move in with you and we'd manage very well.'

'I know you're very, very good with them – but it's too much to expect from you: three of them, all the time, on and on.'

'I'm very willing to do it. I want to be with you all the time. I can't bear to think of you there with him, at his mercy.'

'It's all the more magical when I escape to be with you.'

'Magical, yes. But not very real. I want to be real. I understand the commitment. Please, Jean, please think about it. Stay tonight. Just go home in time for breakfast, and if he kicks up rough about it tell him you want a divorce.'

'Oh, it's so tempting; especially now when I'm lying here with you feeling warm, secure and happy and the last thing I want to do is go out into the cold and back to a house where I have to creep into bed beside a man I dislike and despise. Oh – what shall I do?'

'Do as I say. Stay here and then see what happens when you go back in the morning. Let me help you decide to stay – and then leave it to fate.'

CHAPTER THIRTY-FOUR

When Mrs Davies had left the tall house in the narrow street with a final promise to send her cousin 'and Derek' round straightaway, Julia steeled herself to go up to Astrid's erstwhile room and make it as presentable as possible for the prospective help to look at. She didn't want to think any further than immediately necessary. She had to sort out practical difficulties; emotional ones could be faced later. About Jeremy she felt nothing but a blank numbness. She set to work to clean the room with speed and thoroughness, determined, with an anger that gave her remarkable energy, to remove every trace of Astrid from the premises. Cold though it was, she opened the windows wide. It was a large, light, airy room, with a good single bed and a sofa long enough for 'Derek' to sleep on.

By six o'clock, when Jeremy arrived home, Mrs Thomas and her son were already moving in. Their possessions were very few and their delight in their new accommodation very apparent. Jeremy stared at them uncomprehendingly and escaped into the kitchen to keep out of the way. The children had finished their tea and were watching television in the dining room. Julia lingered a little upstairs with the new arrivals, ostensibly to welcome them and go over details, and actually because she had so little desire to come face to face with her husband. She finally went downstairs with the intention of doing so, but instead went into the drawing room and began to play the piano. She was not very well in practice but still able, with steady concentration, to play one of Bach's French Suites. She had always loved its logic, its precision, its sense of certainty and intellectual clarity. She became quite absorbed in it and when Jeremy came into the room she didn't stop playing. He stood beside her for a long minute and then said

'Can't you stop playing that?'

'No.'

'I want to talk to you.'

'I'm not sure that I want to talk to you.' Julia went on playing and Jeremy was silent.

'Well?' she said finally. 'What have you got to say?'

'She gave me a bottle of whisky,' Jeremy faltered out. Julia almost laughed.

'Is that a reason or an excuse?'

'Both. I don't know.'

Julia looked at Jeremy in disbelief. Could he really have been saying anything so ridiculously inconsequential? She stopped playing the piano and went on staring at him, waiting for him to say something to the point. He said nothing.

'Well,' said Julia – finally, and as a real question - 'are you sorry?'

'Sorry?' he said. 'SORRY?! I'm more than sorry. I'm hurt.'

'You're hurt! YOU'RE hurt! I don't know how you dare say that. How do you think I feel?'

Jeremy shook his head dumbly. He gave the impression of being so immersed in his own misery as to be incapable of considering how Julia felt. Come to that, thought Julia, I don't know how I feel either. I haven't any words to describe them apart from shock, perhaps. Jeremy looked at her again.

'Do you want to go out?' he asked. 'Would you like to go to the pictures?'

'The pictures?!'

'Well, you're always saying we should go to things like that together. I thought you might like to.'

'What a ridiculous ...' Julia began, then she stopped, realising how long it was since Jeremy had suggested such a thing and how far it showed an intention to make amends. The whole situation seemed completely bizarre. What sort of marriage was it when an invitation to the cinema was intended to make up for so blatant, so irresponsible an infidelity?

'What else can we do?' said Jeremy. 'I don't want to go out and leave you.'

Julia registered, somewhat grimly, that that was at least a change, and began to consider alternatives. How else was the time between now and going to bed to be filled in? A situation where she and Jeremy could be together without the necessity of speaking to each other had something to recommend it.

'It's impossible' she said aloud. 'How can I leave Mrs Thomas to babysit on her first night here?'

'Who's Mrs Thomas?'

Julia had forgotten that Jeremy didn't know. The events of the day seemed to have been spread out over a period of weeks.

'Mrs Davies's cousin. She and her son have come to live in and do the housework – and so on. Very fortunately. That must be her in the hall.'

There was a sliding, padding sound. Julia opened the door. It was Mrs Thomas in her carpet slippers, looking immensely cheerful.

'Derek and me's had somefink t'eat,' she announced. 'Why don't you let us put the children to bed and get to know them. There's somefink Derek particularly wants to watch on the telly. Could he watch it in your dining room just this once? We 'aven't got our telly yet. Tell yer what, why don't you and your husband go out and celebrate, now you've got us to see to things?'

Julia and Jeremy were so nonplussed at the turn of events, so totally at a loss to consider any other course of action, that they in fact did as suggested and went to the cinema.

It was a terrible film about a man whose wife laughed all the time and it got on his nerves to such an extent that he killed her. This was scarcely cheering but neither Julia nor Jeremy was in a mood to be cheered and it gave them something external to themselves to talk about, made them act in the presence of the other cinema-goers like a normal couple. On the way home they had a hotdog from a street stall and found they were hungry enough actually to enjoy it. Lying in bed late, Julia reflected that at least Jeremy wasn't drunk or snoring for once. How very strange, she thought, that I owe it to that awful girl that my husband's taken me out for the evening.

CHAPTER THIRTY-FIVE

Jean unlocked the back door quietly, very quietly, at a little after seven in the morning. There seemed to be no sound in the house so far, but the boys would be awake soon. She decided to make porridge for a treat; she felt like giving everybody a treat; she felt jubilant and exulting. She had expected to feel anxious, or at least apprehensive, regarding Everard's reaction to her absence. But she didn't at all! She executed a little pirouette on the floor of the kitchen to express her exultation. She was even with Everard!

The boys filtered down into the kitchen, attracted by the smell of porridge and the cheerfulness of Jean's singing.

'You look very happy, Mummy!'

'Yes, I've made you some porridge and you can have lots of brown sugar.'

'You've got a new dress on, Mummy.'

'Oh – yes – well,' Jean had forgotten that she was wearing something not normally associated with cooking a weekend breakfast, 'it's a nice day.'

Everard woke up to the realisation that he had a headache and that somehow all was not well. After putting the boys to bed the previous night he had sat down and rather grimly drunk the best part of a bottle of port. He enjoyed a glass or two of port in the general way at the end of a dinner, but was not in the habit of drinking large quantities of it without food. He saw, of course, that Jean was not in the bedroom. He couldn't quite make out if there were any signs of her having been in the bedroom: it was never very tidy. The port had made him sleep very heavily of course. He felt a qualm of anxiety, but stifled it almost immediately and decided that action was the best antidote. He got up, ignoring his pounding head as best he could, and shuffled downstairs and into the kitchen.

Jean was flourishing a porridge pot with an air of exceptional well-being and radiance. She didn't look normal – not for the morning – he couldn't precisely think why. She regarded him with smiling and unmoved contempt. His heavy and morning-shadowed face was certainly not attractive. She congratulated herself on having avoided even half a night in bed with him.

'Do you want some porridge?' she asked blandly.

'Ugh!' said Everard 'I feel awful.'

'You look it.'

'I've got a bad headache. I'm going back to bed.'

Upstairs again, Everard was unable to take his mind off Jean. He was trying to analyse her attitude; it struck him as familiar, but not familiar in Jean. Gradually it dawned on him that she was, somehow, triumphant. He recognised it as something he felt himself after a successful night out with another woman. That was it, of course! It explained everything in her recent demeanour. She had a lover and she'd spent the night with him. His heart began to pound violently and he felt cold with shock. How dared she? He'd divorce her, he'd ... He started up, felt worse pounding in his head and heart, and lay back again with a groan and realised that he had absolutely no idea what to do. For one thing he had no proof; for another she could taunt him with his own infidelities and remind him of their supposedly 'open' marriage. Suppose she left him and took the boys – or didn't take them! Who'd cope with them? Did he want a woman like Alison Greer having a hand in their upbringing? He shuddered at the thought. Flicking mentally through the list of women he'd bedded in recent years he saw that there was not one of them he'd want near his children; he'd never considered them in that light; they were not wife-and-mother material.

Everard was dimly aware that a serial adulterer rarely, if ever, wants to divorce his wife. He wants a stable background against which to operate, to provide the extra excitement of secrecy and deception, initially, and triumph in the long run. His wife must be, eventually, impressed by his sexual exploits and simultaneously show by her suffering what a hold he still has on her.

Jean sent the boys upstairs to get dressed and telephoned Tim.

'Are you all right?' he asked anxiously. 'Did anything happen?'

'No. Nothing. I don't think Everard's realised. He just stumbled into the kitchen, said he had a headache and went back to bed, so that's all right.'

'I think I'd rather he'd gone off the deep end; then you'd have had to leave him or get rid of him. What do you want to do today? Take the boys out for a pub lunch in the country?'

'Do you really think it's a good idea?'

'Yes. I'll come and get you all in half an hour.'

So Jean and the boys were out and away before Everard realised they were going anywhere. He moped about for an hour or more until, oppressed by the emptiness of the house and his own unaccustomed and fruitless anxiety, he went into college for want of anything better to do.

His appearance at lunch was greeted with some severity by the butler. 'We wasn't expecting you in to lunch today, Sir!'

'Well, there's always far too much food anyway.'

'Not at weekends. It makes things very difficult, not knowing numbers at weekends.' The butler gave a sniff and walked off to voice his complaints to the kitchen staff. He'd never forgiven Everard for interfering over guest night dessert.

There were fewer than half a dozen college members at lunch. The Archangel was one of them and Peregrine Forsyth another.

'How are the averages in this week's Gazette, Peregrine?' asked Everard, with an attempt at good humour that sounded merely snide. Peregrine regarded him steadily with a look of objective assessment.

'Can't say you're looking too well today, Lucas,' he remarked. 'How old are you? Just about half your allotted span, I think you said. I must say you look a lot more than that.'

Arthur Middleton spoke up. 'You have to realise, Peregrine, that the Gazette presents a most unrepresentative selection of the population. The poor used to die off early because they didn't eat enough and the rich because they ate too much. Everard obviously belongs to the latter category and things haven't changed a lot there, not to mention that people with no scientific training have little or no understanding of food values. My fiancée does a lot of work with her clients, getting them to eat the right food, and the average life-expectation has increased dramatically overall in the past two or three decades ...'

'Oh Arthur! Stick to car parks, will you! Seen any good ones lately?' Roger effectively silenced Arthur Middleton and returned to his newspaper.

'I didn't know you lunched in college on Saturdays, Roger,' said Everard.

'Why should you? You're not here yourself usually. Is something the matter?'

'Certainly not' replied Everard, with an abruptness that immediately prompted Roger to think there probably was. Some tart must have let him down, thought Roger, sourly. Serve him right. He'd seen that Alison Greer emerging from the direction of Everard's rooms the previous week. Now there was a tart, as everybody knew. What a difference between her and a refined, cultured woman like Julia. He was worried about Julia. She'd looked so dreadful on Friday; no, not dreadful: she could never look dreadful – so distressed; so disproportionately distressed for the departure of a mere au pair. Indeed one of his reasons for coming into college that Saturday morning was to try and contact Julia. But there had been no answer to his several telephone calls. He finished his lunch quickly, decided against having coffee in the SCR and went to his room to try Julia's number again. This time she answered, and Roger found himself at a loss for what to say.

'Julia! I ... you didn't seem well yesterday. Are you all right?'

Julia's mind was so taken up with the trauma of events at home that she was unable to realise who was speaking.

'I'm sorry?' she said questioningly. 'Who …?'

'It's Roger.'

'Oh Roger!' Recent events had driven Roger completely from her consciousness. 'I didn't expect … I wouldn't have thought … It's very kind of you to ring.'

'I tried to ring several times this morning.'

'I do the shopping with the children on Saturday mornings, and I usually have to do two trips because I can't manage everything at once.'

'Doesn't your husband help you with it?'

'He's at school on Saturdays. I have to go on Saturday mornings to get some cash before the post office closes. Banks' opening hours make it very difficult for working women to get hold of cash.' Julia was aware of wanting to keep the conversation on a mundane level. Anything of a relationship between her and Roger seemed completely remote and unreal, even a little ridiculous. She had matters so much more serious to contend with.

'Are you coming in to college on Monday?' Roger continued. 'Have you managed to settle your domestic crisis?'

Julia felt a stab of horror at the idea that Roger knew about it and gasped, unable to reply.

Roger's suspicion that there was something serious the matter was all but confirmed, nevertheless he went on.

'You said your au pair had left suddenly.'

'Oh!' Julie sounded relieved. 'Yes, of course. I mean ... yes, I've found another help; somebody rather better in fact. Thank you. It's really kind of you to think about it.'

'I hope it means you'll have more time for yourself in future.' Roger also hoped that this would include more time for him – but deemed it not the right moment to say so.

'Thank you. Yes. I must go. The children haven't had lunch yet, we spent so long on the shopping. Yes. I'll see you on Monday.'

Julia put down the telephone pondering on how dazed and disorientated she felt. She would have expected a desire to fly to a sympathetic man like Roger, who cared about her; but instead of that she had ceased to think of him and felt completely distanced from him. She felt too ashamed of her betrayal by Jeremy to be able to confide in anybody.

CHAPTER THIRTY-SIX

After lunch Everard sat in his college room trying to work and finding it impossible. He was restless, impatient and unable to concentrate. He decided to ring Alison Greer, reached for the telephone and then paused, uncertain whether she would be in Camford or in the village and even more uncertain what to say if her husband should answer the telephone. He decided to try the village; more likely over a weekend. Alison's husband did answer.

'Oh! Hullo Henry – is Alison about?' There was silence at the other end as if Henry were waiting for an explanation. 'Er ...' Everard continued, 'I – er – just wondered if she'd seen Jean. She should be in but I can't get an answer from the house.'

'Really?' said Henry. 'That's strange. I've seen Jean myself, in fact, about half an hour ago. She went past in a car with a young chap and the three boys. They looked as if they were on their way home, judging from the direction.'

'Oh, that's ...' Everard found himself at a loss to say what it was and ended lamely with 'fine' – an expression he rarely used, considering it too banal and preferring to be witty and dismissive. 'Sorry to bother you. Tiresome of me to worry. Goodbye.'

Henry put down the receiver thinking it was not merely tiresome of Everard but remarkably untypical, and decided not to mention it to Alison unless she asked about the call. She did, almost immediately.

'Who was that?'

Henry considered it wasn't worth lying about it.

'Oh – that opinionated Everard Lucas from down the road; except that he can't be there at the moment. He wanted to know if you'd seen his wife because he can't get an answer on the house phone. I told him I'd seen her going in that direction half an hour ago.'

'Oh – did you?'

'Yes. In a car with the three boys and some young-looking chap.'

'Well well!' Alison was immediately interested and a little amused though not particularly pleased that Everard had been so indiscreet as to try and ring her at home on a Saturday afternoon. She was certainly not taken in by the expression of any solicitude for Jean, unless it should have to do with the 'young chap' in the car. Even Everard might be embarrassed about that. Alison's curiosity was aroused. She found herself wondering if Jean was getting her own back on Everard at last.

She called out to Henry: 'I'm just going down to the Lucases'. I want to see if Jean's all right.'

Henry was surprised. 'What on earth for? She looked perfectly all right when I saw her in the car. In fact, she's been looking a lot better altogether lately. I know your game: you want to find out who she's with.'

Alison laughed and departed without answering. She had no illusions about Everard and no fondness for him; the idea of taunting him with Jean's preference for a younger man appealed to her sense of humour. She reached their house and went to the back door – the only outside door that ever seemed to be used. Not bothering to knock she went in, calling out 'Hullo–o!'. Voices sounded from the sitting room, from which Jean emerged before Alison could go in.

'Alison!' Jean looked as if it was an effort to remember Alison's existence.

'Just came to see if you're all right. Everard rang us to ask if we knew where you were because he hadn't been able to get you on the phone. Henry told him he'd seen you in a car with the boys and some very young-looking chap.' Alison's tone implied that 'the chap' had looked much younger than Jean.

Jean was silent and remained standing with her

back to the sitting room door. She totally disbelieved in Alison's supposed solicitude for her and was fully aware of her curiosity. She had no wish to satisfy it by inviting her to meet Tim. Alison was equally determined not to go until she had met him. Each woman stood her ground, silent for several seconds; but Jean was in her own territory and Alison was not.

Finally, Jean spoke. 'Please thank Henry for his concern,' she said slowly, 'and tell him I'm perfectly all right. I'll come to the door with you. I really should lock it, anyway.'

So Alison had no option but to precede Jean to the back door, go out of it and hear it firmly locked behind her.

'Who was that?' asked Tim when Jean returned to the sitting room.

'Alison Greer.'

'Oh! "Alison Malice" – yes, you've told me about her. So have other people. She's rather notorious, isn't she?'

'I'm afraid so. In more ways than one.'

'What did she want?'

'She said she came to see if I was all right, and also that Everard had rung them because he couldn't get an answer here; not that I believe it. Her husband was in the garden when we passed their cottage. She must have come to see who I was with.'

'It'd be better if people knew, wouldn't it?'

'Yes, I think it probably would; but whatever happens I don't feel I can share a house with Everard any more – let alone a bed.'

'You can't think how glad I am to hear that.'

'We can't really talk now. I'll speak to Everard when he comes home. I need to think about it while the boys are still engrossed in television.' They went into the kitchen and kissed goodbye with a special and even solemn fondness.

After the frustration of his intention to speak to Alison and his unsatisfactory conversation with Henry, Everard felt particularly sour. He sensed that Henry had delivered the information about Jean in the young man's car with more than a hint of satisfaction. Delighted to think he's not the only cuckold in the woods, Everard sneered to himself. Hardly surprising in Henry's case, he went on thinking, everybody knows he's an old queen. Supposed to have been in love with Alison's brother and then took on Alison *faute de mieux*. Maybe that's how their marriage works: they both have their male lovers. Not that there's any evidence about him – but he must be getting a bit past-it anyway. Ugh! Everard had all the heterosexual man's aversion to 'poofters', despite his supposedly enlightened views. He shrugged off his thoughts about Henry and decided to go home as Jean must be there by now.

As he turned into the road leading to their

bumpy drive-in yard Everard saw a Beetle car emerge from it, turn sharp right and sputter away. He felt angry, more angry and disturbed than he would have thought possible, certainly more than his avowed philosophy of life would have considered reasonable. He was beyond even telling himself to be calm. He went inside and saw Jean sitting at the kitchen table looking thoughtfully into the distance. She didn't turn her head until he spoke.

'Where have you been?'

'Why do you ask?' Jean countered coolly.

'Because I want to know!'

'Why?'

'What do you mean, "why"?'

'It's so unlike you to show interest.'

'When Henry Greer tells me he's seen you in a Beetle car with some young man that I don't know about ...' Everard paused, unwilling to show that he cared, 'it ... it makes me feel a fool.'

Jean looked at him in disbelief, remembering the all too numerous occasions when his overtly sexual behaviour with other women, in the same room as herself, had made her look and feel deeply debased and diminished, aware as she had so often been of the many glances of slightly contemptuous pity bestowed on her by the other people present. The ridiculousness of his anger over so comparatively trivial an incident almost amused her. She looked at him dispassionately and smiled.

'Good,' she said.

'How very charming of you' was Everard's sarcastic response. 'So you want your husband to look a fool.'

'You make yourself look a fool so often that you ought to be used to it. The only difference is that now you're aware of it. But I'm really quite uninterested in how you feel and I no longer regard you as my husband. I want a divorce and I won't share a house with you a minute longer than I have to.'

Everard suddenly found that he needed to lean against the table. He stared at Jean for a full minute without speaking and then sat down so awkwardly on the nearest chair that he barely managed to stay on it. He hardly noticed this himself, but Jean gave a pitying smile which conveyed something of the superiority she was feeling in her own coolness and preparedness.

Finally Everard spoke. 'I don't believe it' he said.

'You soon will.'

'You're mad. You've got some young lover and you think you can go off with him … what about the boys?'

'They'll stay here with me and have as little disruption as possible. You can move into college.'

'You needn't think lover-boy's going to stick with you and three children.'

'Possibly. Possibly not. He has said he wants to, but I've come to realise that that's beside the point.'

'And what "point" would that be?' Everard sneered.

'The point is that I dislike and despise you to such an extent that I can no longer make any pretence that a marriage exists between us. I detest everything about you: the way you look, the way you smell – particularly the way you smell' – Jean made an expression of extreme distaste – 'the way you talk; every gesture you make jars on me. I dislike being in the same room with you. The thought of being in the same bed is totally repugnant. I think the sum of this might be considered "the total and irrevocable breakdown of a marriage", don't you?'

Everard was silent. He felt utterly numb, though whether from hurt, shock or anger he couldn't have said. Ultimately his pride came to the surface; he was determined not to show Jean how greatly he was affected, even though he was unable to believe that her decision was final. She'll change her mind, he thought, especially when lover-boy dumps her and she's left on her own.

'I'll ring college and ask for a room' he said aloud, ' – a bedroom – but that won't be a problem. I'll go and pack.'

'Good' said Jean again. 'And when you're ready I'll drive you in, because I'll need the car out here, of course, and you can't want one in college.'

Jean went back into the sitting room to be with the boys, greatly relieved that things had, as she thought, been settled so quietly and immediately. Everard went upstairs and began picking up his clothes from whatever surface they had previously alighted on and bundled them into a suitcase, still too numb to be fully aware of what he was doing.

CHAPTER THIRTY-SEVEN

On Sunday there was little opposition from Jeremy when Julia told him she wanted to go to mass on her own and would he please see to the children. Apart from his feeling that it would be out of place to refuse so reasonable a request, he had some hope that Mrs Thomas would come down and give a hand as she had so far shown herself almost unable to stop working. She was never happier than when scurrying about the house, a cigarette in her mouth when it was not occupied by a boiled sweet, cleaning or polishing something, and amusing the children with songs or rhymes or anecdotes about her own offspring. The children regarded her with fascinated wonder, and even Jeremy marvelled at how she seemed to manage both to smoke and to talk all the time. Jeremy even offered Julia the car but she said she preferred to walk. The day was crisp with the brittle brightness of winter, perfect she considered for a brisk walk and a lot of thought.

She reached the church in relative 'calm of mind', though not, she thought with a hint of a smile, 'all passion spent'. That would take a great deal more time, and even the calm was probably transient. Just inside the gateway Pauline Dickinson was bent over her bicycle, locking it. Julia went up to her.

'Pauline – I'm so glad to see you. I want to talk to you, to ask you, how do I go about taking instruction?'

'Ah!' responded Pauline, with a smile of genuine pleasure. 'Very wise and wonderful. The Jesuits are very good at instruction. Who do you want to do it?'

'I don't know any of them. Who do you have?'

'Fr Smiley.'

Julia looked doubtful. 'Oh dear. My courage is beginning to ooze out at my fingers' ends.'

'As in *The Rivals*!' Pauline picked up the allusion immediately. 'But nobody's going to ask you to fight a duel, my dear!'

'I feel just about as nervous.'

'Yes, I know. One does. I do understand. We Prots in England have had centuries of conditioning to make us feel that anything about Catholicism is strange and alien, not to say dangerous. I suppose you were brought up on "to hell with the Pope", and "never trust a Catholic" as I was.'

'The second certainly. But don't let me keep you

standing in the cold. Can I see you after mass?'

'Of course. Come and have a drink in the bar.'

'The bar?'

'Yes, round the corner. All self-respecting Catholic churches have a bar. See you there.'

Julia went inside and sat by the aisle so that she would have a good view of what was going on in the mass and try to follow it in the missal. She knew Latin fairly well, but the medieval pronunciation was different from the classical style she was used to, and a good deal of it was said too quickly and too quietly to follow without a text. Her mind was fully occupied with the effort to keep up and find the place in the missal, and even during the sermon she thought more about the possibility of instruction with Fr Smiley than anything else. She tried to identify him from among the company in the sanctuary, but gave up as she could barely distinguish which were priests and which were not.

After mass she found the bar with little trouble as a good proportion of the congregation were headed there. Pauline came in almost immediately. 'What would you like? Gin and tonic?'

'Heavens!' said Julia. 'This is an unexpected benefit. Yes please.'

They took their drinks to a small, round, formica-topped table.

'Which is Fr Smiley?' asked Julia.

'He hasn't come in yet. I'll introduce you when he

does.'

'I think perhaps I'd rather you didn't, well, at least didn't say anything about taking instruction. I'd like to have a look at him first ... and think about it. I must say his name's rather off-putting; it gives me this immediate picture of the stock-comic C of E vicar with wringing hands and a rush of teeth to the mouth.'

Pauline laughed. 'Well, he's not a bit like that, and rumour has it that his family name was originally Smellie and that his grandfather, whose unthinking parents had saddled him additionally with the initials P.O., got so sick of the taunts and gibes and jokes this occasioned, that he juggled with the sounds and letters of his surname and eventually decided on "Smiley". I suppose it's an improvement, but a bit much to live up to. Any name that has a meaning must be something of a cross to bear.'

Fr Smiley came in, came over to Pauline, gave her a quick pat on the shoulder, said a few brief words and passed on to another group. Julia saw him only long enough to observe that his smile was quick and real and that he spoke with a refreshingly genuine Birmingham accent.

'Well?' Pauline asked when he'd moved away.

'He seems awfully normal. None of that "Anglican intonement", like most of the vicars I've met.'

'Intonement?'

'My made-up word. I mean they talk the way they

intone parts of the service and it sounds really unnatural. We had a chaplain at school who intoned any information he gave in classes, such as: "There are TWO great EVils in the world: COMmunism and ROman CathOLicism; and the GREATER of these two evils is ...,"' Pauline joined in and they said together, 'R-o-o-o-man Catholicism' and they both burst out laughing. They drew a few glances from nearby tables, but only such as were accompanied by tolerant smiles, as everybody else seemed to be enjoying conversations as much as they were.

'There's quite a party atmosphere in here,' Julia observed. 'It reminds me of Brittany, where all those marvellous older women in starched lace headdresses call out "Bonne Dimanche" as you go past. It feels like Christmas.'

'Oh, we stopped enjoying Sundays here in Cromwell's time, and the Victorians didn't do a lot to improve things, though they did put some spirit back into Christmas.'

'I must go,' Julia said, looking at her watch.

'Heavens! So must I – I'm going out to lunch. See you in college.'

Pauline departed in haste and Julia was putting back the empty glasses when a hand touched her arm. 'Julia! I didn't know you were a Catholic!'

Julia turned to recognise a fellow undergraduate from her college.

'Mary! I didn't know you were, either – I suppose

I thought very little about such things in those days. But I'm not actually, I'm just interested – I might take instruction, if I can summon up the courage.'

'Why should it take courage? You don't have to commit yourself, you know. But look – I haven't seen you for ages, there's a pre-dinner drinks thing in college tonight, why don't you come? I'm teaching there and I've got a room. Can you come just after six?'

Julia had drunk just enough gin to feel euphoric, if not exactly reckless. Besides, meeting a college acquaintance transported her back to days of youth and freedom. 'All right. Thank you. I'd love to.'

That must have been a very long service' said Jeremy when Julia finally arrived home.

'Well it was quite; but it's mainly that I had a drink in the bar afterwards. Apparently it's usual.'

'That seems like a good idea! What did you drink?'

'Gin.'

'I never drink gin' said Jeremy righteously.

'No. You go in for quantity rather than quality.'

'Well I don't know about that —' Jeremy was about to expostulate at length, but Julia cut in.

'Never mind that now. It's done me good; and tonight I am going to my own college with a girl I haven't seen for years. She's teaching there now, apparently. Just for drinks at about six. You can cope can't you? I said I'd go.'

Jeremy was not best pleased, but was too grateful for Julia's good humour and too guilt-ridden to refuse.

The party at Julia's college was highly satisfactory; she was asked frequently about her apparently prestigious position in a men's college and was astonished at the status she seemed to have acquired from it. Perhaps it was even worth having to work with somebody like Everard, she thought. She drank a rather vast quantity of sherry – the only thing on offer – and emerged at something after 8 o'clock (as most of the company seemed not to be going on to dinner) feeling light-headed and light-hearted. A short way down the road she could see the lights of the priests' house next to the church. Almost without her conscious volition she felt her feet carrying her towards it. She walked faster and faster, turned into the gateway, almost ran up the steps, took a deep breath and pressed the bell. It was answered by Fr Smiley himself.

'Hullo!' he said, as if her appearance there was perfectly normal. 'Didn't I see you at the bar with Pauline this morning?'

'Yes,' she replied breathlessly, her heart thumping 'I wanted to see you. I want to take instruction – to – to be a Catholic.'

CHAPTER THIRTY-EIGHT

On Monday morning Julia couldn't wait to go and see Pauline in the library so she went there before going to her own room,

'I had to come and tell you, Pauline, I've done it. I've seen Fr Smiley. I've started!'

Pauline was very genuinely delighted. 'I'm so happy for you. I know just how you feel. Bless you. It's early days, but you won't fail to persevere and if it means half as much to you as it does to me you'll find it's the best thing you do in all your life.'

'Thank you. I'm lucky to have you to understand and I'm grateful.'

'I know you're dashing to a tutorial now, but come back on your way to lunch; I've got some news that might interest you – albeit of a very different kind.'

Julia was almost too elated to be inquisitive about Pauline's news, though she did find herself flicking over possibilities as to its content during the less absorbing paragraphs of her pupils' essays. It was not easy to concentrate and she felt her mind jerked back from another realm when she heard the word 'portentous' read in a sentence where it clearly didn't belong. She made the pupil repeat it.

'You're talking about the person's character, aren't you?'

'Yes, of course.' The pupil was a little piqued at her interruption.

'Don't you think "pretentious" would be better – or even "pompous"?'

'Same thing' said the pupil.

He was a pupil over whom Julia often sighed and about whom Everard was particularly snide. Julia reached for the dictionary, pointed out the difference in meaning and wished she could give Pauline's hint of special news as an example of 'portentous'. The tutorial was not a short one as so many corrections were necessary; not, as with brighter undergraduates, because there was so much of interest to discuss. Julia became increasingly impatient and hoped Pauline would wait for her. It was ten past one when she finally went into the library.

'I'm sorry, Pauline. Ghastly pupil for the last tutorial. Let's go out to lunch. I went for drinks in my own college last night and it made me realise how much I've been missing female companionship.'

'That might be a very good idea. There's a little French place round the corner. Very reasonable – let's go there.'

Over the "very reasonable" lunch, and a bottle of wine which they both felt they needed – or certainly wanted, as it was something of a celebration, Julia elaborated enthusiastically on her encounter with Fr Smiley and then asked to hear Pauline's 'portentous' news.

'It's about your colleague Everard Lucas.'

'Oh dear! I hope it's not what I can guess.'

'It might well be, at least in part. He's moved into college.'

'To live?'

'Yes. His wife's kicked him out.'

'I can't imagine anybody blaming her, but I would have thought he'd have moved in with whoever it is.'

'Some other woman, you mean.'

'Yes. Isn't that why his wife's made him leave?'

'Well, according to the scouts, who know everything, of course – not that any of the dons would have told me even if they knew – it's because his wife's got another man and wants him to move in with her.'

'No! She doesn't look the type.'

'Oh have you met her?'

'Yes. At my first college "ladies' night" dinner. I thought she had that mousy downtrodden look

– though she did become increasingly animated talking to a young man most of the evening. I wonder ... How interesting! He was our lodger at the time and in fact I brought him in to dinner. I never thought anything of it at the time. They both come from the same part of the world, from the north, and I was pleased Tim had found somebody comfortable to talk to; pleased that she had too. Her husband had brought a ravishing blonde graduate pupil in, and it was potentially embarrassing for his wife and for everybody else in consequence. Of course it may not be Tim now. How on earth do the scouts find out about those things?'

'Well, apparently somebody's sister's mother-in-law rents out their erstwhile granny-flat to him – to the young man, I mean, and she's been reporting on the "goings on" for some time.'

'That's it! It must be Tim. That's where he went to from us. I hope Everard doesn't remember I'm the one who brought him in to dinner; that's if he cares, of course. And anyway it serves him right. But we shouldn't be talking like this, should we, as incipient Catholics.'

'Do you really mean "incipient"?'

'No – it's a joke – but honestly, Pauline, shouldn't we be saying that it's all very reprehensible and Jean should stay with her horrible husband till death does them part, whatever the misery of the situation?'

'Oh no. Theirs was only a registry office wedding. Everard's an avowed atheist, as I'm sure you know. It's only the sacrament of marriage that can't be dissolved, not the bond of marriage: that's legal and civil like other bonds. Anyway, I never think we should impose our ideas on people who are not Catholics and haven't the benefit of the sacraments to keep them going.'

'Oh good! I'm so glad I can approve of Jean and Tim. But, you know, if it had been the other way round and Everard had wanted another woman to move in with him, I would have been utterly disgusted.'

'Well, his wife hasn't a college to move into.'

'How sensible you are. But one does almost always sympathise with the wife in these cases.'

'It's generally easier for men to find consolation.'

'That's one problem about being a Catholic.' Julia said thoughtfully. 'One can't divorce and remarry.'

'Well, do you want to?'

A shadow passed over Julia's face and Pauline registered the fact and stored in her mind a question about Julia's marriage.

'No. I don't. Both my parents and Jeremy's are divorced and we know at first hand the effects on the children.'

'Then you admit the Church is right about it.'

'I suppose I do. Paradoxically I couldn't wish that

somebody like Jean Lucas should be prevented from leaving a serial adulterer like Everard and finding happiness with somebody else, even if they had had a sacramental marriage.'

'It's one of many problems we old maids don't have to face,' Pauline smiled.

'You might find you want to marry somebody who's been divorced.'

'I very much doubt it: divorced men are even more suspect than bachelors of my age. Anyway, you can be sure that Everard Lucas is no temptation!'

They both laughed until Pauline had to have some more wine to stop her choking.

As she stepped over the wood under the wicket in the great door leading into the college lodge, with Pauline immediately behind her, Julia was aware of Roger hovering in a shadowy corner.

He came up to her. 'You were not at lunch.'

'No. Pauline and I have been to a restaurant together. I find myself pining for female company.'

Roger looked at Pauline as if not quite sure who she was. Pauline raised her eyebrows, pursed her lips as she looked in Julia's direction and gave a resigned shrug, as if to indicate: "you can see how the dons treat me" and made off towards the library. Roger walked round to the cobbled quad with Julia.

'Are you avoiding me?' he said.

'No!' Julia was surprised.

'I know there's something the matter.'

Julia realised that nothing but an admission of some sort would satisfy Roger's curiosity or relieve his anxiety. She had to admit to herself that the latter was a fairer explanation of his insistence.

'It's just that I've started taking instruction to become a Catholic.'

'What's made you do that?'

'I went to a drinks party at my own college one evening and when I left there I had enough Dutch courage to go and ring the doorbell of the presbytery nearby.'

'Why did you need courage – Dutch or otherwise?'

'It's a very big step; and besides, Protestants in this country are brought up to be fearful of Catholics and Catholic institutions. I once went to lunch with a Catholic family when I was a child and I remember being surprised they didn't speak in Latin all the time. I thought they probably did when I wasn't there!'

'I can't believe it was only a few drinks that decided you.'

'I had been thinking about it for a long time.'

'I'd like to hear about it. Please. Let's go out to dinner again. You've said you have a better help than before and more time to yourself.'

'Thank you. I'll see. Yes. Some time. Oh – I'll be late for my tutorial.'

'Well if you will teach in the afternoons ...'

Julia ran up the stairs to her room and, grateful though she was for Roger's concern, she closed her door and sank into her armchair with a relieved feeling of escape.

CHAPTER THIRTY-NINE

The once-a-term wives' lunch, organised by Barbara Tomlinson, was taking place in Emmaeus College. Mary Crawford, Quentin's wife, was sitting next to Barbara and opposite Shona Otis. 'I don't suppose Jean Lucas is coming. Did you even tell her about it?' she remarked.

'Yes, why not?' responded Barbara. 'The date was fixed ages ago and only the reminder needed to go out. It's not my business whether her husband's living in the same house with her or not.'

'Ooooh! Isn't he?' Shona Otis was all ears and interest.

'Yes, didn't you know?' Mary Crawford implied that everybody else did. 'He's living in college.'

'Why?' said Shona.

'Because his wife's finally had the good sense to get rid of him' Barbara replied succinctly. 'Personally, I'm very glad to hear it. He treated her abominably.'

'Most men treat their wives abominably' said Mary Crawford. looking at Shona pointedly. 'You should know.'

Shona stared at Mary open-mouthed, only half understanding the import of her remark and quite unable to respond to it.

'Now, now Mary!' Barbara frowned disapprovingly. 'Eyes on your own plate, you know!'

Mary Crawford merely gave a dismissive shrug and turned to her neighbour, who happened to be the wife of the Archangel, about whose large, loud mistress everybody knew.

'Don't you agree. Muriel?' Mary said.

Muriel gave her a smile of the utmost sweetness. 'Agree? I'm sorry I wasn't listening.'

Shona Otis found her voice. 'Perhaps Muriel doesn't know either,' she said, hoping Muriel didn't.

'Know what?' replied Muriel, in a tone that suggested patience rather than curiosity.

Shona hastened to explain while Mary Crawford spoke, in an aside, to Barbara. 'Muriel's name should be Patience!'

Barbara couldn't help being amused. 'On a monument, you mean.'

'Yes. Smiling at grief.'

'You never know. She may have other distractions to allay the grief and evoke the smile.'

'I really can't believe that!'

'Who would have thought it of Jean Lucas?'

Shona caught the last sentence. 'Jean Lucas?' she gasped. 'Is she the one who ...?'

'Who's found somebody else.' Mary Crawford completed for her.

'Yes. Apparently. That's the reason for Everard's move into college.'

'Ooooh! I wonder what happened before he moved.'

'That we shall probably never know – if you mean immediately before,' said Mary. 'But it must have been sudden because the butler was annoyed that he hadn't given any previous notice about coming in to meals over the weekend.'

'Everard wouldn't have given previous notice anyway.' Barbara had often heard Roger fulminating about Everard's lack of consideration for colleagues and college servants. 'He's always thought the world revolved round him.'

At home that evening Shona greeted Hector with a slightly aggrieved query as to why he hadn't told her about Everard.

'Everybody else seemed to know about it' she said plaintively, 'I felt really stupid being the only one who hadn't heard.'

'Oh, I didn't consider it particularly intewesting,' Hector responded. 'I weally didn't think about it.'

'Well you might have thought about how I'd

feel at the wives' lunch – not knowing.' Shona sounded unusually aggrieved.

'It's not good for you to get upset about things in your condition. You might have found it distwessing.'

'It's only distressing that everybody will think you don't talk to me.'

'Well, I'm talking to you now. But weally, there's nothing to say; Everard hasn't confided in anybody.' Hector didn't need to indulge in much introspection to realise that his unwillingness to mention the matter to Shona was largely due to his discomfort in realising that Everard – of all people – could be got out of his own home by a wife as unassertive as Jean had always seemed to be, and that she'd found herself a lover. Not that he could remotely imagine Shona doing anything similar; but Everard had definitely let the male side down by allowing his wife to turn the tables on him. The fewer women who knew about it the better.

The children were still being bathed by Mrs Thomas, to the accompaniment of songs and splashes and noises of delight, when Jeremy came home. Julia decided not to remark on his earliness. They were treating each other warily, unwilling to show any feeling, desperate to avoid the one subject they both felt about most strongly. Jeremy immediately resorted to his usual panacea for all ills and opened a bottle of wine.

'Would you like a glass of wine?' he asked Julia, politely.

She was almost startled. Normally he merely poured himself one and took it, and the bottle, to wherever he was going in the house.

'Oh!' she said. 'Yes, thank you.'

They talked inconsequentially while Julia went on preparing the supper, and when they were finally eating it Jeremy said

'I hear your Everard Lucas has left the family home and moved into your College.'

It was a subject Julia had not intended to mention, being a little too near to their own situation for comfort.

'However did you know?' she asked.

'Well, one of their boys is at St George's, remember.'

'No, I'm afraid I didn't remember.'

'We always hear about things like that, in case it affects the children. But surely you know something about it.'

Julia took another sip of wine. 'Well not much,' she murmured unwillingly. 'I've only just heard.'

'It's only just happened, but even so why are you being so cagey about it?'

Julia decided that if he were too insensitive to

see why, her reticence would make the strain between them worse rather than better.

'He's always treated his wife very badly – and now she's found somebody else, and actually I think the somebody else is Tim!'

'Tim?'

'Yes. "Our" Tim. The Tim who used to live here.'

'Can't be. He's too young.'

'Not much. I introduced them when I took him in to dinner on that first guest night, and they certainly seemed to get on very well.'

'That's awful!'

'Is it?' Julia looked squarely at Jeremy and decided he was being hypocritical as well as insensitive. 'I don't blame her at all. Tim's kind, considerate and selfless, and very good with children. I think it's a burden for him but I really hope they'll be happy and it serves Everard more than right.' And she got up from the table and left Jeremy to ponder on her words.

In the early hours of the morning Julia woke up to hear Jeremy crying softly. In spite of everything, her immediate reaction was to comfort him.

'Jeremy! what's the matter?' Jeremy turned over and put his arm round her.

'You won't do that, will you?'

'Do what?'

'Take up with somebody else and leave me – like my mother did.'

'Would you mind so much?'

'Of course I would. I need you. Please.' Jeremy sobbed.

'I don't suppose I will,' said Julia slowly. 'I'm a Catholic.'

'No you're not!'

'I think I always have been.' She disengaged herself gently from Jeremy's arms, gave him a brief kiss and said 'We can't talk about it now. Go back to sleep.'

CHAPTER FORTY

The telephone jangled in Everard's room as he finished reading a pupil's essay and put a large, uncompromising gamma on it. His immediate reaction was to be irritable but in case it was somebody interesting he drawled a low-pitched 'Hulloooo'.

'Hulloooo yourself,' the answering female voice mimicked him. 'So you're living in college now.' It was Alison Greer.

'How did you know?'

'Everybody knows.'

'How very flattering!'

Alison gave a low laugh 'That's not exactly how I'd describe it.'

'Really? You're surely one of the first to agree that if there's anything worse than being talked about it's not being talked about.'

Alison was not so completely pleased with the reply as to pursue that aspect of the subject. 'Have you got a new set of rooms?'

'No, just a guest bedroom at the moment.'

'Well that must be more comfortable than your

sofa or your floor!'

'It's only a single bed. When are you coming to try it out?'

'I could – er – try coming this morning.'

'What? When? I'm teaching.'

'Cancel it. Where's the room?'

'In the new building. Staircase X, 6. Second from the top. But ...'

'But nothing. I'll be there at eleven.'

'The scout may be cleaning it.'

'How exciting. Eleven.'

Alison put down the receiver leaving Everard to wonder whether he felt more excited than exasperated or vice versa. He was not given to cancelling tutorials: it went against the grain. Irritatingly casual as he was to colleagues and domestic staff, he was a conscientious, if acerbic, tutor. His bedroom was a long way from his teaching room, it would look strange for him to be going to it at that hour of the morning. The situation was getting out of control, out of his control, anyway. Alison was taking over what he considered to be his role; in fact he was aware that he had not infrequently spoken to a woman in just the way Alison had spoken to him, and he was not at all sure that he appreciated being on the other end. He considered the possibility of simply not being in his bedroom at eleven o'clock. Then presumably Alison would come to his teaching room. But of course he'd be teaching, so that would be that. It would also, pretty inevitably, be the end of the relationship with Alison, and she was undeniably an excitingly desirable woman.

He was cursing his indecision when the telephone rang again. He half hoped it was Alison, calling off their assignation. But it was not. It was his eleven o'clock pupil saying that he was ill and couldn't come to the tutorial. Everard put down the telephone feeling no less indecisive. He still had more than one option open: he could go to his bedroom – without the hassle of cancelling his tutorial; he could stay in his teaching-room and see whether Alison would come and find him, or he could go out and thus be totally unavailable. He rejected the first option as being too subservient to Alison's whims and the last one as too redolent of being driven out of his own room; the middle way of simply staying in his teaching-room gave Alison the option of finding him, conveyed the intended message that he was the boss, and perhaps most usefully required no action at all on his part.

Having no eleven o'clock tutorial that morning, Julia set off from her staircase to cross the two quads to the library and have coffee with Pauline. She was surprised to see Alison Greer emerging from the neighbouring staircase. It was on the tip of her tongue to ask the obvious "what-are-you-doing-here" question, but Julia decided against it, feeling that she didn't particularly want to know the answer. It would have been redundant anyway as Alison, with a frown and no preliminary greeting immediately addressed her.

'Have you seen Everard?'

So that's it! Julia thought and aloud answered, 'No. Not this morning. I imagine he's teaching.'

'Oh he is, is he?' Alison replied more as a statement than a question and strode off in the direction of Everard's tower.

Julia went into the little cubbyhole just inside the entrance to the library, in which Pauline had a desk, a kettle and little else.

'Sit down – you see I've squeezed in an extra chair. Coffee's ready. Can't have biscuits in Lent, of course.'

'Can't you? Why?'

'You'll have to learn to fast in Lent if you're going to take this great step. Nothing between meals – no food, that is – and only one meal and two collations at that!'

'What's a collation?'

'About as much as you can get on one plate – once.'

'I hope it's a big plate.'

'Oh, certainly. Even so I lose pounds.'

'I'm sure that's an added incentive.'

'Undoubtedly. Of course you can get a dispensation if you're pregnant – or a heavy labourer.'

'Well I'm neither of those at the moment – and I can easily do without a biscuit.'

'Lucky you. I find it extremely difficult' Pauline sighed. She was a large, heavily-built woman and Julia decided to change the subject rather than go on talking about food and weight.

'Do you know Alison Greer?' she asked. 'Her husband's Dean of St Joshua's.'

'I know who you mean' said Pauline with interest. 'It was quite a nine days' wonder when they got married – well, even when the engagement was announced. The Camford Times sported a picture of Henry Greer with a spanking new white sports car and said it was all because he was marrying "undergraduate Alison ..." whatever her name was. He must be twenty years older than she is.'

'That's the one. I've just seen her in the back quad, coming out of the staircase next to mine. She asked me if I'd seen Everard.'

'Well, well. Isn't that interesting! Is that the staircase where Everard's bedroom is, now that he's moved into college?'

'I don't know' replied Julia. 'I've never thought about it.'

'Well somebody else seems to have!'

They both burst out laughing.

Everard had spent an unpleasant half hour or more unable to concentrate on anything other than the possibility of Alison's arriving at his room. He had never agonised over anything similar before and he found it a very trying experience. At a quarter past eleven he decided he could stand it no longer and would put plan three into action and go out. He had almost reached the door when he heard footsteps on the resounding wooden stairs and almost immediately the door was flung open with no preliminary knock and there was Alison. Everard decided to be very cool and collected, especially as Alison looked anything but. 'I thought you might find your way here,' he said.

'You're not teaching!'

'No. My pupil's ill and cancelled his tutorial.'

'Oh yes?' Alison clearly didn't believe him.

'Yes, actually. I didn't cancel it myself.'

'Why not?'

'I don't think I like being told what to do.'

'Which is why you were not in your bedroom.'

'Possibly.'

'What do you mean "possibly"?'

'There could be other reasons.'

'Such as?'

'I leave them to your wit to devise.'

Alison opened her mouth to protest as Everard grasped her by the shoulders, bending her towards him, and kissed her fiercely, inserting his tongue deep into her mouth. She melted into him with a feline movement, rubbed herself against him, felt his erection, swayed towards the sofa, pushed him away a little as if to walk to it – and instead made a bolt for the door, opened it, – and sped clattering down the wooden stairs with a ghost of a laugh echoing behind her.

Emerging from Pauline's cubbyhole Julia crossed the quad to deliver a letter to the porter's lodge and mused on how the company of another woman could be so much more cheering than that of most men. She was so taken up with this mental observation that she failed to notice Everard coming out of his staircase until they had almost collided. She saw that he was looking particularly black and attributed it to his domestic situation – or lack of it. She would gladly have hurried on but felt it imperative to say something.

'Oh – hullo,' she said, 'did Alison find you?' Everard looked completely taken aback.

'Alison?' he said.

'Yes. Alison Greer. She was looking for you in the

back quad.'

'Really? Oh – of course; I'd forgotten she knows you.'

'We were in the same college at the same time'.

Everard gave Julia an up-and-down glance. 'You can hardly have anything else in common.'

'Very probably not. But you asked me something about her at the dinner after the interview – whether I thought I would agree with her assessment of me.'

'And did you?' Everard now remembered the incident with perfect clarity, but somehow the Julia he had got to know as a colleague now seemed hardly the same person as the one he'd interviewed.

'Of course not. You then commented on her malicious sense of humour.'

Everard's face darkened menacingly. 'Did I indeed?'

Julia couldn't resist the jibe she had been too cautious to utter at the time. 'I remember hoping the things she had said about you were as untrue as the things she'd doubtless said about me.'

Julia went back to her room feeling both elated and guilty: elated because she had exorcised a rankling anger of which she'd been conscious ever since the incident, and guilty because she had quite deliberately been snide to Everard who was hardly in the happiest of situations. She might have felt more elated and less guilty had she known of Everard's most recent encounter with Alison.

Everard went back to his room in a state of unsatisfied lust and obsessive animosity which was only partially palliated by sadistic visions of what he'd do to Alison next time he had her in his room.

CHAPTER FORTY-ONE

After little more than a week of coming home early and sober every evening Jeremy was beginning to show signs of restlessness. He would come back for supper and then go out again, full of urgent things to be done at school and how hard he had to work. Then he would come back too late for supper, increasingly late. Julia herself was doing so much teaching during the day, and spending so much time with the children in the late afternoons that her evenings were spent perforce in preparation and marking and she was not always sorry to have them to herself.

Nevertheless, when Jeremy returned at two o'clock one morning and crept into bed very quietly and not very drunkenly, Julia found herself unable to go back to sleep and beset by anxieties and suspicions. At half past two she could stand it no longer. She stealthily eased her way out of bed and crept downstairs. Having got so far she was at a loss what to do next. She'd often been sleepless while pregnant, and generally dealt with it by making a hot milk drink spiced with cinnamon and nutmeg and a dash of brandy if she could find any; but now she felt she must stay awake, must search for something, some explanation of Jeremy's behaviour. His waxed jacket was hanging over the end of the bannisters. She looked in the pockets and found a very dirty handkerchief and a crumpled receipt for a restaurant dinner. A very expensive one, Julia thought grimly, but that was nothing new. In another pocket was a bunch of keys, including the car key. She put her bare feet into gumboots, the only footwear in the hall, and went out to the car, which was standing on the so-called driveway in front of the house, taking up all the space not devoted to the narrow tiled path leading to the front door.

She sat in the passenger's seat, quietly pulled the door to and switched the light on, then knelt on the seat to look into the back of the car. There was an empty wine-bottle on the floor. She was alarmed. Surely Jeremy wasn't so far gone that he had to drink even in the car! She turned to the front again and opened the glove box. In it were two wine glasses. She took them out. One was marked with a clear impression of red lips. She put them on the driver's seat and felt further into the glove box. She brought out a packet – a Durex packet – torn open. She felt so sick and her heart pounded to such an extent that she couldn't move for more than a minute. So. What she had fondly thought was a one-off, for which Jeremy was deeply sorry and fully contrite, was a full-blown, ongoing affair. She began to shiver, uncontrollably and with increasing violence until her teeth were chattering and her whole body in a continuing spasm of trembling. It was at least another five minutes before she could summon the resolution or the steadiness to get out of the car. With her she took the glasses and the torn packet. She didn't lock the car. It didn't seem to matter. Inside she went up to her bedroom, where Jeremy lay asleep, and put the incriminating items on his bedside table. Then she took her pillow and went downstairs again to lie on the sitting room sofa under a couple of coats.

When the electric alarm-clock, which was on Julia's side, went off and nobody stopped its penetrating buzz, Jeremy gradually woke up and wondered, somewhat angrily, why the horrible noise was going on and on. Finally he rolled over to Julia's side and pressed the clock's stop-button so heavy-handedly that it fell to the floor with a thump.

'Sod it!' he said, picked up the clock and got out of that side of the bed. He went to the bathroom, surprised to find it open and unoccupied by Julia. He went down to the kitchen and put the kettle on, went into the dining room, then the sitting room and was astonished to see Julia asleep on the sofa. He would have sworn that she'd been in the bed when he'd got into it himself. He looked more closely and saw that one of the coats she'd used as a covering had slipped most of its material on to the floor. He picked it up and was putting it over her when she woke. She seized the coat from him and clutched it to herself protectively and shrank away from him.

'What on earth's the matter?' he asked.

'How can you ask?' Julia recoiled from him even further.

'Because I don't know.'

'Didn't you see anything on your bedside table?'

'No.' Jeremy seemed genuinely puzzled.

'Then you'd better go and see now.'

Jeremy gave her an uncertain look and decided to do as she said.

She closed her eyes and waited for him to come back, feeling unable to move and breathing as if every breath was a conscious effort. Jeremy returned to the sitting room, looking shamefaced and avoiding Julia's eyes.

'It wasn't me,' he said. 'I lent the car to Spatters.'

'And who might "Spatters" be?'

'You know – Spatters Walsh – History – Lower X.'

'You shouldn't try to lie, Jeremy. You're not intelligent enough to do it properly and I find it insulting.'

'I did lend it to Spatters.'

'Until two o'clock in the morning?'

'He was late back.'

'And what did you do in the meantime?'

'Watched a match in the Common Room.'

'You can't expect me to believe that.'

Jeremy closed his mouth tightly, set his face into a cast of stubbornness and left the room.

Julia decided she had to speak to him again before the children got up so she put on one of the coats and went into the kitchen where Jeremy was pouring a lot of milk into two mugs of tea.

'You must be honest with me,' she said. 'You're still seeing that girl aren't you? You must tell me the truth.'

Jeremy's face set harder and his silence was unbroken.

'Will you answer me!' Julia shouted.

Jeremy picked up his mug of tea and began to walk out of the kitchen.

'Jeremy!!' Still no response. Enraged, Julia picked up the wet dishcloth and hurled it at him, hitting him on the side of the head. He turned swiftly and threw his mug of tea at her. It hit her in the face, spilled most of its lukewarm contents over her and crashed into pieces on the floor. Then he left the kitchen as if nothing had happened. Julia bent to pick up the broken crockery but instead went sprawling with her head against the leg of the kitchen table. Feeling utterly defeated she remained there, sobbing bitterly. She hadn't moved when, minutes later, Mrs Thomas came into the room.

'Coo-er! Whatever's 'appened 'ere?' was her immediate reaction.

Julia made an effort to recover. 'I don't know. An accident – I slipped on the floor – a mug of tea.'

'Hmmm. Yes.' Mrs Thomas was not slow to take in the situation.

'Looks as if you got it full in the face! Never you mind, luv, sit down proper on a chair and I'll make you another cuppa – with lots of sugar in it.' She raised Julia from the floor and eased her on to a chair as if she were as light as a child. Julia put her head on her hand and let her tears dribble on to the table. Not many moments later Mrs Thomas put a cup of very sweet, very milky tea in front of her.

'Now, you just drink that down and don't worry. I'll get the children up!'

Julia's gratitude for such tact and kindness overflowed into more tears, but she drank the sugary tea and began to feel a little better. Before she'd finished it she heard Jeremy run down the stairs and leave the house, at which she was sufficiently heartened to go up and wash and dress herself. She was somewhat aghast to see in the mirror that the right side of her face was very red and her upper lip was swollen and beginning to show a hint of blue. She was not given to using a lot of makeup, but put on as much cream and powder as she could apply and went down to deal with the children, already dressed, breakfasted and entertained by Mrs Thomas.

'You're a marvel,' Julia told her, 'in more ways than one.'

Julia was actually early in college; she couldn't imagine how, the morning seemed to have gone on for hours and hours already. As she was collecting the contents of her pigeonhole from the porter, Pauline eased her solid form through the wicket.

'Hullo!' she said brightly. But the brightness faded when she saw Julia's face. 'Are you all right?' she asked anxiously.

The porter froze to listen and made no movement to close the lodge window.

'Oh yes,' said Julia, managing a very slight smile, 'it's nothing. Just more thorns than honey.'

CHAPTER FORTY-TWO

Before going to lunch Julia anxiously examined her face in the mirror and wondered whether it would pass muster. She was ready with her story of slipping on the kitchen floor and banging her face on the table if anybody should make a comment. She needed to feel as normal as possible. She couldn't hide from her pupils; she didn't want to hide from her colleagues. It would be too easy to become completely introverted and dwell on nothing but her troubles.

At the lunch table Julia sat with a small tabloid newspaper propped in front of her, as did most of the others. She kept her eyes down towards it as much as possible and hoped that she was only imagining the series of curious glances that appeared to come her way. Nobody spoke to her at all. She was, in fact, giving out an aura conveying a powerful signal of "do not disturb". Roger was particularly aware of this and more convinced than ever that something had gone very wrong;

but Julia met none of his enquiring glances and kept her eyes on her newspaper. I suppose, she thought to herself grimly, this is precisely what's known as keeping a low profile. With no interruptions for conversation, she finished her lunch quickly and went back to her own room to have coffee there. She was sipping it thoughtfully when there was a knock on her door. Automatically she said 'Come in'.

Roger entered, sat in the chair next to hers and put a hand on her shoulder. 'Please – tell me what's the matter.'

To her own intense annoyance Julia found herself crying.

'I can't,' she said.

'It's not anybody here, is it?' Julia shook her head.

'Something to do with the vanishing au pair?'

'She hasn't vanished. Jeremy's still seeing her.'

'Ah!' Roger felt strongly relieved. 'So that's it. Do you mind so very much?'

Julia crumpled into sobs.

'I see you do.'

'I feel so ashamed.'

'Can't you regard it as giving you some freedom?'

'Freedom? No. I can't think about anything outside it. Everything else seems distant and unreal. I need to protect the children from it, to maintain some stability for them.'

'Did Jeremy ever help you to provide that kind of stability?'

Julia thought for several moments before replying. 'I suppose not, really. It was more as if he were one of them. I thought he needed me.'

'Perhaps he still does,' said Roger, unwillingly.

'He won't talk to me. He only tells lies about it.'

'Well at least he's not boasting about it and throwing it in your face.'

'Throwing what in my face?' said Julia in alarm.

'This affair with the girl.'

In spite of herself Julia smiled. 'No. The only thing he's thrown in my face so far is a cup of tea!'

'Is that ...?' Roger looked at the blue mark near Julia's mouth. She nodded. Roger got up and paced the room, hardly able to contain his anger.

'That's intolerable. You can't let yourself be subjected to violence. You'll have to leave him. Move into college.'

'Like Everard? Ugh!' Julia flinched dismissively. 'Anyway, you know I can't "live in".'

'Come and stay with us then.'

'And bring my three children?' Julia had visions of them rushing about in Barbara Tomlinson's beautifully kept, childless house. 'You're being kindly ridiculous.'

'Not ridiculously kind?'

'Worse than that; more impossible.'

'Can you make him leave?'

'How? Take out an injunction against him? Start divorce proceedings?' Julia realised with surprise how little she wanted to do that. 'I'm not giving up yet,' she said.

'Well, at least let me take you out tonight, so that you don't have to go home till late.'

'Oh, you are kind. Thank you. But no. I must go home this afternoon. I've been glad to come here today, to get away for a little while, but I feel the need to see that the house is still there, somehow; especially to see the children.'

There was a knock on the door.

'Oh God!' said Julia. 'My pupils already!'

'Let me send them away. I'll say you're ill.'

'No – just ask them to wait a few minutes. Say I'm on the telephone. Then I can wash my face and put myself to rights. Teaching's good for me – concentrates the mind wonderfully. Thank you.'

In the Senior Common Room Hector Otis and Peregrine Forsyth were playing chess.

'Very quiet lunch today,' Peregrine observed. 'A nuisance having a woman there, of course. Limits conversation. Not that Mrs Leslie stayed long. Didn't look well, did she?'

'You're always hoping people don't look well, Peregwine,' said Hector a little testily. 'Though it's twue Julia did seem wather forbidding today; she looked too engwossed in her newspaper to speak to anybody. Pwaps she's had a wow with Woger. Tee hee!' Hector ended with a faint giggle. 'Eveward's looking as black as the devil these days too. Now that is a blight on conversation. Nobody wants to embark on any subjects welated to cuckoldwy. Weally it's quite a stwain. Check!'

'Didn't see that,' Peregrine grumbled. 'Don't know how you can talk so much and play chess at the same time, Otis. You must be more intelligent than you look.'

Hector smirked at the compliment and left Peregrine to peruse the obituaries in the latest Gazette.

When the last pupil for the day had left the room Julia remained in her chair, immobile. Despite her brave words to Roger she dreaded going home. She really envied Everard's male ability to up stumps and move into college when his position at home became untenable. A thought struck her. She pulled back the cover from the bed in her room and saw that it was made up with sheets and blankets. She told herself she must have known this before, but never registered the fact. Another night on the sofa was not a pleasant prospect, and a night in bed with Jeremy an even less pleasant one. Taking nothing but her coat and handbag and leaving behind her books and the essays to be marked for the following day, she set off for home.

When the children had had their tea, Mrs Thomas came down to help bath them and put them to bed. 'How are you bearing up, luv?' she asked Julia. 'Nasty shock you had this morning, but you're looking better.'

'Yes, I am, thank you; but I'm afraid I've left my work in college and I'll have to go back and get it: it's for tomorrow morning.'

'That's all right luv, I'll be here. Me and Derek's got a lot to watch on telly this evening. Stay out all night if you like!'

Julia smiled. 'I might just do that,' she said, 'but I'll see the children in bed first.' She went upstairs and swiftly packed clean clothes, sponge bag, night things and travel clock. She was anxious to be away before Jeremy came back, but she kissed the children goodnight and told them to behave perfectly for Mrs Thomas before thankfully leaving the house.

A neighbour was opening his car door as she passed.

'Hullo!' he said. 'What are you doing with that big case?'

'It isn't very big: just some things I need to take into college.'

'I'm going into town. Would you like a lift?'

'Oh, I would be grateful. Thank you so much.'

'Where's college then?' Julia wondered why she was surprised that the neighbour didn't know. She should realise, she told herself, that few of Camford's native inhabitants who were in no way connected with the university knew one college from another.

'Anywhere near the Broad will be all right.'

'Oh! Broad Street. That's where I'm going to park.'

Julia went in through the back gate to avoid passing the porter's lodge. It was still so early that no colleagues need think it strange to see her coming in to college rather than going out of it, but she was wary of giving the college servants any food for gossip or speculation. As far as she was aware nobody saw her cross the quad or go up the staircase to her room, and she felt a thrill of excitement and achievement as she reached it: she was doing something strictly against the canons of the college, something secret which nobody was to know about.

Roger decided against dining in college. There would be very few people in and conversation was considered more obligatory at dinner than at lunch, and his preoccupation with Julia made him feel unequal to it. He'd help himself to some bread and cheese when he got home. He was making his way across the back quad, wondering what Julia might be doing at that moment, when he looked up at the window of her room and saw the curtains drawn and a light glowing behind them. He stopped short, then changed direction, made for the corner staircase. Upstairs he knocked on Julia's door. No answer. He knocked again and in a fit of sudden anxiety tried the door handle. The door was locked.

'Julia!' he called quietly. 'Julia – please – open the door.' After another silence that seemed to last a full minute the door opened.

'Oh! You're all right!' he sighed with relief. 'You said you were going home to see the children.'

'Yes. I've been home. I left my work here. I've come back to do it.'

Roger could see that Julia had been working at her desk, but his eyes travelled to the small suitcase on the floor by the bed. He looked questioningly from the case to Julia.

'You're staying here.' he said. 'Staying here for the night.'

'I know it's not allowed – but you did suggest it.'

'I did?'

'Well, not exactly, but I think you gave me the idea. You suggested I move into college. But of course it's only for the night. I'll go home before breakfast.'

'I don't suppose you've had anything to eat.'

'I had lunch.'

'Yes, I saw. A very small lunch, eaten very quickly.'

'I'm not hungry.'

'What about thirsty? You can't stay here on your own all evening – thinking.'

'It's what I do most evenings – that and working.' Julia's thoughts had formerly centred on Jeremy in the school bar, but now there was the much worse alternative thought of Jeremy with Astrid.

Roger saw the pain in her face. 'Come on,' he said, 'we're going out.'

Julia was aware of the nightmare vision of Jeremy and Astrid receding a little. 'Sauce for the goose ...' she murmured, and then took her coat from the hook on the door.

CHAPTER FORTY-THREE

'Do you know where we're going?' asked Julia, as she and Roger ambled companionably into the core of Camford.

'Same as last time?' Roger's answer asked.

'If there's a dark corner where we won't be noticed.'

'Are you worried about our being seen together?'

'I think I just don't want to be seen at all. I want to hide myself away somewhere.'

'Do you know why?'

'Shame. I feel it's written all over me: a wife who can't keep her husband; a wife who shows the marks of his violence. It's so sordid and degrading.' Julia suddenly stopped and stood still. 'I'm sorry Roger. I don't think I can go out ... have dinner ... I haven't the courage. I'll have to go back.'

'No you won't,' said Roger gently. 'But we'll go somewhere else. There's a dimly lit Indian place where each table's in a kind of alcove formed by high-backed benches, so it's very private.'

Julia began to move forward slowly. 'That sounds better' she said.

As soon as they were ensconced in their alcove Roger ordered a bottle of wine. Julia drank down the first glassful with unusual rapidity.

'Better?' asked Roger.

'Thank you, yes, I feel anonymous and unnoticeable – the way I try to feel in college.'

'Do you really? I'm afraid you don't quite succeed there!'

'No, probably not. But when I'm in the darkest corner of the dark panelling I do at least have the illusion of it.'

'You mean always? Not just as things are at the moment?'

'Oh yes. I've always been aware that the majority of the men in the SCR would prefer me not to be there at all.'

Roger was too aware of the truth of this to attempt a denial. 'It can't be easy for you' he said slowly, realising that he had never quite appreciated the difficulties of her position: married to a husband who resented her superiority, separated from her colleagues by her sex, and from her husband's colleagues and their wives by her situation. 'I hope some of the pupils make it worthwhile' he added.

'They certainly do. I can relate to them – they accept me much more readily than most older men.' Julia went on talking about her pupils. As Senior Tutor, Roger knew most of them, at least by sight and name and reputation. The effect on Julia was similar to that of teaching: she lit up with enthusiasm and interest. Roger saw to it that her glass was refilled frequently and she drank the wine as if without noticing. As the meal progressed Roger was increasingly aware of the fulfilment of the promise she had shown in her interview the first time he had seen her, and of how deeply he was attracted to her.

'Let's go and have coffee at home,' he said as they finished their meal. 'Indian coffee's awful.'

'At home?' Julia looked aghast.

'I mean in college – our only mutual home,' Roger amended quickly.

'Oh yes!' Julia gave a little laugh at the absurdity of the idea, but at the same time gave Roger credit for making her feel that she belonged. Roger paid the bill and they got up from the table and left the comfortable alcove. Julia became aware that she was a little unsteady, but in contrast to her former mood she felt almost elated.

'I've had too much to drink, of course,' she murmured to Roger.

'Good!' he said and took her arm and supported her down the narrow staircase and into the street. Almost immediately he hailed a taxi and helped her into it.

Julia protested feebly. 'Oh really, Roger! A taxi! It's

only five minutes' walk away.'

'Never mind.' Roger drew Julia towards him and made her head rest on his shoulder. Julia found this posture significantly easier than keeping her head upright.

'Nice Roger' she murmured.

There was barely time for Roger to kiss her hair before the taxi stopped. From it they went to Julia's room, each with one arm round the other. Roger took the key from Julia and let them in and they resumed their comforting and comfortable back-seat-of-the-taxi position on Julia's bed, but soon found it was better suited to lying down than to sitting up.

Roger stroked Julia's hair and kissed her. 'I love you, Julia. You know I do, don't you?'

Julia heard his words in a haze and murmured 'I love you too.'

She nestled happily into his arms, kissed him fondly and made no resistance when he began to undo her clothes.

At half past five in the morning Julia woke up suddenly for no better reason, as far as she could fathom, than that she was gasping with thirst and had a throbbing headache. She reached out her left arm to switch on the bedside light and hit the wall instead. Frightened, she sat bolt upright, wondering where she was. Memory came to her gradually and she sank back with a groan, realising not only that she was in the single bed in her room in college, but that in her last conscious moments she had been making passionate and abandoned love in it with Roger! She groaned again and began to cry, but her thirst was as strong as her grief and rather more easily remedied, so she forced herself to get up and have a very long drink of water. 'Thank heaven I've got a modern room with a basin in it,' she murmured to herself, 'and a loo right next door.'

Her throbbing head drove her back to a prone position in bed, where she tried to think what to do next. She could go home, creep in quietly and lie on the sofa, or she could simply stay in college and not go home until the usual time in the afternoon. It might be easier, too, to say that she'd spent the night with a friend (and pretty near the truth, she thought grimly), than to explain why she'd got home so late at night – or so early in the morning – if anybody saw or heard her come in. Her aching head made the thought of any immediate physical effort very unpleasant, but her anxiety as to what the children would feel and say if "mummy wasn't there" was paramount.

Reluctantly, therefore, she washed and dressed; finished marking the essay she'd abandoned (now that really shows devotion to duty, she thought); telephoned a taxi – blessing Roger for getting her a telephone, as she did so, put on her coat and went to the back gate. She went to open the wicket and discovered, horrified, that it was locked. Of course! The undergraduates were supposed to be in by midnight – the gates were locked then by the porter. Only the dons had keys to the wicket and the great double doors were bolted. Julia had no wicket key because she'd never been in college so late. But the bolts – surely they could be undone from the inside. She found them: one in the middle of the door and one going into a hole in the ground. They were heavy, but well-oiled and manageable. The great door opened and she emerged into the street and tried to pull them closed behind her. No use. They'd have to stay unbolted for what remained of the night and the porters could scratch their heads over them in the morning to no avail.

The taxi drew up and Julia got into it. To her relief the driver was wooden-faced and uncommunicative. She'd been in fear of landing a cheeky one who might make snide hints or ribald comments. She had him stop the cab on the main road near the corner of her street and turned into it only after he'd driven away. Her every footstep seemed to echo accusingly in the silence. She stopped and glanced round quickly. No windows were lit, no movement to be seen. She slipped off her shoes and went inaudibly to her door, opened and closed it without mishap. In the sitting room she found a blanket and a pillow on the sofa. Blessed Mrs Thomas, she thought. She took off her outer clothes, threw them over the nearest chair and lay gratefully on the sofa. In barely more than a minute she was asleep.

CHAPTER FORTY-FOUR

In the morning Julia managed to take her pillow and blanket from the sofa to her bedroom, find her clean clothes and change into them in the bathroom without speaking to Jeremy or alerting the children to anything unusual. Mrs Thomas responded to thanks for her thoughtfulness with a knowing but sympathetic grin and the advice to have a cup of tea.

'Nothing like it,' said Mrs Thomas, 'though there was this lady I worked with in the hospital, you never saw her without a cup of tea or a teapot in 'er 'and. She got quite poorly because of it and the doctor said she was a tea-avadict. Fancy that – a tea-avadict! You wouldn't think it would you?'

'Cheaper than alcohol or tobacco, anyway,' Julia replied, and despite her headache and distressed state of mind made a mental note to ask one of the medics if this were possible and whether it resulted in cumulative tannin poisoning.

'You are a marvel, Mrs Thomas,' said Julia gratefully.

'Do you have to go to work today, love?' Mrs Thomas realised the reason for the compliment rather than the substance of it. 'You look ever-so poorly'.

'I didn't have a lot of sleep,' Julia murmured, and closed her eyes in painful awareness that she wished neither to go into college nor to stay at home. She felt totally unequal to any encounter with Roger, but hated the idea of cancelling tutorials and in fact welcomed them as a distraction and a means to mental absorption in something other than her own problems. Aloud she said, 'I'll be all right. It'll probably make me feel better.'

Once in college, Julia telephoned to Pauline in the library.

'Can you come and have lunch with me? I can't face college lunch today, and I do want to talk to you.'

'Lovely' said Pauline. 'What time?'

'I finish teaching at one – or should. Could you come over to my room? That'll make it easy to end the tutorial on time.' And also to avoid running into Roger, she added in her mind.

She was already teaching when the telephone rang. It was Roger.

'Oh – hullo.' Julia felt that her voice was shaking but tried to sound normal. 'I'm afraid I'm teaching at the moment and all morning, in fact.'

'Oh dear! Never mind. I'll see you later.' Roger

sounded disappointed and added 'I love you' in a low whisper. It was Julia's turn to say 'Oh dear', leaving it to be interpreted in any way possible, before she put down the receiver and returned gratefully to the lesser complications of her pupil's essay on courtly love in French romance.

Over lunch in the very-good-and-not-expensive French place, Pauline remarked that Julia wasn't looking as well as she might.

'Oh – it's nothing physical,' Julia replied evasively.

'Just more thorns than honey?'

'No honey at all – well,' Julia corrected herself, thinking of the children and Mrs Thomas and the roof over her head and her reasonably- sized house, 'not quite enough to compensate for the thorns.'

'Have you told Fr Smiley?' Pauline asked. 'He'd be the first to say "we're here to help you whenever you need us" you know. You are still seeing him, aren't you?'

'Yes – I'd forgotten – in fact I think it's tomorrow. No "forgotten" isn't the right word, but I've thought of him as in a different dimension – outside the honey and thorns aspect of my life.'

'That's a very un-Catholic way of looking at things,' Pauline rejoined. 'You'll see. He'll help you to integrate things and put them into perspective. And while I'm on the subject – more or less – what about coming on the pilgrimage to Lourdes with me? It's only a few days and very soon after the end of term, just after my reception in fact. Please do. I'm sure your marvellous Mrs Thomas could manage while you're gone.'

'Oh no,' Julia was aghast at the thought. 'I couldn't. It's something I've always wanted to do – ever since I saw The Song of Bernadette when I was a child – but I couldn't now – I'm too sinful.'

'And that's a very un-Catholic attitude too,' said Pauline briskly. 'Our Lord never ceased telling people that he'd come into the world to save sinners; and one of Our Lady's titles is "Refuge of sinners".'

'I didn't know that,' said Julia humbly, and to her dismay she began to cry, quietly, with little gasps and large tears. Pauline handed over her paper napkin for use as a tissue and said sensibly, 'Clearly it's exactly what you need.'

'The paper napkin?' Julia managed a smile.

'Now you are being naughty! The pilgrimage, of course. Tell Fr Smiley when you see him.'

Julia wiped her eyes, blew her nose and found that she'd stopped crying. 'Thank you, Pauline. You're absolutely right – and I feel much better, though I hardly know why.'

'A sudden shift of perspective, probably.'

'That's true. All thought of seeing Fr Smiley – of taking instruction – was so far in the background as to be almost negligible, and now it's the most important thing in the forefront of my mind and everything else has become relatively insignificant. I'm amazed – and relieved – and grateful. Let's go back to college and have coffee in my room instead of here.'

Strengthened though she felt, Julia decided she would prefer to avoid Roger until after she'd seen Fr Smiley; and Pauline's company, continued until the arrival of the next pupil, would usefully render any confrontation impossible.

When she'd finished teaching and was putting on her coat to leave college and dash away to fetch the children on her way home, Julia's telephone rang. She shut her ears to it and left her room precipitately. Once home with the children, she found herself in surprisingly good spirits.

'Well, it 'asn't done you any 'arm going to work, I must say,' Mrs Thomas commented.

'No,' said Julia. 'I enjoy my work; and I had lunch with a very nice friend, practically the only other woman in the college – and that made me feel much better.' Julia was still feeling much better even when Jeremy came home, amazingly, in time for supper.

'Oh hullo,' she said, regarding him dispassionately. She realised she no longer felt any animosity towards him.

He returned her regard with an air of anxious uncertainty. He opened his mouth, closed it, opened it again and finally spoke, almost accusingly. 'You look happy.'

'Ye, I am, thank you,' Julia replied calmly. 'I feel free.'

'Free from what?'

'Oh – I don't know. Perhaps "the storms of passion, the murmurs of self-will".'

Clearly uncomprehending, Jeremy decided not to pursue the subject and Julia went into a brown study, reflecting on the astonishing advantage of being unmoved by Jeremy and his behaviour. I hope it's not just because I've got my own back, she pondered, but I don't think so. I think it's because I've found something that transcends "the changes and chances of this transitory life," something ... somebody ... "whose service is perfect freedom." What a relief! I've heard those phrases so often; I'm fortunate to have them to call to mind, to express what I feel now that I realise their meaning. If only I can maintain that sense of imperturbable equanimity, or even return to it occasionally, knowing that it's attainable, the rest of my life should be much less difficult. As Julia's life had not yet reached quite half its allotted span this was an optimistic assumption, but at least she maintained it for the rest of that evening and went to bed, beside Jeremy, free from turmoil and distress, which was a considerable achievement.

In the night she was aware of Jeremy's arm over her and his breath on her face.

'No, Jeremy,' she said calmly, 'please not.'

'No,' Jeremy replied, 'I'm sorry. Too soon. But at least you know I want to.'

Still unperturbed Julia sank back, almost immediately, into a dreamless sleep.

CHAPTER FORTY-FIVE

Among other envelopes in her pigeonhole next morning Julia saw one addressed in Roger's unmistakable handwriting. She was relieved, as she considered writing the best means of communication in the present circumstances. She delayed opening it until she was sitting down with her pre-tutorial cup of coffee.

Dear Julia,

I've spent the most wretched day trying, and failing, to find a chance to speak to you. Clearly, you have not wanted to speak to me. Are you very angry with me? I've been over and over everything in my mind and I realise it must seem to you that I plied you with wine when you were distressed and vulnerable and then took advantage of you. I know it must seem like that, but truly, truly it was not, is not, not then, not now, not ever. I love you and I want to look after you. Please let me come and see you and talk to you. I can't rest until I do, until everything is right between us.

I love you, Roger.

Julia sighed. 'Poor Roger' she murmured. 'He sounds more distressed than I am. I'll drop a note into the lodge quickly and tell him to come in my free hour this afternoon.' That done she settled in to the morning's teaching with enhanced interest and enthusiasm. Only when walking over to lunch did she ponder on her own letter to Roger, hoping it was kind enough to allay his worst fears without sounding too encouraging. 'Dear Roger' was certainly a safe enough salutation, and 'Please don't worry, I'll be happy to talk to you in my free hour' reasonably non-committal. Finishing it with 'In haste, Julia' might sound rather cool, but better than erring in the other direction.

Over lunch Roger was not sitting near enough to Julia to speak to her, but he was able to hear Hector Otis. 'You're looking very well today Julia, if I may say so,' and Julia's reply 'Thank you Hector, I'm feeling very well in fact. I've been a bit off colour lately but I think I've quite recovered.' And Julia smiled a general smile and Roger sighed with audible relief amid the quizzical looks of his nearer colleagues.

A few minutes into Julia's "free hour" Roger reached her room just as her pupil was emerging from it. She was glad of the third person's presence to necessitate a non-committal tone to her greeting.

'Oh Roger – come in.' Roger came in and Julia put

the kettle on. 'I'm not angry, you see.'

'I do see.' Roger stared at her. She seemed to radiate a quality he'd never previously observed; he couldn't find the word to describe it. 'You look ...' he hesitated '... I want to say "wonderful" but that sounds far too trite and ordinary. It's much more than that, perhaps "serene' is the nearest.'

'Thank you – very perceptive. That's how I feel.'

'And what,' (Roger tried not to sound too hopeful) 'what's made you feel like that?'

'Faith' said Julia.

Roger was non-plussed, 'Faith in what?'

'In the holy Catholic Church and all it stands for. It's a gift. You can't become a Catholic without it; but I've received it so now I can.'

'When? How?'

'When my instruction's finished.'

'No – I mean, when did you receive it? It seems odd ...' Roger's voice trailed into an unfinished sentence.

'Yes' said Julia reflectively, 'it does seem a very odd reward for committing adultery.'

Roger flinched a little. 'Adultery's an ugly word.'

'Don't expect me to use mealy-mouthed euphemisms, please! What else would you call it?'

'It's not how I think of it – not with you.'

'I suppose the Lord can always make good come out of evil – as long as one stays on the right side somehow and doesn't let the evil become overwhelming and swamp everything else.'

'Do you think it'll last?'

'What – the good?'

'The faith, the serenity you've acquired. Isn't it just a state of mind, a reaction perhaps?'

'I don't think so, but it might be presumptuous to be too sure. All I know is that there are two things I want to do now: complete my instruction and go to Lourdes.'

'To Lourdes?'

'Yes, why not?'

'I know very little about it, of course, but I've always heard that it's full of tourists and horrible religious kitsh.'

'Yes, I've heard that too; but also that people who've been daunted by such reports have been completely won over by the reality of the whole Lourdes experience.'

'When are you going?'

'Almost immediately after the end of term. Not too long to go, now.'

'Your mind's really set on it, isn't it? I can see there's no mistaking your sincerity now, however temporary it may prove to be.'

'Well, everything in this world is transient; but "There abideth faith, hope and charity …'

'Faith, hope and love,' Roger interrupted, 'and the greatest of these is love.' Julia laughed and Roger couldn't resist a little chuckle at his own quick-wittedness.

'That's because faith and hope are no longer needed in heaven, Roger, where we come into the reality of all we've believed in and hoped for – and live in love forever. But I don't think it's quite the kind of love you mean.'

'I wouldn't count it out.'

'No, perhaps not; but if in heaven there's no marrying or giving in marriage it certainly stands to reason that there's no possibility of adultery either!' They both laughed again and Roger's tension was eased out of the atmosphere or resolved into companionability.

'Anyway,' said Julia, 'let's have a loving cup of tea!'

Hector, Everard, Peregrine and Julian Holloway-Smythe were still in the Senior Common Room. It was not generally Everard's custom to spend a great deal of time there, but he was not in a mood to be particularly happy with his own company. His attitude to Julian was still inclined to be defensive rather than conciliatory, though his pangs of guilt over the illicit borrowing of Julian's car were receding with time and the pressure of other events. Nevertheless he'd had a disturbing lunch with Arthur Middleton holding forth about his fiancée having to spend the day in a Camford court looking after a client of hers who was 'up for TWOC'.

'Pray enlighten us,' Julian had intoned. 'You can hardly expect, Middleton, that many members of a Camford college are familiar with the parlance of the criminal classes.'

Arthur Middleton had with difficulty resisted the temptation to launch into one of his diatribes on the iniquities of the English class system and managed to reply that it meant Taking Without Consent – 'taking vehicles, that is. You should be aware of it, Julian, your car's very valuable, and I've seen you even leave it with the keys in the ignition, simply asking for it to be taken. It's a very serious offence and you're putting temptation in the way of people less fortunate than yourself. There should be far more care taken in places like this: they provide what the welfare service describes as a "target-rich environment". Not that they should exist at all, of course, but as they do ...'

'Thank you Middleton,' Julian had interrupted, 'I appreciate the warning, if not the attitude that prompts it. The only people to have any opportunity to take my car would be colleagues with a key to the courtyard barrier, wouldn't you agree?' Then noticing that Everard was listening intently to this conversation had added, 'Few of us quite come into that category of criminality and deprivation, do they, eh Lucas?'

Though in fact singled out only because of his obvious interest, Everard had undergone a gut-lurching pang of guilt and fear that Julian was already accusing him. He'd felt himself shaking but replied as suavely as he could manage. 'Speak for yourself, Julian. You're always condemning those who make sweeping generalizations – like Arthur!'

This had effectively brought the conversation to a halt and left both Julian and Arthur feeling aggrieved.

In the common-room later, Everard asked Hector, 'How's your wife keeping?' and Hector replied 'Pwetty well, considewing; but she has to west a good deal and that's vewy tiwing for everybody else.'

'Hard labour for you, you mean – not used to it.' Everard couldn't help sounding snide.

'Come to that, Lucas, how's your wife?' Julian cut in, to the shock reaction of the others. 'Nice little woman. Don't seem to have heard much about her lately. Had her in to the first women's night last term – she spent the evening talking to that guest of Mrs Leslie's, I remember.'

This was greeted with an incredulous silence during which Hector gave Julian a poke and mouthed at him the words 'Don't you know?!'

'Of course I know,' said Julian aloud. 'Everybody knows. I can't stand this ridiculous hush over it, that's all. It's ruining common-room conversation because we're all treading so warily round it; far worse than having a woman in the place. That's the chap who's bowled you out, isn't it Lucas? The male guest at the women's night.

Can't say I blame your wife in the slightest. You would have bowled her out with that blonde bit you brought in – if you'd had half a chance. High time it was all out in the open; stop all this pussy-footing about pretending to be in deepest sympathy with you. Always thought you were nothing but a cad.' With that last word Julian Holloway-Smythe rose from his seat, towered over and glowered at Everard and embarked on a dignified exit. Hector was the first to break the ensuing shocked silence.

'Well weally!' he gasped 'we all know Julian's an old queen and can't be expected to understand anything about mawwiage – but weally! This is – that was – well – unnecessawy!'

CHAPTER FORTY-SIX

For the rest of the term Julia saw herself as engaged in a tripartite balancing act involving home, college and Catholicism. The last of these took up the least time in itself but increasingly, Julia felt, pervaded the other two. Although Mrs Thomas had largely absorbed the basic domestic chores of home, Julia was still too well occupied with reading to the children at bedtime, doing the marking and preparation necessary for teaching, going out to instruction or the occasional evening with Pauline, to be unduly distressed over the vagaries of Jeremy. She had to admit that having 'got her own back' as she put it, she felt much more philosophical about his behaviour. There were now so many other things in her life that she could regard him with an almost uncritical detachment. Roger rang her every morning just before her first tutorial and she began to accept his concern as a strength rather than a problem, though she responded to any invitations to dinner with a flat negative.

'Don't ask me. You know I'm taking instruction and working up to the pilgrimage to Lourdes – and I want to see the children in the evenings.'

'Well, at least let me take you to tea at the Randolph,' Roger finally countered. 'You can hardly come to any harm there!'

Julia laughed. 'That's something I've never thought of doing.'

'Coming to any harm?'

'Well – that too – but I meant having tea at the Randolph. It does sound deliciously – and harmlessly – luxurious!'

It was. 'What a wonderfully comfortable sofa,' said Julia. 'This beats even our "loving cup of tea" in college.'

'No' said Roger. 'Nothing beats that. I've felt so much closer to you since that afternoon – strangely. I can't share the way you feel, but I can understand it, and even admire it. I'll never forget how you looked and spoke. If I'd been French I would have said 'Elle brille!'"

'Thank you. That's the best compliment I could ever wish for. I only hope it lasts – the shining, I mean.'

'I hope Lourdes isn't going to put you off – says he, in his new unselfishness! Once I could have hoped it would! I suppose I still do in a way.'

'I don't really know what I expect to find there;

but I know I've always wanted to go.'

The waitress came up to ask if everything was all right and would they like some more hot water? They would, as it happened, and they then settled back happily, with their renewed cups of tea, to a comfortable conversation.

The time for reading end of term reports came round, it seemed to Julia, with unusual speed. For these the dons sat, gowned, in the Senior Common Room with the Rector in their midst. The undergraduates, also gowned, came in one by one from the hall, down the polished wooden stairs and to a conspicuous seat facing the dons. Used to a women's college, where reports were merely read in private by one's moral tutor with nobody else present, Julia found this ceremony dauntingly impressive. It was certainly an incentive for the men not to slack off in their work during the last few weeks in term. The scholars in each subject came first, followed by the commoners in alphabetical order. Hector's lot began the proceedings. All went well until gentleman number five took the conspicuous seat. (Julia had noted with some amusement on arriving at Emmaeus that undergraduates were always addressed as "gentlemen" in tutors' notices).

Hector began reading. 'Jenkins has really been showing his alpha this term ...' (there was a very slight sound of a snigger from among the dons,

Julia thought it might have come from Everard's direction) '... this term,' Hector repeated, 'a welcome, if tardy, indication of his real capabilities in this subject.'

He was about to go on when the Rector cut in, addressing the young man. 'But you're not Jenkins are you?'

'No, I'm Higgins,' he replied, in a tone between apologetic and amused.

Hector was clearly at a loss for anything to say and, sitting behind him as she was, Julia could see his colour rising slowly into his hair line, then into his ears. The atmosphere was so tense that Julia longed for somebody to burst into laughter and lighten it, but nobody did.

Finally the Rector spoke somewhat heavily. 'Well, if Higgins's reports could be read, please' and Hector, clearly more discomposed than the undergraduate, began to read the first of the appropriate reports.

'Well really, Otis,' said Julian Holloway-Smythe at lunch, 'you quite excelled yourself this morning. First you've got a chap "showing his alpha" – and then it's the wrong chap "showing his alpha"!'

There was something of a general guffaw, although Peregrine Forsyth gave a warning cough and an expressive glance in Julia's direction. It's moments like this, she thought despairingly, that make me feel less like a fly on the wall and more like a sore thumb. Do they expect me to be shocked or embarrassed or something? There's nothing I can say or do without making it worse. Can't they realise I think it's funny too? Except that I do feel a bit sorry for Hector.

The end of full term, for Julia, meant that her departure for Lourdes was very imminent. Jeremy seemed at a loss to know what to say about it. Finally he managed 'Do you have to go?'

'I think I do, really,' she answered slowly. 'Don't you want me to?'

'You know I don't.'

'In fact I didn't know. But as it's the first time since we've been married that I've been anywhere without you or the children I suppose it's not too surprising. But actually you should be grateful.'

'Grateful? Why?.'

'Because if I wasn't thinking about this I might have been thinking about divorcing you.' She looked at him squarely. 'Is that what you want?'

Jeremy turned white. 'No!' he said urgently. 'No! And it wasn't me!'

'What? Julia was not unaccustomed to Jeremy speaking inconsequentially, but this time she was quite unable to follow his train of thought.

'In the car' Jeremy gasped 'what you found. It wasn't me – it was Spatters!'

'Oh Jeremy! Don't insult my intelligence!' Julia sighed and turned away, but in trying to look at the matter dispassionately decided that a lie showed a better disposition than a boast.

In the event Jeremy even drove Julia to the church on the departure day, leaving her to join Pauline and the other pilgrims and attend mass before they set off for Lourdes.

CHAPTER FORTY-SEVEN

Arrived in Lourdes, the bus took them to their hotel, a small 2-star establishment a short walk away from the 'Domaine'. Julia and Pauline asked the more seasoned Lourdes-goers what the Domaine was and were told it was the strictly 'religious' part of the town and contained the grotto, the church and the vast area given over to pilgrims' processions. The baths, where one could be dipped in the holy water of Lourdes, were there too, and nothing was sold, except candles to light at the grotto. They were to go there in the evening and take part in the procession.

Summoned to the *salle-a-manger* for dinner they found they were required to help themselves to fine slices of garlic sausages of various colours and textures along with some grated carrot and lettuce leaves.

'Well,' murmured Pauline, 'I know it's still Lent – but one won't get fat on this!' Having finished that course, however, they were a little surprised to be served with veal escalopes and chips.

'Oh dear! They look awfully irresistible' said Pauline, taking a chip in her fingers. She devoured it rapidly. 'Oh yes, in fact they are,' she murmured guiltily and took another.

'Never mind' said Julia. 'We've got to walk down to the Domaine after this and then go in a procession – that'll offload a few calories!'

'Of course it will' said Pauline, relieved, and took a large helping.

After dinner – including a pudding which was fortunately not too substantial – Julia and Pauline met the rest of the pilgrims at the hotel entrance and volunteered to push the wheelchairs of those too old or too incapacitated to walk the distance.

'You're better off pushing a wheelchair,' one of the seasoned pilgrims volunteered. 'The crowds part before you like the Red Sea before the Israelites – and you get closer to everything and have a good view.'

At the entrance to the Domaine they were furnished with candles in small blue and white shades carrying the words of a hymn to Our Lady. Pauline and Julia were more aware of the vast numbers of people taking part in the procession than of anything else. Protestants from a Protestant country, they had never before seen any kind of religious observance on such a scale and were unprepared for the uncountable thousands of people thronging the Domaine and singing the refrain 'Avé, Avé, Avé Maria!' with their shaded candles raised as high as their upstretched arms could ascend on the second syllable of each 'Avé'.

'I can't imagine anything like this in England' Pauline mouthed to Julia at the end of the hymn.

'No! Julia replied, oblivious of the tears that were pouring over her cheeks 'It's so wonderful I don't want it to end.'

One of their wheelchair passengers turned to them. 'Since you're pushing invalids in wheelchairs you can go into the grotto with us and touch the stones where Our Lady appeared to Bernadette.' So they proceeded to the grotto, which was lit by tier upon tier of candles in an ascending spiral lighting up the flower-decked altar and the statue of Our Lady on its natural shelf in the rock above it. Round and behind the altar they wheeled the invalids, pausing to touch the smooth, cold rock, and emerged into the countless crowds which, as promised, parted before the wheelchairs and let them through with ease.

'This is a miracle in itself,' said Julia, 'to see such crowds so orderly and so charitably disposed.'

They pushed their charges out of the Domaine and back to the hotel, along the red lanes reserved for wheelchairs.

'What I think's marvellous,' said Pauline, 'is to

see a place where the sick and the disabled are such VIPs. Generally they're the outcasts of society, regarded as a useless burden, but here they're all-important. I know there have been wonderful cures, however strict they are about verifying them, but in a way that's nothing to the whole shift of attitude, making the sick and dying the ones who matter most.'

Julia said nothing; she could think of no adequate response.

In the morning after breakfast Pauline and Julia were to take their wheelchair charges down to the Domaine to bathe in the holy waters. They were gleaning information about it over breakfast. The morning was chilly and held a threat of rain. Julia and Pauline had some misgivings despite their elation of the previous evening.

'It's the water that started flowing when Our Lady told St Bernadette to drink it, isn't it?' asked Julia. 'I remember it in the film. She started scrabbling about in the mud and putting it in her mouth and everybody thought she was mad – until it started flowing properly. It's not still muddy is it?'

'No, it's perfectly clear' said Mary, a veteran Lourdes pilgrim. 'And remember you're not to take a towel. You won't need to dry yourselves.'

Pauline and Julia were aghast. 'Why ever not? Of course we must take towels.'

'Well they won't let you use them.'

'But that's ridiculous – and on a damp, chill morning like this!'

'Oh, you'll see,' replied Mary in the most matter-of-fact tone. 'You won't feel cold and you won't feel wet.'

Pauline and Julia exchanged disbelieving glances, then looked again at Mary, a plump, motherly, sensible woman in her fifties. She was hardly the stuff of which fanatics were made. Nevertheless, before setting out, towelless as instructed, Julia put on a dark blouse so that the water stains wouldn't show.

Arrived at the Domaine they were grateful to be able to push their chair-bound charges to the special place reserved for 'Les Malades' and bypass the queue, already very numerous, of women seated and waiting – for anything up to three hours – to be received into the bathing rooms. There were groups saying the rosary – groups singing hymns and none showing a sign of impatience. In their privileged position, however, Julia and Pauline barely had time to exchange words with a Chinese woman in a wheelchair next to them; she had cancer, she told them, in tones of complete serenity. Almost immediately they were ushered in, given a large tent-like wrap, and told to divest themselves of their clothes while suitably dressed nurses helped the invalids. Julia felt herself shaking, though not with cold, as she went through the opening leading to the large stone bath, took off the wrap, and descended the stone steps into it, guided on each side by a woman attendant. Before she went into the water they wrung out, between them, an oblong of what looked like white muslin, and placed it over Julia's body from above her breasts to below her knees. Then she waded through the water repeating the prayers they prompted and reached the end of the bath, where a small statue of Our Lady of Lourdes was placed. 'Kiss Our Lady!' commanded the attendants. Julia did so and was immediately and firmly immersed in the water up to her neck. She was then turned round and helped up the steps again. She relinquished the white muslin and a dark thin cape of some shiny, unabsorbent material was placed round her shoulders and she was told to dress herself. Remembering days at the seaside when she'd tried to put on her clothes without drying herself properly she feared this might be difficult, but to her astonishment her clothes went on without sticking and showed no sign of wetness. She needn't have put on the dark blouse after all. She and Pauline collected their charges, wheeled them out past the ever-increasing queue and along to the grotto to gaze with wonderment and give thanks. The invalids sat in their chairs looking peacefully, contentedly happy.

Pauline looked at Julia. 'You're glowing,' she said, in a tone between a statement and an accusation.

'I feel as if I am,' Julia replied. 'And I don't feel wet or cold, either, do you?'

'No, I don't,' replied Pauline wonderingly. 'I feel warmer than I did before. Inexplicable, isn't it?'

Pauline and Julia sat with Mary at lunch.

'Well, I can see you've emerged glowing from the water,' she re- marked. 'How was it?'

'Incredible,' said Pauline.

'Ineffable,' said Julia.

'Yes,' Mary went on reflectively. 'It always happens. I've seen it so often. People go in looking reluctant and full of fear and come out absolutely radiant. Perhaps you'd better not go to the shops, though, you'll find them very tawdry. Even the more expensive things are only bigger and more vulgar than the cheap ones.'

'Well, at least we won't be tempted to spend too much,' said Julia.

Later, in the small town with the bridge and river and cluttered, hilly streets, its conglomeration of absurdly numerous offers of accomodation, Pauline and Julia gazed into shop after shop overflowing with "religious" artefacts.

'Look at these rosaries,' said Pauline. 'Did you ever see such violent colours? And what on earth are these little plastic things?'

Julia picked one up and discovered that it was a small bottle, in the shape of Our Lady of Lourdes, with a screw top emerging from her head.

'I believe,' she said slowly, in a tone indicating that such belief was difficult, 'I think it's a bottle for putting Lourdes water in! How funny! But I'll take one home for Emma, all the same.'

'Oh, you can't!' Pauline sounded shocked.

'Why not?' Julia countered. 'This place caters for, literally, a world of Christians – of Catholics – and the world contains a great many children and childlike people with what we'd call appallingly bad taste. Things like this make religion reachable and relevant to them. Why shouldn't they have religious objects that appeal to them as much as the other things they admire and put in their houses? How can they be expected to make their religion part of their daily lives if its only visible face seems to be outside their sphere of appreciation and understanding? Our Lady appeared to one of the humblest and least educated girls in France – St Bernadette was considered too stupid to be confirmed because she couldn't learn her catechism! She didn't appear to an educated lady of refined taste. I love this exuberance of religious kitsh. It goes against everything I was brought up to admire and appreciate, but it shows something of the happy piety of the middle ages, part and parcel of the everyday lives of people of all sorts and conditions.'

'You're very persuasive,' Pauline laughed, 'you must be a powerful teacher; but do look at these before you say any more.'

Julia paused to take in the objects Pauline indicated. They were roughly hewn out of some substance that looked rather like solidified washing-soda; so roughly hewn in fact that it was not at first easy to discern that they were – of course – statues of Our Lady of Lourdes. In colour they ranged from very light blue to middle mauve. Puzzled, Julia read the notice in French at the end of the shelf.

'Oh no!' she gasped 'This time I really don't believe it. 'They're supposed to show what the weather's going to do according to what colour they turn!'

'You're quite right not to believe it," Pauline laughed, 'considering the range of colours they're showing on the same day and in the same place. Not that I've ever has much faith in the accuracy of any barometers. My cat washing behind its ears is the only thing I go by.'

CHAPTER FORTY-EIGHT

The children were in bed when Julia arrived home but Jeremy was up and waiting for her.

'I've really missed you,' he said. 'Have a glass of wine.'

Julia wished she could say that she'd missed Jeremy, but realised that she hadn't at all, not in any way. Nevertheless she accepted the glass of wine and sat down companionably, asking how the children had been, not that she really expected Jeremy to know.

'I read them a story every night,' he said, 'or told them one I made up. They seemed to like them.'

'I should go away more often,' Julia smiled. 'It's clearly done you all a lot of good.'

'It was very strange here without you.' Jeremy looked at Julia almost pleadingly. 'I didn't like it. Sometimes I felt the way I did when I was little – at night – I used to be in a dark room and I was sure nobody would ever come into it again.'

Julia went and sat on the arm of Jeremy's chair

and put her own protecting arm round his shoulders.

'You know you don't need to feel like that now.'

Jeremy clasped her round the waist and buried his head in her breast. She felt him shaking. 'Don't ever leave me,' he whispered. 'Please, please, Julia, I need you so much.'

Julia sighed deeply and put her head on his. 'I know you do,' she said sadly.

Over lunch in the tiny North Camford terraced house Pauline shared with her mother, Julia and Pauline were reliving their Lourdes experience.

'How did the children like their presents?' Pauline asked.

'Better than I expected, actually. I was very relieved. The do-it- yourself poster with the stick-on stars and moon went down very well – better than the colouring books – and the glow-in-the-dark rosary beads are particularly popular.'

'What about the glass domes with Our Lady and St Bernadette in a snowstorm when you shake them?'

'Oh yes. They really like those, and even seemed quite interested in the story. If Song of Bernadette's ever shown again when they're older I'll take them. But that reminds me, there's something I bought for you.' Julia fished in her compendious handbag. 'Here. I hope you like it.'

'No, but why?... when?... I must open it now. How exciting.' Pauline undid the light, soft package and the tissue paper inside it and took out a black lace mantilla.

'Oh Julia! How did you know how much I wanted one?' Pauline shook out the gauzy folds and gasped 'and particularly this one!'

'I saw you holding it up in the shop – and I knew you'd already bought that expensive scent for your mother and nothing for yourself but a garlic plait.'

'Yes, the mantilla was so expensive. Oh, you shouldn't have, you really shouldn't have.'

'Nonsense. It's considerably less than I owe you in so many ways – and you can wear it when you're received.'

'I don't think I've ever had anything so beautiful. I can't thank you enough.'

'Well I want to thank you for this extremely good lunch. I shan't be able to reciprocate, it's too noisy at home with the children. I must say there are advantages to living on your own; well, I know your mother's here too, but I presume she has her meals separately.'

'Not exactly; but she tends to want them earlier than I do, sometimes at rather strange hours, and she likes quiet simple food. So I often give her something before I have my own meal, especially if I've got someone coming.'

'You really are saintly, Pauline, as well as being

extremely well organised!'

During vacations Jeremy could muster few excuses for being out in the evenings and absent from supper, so Julia could hardly attribute his presence at home to any change of heart or habits. Nevertheless, he had been flattered, and she greatly gratified, by the children's vociferously expressed hope that Daddy would go on telling them stories even though Mummy was home now. Julia reflected that she had probably never insisted enough on his being involved with the children, had given up too easily and done too much herself, with the vicious-circle result of distancing Jeremy even further. Now, increasingly, the children's delight in his stories, and his own in telling them, provided a very positive incentive to be at home. He was naturally inventive and amusing and the children's appreciation was stimulating and good for his self-esteem.

One evening over dinner he suddenly asked Julia, 'Would you like to go away for Easter? Take the children to the seaside?'

'Oh, not for Easter, please. After Easter if you like. Pauline's being received just before Easter and I want to go to the Easter services.'

'Received?' Jeremy queried, puzzled.

'Into the Church. She's becoming a Catholic.'

'So I suppose that's more important than taking

the children for a holiday.'

'In a way I suppose it is. But I didn't mean that. We don't need to go away over Easter when everything's crowded with people who have to work on either side of it. We'll still have time after, before term begins. It would be very nice to go then.'

'All right.' Jeremy appeared mollified. 'Let's do that then. There's that pleasant guest-house right on the sea-front, where we stayed when Jamie was a baby.'

At ten o'clock the next morning Jeremy answered the telephone. 'Yes. Who shall I say is calling?' He told Julia in a tone hovering between the impressed and the exasperated that it was 'The Senior Tutor of Emmaeus College.'

Julia made a conscious effort to appear more calm than she felt.

'Oh, hullo Roger!'

'How are you Julia? It seems so long since I've heard from you. Have you been into college? I've left some letters in your pigeonhole.'

'Oh I'm sorry, Roger. I'm afraid I tend to be rather remiss about college during vacations.'

'When can you come in? I do want to see you.'

'I could come in this morning. My help's on duty and Jeremy's here.'

'Please do. In about an hour? I'll be in my room.'

'I suppose you're going into College,' said Jeremy, when Julia had put the phone down.

'Yes. I'm afraid I'm not used to having a proper job which spreads over vacations. It wasn't necessary when I was just a 'hired help' doing some teaching for a college. I'd better get ready and go.'

She was glad not to have too much time to anticipate meeting Roger. Nevertheless, once in college, she picked up her post from the lodge and went to her own room to read it before going to see him. There were some official missives from the faculty; a brief, perfunctory note from Everard about the time and date of the pre-term meeting, a couple of Gazettes and three letters from Roger. She read these first. They were all rather similar in expressions of how much he was missing her, anxiety about her health and happiness, and increasing distress at not having heard from her, interspersed with intimations of desire and affection. They did little to diminish her unwillingness to see him face to face and she found herself dawdling through one of the Gazettes as a delaying tactic. A paragraph in one of the blue pages advertising vacant positions caught her eye. It was from one of the women's colleges, requesting applications for a lecturership in just her own subject and field. It seemed like an answer to prayer; a way out of present difficulties; a position similar to the one she had but less threatening to her marriage, if only she could get it. Strengthened by the mere possibility she set off immediately to see Roger.

CHAPTER FORTY-NINE

Roger answered 'Come in!' to Julia's knock, bounded to the door, took both her hands in his and kissed her forehead.

'A very chaste kiss' he said.

'Thank you.' Julia smiled, surprised at how glad she was to see him.

'I needn't ask if Lourdes was a success, I can see it was. But you didn't send me a postcard.'

'No. It didn't seem appropriate, somehow.'

'Did it come up to your expectations?'

'It surpassed them. It was beyond my power to imagine. I don't think you can envisage something so far above anything you've ever experienced.'

'What about the religious kitsch?'

'I loved it. I brought some home for the children. I won't go into my spiel about the justification of it – Pauline says I sound as if I'm giving a lecture on a favourite hobby-horse – but I will say that it's a mistake to equate bad taste with bad faith and I think it's arrogant and presumptuous to do so.'

'Have you read my letters?'

'Yes, and thank you for them.'

'Then I needn't tell you again how much I've missed you. How is it being home again?'

'Better, actually: quite a lot better, though there's no knowing how long that will last.'

'Julia please, please think about it. Can you really stay in that marriage?'

'What's the alternative?'

'You know very well. Get a divorce; it wouldn't be difficult, you've certainly got grounds for it; and then marry me.'

'Roger, you've got a wife.'

'She's a very self-sufficient woman; she'd cope very well. And we haven't any children to complicate matters.'

'I have, though, and Jeremy's their father, nothing can change that. You know I'd never leave them myself and I know, too, that you simply can't imagine what a house with three children in it is like to live in. It has to be experienced to be believed – and it's not the sort of experience to be thrown into all at once. At least with your own children it comes on gradually over the years! Truly – I could simply make it a virtue of necessity. But there's more to it than that. What I most want to do now, with all my heart and soul, is to be a Catholic and bring up my children as Catholics. How could I do that in the middle of a divorce or after it?'

'I believe it's possible to get an annulment once you're divorced.'

'That may be so, with a lot of difficulty and a lot of time consumed. But you'd have to get one too. Besides, I simply know it wouldn't work. And Jeremy needs me. There's some relish of salvation in him now, and I don't know that there would be if I left him. I still care about him, even love him in an odd despairing sort of way.'

Roger groaned. 'Why didn't I meet you and marry you years ago, before either of us was tied up?'

'Well, for one thing you were already married before I left school!'

'So that's it! You just don't want to marry an old man!' Roger was half in jest, half in earnest.

'I don't want to inflict three young children on him, that's more to the point.'

'How can I go on seeing you?'

'You'll see me in college – almost every day.'

'That's what I mean. I don't think I can bear it.'

'Oh I see. I know you meant a different kind of "seeing" and that's out of the question, so I was trying to pass it off lightly. But in fact there's a lectureship going at St Etheldreda's, exactly in my field. I intend to apply for it.'

'Oh – I wondered if you'd seen that. I rather hoped you hadn't, illogically.'

'Of course, I might not get it.'

'No. But we'd have to give you a very good reference.'

'It would solve a lot of problems. Jeremy wouldn't feel so jealous and – what can I say – diminished if I were in a college with other women, and I wouldn't be tempted to make comparisons between him and his status and that of my colleagues here. Though when I think of some of them! And I can't say I'd be sorry to give up working with Everard – or working against him as I often feel I have to. Is he still living in college?'

'Oh yes. Chatting up the secretaries in the absence of other fodder. But there'll be a new crop of graduates for him to lope after soon.'

They both laughed, but Roger looked at Julia sadly.

'I don't think I meant it about not being able to bear seeing you in college. It's better than nothing. But I feel as if there's a great blank gap in my life. I wish I could fill it with a new faith, as you're doing.'

'Yes,' said Julia thoughtfully. 'I can really see the point of that story about the man who got rid of one devil and swept his soul clear and clean and empty – only to have seven devils decide it was a perfect place to live in and inhabit it accordingly. I've seen it happen to women of my mother's generation. They get rid of a husband; then take another just the same or worse; then have a series of lovers – usually faithless and unfulfilling – and end up with an embittered emptiness worse than they started out with.'

'I hope you're not thinking of me as a devil!'

'Of course not – well, not personally! But even good things and good people can be a temptation to evil, and I can only regard it as evil to take another woman's husband and break up one's own family, whatever the world says to the contrary. But you know that.'

'Yes. You've made it very clear, and in my heart of hearts I know you're right. But I can't stop loving you. Just – just believe that I'll always be here if you need me.'

'Thank you.' Julia stood up, put her hands on Roger's shoulders and kissed his forehead.

'My chaste kiss for you,' she said. 'Goodbye.'

She left him sitting with his head in his hands and made her way back to her own room, taken too unawares by the tears that were streaming down her face to be able to do anything about them.

CHAPTER FIFTY

Julia got the job at St Etheldreda's. It was in University News in The Times half way through the summer term. Julian Holloway-Smythe pointed it out at lunch.

'So you're leaving us already, my dear,' he boomed, after voicing the customary congratulations. 'You got fed up with us very soon, it seems.'

Julia smiled. 'Only some of you,' she replied politely.

'Leaving us to guess which ones, eh? No prizes for one I can think of!'

Everard looked up, looked black and looked down again. He was tempted to say "If you mean me I assure you it's entirely mutual" but decided to save it up till he'd thought of something more witty and cutting.

'Oh dear, what a shame!' said Hector Otis. He'd been looking forward to regaling Julia with the more interesting of his wife's gynaecological details and some account of the enormous sacrifice he was making in order to help her at home.

'Very sensible,' said Arthur Middleton. 'At least

you've got some prospect of becoming a Fellow in a women's college. Personally I think this sex discrimination's elitist and outmoded. Now in Russia ...'

'Yes, yes, Arthur,' Hector Otis cut in, 'we all know you and Russia believe in women doing everything men can do everywhere they do it. You want us to have women undergraduates, women Fellows; if you had your way we might even have a woman Rector!'

There was some laughter at that, varying from the snigger to the guffaw. Julia held her peace and thought thankfully of St Etheldreda's.

Having coffee in the Senior Common Room after lunch Julia was surprised when Stuart Gregson came purposefully towards her and sat down beside her.

'Congratulations on your appointment,' he said. 'I'm sorry you're going. You've always been very nice to me.'

'Have I?' Julia tried to think in what way, realised she might have sounded rude and went on, 'I mean, it's never been the result of conscious effort, or any effort at all in fact. Why shouldn't I be nice to you?'

'Well, it's not everybody that makes me feel as if I belong here.'

'Ah, well,' Julia was sympathetic. 'I think perhaps I'm the president of that club!

Stuart smiled. 'I hope you're coming to the ladies guest night.'

'Oh yes, I think I must. It'll be my last one.'

'I'm really glad, because you see I'm bringing in my fiancée.'

'Oh, how nice! I didn't know you were engaged.'

'Yes – very recently – at Easter.' Stuart looked pleased and proud and embarrassed all at once. 'I really want to bring her to dinner but she's very nervous about it.'

'That's natural enough, if she hasn't been to one before.'

'Well, she has, as a matter of fact. That's the trouble. It's Everard you see, Everard Lucas. He used to be her supervisor and she didn't like him at all and asked to change to somebody else, so it's a bit awkward.'

'Did she come to dinner here with Everard?'

'Yes.' Stuart was endeavouring to speak quietly, but his high Australian vowels rendered his voice noticeable and fairly audible to all around. Julia was aware of this but felt that telling him to keep his voice down might make matters worse. She compensated by speaking very quietly herself.

'Who is she? What's she like?' she asked in a voice little above a whisper – but in vain. In his enthusiasm Stuart's tones became more carrying (strident, Julia was inclined to think) than ever.

'Well, she's American and her name's Emily Matheson and she's doing a DPhil in French – modern – and she's very beautiful!'

Julia saw that everybody's attention, and Everard's in particular, was drawn to their conversation and gave up on caution. 'Oh, I believe I've met her, at my first guest night in fact, in the Autumn term. Yes, she is very beautiful, isn't she? Congratulations! She seems a very attractive girl in every way.'

'Yes, she is, and she's usually fine in social situations but I don't think she enjoyed that Ladies' Night very much and it's sort of put her off them.'

Julia was aware of Everard looking particularly sardonic and hastened to end the conversation by promising to do everything she could to make Emily feel at ease, 'though I'm sure,' she concluded, 'that she'll be perfectly happy here with you.'

Julian Holloway-Smythe turned on Stuart with alacrity. 'What's this, Gregson?' he boomed. 'Bringing your fiancée? That's really not on you know, one should bring in colleagues from other colleges, academic women, you know, not wives or fiancées.'

'Well,' countered Stuart, heartened by Julia's support, 'she has been here before, you know.'

Emily's identity clicked into focus in Julian's perceptive mind. 'Ah yes, of course,' he boomed. 'Lucas brought her in, didn't you Lucas? First

Ladies' Night in Autumn. And now here's this young chap carrying her off to Australia. Isn't that interesting?'

Everard longed to say something cutting about Emily that wouldn't sound too much like sour grapes. 'Is it?' he countered in a voice indicating a lazy lack of interest. 'Well, do look after her. See she doesn't make herself sick.'

To Julia's relief Stuart looked puzzled rather than embarrassed by this. She herself shot Everard a look of disgust and, rejoicing in her freedom from him, said 'There are some kinds of men who might well make any decent girl sick! Don't worry, Stuart. Bring Emily to my room for a drink before dinner and we'll all look after her.'

And she left the room and Everard to his reflections, which were anything but pleasant. He had severed relations with Alison Greer after a thoroughly nasty encounter during which they competed in malicious accusations and observations about the other's character and appearance and any other proclivities they could think of. As each of them was very well practised in this art it had resulted in a pyrrhic victory with some deep wounds on either side. Moreover Everard's reputation among this year's crop of women graduates in his field was sufficiently damaged to deter all but the most desperate, so that he could make little headway in that direction. He was a great deal more distressed and disturbed by his divorce proceedings than he could have thought possible, and it was unfortunate for him that his sardonic posings and general arrogance repelled sympathy.

A little after the end of term, when Roger was feeling what he called his 'great, blank gap' even more acutely because Julia was no longer coming into college, he returned home to be greeted by his wife. 'Oh Roger, a rather strange invitation's been sent to us. It is to both of us, though it was very properly addressed to "Mrs Roger Tomlinson".'

'Really? What's so strange about it? What does it say? Who's it from?'

'From that young woman at your college who told me you'd been very kind to her. I suppose that's why she's asked us. You know – Everard's lecturer. Though I must admit it took me a few minutes to work out who she was. She's invited us to attend her reception into the Church – it gives the name of the church, some saint I've never heard of – and a small celebration afterwards. Apparently all her three children are going to be received too!'

Roger paused until he felt he could make a reply that sounded natural and casual. His wife put it down to a puzzlement similar to her own.

'Look!' She showed him the invitation.

'Yes,' he said, 'I know what it is. She's becoming a Catholic – being officially received into the Roman Church. It's very significant for her – and her family – and we're asked to "rejoice and be glad" with her.'

'You surely don't want to go. I'll write a refusal, shall I?'

'No! I want to go.'

'Good heavens, Roger! I would have thought you were the last person …! Why should you or I rejoice because an intelligent young woman with her life before her is becoming a Roman Catholic?'

'I'm not entirely sure that I do rejoice' said Roger slowly, 'but I think *you* should!'

EPILOGUE

Shona and Hector Otis did manage to produce a son, who duly went to St George's along with his sisters; but it was the girls who distinguished themselves academically, both by becoming Fellows of colleges at a very young age and one by becoming a Professor and a D.Litt. The boy was content to be a schoolmaster.

Peregrine himself died before retirement age and thus improved his averages for that week considerably. His colleagues were unanimous in regretting that he was no longer there to appreciate the fact.

Tim and Jean got married as soon as her divorce came through and lived nearly as happily-ever-after as can be achieved in this world. Tim took a Senior Lectureship in a northern university and they moved there before their own children, both girls, were born. Efforts were made for Everard to maintain contact with his boys but visits became increasingly sporadic especially after he married a graduate student he'd been supervising. The marriage lasted a few years before his wife, who was teaching in a mixed college, left him for one of her colleagues. They had no children.

Julia and Jeremy had two more children, both girls, and needed to move into a larger house. Jeremy's father was so considerate as to die and leave them a surprisingly large amount of money. He'd done clever things on the stock market. They gladly abandoned the tall house in the narrow street for a much pleasanter one in a prestigious neighbourhood, which was, moreover, a stone's throw from where Roger and Barbara Tomlinson lived. Roger hastened to welcome them and soon became a friend of Jeremy's. They had chess and wine as common interests. Julia and Barbara got on extremely well and the childless couple became very fond of the Leslie children—in suitably small doses. Roger particularly loved the two youngest girls, who were always most flatteringly pleased to see him. He and Julia rarely met without any other company and if their relationship didn't always remain on terms of the purest friendship they managed to keep it strictly to themselves. Barbara was astute enough to realise why Roger had said she should rejoice that Julia had become a Catholic and moreover, was sensible enough to agree with him. She felt that the relationship involving the

Leslies was a safety valve. The couples sometimes went on brief holidays together and Barbara thus saw rather more of her husband than she had previously.

They stayed together in considerable harmony until Barbara died, some thirty years later. Roger coped very well on his own and even learned how to use the washing machine. Julia helped him as much as she was able to when not needed to help with a rather large number of grandchildren. Some of the younger of these befriended a pair of twins at the Catholic school they attended before they were old enough to go to St George's. They were nice, well-behaved children with an American mother and a recently dead father. Julia was saddened to hear of this but was informed that he'd been awfully old, over seventy in fact. 'Even older than you, Granny!' Certainly the twins, Polly and Paul Lucas, seemed to be happy, well-adjusted children, who enjoyed an excellent relationship with their mother's amazingly young-looking parents, who, on better acquaintance told Julia the story of their son-in-law dying in his young wife's arms. 'Of course,' they added, 'Everard was getting on; he was quite a bit older than we are!'

On further enquiry from adult and reliable sources Julia ascertained that the twins and their even younger sibling were the children of

Everard Lucas by his third wife, some thirty-five years younger than he was! This was amazing enough, but even more amazing, in Julia's eyes, was the fact that these children were being brought up Catholics. The boy twin was often to be seen serving mass. Whenever she saw him Julia offered up a prayer for the soul of his father, her old enemy, and decided that the mystic Mother Julian was right when she pronounced that 'all shall be well, and all manner of thing shall be well.'

ACKNOWLEDGEMENT

My heartfelt thanks are due to the many kind people, friends and members of my family, who have given me appreciative encouragement and help. My granddaughter Mary Bowen has done sterling work in providing an eye-catching cover illustration and I must give due and proper thanks to Jim Williamson, who, when helping us incompetent oldies to cope with the mysteries of our computer, came across the beginnings of this book and encouraged me to continue with it and increase my mastery of keyboard and screen.

The prime mover in the publication is of course Joanna Frank, without whose kind and patient help this book would never have managed to appear in a readable form.

ABOUT THE AUTHOR

Elizabeth Longrigg

Originally from New Zealand, Elizabeth Longrigg has lived for many years in Oxford where she raised her five children. She has taught English Literature at several Oxford colleges and her former students include Philip Pullman, Val McDermid and Tina Brown.

BOOKS BY THIS AUTHOR

The Oxford Pot

The Incident

The Inconsistent Widow

Printed in Great Britain
by Amazon